'Chris Simms combines psychological insight with gritty realism to give the reader a genuinely exciting story'

*Crime Time*

'Simms keeps you guessing' *Daily Telegraph*

'An exciting new psychological thriller' *Daily Mail*

'Gritty, grimy and deeply absorbing, *Hell's Fire* keeps the reputation that Simms is fast earning for himself as one of the UK's finest exponents of the crime-writing art firmly intact. This is tight, eminently readable stuff that will have the pages racing by in a whirl' *Shots* magazine

'Simms homes in on very human evil' *Guardian*

'A promising debut ... the characterisation is merciless, convincing and very gripping' *Morning Star*

'Simms's fresh approach, and the way the story weaves between three viewpoints, makes this one of the most promising debuts in crime for some time. From the prologue's brutal first pages to the satisfying crunch of the final chapter, the prose is spare, lean and mean' *City Life* (Manchester)

'A thriller should, ideally, star characters one can care about, move briskly without any signs of sagging, and leave an indelible impression long after the last page is closed. On all counts, Simms succeeds marvellously ... a wonderful display of talent from a soon-to-be star of the crime fiction world' *January* magazine

'A very robust and creepy tale that had me riveted for an evening with dark characters that still reverberate in my head ... a rapidly developing talent in the world of crime fiction' *Deadly Pleasures*

'An ingeniously plotted psychological thriller ... reading Chris Simms is like watching a Danny Boyle film – strong characters in a present-day setting, enlarged with splashes of violence' *Ottakar's Bookshop*

*Hell's Fire* is Chris Simms's fourth novel in this compelling series set in Manchester, featuring Detective Inspector Jon Spicer. Chris was picked by Waterstone's as one of their '25 authors of the future' and he has been nominated for both the Theakstons Crime Novel of the Year and a Crime Writers' Association Dagger. Chris lives near Manchester with his wife and four children. Visit his website at www. chrissimms.info.

*By Chris Simms*

Outside the White Lines
Pecking Order
Killing the Beasts
Shifting Skin
Savage Moon
Hell's Fire

# HELL'S
# FIRE

Chris Simms

An Orion paperback

First published in Great Britain in 2008
by Orion
This paperback edition published in 2009
by Orion Books Ltd,
Orion House, 5 Upper Saint Martin's Lane
London, WC2H 9EA

An Hachette UK Company

1 3 5 7 9 10 8 6 4 2

A CIP catalogue record for this book
is available from the British Library.

ISBN 978-0-7528-8416-5

Typeset by Deltatype Ltd, Birkenhead, Merseyside

Printed and bound in Great Britain by Clays Ltd, St Ives, plc

The Orion Publishing Group's policy is to use papers that are natural,
renewable and recyclable products and made from wood grown in sustainable
forests. The logging and manufacturing processes are expected to
conform to the environmental regulations of the country of origin.

www.orionbooks.co.uk

To Mum, who sneaked out that rear door
and never looked back.

*Men never do evil so completely and cheerfully
as when they do it from a religious conviction.*

Blaise Pascal 1623–1662

# Chapter 1

Jon Spicer reached up, turned on the interior light and examined the top third of his face in the rear-view mirror. He sighed. It looked like a fine red gauze had settled over each eyeball.

He turned the light off, soothed by the dark, glad to be back in its comforting folds. A minicab ghosted past his parked car, its driver scanning the deserted streets for one last fare, but the clubs had kicked out over half an hour ago. Jon glanced to his left. Even Canal Street was devoid of life. As the cab neared the set of traffic lights in front they switched to amber, then red. The vehicle's brake lights glowed briefly in response, but there was nothing waiting to emerge from Sackville Street and the rear lights died as he scooted through anyway.

'Naughty, naughty,' Jon muttered, leaning to the side and looking up the front steps of the renovated warehouse. Come on Rick, the bloody church will be a pile of ash at this rate.

He tapped his forefinger impatiently on the knob of the gear stick. His presence here in the middle of the night was part of a pre-arranged plan of action. Three local churches had been torched in as many weeks and evidence of satanic rituals had been discovered in the smoking remains of each one. The Christian community was outraged and media interest had reached national levels.

Following a meeting of senior officers of the Greater Manchester Police, it had been decided that if another church was attacked the Major Incident Team would take over the investigation. Jon was on call when this latest fire had been reported forty minutes earlier. He glanced at the building again. Where was Rick? He considered tooting his horn, but then remembered how much it annoyed him when taxis resorted to that tactic outside his house.

Leaning his head back, his eyes drifted to the rear-view mirror where they caught on the reflection of the child's seat behind him. Holly. He thought of her at home, asleep in her cot. Christ, was she really nine months old already? He smiled to himself, picturing her high-speed crawl round their house, determined to open every cupboard, explore every corner. He almost laughed aloud, thinking of her frustration with the stair gate, which denied her access to the top half of her miniature universe. How simple his daughter's life was. How free of concern and complication. If only he could keep it that way for ever, save her from the shit which one day would inevitably find her. The thought of someone or something making her cry caused a clenching in his chest. At times, he concluded, that was the real consequence of parenthood. A continual low-level hum of anxiety – increased by every unguarded plug socket, every swinging door, every flight of open steps. God, what will I be like when she can walk? Go to the playground on her own? He shook his head. Too much even to contemplate.

Movement to his side. The door to the building was opening. The limited view through Jon's side window only allowed him to see a very shiny pair of black shoes emerge on to the top step. As the wearer began jogging down, perfectly creased suit trousers were revealed, then a light overcoat, smooth as though it had just been pressed. Definitely Rick and, shit, would he regret coming out in his best gear! Next into view was a crisp shirt and perfectly centred tie. The side door opened and Rick leaned in.

'Morning.'

Jon took in the clean-cut looks and slightly damp hair. 'You been in the fucking shower while I've been sat out here?'

Rick slid into the passenger seat. 'I dipped my head in a sink of cold water. Needed something to wake me up. Four thirty in the morning. Christ.'

'You asked to come along if a church went up on my shift.'

'Yeah, I know.' He pointed a finger upwards. 'I could see the glow from my windows. Looks like a big bloody blaze.'

Jon put the car into gear and pulled away from the kerb, thinking of Rick's penthouse apartment, wondering how much it cost. 'The Sacred Heart, a Roman Catholic church in Fairfield. All those fancy altar cloths and wooden carvings no doubt.'

'From the direction I thought it was the big empty one by the side of the track if you're on the train going out of Piccadilly. Next to Ashburys station, I think.'

'The huge great thing with the green spire? That's Gorton Monastery.'

'Is that what it is? A monastery?'

'Was. A load of monks used to live there. They built the church part and a school too. It was a kind of a religious centre for the local community.'

'But no longer, I take it.'

'No. Like so many churches round Manchester, it's been derelict for a while now. My mum used to attend Mass there right up to the eighties. She could tell you all about it. Where we're heading is about a mile east, along the Ashton Old Road.'

Waiting at a set of lights, he stared across towards the figures huddled on Fairfield Street as it ran round the back of Piccadilly Station. 'Working girls are still out.'

'Quick handjob to put you in a good mood for work, sir?' Rick said in a high voice.

Jon smiled wryly. He knew that in a few hours many commuters would be receiving that exact offer as they walked from the station towards their sterile city-centre offices. Some must accept, or the girls wouldn't keep asking.

'No need for any of that,' he replied, imagining Alice curled up in bed, strands of her long blonde hair lying across the pillow. Thank God their sex life was on track again after the long drought brought on by Holly's birth and his wife's subsequent post-natal depression. She'd been back to her old feisty self for a few months now, though it would be a couple more before she was weaned off her medication completely.

'Oh yeah?' Rick smirked.

Jon glanced at his partner, about to ask if he was getting any action in the sack, but the fact that Rick was gay caused the question to sink back. Try as he might, Jon just couldn't chat to him about anything sex-related without feeling awkward.

3

The unanswered question lingered in the car and Rick turned away to look out the side window. Idiot, Jon cursed himself. Now on the A6, they passed the gently undulating glass front of the old BT offices, reflections of street lamps gliding across the smoky panes like comets crossing a night sky.

'So, looks like he's added a fourth to his list,' Jon said, taking refuge in the safety offered by work.

'Suppose so. When did the call come in?' Rick was now looking ahead as they sped along the empty road.

'An hour or so ago. There are three fire engines at the scene.' A few minutes later Jon tapped a knuckle against his side window, just able to make out the tapering point of Gorton Monastery's spire as it thrust up against a sky tainted orange by the massed city lights. 'That's the monastery. See the silhouette?'

Rick leaned forward. 'God, it's massive.'

Soon a bright patch of light became visible up ahead. It shimmered slightly against the bruised amber sky, the occasional spark carried heavenwards by hot air billowing up from below.

'That'll be our church,' Jon said, turning off the main road. They passed a couple of playing fields, and then the road jinked to the right round some houses before revealing what looked like a massive bonfire celebration gone wrong.

The church was burning fiercely, flames emerging from its many windows and shooting out of the roof at one end where it had begun to collapse. Three fire engines, two police cars and an ambulance were parked up, their flickering blue lights muted by the glare of the blaze. Several dozen residents stood beyond the cordon that stretched across the road, many in dressing gowns and slippers. A group of children were dancing in the puddles by the hoses, which snaked along the road before disappearing down open manholes. Jon pulled up behind the last emergency vehicle.

'Quite a sight.'

Rick nodded. 'No more wine and wafers in there for a bit.'

They got out of the car, and a faint wave of heat hit their faces, even though they were a good hundred metres away from the flames. Mixing with the low roar created by the blaze itself

4

was the diesel chug of the idling fire engines and, above that, occasional groaning sounds of wooden timbers being tortured by the heat.

'Should have brought some marshmallows,' Jon said, holding his palms towards the church and then rubbing them together.

Rick looked him up and down, taking in his ragged coat, old rugby shirt and battered jeans. 'Dressed like that, you're lucky it's not November. They might have mistaken you for the guy and chucked you on the bloody fire.'

Jon held his sides and mimed a ho, ho, ho. 'Never attended a fire, have you?'

Rick's grin faltered. 'No. Why?'

Jon nodded at his partner's suit. 'That'll need to be dry-cleaned for a start. Something about jets of water hitting red-hot mortar, brick and wood. Creates a right stink.'

Rick turned towards the church, registering for the first time the billows of steam, black smoke and fine particles of ash drifting down all around them. 'Bollocks.'

Chuckling to himself, Jon began to survey the onlookers, searching for any lone males who hadn't obviously just pulled on a tracksuit over their pyjamas. Profit, vanity, vandalism, crime concealment, psychological compulsion, prejudice, revenge: Jon knew the motives for arson. But these fires weren't about any jilted lover getting back at his ex. They weren't an insurance job, nor were they lit to hide an earlier crime. Prejudice seemed the most likely reason; someone harbouring a deep-seated hostility towards Christianity. The satanic symbols further backed up the theory. Jon also knew many arsonists couldn't resist hanging round the scene to witness the results of their actions. Some, he gathered, even got sexual satisfaction from seeing the blaze. He and Rick headed towards the uniform with the clipboard, 'DI Spicer, DS Saville, Major Incident Team.'

The officer looked at their warrant cards, signed them in, then stepped aside, allowing them through to the inner cordon.

'Who's in charge?' Jon asked.

'Sergeant Thompson, sir. Over there talking to the Fire Investigation Officer.'

'Cheers.' Jon led the way towards the two men, pausing to address a firefighter who was filming the scene through a camcorder. 'Got some footage of the crowd?'

The firefighter tilted his head to the side, camera still trained on the church. 'Yeah, I'll do another sweep in a second.'

Jon nodded, then stepped over to the pair of men. 'DI Jon Spicer, MIT. This is my partner, DS Rick Saville.'

The two men turned to him, their faces glowing in the heat, and introduced themselves. Sergeant Andrew Thompson was a slim man with thinning hair; the Fire Investigation Officer, Station Commander Dean Webster, was a stoutly built bloke of about fifty with black hair shorn short – a style so many in the police and fire service seemed to favour. Jon noticed his olive skin and the slight slant at the edges of his eyes. It gave him the look of a Pacific Islander, someone from Fiji or Tonga, or perhaps Samoa. Jon couldn't help wondering if the guy had played rugby.

'So what's the sequence of events?' he asked as they shook hands.

Sergeant Thompson spoke up. 'The occupant of number seven on the road behind us called in at twenty-five past three. She'd noticed the glow of flames on her bedroom ceiling, looked out the window and saw the side windows of the church were alight.'

'As in the flames were on the inside of the church?' Rick asked, wrinkling his nose as a wave of acrid-smelling steam washed over them.

'Correct. She rang nine nine nine immediately.'

'Our first appliance arrived fourteen minutes later,' Webster said. 'After assessing the situation, they called for back-up. By then the fire was well established. Residents in the nearest homes were evacuated and we commenced containing the fire within the church itself.'

Jon surveyed the stricken building, with its narrow graveyard and pleasant-looking presbytery to the side. A fireman stood in front of the house, playing a stream of water over the windows, dampening the wooden frames in case of stray sparks. 'Any sign of the priest?'

'None.' Sergeant Thompson shook his head. 'His phone number is on the noticeboard at the front gates of the church. No reply on his phone and no response from hammering at his front door. I requested an ambulance as a precautionary measure.'

'What's his name?' Jon asked, eyes on the deserted property.

'Father Ben Waters.'

Turning back to the church, he said, 'Reckon the same guy set this one alight?'

Webster shrugged. 'Seems likely. Once it's burnt itself out we can go in and get some answers.'

'How soon do—'

A loud cracking sound came from the church and the exposed timbers in the roof shifted. Suddenly the beams collapsed with a massive crash. A cloud of sparks surged up, veering off into the night like a plague of angry fireflies. From the crowd behind them came a couple of whoops.

'Not long, now that's come down,' Webster replied. 'Just a case of pumping in enough water through the windows.'

Jon thought about the crime scene, any evidence obliterated by a flood of biblical proportions. A young officer appeared at their side, an agitated man standing just behind him. Jon spotted the white dog collar round his neck. He appeared to be in his early fifties, though the anguished look on his face was adding a good few years to his appearance. His neat, side-parted hair could have been blond, or maybe light brown and tinged with grey. It was difficult to tell in the unnatural light.

'Sir, this is Father Waters. It's his church,' the officer announced.

'Father. We're glad to see you. We were getting worried you might have been inside the church,' Jon said.

The priest raised a hand and rubbed at a spot just above one eyebrow. 'No. I've been with a parishioner. St Mary's Hospice.' The hand dropped, then was held outwards towards the burning building. 'What on earth has happened? Was it deliberate?'

Gently, Jon took him by the shoulder and tried to turn him away from what remained of his church. 'We're not sure yet. Can we talk somewhere more quiet?'

'I just can't understand ... I mean, someone has done this, have they not?'

Firelight caught in the lower rims of his eyes as tears welled up. At the edge of his vision Jon saw Webster turn away in embarrassment at the priest's show of emotion.

'Sir ... I mean Father, let's sit down somewhere.' Jon looked about. No incident wagon was at the scene. He started back towards his vehicle, the priest alongside, shoulders sagging in defeat. Rick behind the both of them.

'We can sit in my car and I'll run through what I know. I'm sorry you've had to suffer this shock. How long has it been your church?'

'Twenty-one years.' The reply was flat, all emotion now drained away.

Jon was familiar with the tone. It was that of someone who'd just been informed a loved one was dead. He thought of how the priest had come from the bedside of a dying parishioner. How to console a person who spent his life comforting others? 'Did you walk here from the hospice? I'm not sure where St Mary's is.'

'About a mile away. No, I drove. I've only just parked ...'

His words fell away and Jon turned in the direction of the man's crestfallen stare. A blue Volvo estate was parked at the opposite side of the road to Jon's. Shattered glass lay like jewels on the tarmac by its back wheels.

'My car.'

Jon looked about. Everyone's attention was on the church at the end of the close. If anything, the fire made the shadows behind the vehicle deeper, creating an inky space into which a thief had obviously crept. The little bastard, using an incident like this for a bit of robbing. And of all the fucking cars to choose. 'What was in your boot?'

The man's head was bowed and Jon could see his shoulders rise and fall as he gulped in air. 'A sports bag full of hockey gear.'

Jon was impressed the man was still playing. He was about to say so when the priest took a step backwards, hands going to his chest.

'Father?'

The priest looked at him and Jon saw pain and fear in his eyes. Oh shit no, not a heart attack. Jon grabbed his shoulders. 'Rick! Get the ambulance crew.' He hooked an arm around the other man. 'Can you walk? Would you like to sit?'

'Can't breathe ...'

'It's OK, we're getting the ambulance. They'll have oxygen.'

He'd half carried him ten or so steps when the paramedics ran over.

Jon lowered the priest to the tarmac, keeping a hand between the man's head and the surface of the road. Fragments of gravel dug into the back of his hand as the female paramedic began to loosen Waters' dog collar and unbutton his shirt. The priest squirmed under her touch, short gasps coming from his half-open mouth. He clamped a hand over the paramedic's wrist, preventing her from undoing the next button down.

'Sir, please try to relax.'

The priest's eyes were shut tight.

'Sir, what can you feel?'

'My chest is tight,' he panted in reply.

The male paramedic crouched down and placed a finger on the side of the priest's neck. 'Any pains in your chest?'

'No.'

'Tingling in your arms?'

'No.'

'Just shortness of breath?'

He nodded.

The paramedic looked at his colleague. 'Arrhythmic heartbeat. Let's get him to hospital. We'll put an IV in en route.'

'Which hospital?' Jon asked.

'Manchester Royal Infirmary is closest.'

The female paramedic extricated her wrist from the priest's grip, ran to the ambulance and returned with a stretcher. She and her colleague lifted him on to it, raised it up and then wheeled him to the back of the ambulance.

'We'll take care of your car. I'll check with you later,' Jon said through the rear doors, noting that the oxygen mask which hid the lower half of Waters' face only emphasised the alarm in his eyes. Seconds later the vehicle accelerated away.

'Poor sod,' said Jon, watching the flashing lights until they disappeared from sight.


As he crammed the last of the pizza into his mouth a shiver sent his arms into miniature spasm. End of April and still so fucking cold. He chewed with his mouth open, watching the vapour of his breath as it curled into the freezing air. The temperature always seemed to drop to its lowest point in the final hour before dawn. It was the night's parting shot, like an army forced into retreat trying to ruin the territory it had occupied.

He knew that the horizon would soon begin to materialise and sunlight would warm the earth. But that would make little difference in his tomb of curving brick. In the shadows by his side, his sleeping bag lay like a giant insect's sloughed-off cocoon. He'd forgotten to roll it up again.

Straightening it out, he saw the slugs gathered in its folds, flaky trails of silver criss-crossing the nylon. He plucked their plump forms off and tossed them into the blackness that lurked beyond the weak glow of his lamp.

After removing his army boots, he climbed in and zipped up the bag as far as it would go. Inside, his hand ferreted in his army coat, searching the breast pockets for the lighter. He brought it out, flicked the wheel and held the flame to the black candle. The wick seemed to suck the yellow glow across, absorbing its power so the lighter's flame shrank down momentarily. He snapped the lid of the Zippo shut and listened to the peaceful whisper the burning candle made.

Staring into the source of light, he thought about his dead mother and where she was now. Would the tongues of flame really be licking her flesh soon? Scorching and blistering her skin but never actually destroying it, so that she would writhe in eternal torment?

Tears stung his eyes as the memory of returning from school and finding her in the bedroom flooded back. At first he hadn't understood what was keeping the door shut. As he pushed harder, the tape on the other side began to crackle and tear as it came away from the frame. Finally he'd broken the seal she'd created and the door swung open to reveal her lying on the bed. The windows were closed and the air that washed over him was heavy with the aroma of burning. In the corner of the room was their barbecue from the garden, half the charcoal on it reduced to white ash.

The police and firemen had been reluctant to explain, but the internet had answered his questions. Carbon monoxide poisoning – a seductively gentle death.

But her serene appearance was misleading, his father explained. Though her bodily remains were unscathed, her soul was facing an entirely different fate. Stuck in limbo for the moment, hell would eventually claim it, and hell would keep it for ever. Judgement Day, when it came – and his dad said that time was getting ever closer – would see to that. She had committed suicide and there would be no forgiveness from God.

He extended a freezing finger into the flame and watched impassively as an angry red bump began to push slowly up from his skin.

# Chapter 2

Jon unzipped his jeans and let them drop to the kitchen floor. As he stepped out of them he pulled the rugby shirt over his head. Then, in just a pair of boxer shorts, he crouched down and opened the washing machine door. 'Christ, that smell of burning's horrible.'

'Not with the baby stuff,' Alice said, mashing Weetabix up in a bowl.

His eyes took in her hair, casually pinned up with a tortoise-shell clip. It amused him to think that, however stunning she might look on the rare occasions they went out, seeing her barefoot in an old T-shirt and the cut-off tracksuit bottoms she wore at her kick-boxing classes was a far sexier sight. Ducking his head, he peered into the drum. A pile of dirty bibs and grimy Babygros was already inside.

'Just leave them on the floor, I'll do another load later,' she added, now sitting down and holding a plastic spoon piled with mushy cereal to their daughter's mouth. Holly leaned back in the high chair to examine it for a second. Her mouth opened and Alice popped the food in. 'Good girl.'

As he piled his clothes neatly on the lino, he felt Alice's fingers gently tracing a line down his back. The tingling sensation radiated outwards, causing him to breathe in. 'Those stud marks are still red.'

He lifted an arm to examine the angry row of welts that followed the curve of his ribs. 'Traditional Scouse welcome, that,' he replied, thinking of the stamp he'd received that Saturday from a Newton-le-Willows player. It had set the tone for an afternoon of violent play that eventually erupted in a thirty-man brawl. In the mêlée, Jon had sought out the prop who'd caused his injury and landed a punch in the opposition player's face that had sent the man staggering backwards like a comedy drunk. Finally his knees buckled and he ended up on his arse in the turf. It was a sweet shot, as the prop himself grudgingly admitted in the bar after the match.

'Bloody stupid game,' Alice stated for the umpteenth time.

Jon didn't bother replying. His love for the sport was a subject he'd given up trying to explain to her long ago. His boxer dog, Punch, was edging on his belly across the lino, positioning himself beneath the high chair in the hope a fragment of food might fall down. Jon ran a hand over his head, then scratched behind the animal's ears. Punch's eyes didn't waver from the pair of chubby legs swinging above. 'Pig of a dog.'

As he shut the washing machine door, the eight o'clock news came on the radio that was on in the background. Alice waved a hand. 'You'll be on this!'

'How do you know?'

'Because I heard it at seven. Listen. You sound quite professional for once.'

Jon turned towards the radio, seeing his wife's bottle of fluoxetine beside it. As usual, he caught himself wondering how much of her upbeat mood was down to the anti-depression pills. The fire was second story on Key 103, beaten to the top spot by a report on evidence emerging that the US illegally dropped massive amounts of white phosphorous on the civilians of Fallujah during its assault on the city.

*Police and fire teams are investigating the cause of a blaze that completely gutted the Sacred Heart Church in Fairfield early this morning. Our reporter at the scene had this to say . . .*

Sound quality dropped as the studio switched to the outside recording.

*'Local residents reported that the church was on fire at around three o'clock this morning. By the time fire crews arrived quarter of an hour later, the building was beyond rescue. This is the fourth church to have burned down in the last month and, at this time, police are refusing to rule out that the blaze is linked to the three other attacks. However, the presence of officers from the city's Major Incident Team could indicate*

*that we have a serial arsonist at loose in the city. I put that question to Detective Inspector Jon Spicer, MIT's officer at the scene.'*

Jon then heard his own voice.

*'I'm afraid we can't say. The site has been sealed off and fire investigation officers will conduct an examination alongside our own forensic team once it is safe to do so.'*

*'But is it true that the same satanic symbols found spray-painted on the walls of the other three churches were also found here?'*

*'No one's even been near the inside of the church yet, so I really can't say.'*

*'We understand the priest of the church suffered a heart attack as a result of this act. Will it be a murder investigation if he dies?'*

*'I really can't comment on that. Thank you.'*

The link switched back to the studio.

*We'll bring you more on that story as it unfolds. Now on to sports news and a brilliant victory for Belle Vue Aces at Kirkmanshulme Lane last night—*

Jon turned the radio off. 'That wasn't too bad, was it?'

Alice smiled back. 'You sounded very on the ball. How is that poor priest?'

'Not sure. I'll drop by before I report in to the incident room.'

'So is it Satanists doing this?'

Jon ran a hand through his cropped brown hair. 'Probably. How often do churches burn down of their own accord?'

'That's awful.'

'Yeah. I thought those sorts of beliefs had died out in the Middle Ages too,' Jon replied, filling the kettle with water.

'You're joking aren't you? Alternative religions have never been so popular. Look at Ellie. Which reminds me, your mum wants to speak to you about her.'

'What the hell am I supposed to do? Jesus Christ.' He banged the cupboard door shut and placed two cups on the worktop.

'Jon, losing your temper about this is the last thing we need. You should sit down with Ellie and sort something out.'

Jon kept his eyes on the cups. For fuck's sake! Why did he have to play the middle man here...?

'I spoke to Ellie yesterday night,' Alice continued. 'She's coming round for tea. Maybe you two could have a chat then.'

Jon turned to his wife, sensing that she'd set the meeting up.

'Don't look at me like that, I'm only trying to help.'

He sighed. 'Yeah, sorry. It pisses me off though. I always seem to get stuck as some sort of mediator.'

'The pitfalls of being the eldest child.'

Jon thought back to when they were all kids. It was true. Being the eldest had so many disadvantages. There was no doubt his parents had been strict with them all during their early years, but only Jon had suffered the same treatment right the way through being a teenager. In by ten o'clock until he was seventeen, not allowed to the pub until eighteen. Then along comes Dave, his younger brother by four years. Allowed to stay out far later, far younger. In the pub by the time he was sixteen. Then Ellie, the youngest by seven years. He couldn't believe how much she'd got away with. Had his parents grown tired of enforcing discipline by the time she'd reached her teenage years? No wonder she drifted through life, swayed by any hippy-dippy shit that came her way. His thoughts turned back to Dave. The black sheep of the family who'd left home to live in squats, dabbling in minor crime and, in all probability, drugs. As usual, he was nowhere around, safe from all this family shit. 'When did Mum ring?'

'Yesterday. You got in too late last night for me to mention it then.'

Jon reflected on the latest crisis to hit his family. During Sunday lunch at his parents', Ellie had announced that she was starting to follow a religion called Wicca. She had described it as a set of pagan beliefs that pre-dated Christianity and were based around respect for the natural environment.

Their mother, Mary, a devout Catholic, had hit the roof. In the ensuing argument she had asserted that Wiccans were actually witches, and Wicca was a religion that would lead its followers straight to hell.

Ellie had responded with a description of the part the Church had played in burning thousands of women during the seventeenth century. Now, as an integral part of the Establishment, the Church was meekly allowing government after government to help wreck the planet through policies based on pure greed.

Jon had lost track of what Ellie was on about after her first three sentences. Concentrating on his roast beef and Yorkshire pudding, he'd hoped the dispute would settle itself down, but things had got more and more heated, culminating in Ellie storming out of the house.

He could understand why Mary had reacted so strongly. Increasingly he believed that his mum's faith had become the most important thing in her life. She'd tried to impress it on each of them when they were young, and about the only advantage of being the eldest was that it had enabled him to escape the forced attendance at Sunday school. She'd tried to make him go, but he'd been so miserable, she reluctantly gave up, allowing him to spend Sunday mornings at the rugby club where his dad coached the Junior Colts. Soon Jon had taken up mini-rugby himself and was safe from his mum's clutches.

But Dave and Ellie hadn't been so lucky. Jon's memories of the time were pretty vague, but he remembered smirking at his younger siblings as they were driven to a dreary church hall while he and his dad set off for some exercise in the open air.

After Ellie had stormed out of his parents' house, Alice had quietly said, 'Mary, there's a difference between Wiccans and Satanists.'

His mother had dabbed at her eyes with a napkin. 'Is there? They claim that, but is it really true?'

Alice had proceeded carefully on. 'Wiccans worship Mother Nature, Satanists worship the Devil. Surely that's a big difference.'

'It doesn't matter in the eyes of the Lord. She'll be damned if she doesn't accept Christ as her true saviour.'

Jon rolled his eyes, then turned to his dad, but over forty years spent under the same roof as his wife had taught him to keep his mouth shut when talk turned to religion.

Jon spooned coffee into the cups as he waited for the kettle to boil. 'What does Mum want me to do? Persuade Ellie to renounce evil and start going to church so her soul can be saved?'

Alice placed the empty bowl on the table, then removed the bib from round Holly's neck. A blob of damp cereal fell to the floor where it was instantly hoovered up by Punch. 'She wants you to talk to Ellie, try and get her to at least answer your mum's calls.'

Jon tilted his head in semi-agreement. 'I can try and do that, but you know Ellie. She'll have probably found another fad in a month's time. It'll all blow over.'

'Don't bet on it. She's discovered a new friend. A girl who belongs to a coven. I get the impression she's made quite an impression on Ellie.'

Jon glanced at his wife. 'You mean Ellie's being brain-washed?'

'She's twenty-eight, for Christ's sake. I think she's old enough to think for herself.'

'But you implied this girl ... who is she anyway?'

'She works in a New Age shop on Oldham Street.'

'New Age? Selling what?'

'You know. Healing crystals, tarot cards, candles, books on mysticism. All that kind of stuff.'

'And the Wicca thing. Is it really just a front for Devil worship-pers? I mean, if it is and they're torching churches round town, we don't want Ellie getting involved. She's gullible enough as it is.'

'Jon, she's not gullible. A bit naïve maybe.'

'Naïve? She's got her head in the clouds. Always has had. You never saw the collection of fairies she had as a kid. A dreamer, that's what she is.'

'Well, there are people who do use Wicca to hide more sinister beliefs ...'

'Bloody great.'

'But it was Ellie who told me that on the phone last night. She knows the difference between right and wrong. She'll be safe.'

'How can you be so sure? I mean, you're in the middle of

nowhere, dancing around in some field, and the lead guy suddenly announces it's time for an orgy. If Ellie was there voluntarily . . .' His eyes swept the ceiling. 'It worries me. You know how hard this sort of stuff is to prove in court.'

'You're talking about rape? Jon, you need to chat with Ellie. I don't think being a Wiccan involves free love with the other followers.'

Jon poured boiling water into the cups. 'I've got to get ready for work. The fire investigation officer and forensics are coming to the station at ten for a strategy meeting.'

'By the way, I've been looking at nurseries for Holly.'

Jon paused. His wife wanted to return to her job in a beauty salon for a couple of days a week once Holly reached her first birthday. The earnings would barely cover childcare costs, but Alice wanted to avoid becoming a stay-at-home mum. She had friends who'd chosen that role and she worried that, like them, eventually she'd only be able to talk about baby-related issues.

'So which ones look like the best for Holly?' he said, turning round in the doorway.

She handed a beaker of apple juice to their daughter. 'Well, the best one by a mile is called Sunshine, it's connected to St Martin's Church.'

'The Church of England place?'

'Yes, I know it's a bit happy clappy, but it's got very good links to the primary school near to it. I'm thinking long term here, but it will set her up perfectly for when we look at secondary schools.'

Jon's mind reeled. 'Hang on, we were talking about nurseries just now.'

'I know, but we need to think ahead.'

'Jesus Alice, she isn't even one yet.' Why did no one warn him having kids made everything so bloody complicated?

She shook her head. 'I never thought I'd be one of those horrible calculating parents, but you don't want her ending up at the Dalewood do you?'

Jon thought about the nearby comprehensive. Uniformed officers were called out to it most days and the most recent talk was about the school employing private security to try and keep control. 'No.'

'Which leaves Trinity. If Holly has been educated in faith schools, she stands a far better chance of getting in there.'

Jon looked at her. 'You'll be telling me we'll start needing to go to church next.'

Alice glanced away. 'When the time comes, it'll certainly help.'

Jon felt his eyes widen. 'Tell me that's a frigging joke.'

'It's an hour of your Sunday, Jon. Hardly much to ask.'

Not if we've had a boy by then and I've started taking him to mini-rugby, thought Jon. He pointed a finger. 'Anyway. Who says we'll still be in this little terrace by the time Holly starts Sunday school? I could have been promoted and we'll be living somewhere out in Cheshire. Hale or round those parts. There are no sink schools out there.'

Alice raised an eyebrow. 'Maybe if you didn't punch your senior officers that would be a possibility.'

Jon cringed at the memory of the incident with McCloughlin. 'OK, it might not be happening any time soon.'

Alice smiled. 'Come on, Jon. You and desks don't go together. Running an incident room would make you miserable as sin, and you know it.'

As usual, he thought, she had him totally sussed. Which left them living here and aiming for the local Church of England place. His thoughts turned again to his childhood and how much Dave and Ellie resented being made to attend Sunday school. And look at how things had turned out. Dave living God knows where and Ellie wanting to become a witch. 'One thing, Ali. If we end up going down that route, we make it perfectly plain to Holly – and any other kids we have – that we don't believe in any of that God stuff, all right?'

'What if she wants to believe in it?'

Jon shrugged. 'If she does, and it's of her own free will, fine. But if she starts parroting Jesus Loves Me shit, I reserve the right to step in with my own thoughts on the matter.'

'And explain that Mummy and Daddy only went to church to

get her a place at a good school?' Alice smiled provocatively.

Jon looked at his daughter sucking noisily on her beaker, a nappy bulging out from beneath her Babygro. 'She'll have to learn everyone bullshits a little bit to get by.'

Alice laughed. 'I'll let you, the fine upstanding policeman, tell her that.'

He went upstairs. In their bedroom, he paused in front of the mirror. Thirty-five years old. He examined himself. Six feet four, fifteen and a half stone. The fine upstanding policeman, according to Alice. A hand went to his stomach and he pinched a slight roll of fat. It was beginning to build up, no matter how much time he spent training. He reflected on his dad, still in decent shape having just pipped sixty. 'Fingers crossed, Jon,' he murmured, reaching for a towel.

# Chapter 3

He pulled into one of the car parks bordering the Manchester Royal Infirmary fifty minutes later. It took him another ten minutes to find a space, competition for slots being fiercer than at any supermarket on a Saturday morning.

As he walked across the car park he looked at the row of trees lining one side. Tips of leaves were fuzzing the ends of their branches with a delicate green. Dandelions had recently erupted with miraculous speed through the cracked concrete of his own back yard and, as Jon stepped over the verge at the top of the hospital parking ground, he saw masses of the yellow flowers dotting the grass. A glance up revealed clumps of fluffy greyish cloud, edges lit white by the sun hidden behind them. The sky beyond was iridescent blue and he breathed in the light breeze, relishing the way spring always managed to lift his mood.

The usual smattering of smokers were gathered in their dressing gowns, on either side of the main entrance. For a second, the familiar urge hit him. But then he saw a stick-like woman raise her bony wrist. A half-smoked cigarette was between her thin fingers and a tube emerged from the back of her hand, looping upwards to an intravenous drip she'd wheeled out with her. That is bloody horrific, Jon thought, and strode through the sliding doors to the reception desk. There, he asked for the whereabouts of Ben Waters. The receptionist consulted a computer screen. 'Are you a relative?'

He held up his warrant card in reply.

'He's in the cardiac suite, down the corridor, turn right at the end.'

As Jon turned to go he heard a familiar voice. 'DI Spicer, nice morning isn't it?'

He thrust his hands into his trouser pockets and turned round. Carmel Todd, crime reporter at the *Manchester Evening Chronicle*. She'd cut her blonde hair short since he'd last seen her. It was a good move, he thought, settling on green eyes that now seemed larger and more friendly. 'Hi, Carmel.' He noticed the notebook and pen in her hands. 'Here visiting a poorly aunt?'

She gave a quick smile, but it didn't ring true. Fair enough, Jon thought. It was a crap attempt at being funny.

'Is he still alive?'

'As far as I know.'

Her lips tensed, then the expression was gone. 'Chances of survival?'

'Am I wearing a white coat and stethoscope? Christ, Carmel, give us a break, will you?'

Her shoulders relaxed and he controlled the urge to smile. Since the Monster of the Moor case, they'd reached a grudging sort of agreement. He kept her up to speed on his cases, she kept off his back while he went about his job.

'I'll let you know more once I know more.'

She lowered the notebook and nodded to the side. 'I'll be in the canteen bit just down there. There's a free tea in it for you.'

'Oooh, I can't wait.' She shot him an uncertain look and he raised his eyebrows to show he wasn't serious. 'I'll duck by on my way out.'

He set off along the corridor, stopping at the reception desk for the cardiac suite a minute later. A nurse took him to a side room where a very calm-looking Waters was sitting up in bed reading a book. That's some change from last night, Jon thought.

As he entered the room he couldn't help but glance down at the priest's hairy chest. His pyjama top was open and in the middle of each of several shaved patches of skin was a circular plaster. A wire from each one ran into a small black box on the bedside cabinet. Jon looked for a screen or any other beeping machinery.

'Everything's beamed to a monitoring room somewhere else,' Waters said, with a casual wave. 'It had me confused too.'

Jon pictured a darkened room with a row of anonymous medical staff sitting before a bank of glowing monitors. 'Technology nowadays. Not sure if it makes me more relaxed, or less.'

The priest smiled. 'I quite agree. I found it unsettling too. Please, sit down.'

Jon eased his frame into the soft chair by the side of the bed, noticing the cover of Waters' book as he did so. *The Pilgrim's Progress*, by John Bunyan. 'So, how are you feeling?'

The priest lowered the open book, revealing the title at the top of the page. *The author's apology for his book.* 'Quite a bit better, thanks.' An earnest expression came over his face. 'I'm sorry I couldn't stay around to answer your questions.'

Jon didn't know how to answer. Why did religious types always have to be so bloody meek? The guy was on the brink of a heart attack and here he was apologising for it. 'Hardly your fault, sir.'

The priest went to say something, stopped, then started again. 'I've had these things once or twice in the past.'

Jon raised his eyebrows, not wanting to use the word coronary.

'They're palpitations.' Waters explained. 'Stress related and nothing too serious I'm relieved to say.'

Are you sure, Jon thought. You weren't too good when you realised your car had been broken into.

'They're keeping me in for twenty-four hours' observation, then I'm free to go.'

Jon sat back. 'Well that's a relief. I was very worried last night.'

The priest nodded, then lowered his eyes. 'My church is gone.'

The sudden tremor in his voice made it impossible for Jon to discern whether it was a statement or a question. 'Yes. The roof collapsed. I understand the fire is now out, but the remaining structure is badly burned.'

Waters sighed. Jon pictured startled technicians gathering around a screen, studying the sudden change in the priest's pulse. But the other man didn't seem overtly distressed as his eyes drifted to the opposite wall. 'It was obviously God's will. He has, I can only hope, other plans for me.'

Well, Jon thought, if believing that makes you feel better … 'Oh, your car is secure by the way. We moved it next to the scene of crime unit, and uniformed officers are scouting the area for your kitbag. It'll probably show up dumped in a nearby bin. What will you do now?'

'Contact my bishop. To be honest, I'm torn between getting back to work and asking for a little time off. Sometimes I think I need time to recharge my batteries. Perhaps I'll apply for a posting in a country parish. The fabric of society in our inner cities really is starting to unravel, you know. I frequently fear for our future, I really do.'

Jon had to purse his lips to stop an enthusiastic agreement popping out. 'Have you had much trouble at your church then?'

A ghost of a smile passed across Waters' lips. 'Shall I start with the most recent incident?'

'Sorry,' Jon said, cocking his head to the side. 'Which incident?'

'The attempted break-in three weeks ago. I scared them off that time, but they obviously came back.'

'How do you mean, scared them off?'

'A police officer noted all this down. Once he turned up.'

Jon caught the implication of the comment: it was probably hours before a patrol car got there. 'I'll get a copy of your statement, but could you run through it for me now?'

A slight shiver passed through Waters' shoulders. Again, Jon wondered how long before someone from the monitoring room came to see what was happening. 'It was in the early hours. I was up, jotting down ideas for sermons. They often occur to me in the dead of night, wake me up sometimes with their urgency. Anyway, I heard the noise of metal on metal. Somehow I knew it was someone breaking into the church, so I turned off my reading lamp and drew back the curtain in my study. When I peered out the window I could see them. Three figures, all in black. They were working at the grille on one of the side

24

windows that face the presbytery. I called the police, was told a patrol car would be on its way.'

Jon knew that in each attack so far the arsonists had gained entry into the church by prising away a side window grille, probably with a car jack. Then they'd smashed through the window itself, climbed in, vandalised the altar and spray-painted the walls. Lastly they'd set a fire using hymn books, broken pieces of pews, altar cloths and anything else that was to hand. 'What happened next?'

'They bent the grille right back. Still no patrol car. When they smashed the first pane of glass, I had to intervene. It's over a hundred years old. Stained glass is very expensive to replace.'

'How did you intervene?'

'I got a torch and went outside. Shouted that the police were coming, told them they'd best clear off straight away. Which they did.'

Jon wanted to tut-tut. It was a stupid thing to have done. What if they hadn't fled? The priest obviously believed God was on his side, so the thought of being kicked to death in his own graveyard probably hadn't occurred to him. 'Did you see any of their faces?'

Waters shook his head. 'They were covered. Balaclavas, I suppose.'

'Were they male or female in your opinion?'

'Male, most certainly. Fairly young too, the way they sprinted off across the graveyard. Their movements were those of young men. I coach under-seventeens at hockey, I should know.'

'Did you see what they were using to bend the grille back?'

'One was carrying some sort of a tool.'

'Could it have been a car jack?'

'Yes, I suppose so, they were pumping it up and down. I thought it was some sort of a crowbar, but now you mention a car jack, that seems more likely.'

'Any of them carrying anything else?'

'Yes. One had a container. Plastic. I heard it when it bumped against a headstone.'

Jon wondered if the uniformed officers who had been investigating the arson attacks so far were aware of the incident. He had a nasty feeling they weren't. If the attending officer had filed it as an attempted burglary, his report may have gone unnoticed. 'What did you do next?'

'Inspected the damage, then waited for the promised patrol car.'

'Which arrived ...?'

'Two hours later. Just as dawn was breaking. The policeman looked in need of a good sleep. I think I was his last incident before he clocked off. Anyway, I made him a cup of tea and he noted everything down.'

'You say this was three weeks ago. Do you recall the exact date?'

Waters bowed his head. 'Let's see. It was a Sunday night.'

Jon counted back three weeks. 'The fourth of April?'

'Yes, it must have been.'

Two nights before the first arson attack on a derelict church in Swinton. Shit, this could have been their first attempt. 'From what you said just now, I got the impression there have been other incidents in the past. Is that so?'

The priest placed his book to one side and raised the left sleeve of his pyjama top. A thin scar ran along the underside of his forearm, dots still visible on either side where the stitches had come out. Jon took in its angle and position. Classic defence wound. 'Someone tried to slash you?'

Waters nodded. 'When I wouldn't give him cash or alcohol. You get used to people hammering at the door in the dead of night. The addicted and afflicted I call them. This individual was both, it seemed. They aren't interested in spiritual guidance, just money for their next fix.'

Jon shook his head. Most police officers would only approach someone like that if they had a stab-proof vest and can of pepper spray at the ready. This poor bastard was opening his door to them with nothing but a dog collar for defence.

'But it's not just those people.' Waters was speaking a little faster now. 'The front of the church is showing signs of subsidence. Not such an issue any more, I suppose. Anyway, I advertised locally to raise funds. Next thing, I'm being hounded by builders claiming an expertise in stone masonry or architectural restoration. Leaflets, phone calls, free quotes. Where do they think the money's coming from?' He seemed to shrink into his pyjamas. 'The congregation hardly fills the front pews. Another decade and they'll all be dead.' He stopped, his hands searching out his book, cradling it protectively. 'Forgive me. I'm feeling rather maudlin at the moment. I shouldn't let such a gloomy outlook beset me.'

Jon studied him. He hadn't thought of priests as businessmen, in charge of something that required finance to survive. But, like any building, a church needed to be heated, lit and properly maintained. His mind went to Gorton Monastery, a magnificent building left to rot once donations dried up. He leaned forward in his seat. 'When did that attack occur?'

'Last month.'

Jon wondered if the incidents could somehow be connected. 'Was your attacker caught?'

'No, I've heard nothing more.'

'Description?' He caught himself lapsing into interrogator's role. 'Sorry. What did he look like?'

'About six feet tall. Thin, shaved head. Gaunt in the face. He was wearing a shiny top, like a cagoule.'

Jon knew the uniform well. Below that there would probably have been a pair of nylon tracksuit bottoms that had ridden up around spindly ankles, revealing dirty socks and trainers. Your standard scrote, hopelessly hooked on crack or crystal meth or heroin or speed. Maybe all four. A walking corpse, destined to cheat, lie, rob and steal before something finally snuffed him out. Take your pick: a bad deal, a dirty syringe, or a double-decker bus for all Jon cared. 'What did he say?'

'He had the usual speech prepared. His faith had lapsed, he still wanted to believe, he would start coming to church, refind his path. But – and there's always a but – could he just have some money for the night. I've heard it so often. He'll have needed to eat. Or his pregnant girlfriend would have needed to eat.' He paused for a second to lick his lips. 'There's usually a female involved somewhere.'

Jon blinked. That was, he thought, a heck of a lot of bitterness you just packed into the word female.

'Sometimes,' Waters carried on, 'their baby's short of formula. I even keep a box of milk powder ready. Of course, it's never the right type. So it must be cash. Ten pounds, five. Anything. Always the same.'

'So you turned him away?'

'Yes. I stood firm. Food and nothing else. He got agitated and the next thing went for me with his knife. I pushed him off my step and slammed the door.' A cynical note entered his voice. 'Funny, he never did turn up to any service.'

The guy needed cheering up. Jon looked for a wedding ring. Saw none. 'You get on to your bishop. I think the least you deserve is that break. Where would you go if you get it?'

'There's a retreat in Spain I love,' Waters replied, his face brightening. 'It's near to Salamanca. Have you ever been?'

Jon shook his head.

'Stunning place. So full of history.'

'Good, keep your mind on going back there. Stay positive. In the meantime, can I send an officer to take a statement for last night?'

'Yes.'

'Great. I'll release a comment to the press. Once they realise you're fine they'll soon disappear. They're like vultures in that respect.' Jon stood and held out his hand. 'Take care. I'll keep you posted of any developments.'

The vicar was turning to his book as Jon set off for the canteen. Unlucky Carmel, he thought. No corpse for you on this case. Not yet at least.

The hospital canteen smelt of fried bacon and only a few tables were occupied, a couple of doctors in earnest discussion at one. What looked like a family were at another, the mum looking strained, the two kids glued to handheld games consoles. Carmel beckoned to him. She was sitting at a corner table near the till.

'I've already paid for your drink,' she said, gesturing towards the elderly lady by a stainless steel urn.

'Tea or coffee?' The woman smiled, reaching for a cup and saucer.

'Coffee, thanks. Black, no sugar.'

She handed him his drink and he made his way over to Carmel. She'd taken her overcoat off and was wearing a lilac fitted shirt and black trousers.

He sat down opposite her. 'How're things then?'

She continued running a varnished purple nail round the rim of her cup. 'Apart from this church business? Slow. Nothing doing on Crocodile Dundee?'

Jon shook his head. A lone male had taken to cycling up behind elderly women in Wythenshawe, cutting through the straps of their handbag with a razor-sharp blade, then pedalling away with their possessions. Two weeks ago an old lady had put up a struggle and ended up being stabbed five times. The pathologist had calculated the blade to be ten inches long with a serrated upper side. Hence the Crocodile Dundee moniker. 'No, it'll be signed over to McCloughlin's syndicate now we've got the church case.'

Her eyebrows arched a fraction. 'All settled with him then?'

Carmel was the reporter McCloughlin had leaked details to about the Monster of the Moor case. Jon's discovery of the fact had led to him laying out McCloughlin in the stairwell at Longsight police station. Since then they had steered cautious paths, locked into mutual silence by the dirt each had on the other.

Jon crossed his arms. 'Looks like it for the moment. I'm still watching my back though.'

'So you should. These churches – teenage kids, or something more sinister?'

'Off the record?'

She nodded.

'Teenagers. The priest recently spotted three lads trying to force the grille on one of his church's side windows. Scared them away, but they obviously came back.'

'Graffiti on the walls of this last one?'

'I'm finding out straight after this.' He glanced at his watch. 'Shit, I'd better go.' He took a gulp of his coffee and grimaced. 'Think I'll pass on that.'

'How's the priest doing?' Carmel asked as he got up.

'Burnt out. Like his church in fact.'

She acknowledged his play on words with a little nod. 'But he'll survive?'

'Seems so.'

'Let me know what's happening, won't you?'

'No problem,' Jon replied, already heading for the exit.

# Chapter 4

The incident room at Longsight was all but empty. Jon looked about for anyone who might know what was going on.

'Buchanon's moved the meeting to the room at the end of the corridor,' an indexer replied from behind his computer screen. 'Everyone's in there.'

Jon thanked him. As he walked back out the door he reflected on Mark Buchanon being his Senior Investigating Officer. They'd got into the MIT at the same time, and were almost the same age. Buchanon had joined the Greater Manchester Police four years ago, having spent his career until then with the Met. Apparently his wife was an expert in photon science and had been contracted by Manchester University to undertake a big research project at Jodrell Bank, the huge observatory out on the Cheshire plain near Macclesfield.

Jon found Buchanon himself a bit cold as a person. Efficient, no doubt about it, conscientious and committed too. But there was a slight air of detachment about him. Jon hadn't really analysed it until his colleague had successfully applied for promotion to DCI, then almost immediately been given Summerby's position when the old boy retired at the end of last year.

Buchanon, it was rumoured, was tipped to go a lot higher than heading up one of the MIT's syndicates. It didn't surprise Jon. The guy obviously had brains. Just as importantly, he also kept calm and collected on camera – a valuable attribute for a senior officer these days. Just a shame, Jon thought, about the tightly fixed crimps that made his short brown hair look like an electric current had just passed through it.

It made sense to hold the initial briefing in the big conference room. Any suspicious fire prompted a multi-agency approach and Jon knew that, along with members of the MIT, there would be the crime scene manager, forensics, representatives from the fire service, and the uniformed police officers who'd been handling the case up until now all crammed in.

Jon opened the door to a buzz of voices. No seats left at the central table. He plonked himself down in one of the chairs lining the side of the room and looked around him. Buchanon was at the top of the table, conferring with Webster, the Fire Investigation Officer from the church. Next to him was a dumpy-looking woman with several bulky files, probably a forensics officer with specialist knowledge of fires. To her side was Nikki Kingston. She was staring at him and Jon realised she must have been waiting for his gaze to move round to where she was sitting. As soon as their eyes met she looked back to her colleague with the files.

Guilt flared in Jon's head. Christ, this was her first case as Crime Scene Manager since being signed off for stress. Jon's mind went back to the Monster of the Moor case and the night he and Nikki went searching for evidence in the gully by Black Hill. What a fucking mistake. Possibly the stupidest decision he'd ever made as an officer, and made all the worse by the fact it had involved Nikki.

His eyes lingered on her profile a moment longer. Her face seemed slightly thinner, adding an air of vulnerability to a woman who, until recently, had an aura of self-confidence that Jon found more than attractive.

His gaze wandered on. There were several of his syndicate colleagues, including Gardiner and Adlon and, next to them, Rick, who was now wearing another suit. Jon grinned, straightening the lapels of his jacket as he did so. Seeing the gesture, Rick flicked his middle finger up for an instant. The rest of the table consisted of uniformed officers and a few people in civilian clothes.

Buchanon looked at his watch. 'OK, let's get started. As you'll all be aware, an emergency call was received at three twenty-five this morning. Fire services arrived at the Sacred Heart in Fairfield at three forty. They contained the blaze, but could not prevent it from completely gutting the church.'

Buchanon nodded to his side, his hair not moving a millimetre as he did so. 'This is—' he paused. 'Sorry, I'm not sure what your title is nowadays.'

Webster smiled. 'Neither do any of us in the fire service. I was an assistant divisional officer, but that rank has now become station commander.'

Buchanon nodded. 'Thanks. Station Commander Webster is the fire investigation team manager for the Greater Manchester Fire and Rescue Service.'

Webster put his elbows on the table. 'As you all know, this is the fourth church to burn down in under a month. Our initial examination indicates this one bears the same hallmarks as the other three. Entry appears to have been through a side window, the protective grille of which was forced back. This we can now assume was by a car jack.'

He looked at Nikki, who flinched slightly in her seat then quickly bent to the side. Plastic crackled as she lifted a large evidence bag. Inside was a car jack, almost fully extended. As she attempted to steady it, Jon could see the smallest of trembles in her fingers.

She looked up, her usual air of decisiveness lacking. 'My name's Nikki Kingston and I'm managing the crime scene. This was found in the grass below the side window which had been forced open.' She held up a smaller evidence bag which contained several pieces of broken glass. 'These fragments were found in the same spot. Their jagged edges indicate the pane of glass was smashed, rather than fractured as a result of heat from the fire. Also their undersides are clear of soot or smoke damage, indicating the window was broken before the fire started.'

Buchanon leaned forward. 'We need to be thinking about why this car jack was left behind. Carelessness, or maybe they were disturbed. What we can say is that our arsonist or arsonists entered, and probably exited, the building through the side window. Fragments of glass will most certainly be embedded in their clothing. Station Commander, please continue.'

Jon detected a glimmer of relief on Nikki's face as the fire officer took over. 'The church walls do not appear in danger of collapse, so the building was entered at first light. The fire caused the roof to fall in, covering the entire scene in a layer of roof timbers and slate tiles. Although some supporting trusses are still in place at the tops of the church walls, those on the right-hand side at the altar end of the church have been almost completely burnt away.'

The dumpy woman with the files looked up. 'This fact, along with the V-shaped burn pattern at the base of the wall below that spot, suggests the fire originated there.'

Webster nodded. 'I instructed my crew to leave that area untouched and begin excavating larger debris from the rest of the building. The roof timbers are of considerable weight, so we moved a mini crane on site to start lifting those items over the church walls. This is happening as we speak and I anticipate the scene will be safe enough for a forensic examination by lunch.'

Jon didn't envy the task forensics faced. Identifying exactly how and where the fire started would require the type of finger-tip excavation employed at an archaeological site. Every bit of debris would have to be sifted through, identified, recorded and packaged in case it counted as evidence. Trapped in the waterlogged ash would be that acrid smell, ready to be released as soon as it was disturbed.

A thickly built uniformed officer at the other end of the table half-raised a hand. Buchanon gestured for him to speak. 'Inspector Mather, Trafford Division. I've been co-ordinating the investigation into the previous attacks. Any sign of vandal-ism inside the church?'

The fire investigation officer nodded. 'We could see evidence of graffiti on the walls at the altar end of the church. Symbols, shapes, I'm not sure what; smoke damage is severe.'

Mather leaned his square shoulders forward. 'Pentacles?'

'Sorry?'

'Five-pointed stars?'

'Possible, the shapes were certainly jagged.'

The Inspector gave his colleagues in Trafford Division a meaningful look.

'This is as good a time as any to look at the previous attacks,' Buchanon announced. 'Inspector Mather, it's all yours.'

The officer opened a file. 'First attack occurred on the sixth of April, a derelict Methodist church in Swinton—'

'Sorry to interrupt.' Jon felt all eyes in the room turning to him. 'I've just come from the hospital bed of the priest whose church burned down last night. Are you aware he chased three people trying to break into it on Sunday the fourth of this month?'

The Inspector looked uneasy and Jon knew he'd inadvertently put him on the spot. 'No, I wasn't.'

'Not your fault,' Jon quickly replied. 'I suspect the attending officer logged it as an attempted B and E. Thing is, they were bending back the grille of a side window using, as the priest said, a piece of equipment.'

'Could he give a description of the people trying to break in?' Buchanon asked.

'I haven't had a chance to dig out his statement yet,' Jon replied, 'but he said they were three males, all dressed in black. Faces concealed, but he thinks one fled carrying a large plastic container.'

Buchanon turned to one of the civilian assistants taking notes. 'Janet, get on the system would you? An incident involving the Sacred Heart, Fairfield, fourth of April. Check the next day too – the report may not have been filed straight away.'

As the woman hurried from the room Buchanon turned back to Jon. 'How is the priest, by the way?'

Jon's hand see-sawed from side to side. 'Not so good. Devastated, actually. He's been through some rough times recently. Assaulted in the presbytery not long ago, sustained a knife wound to his forearm in the incident.'

'Was it a heart attack he suffered last night?'

'No. His pulse went haywire, but just palpitations apparently. I think he needs a good holiday.'

'Sounds like it,' Buchanon replied, looking back to Mather. 'You were recapping?'

'The first arson attack occurred on Swinton Methodist Church on the sixth of April, a Tuesday. Next was St Thomas's, an Anglican church in Pendleton, five nights later on Sunday the eleventh.'

'If it was them at the church in Fairfield three weeks ago, they tried to burn down the first church on a Sunday night too,' Jon interjected.

'Good point,' Buchanon said. 'Dates of the third and fourth attacks?'

Mather consulted his notes. 'Then we have a gap of eleven nights before a Church of England building, All Saints in Whalley Range, went up. That was on a Thursday, the twenty-second. Then we have last night's, Monday the twenty-sixth. No witnesses to the first three attacks. The only thing we can find to link them is their relatively secluded locations. None are on main roads, all are tucked away in quiet residential areas. We've been working on the theory that the culprits are driving around during the day scoping potential targets, then returning in the early hours of the morning to carry out their attacks.'

'So they've got transport,' Buchanon said. 'No trains or buses that time of night. How about door-to-doors in the neighbourhoods? Any reports of unfamiliar cars cruising the area? Three males loitering in church grounds?'

'Nothing so far.'

'And no significant evidence from the crime scenes either?'

'Very little. The accelerant being used is petrol; that's now been confirmed by a forensic chemist for all three cases. They're building a pyre using anything combustible that comes to hand. They always position it at the side wall of the church, at the base of wooden panelling in two instances. In terms of—'

He was interrupted by the ringing of the phone in the corner. Buchanon mouthed a silent curse, then flicked a finger to the officer nearest it. The man picked it up, eyes straying to Jon before he lowered the handset to address Buchanon. 'It's the front desk, sir. A member of the public is downstairs. He says he's got evidence that's vital to the arson attacks. He wants to speak directly with DI Spicer.'

Buchanon looked at Jon, eyebrows raised.

Jon returned the expression. 'Maybe because the local radio gave my name.'

'Yes, probably. Who is this person?' Buchanon asked the officer holding the phone.

'A Mr Henry Robson, sir.'

From the corner of his eyes, Jon saw the uniformed officers from Trafford Division exchange glances. One raised a hand to cover his mouth.

'Well, Jon, you'd better see what he's got.'

'Sir.' Jon stood up and headed downstairs.

# Chapter 5

In the station's reception area was the usual collection of people. Some glum, some impatient, others slouched with legs thrust out. One man, however, was standing by the counter, rocking slightly as he transferred his weight from one foot to the other.

Jon looked him over. Late forties, greying hair, neatly cut. He was wearing the kind of slightly padded, light brown coat usually favoured by pensioners. Jon's glance returned to the man's head. He was staring at the notices on the wall with an intense expression, as if studying a higher-than-expected restaurant bill. Jon leaned towards the officer behind the counter. 'Is that Mr Robson?'

The person rolled his eyes. 'It is.'

Jon stepped round to the security door, buzzed the lock and pushed it open. Robson was holding a leather satchel. 'Mr Robson? Please step this way.'

The man suddenly came to life, transferring the satchel to one hand and striding over with his eyes fixed on Jon. 'DI Spicer?'

Jon nodded and the man thrust his hand out. With slight reluctance Jon offered his and felt it enthusiastically shaken up and down. 'I hope we can get to the bottom of this together.'

Oh fuck, Jon thought. Headcase. He recalled how the Trafford officers upstairs reacted to the news a Mr Robson had turned up. Was it a smirk one had quickly concealed with his palm? Suddenly Jon was loath to show the man into an interview room, fearful of how long it would take to get him back out. 'You have some evidence you believe will be of interest?'

The man tapped the satchel, then glanced down the corridor. 'Where can we talk in private?'

Suppressing a sigh, Jon opened the nearest door. 'Here will be 'fine.' He motioned to a chair, then took the one on the other side of the table.

Robson lowered himself into the seat, unzipped his overcoat enough to reveal a plain blue tie and cheap-looking white shirt, then placed the satchel on the scratched surface of the desk. 'They've struck again.'

'Who would that be, sir?'

'The Satanists. They've destroyed another of God's houses.'

Shit, I should have guessed it. Slightly manic stare. Too severe a side parting. Anorak. He's bloody God Squad. The walls of the room seemed to inch in. 'I can't say at the moment. What evidence do you have?' The man's eyes bored into Jon's and he had to lower his gaze. 'Something in that satchel maybe?'

Robson undid the brass buckles and slid out a pile of documents. Topping them was a photo of three young men. They'd been snapped sideways on in the street, seemingly unaware their picture was being taken. All wore black clothes and tattoos were visible on the two in T-shirts. The one in front wore a full-length leather coat and sunglasses. Jon noticed the café behind them. On The Seventh Day. The hippy-type place near the university. The lads were local.

'Satan's Inferno. These people have corrupted my son, lured him from the true path and, increasingly I suspect, sacrificed him to the Devil. They are, DI Spicer, evil. And you need look no further to find those responsible for last night's crime.'

'Sorry, they're who?'

'Satan's Inferno. You're not familiar with them? Or with the music known as Death Metal?'

Jon held his hands out. 'Afraid not.'

Robson sat up, eyes on the Neal twin-deck recorder. 'Does that machine play CDs?'

'Sorry, it's only capable of making tape recordings,' Jon said, relieved the interview wasn't about to branch off in another bizarre direction.

'No matter,' Robson replied. 'I have a player in here.'

Jon's eyes slid to the foam panelling stuck to the walls. How soon before I'm bouncing my head off it? From his bag Robson produced a Walkman and pair of headphones, the earpieces worn ragged at the edges. Then he retrieved a CD case from the bottom of the satchel and slid the CD into the machine. 'Here, put these on,' he said, holding the manky earphones out, his eyes glued to Jon's once again.

Bollocks, Jon thought, glancing at the headset and imagining dead flakes of the other man's skin embedded in the deteriorating foam. Robson thrust them a little closer, as if encouraging a reluctant animal to feed. Gingerly, Jon placed them over his ears.

Robson pressed play and a sound like someone scraping an iron file across a guitar's strings filled Jon's head. A drum was struck again and again, before a mangled voice began to scream, 'Kill, kill, kill!'

Jon reached for the volume control and turned it down. 'Jesus Christ. Is that meant to be a song?'

'Please don't blaspheme. They claim it is music.'

Jon listened for a few moments longer. Nothing changed, except for the loudness. The same monotonous beat, the same tortured chant. He took the earphones off. 'That's awful, I agree, but what's it got to do with these arson attacks?'

'My son, Peter, disappeared four weeks ago. He was, until that time, the support guitar for Satan's Inferno. Six months ago, he was playing in our church band. Then he went along to an organisation that claims to be a college. It teaches you how to commune with spirits, read tarot cards and predict the future, among other things.'

'What's this place called?'

'The Psychic Academy. Here.' He took out a small booklet which Jon could see was a prospectus. Robson began reading from the contents page. 'The secrets of heart-centred healing. Clairvoyancy – connecting with the other side. Psychic powers – unlock yours. Tarot – learn the art. I could go on. In my opinion, this is nothing more than a front for an occult organisation, exposing people to forces they don't know are dangerous until it's too late.'

Jon crossed his arms. 'You're losing me here. How does this

academy link to Satan's Inferno?'

'Peter met the singer from Satan's Inferno on a course at the Psychic Academy.' He tapped the photo. 'This person is the new support guitarist. I fear my son may no longer be alive.'

Jon sat back. He wouldn't be getting out of here in a hurry. 'You've reported him as a missing person?'

Robson nodded.

'And how does this link to the arson attacks?'

'May I quote you a passage from one of their songs?'

In for a penny, in for a pound, thought Jon. 'Go ahead.'

Robson unravelled the CD's sleeve notes and started to read:

> *The beast will be among us soon,*
> *The night shall be torn asunder,*
> *Let us light his way with burning spires,*
> *As the air cracks loud with thunder.*

'That sums up the message of Satan's Inferno,' Robson continued, lowering the cover. 'They actively encourage people to destroy churches and embrace Satan.'

Jon held out a hand and Robson passed him the photocopied piece of paper. The album was called *Raging Spires* and on the front an enormous demon towered over a skyline that Jon quickly recognised as Manchester's. There was the dome of the central library, the Gothic turrets of the town hall, the ugly edifice that was the Jarvis Piccadilly hotel. The horns from the creature's head curled up into a night sky that was laced with forks of lightning. Flipping the poorly cut-out piece of paper over, Jon looked at the album's lyrics. Though the words were slightly smudged, he could see an emphasis on the Devil, death and destruction. 'Nice,' he murmured. 'I take it this lot are still searching for a record deal?'

'They play at plenty of venues around Manchester. And their following grows at a frightening pace. The ringleader is, without a shadow of a doubt, the singer. This one.'

He produced another photo. It was of the band member

wearing sunglasses. This time the shot was head-on, though an out-of-focus shape in one corner made Jon suspect it had been taken from some distance, then blown up.

The man appeared to be in his early twenties, straggly dark hair tied back, sideburns tapering into a thin line of stubble that ran along his jaw before connecting to a goatee. Jon squinted. 'What's that on his forehead?'

'A tattoo. It's an inverted cross, the sign of a devil worshipper.'

'You're serious? He's had that tattooed on his forehead?'

Robson stared grimly back and Jon's gaze returned to the photo. His dark looks and black leather waistcoat gave him a Latino air. 'What's his name?'

'Serberos Tavovitch.'

'That a stage name?'

Robson shrugged.

'Where's he from?'

'He claims to be descended from Romanian gypsies. His soul is lost. He exudes profanity from every pore and he despises all that is decent and Christian. I have seen him drink blood on stage then pass it from his lips into the mouth of a female plucked from the audience. They decorate the stage with severed pigs' heads. They are wicked.'

'Well,' Jon replied. 'Health and safety may have something to say about that, but it's not really my area of expertise. I'm more interested in your assertion that they're burning churches. How can you prove that?'

Robson pointed to the sleeve notes. 'They confess to it here.'

Jon handed back the piece of paper and the photo. 'I need more than that to take this further. Have you video footage of them near one of the churches that's been attacked? A recording of them talking about setting one on fire? A letter or a note?'

Robson shook his head.

Jon looked at the pile of documents. 'What else have you got there?'

'I've been tracking them. Dates of their concerts, what they do during the day. Which shops they visit.'

'Are they aware of you doing this, sir?'

He waved a hand. 'Sometimes.'

Christ, the guy's a loony. 'Do you know where they were on the night of each attack?'

'Only the third one.'

Jon looked up. 'And where were they?'

'Leeds. Playing a concert there. They stayed in a Travelodge in the city centre.'

'On the night a church was burned down in Manchester, the entire band was in a hotel in Leeds?'

'Yes. But one of their acolytes could have done it. They are legion, you should see the crowds at their concerts. They worship them, such is the band's power.'

Right, time to wrap this up, thought Jon. The guy's got an obsession. 'Thank you, sir. I'll look into it.'

'Will you arrest them? Search their houses?'

'Not at this stage of the investigation. I'd prefer to gather some evidence of my own first.'

'Well, take my dossier. I have copies of everything. It will give you plenty to consider.'

Jon accepted the stack of sheets. 'Thanks. I'll go over it.'

'When?'

'As soon as I get the time.'

Robson just sat and stared. God, thought Jon, I need to get out of this room. He resorted to a tried and tested tactic. 'If I could take your number, sir. I'll be in contact in due course.'

Jon jotted it down and was putting his notebook back in his jacket when Robson said, 'Do you have a card? The other officer had a card with a number on where I could reach him.'

'Other officer?'

'Inspector Mather. From the Trafford Division. Not that he returns my calls.'

The bastards, Jon thought. They let me walk straight into this. He reluctantly held out a card as he stood. 'Thanks for your help, Mr Robson.'

Robson reached for it, but latched on to Jon's hand instead. 'Will you pray with me, detective?'

Jon tried to pull free of his grip, but the man's fingers dug in. 'Sir, let go of my hand.'

'You will not pray with me?'

'I'm very busy.' He saw something register in the other man's eyes as Robson released his grip and took the card without a word.

Once he'd shown him back to reception, Jon bounded up the stairs two at a time. He opened the door and knew immediately everyone was now in on the joke.

'Has he converted you yet?' Mather asked innocently.

Chuckles broke out all round. 'Yeah, yeah, good one, you tosser. Christ, he's a bit scary.'

'I hope you didn't use profane language like that in his presence?' Buchanon said.

The laughter picked up a level. Great, thought Jon. Even Buchanon's managed to crack a joke at my expense.

Still smiling, Inspector Mather said, 'Did he ask for a card by the way?'

'He didn't give me much choice.'

'Thank God for that, maybe he'll stop ringing my number now.'

More laughter.

Jon sat down and placed Robson's sheaf of papers on his lap. 'So what's the score with his son? Has he really vanished?'

'Has he, heck,' Mather replied. 'We made some enquiries following the father's allegations that Satan's Inferno were behind the arson attacks. It took us less than two hours to track down the missing son. He was kipping on the sofa of that Serberos fellow's flat. Robson had left home, unable to take any more grief from his old man.'

'Was kipping there?'

'According to Mr Robson, his son is no longer at that address.'

'So when was the last time anyone saw him?'

Mather lifted his eyebrows. 'I don't know. Around three weeks. He'll be hiding from his dad, and I don't blame him.'

'True. Does the dad work for the church or something?' Jon asked.

'No. He's in charge of all the machines at a printing company near Urmston.'

'But manages to combine it with a good bit of bible-bashing.'

'Absolutely, real fire and brimstone. Evangelical, I think. The world's about to end and only true Christians will be plucked from the face of the earth and levitated up to a life of bliss in heaven. The rest of us get dragged down into the pits of hell for an eternity of torment.'

Jon thought about how his mum had fallen out with Ellie. 'His son joining Satan's Inferno didn't go down too well.'

The team from Trafford nodded their assent. 'His dad tried to take a belt to him on several occasions. The local nick attended more than one disturbance at the family home. The son refused to press charges each time.'

'Where's the mum?'

'Committed suicide about six years ago. Small surprise, being married to that nutter. The lead singer of the band is also taking out a restraining order on Mr Robson. Repeated harassment, emails, phone calls. He's barred from all their gigs too, after he climbed on stage and threw holy water over an amp.'

Jon opened his notebook. 'Shall I just tear out his details now?'

Mather laughed. 'Keep them. I don't think that's the last you'll hear from Mr Robson.'

'Right, back to business,' Buchanon cut in. 'I want door-to-doors on the neighbourhood of the Sacred Heart. Gardiner and Adlon, can you take another statement from Father Waters? Cover last night's entry, the incident from the eleventh and the assault DI Spicer mentioned. The rest of you—'

Someone's mobile began to ring.

'If it's a Mr Robson, I'm out,' Jon stated.

Frowning with irritation, Buchanan fished his phone out of his jacket. 'Buchanon here.' His face grew more serious. 'No sign of ID? OK, clear the scene until we get there.' He snapped his phone shut. 'We'll be needing a forensic pathologist. A badly charred body has just been found inside the Sacred Heart.'

# Chapter 6

The mini crane stood motionless, its arm leaning over the side wall of the church. Jon looked at it, thinking how much these towering pieces of machinery had become a part of Manchester's landscape over the past decade.

As soon as one part of the city centre had been revamped, work seemed to shift immediately to another. He'd walked out of the Printworks the other week to be confronted by a colossal building site directly opposite. He'd racked his brain trying to remember what had been there before. The arse-end of the grotesque Arndale Centre? Probably. Things changed so fast it was hard to keep up. Now, according to the posters on the hoardings, it was going to be a massive Next.

They'd skirted round the perimeter to Shudehill tram stop. Behind it was another enormous building site on what used to be waste ground. Soon the city would have a gleaming new bus terminal and multi-storey car park right on that spot. But for now it was just a cluster of cranes. Each one was lowering vats of concrete down to workmen who waited by the side of canyon-like foundations. He watched the men, catching fragments of the unfamiliar languages they spoke. A century ago it had been generations of his family who had helped build Manchester up into an industrial giant. Now those Irish navvies had been replaced by workers from Poland, Romania and other countries from eastern Europe.

Jon turned to the remaining fire crew, now all relegated to the outer cordon. A lady from a nearby house was walking over to them, carrying a tray laden with mugs. They gathered round her and she beamed with pleasure at their grateful smiles.

Nikki was over by the crime scene caravan where a forensics

officer was pointing at a row of nylon bags, the necks of which were tightly closed with plastic ties. Jon knew each would contain samples from inside the church along with a quantity of air. This would allow forensics to gently warm up the bags back at the lab, then draw off a sample of the vapours inside. Gas chromatography would quickly identify whether the type of accelerant used to light the fire matched the one used to burn down the other churches.

Buchanon was tapping his foot. 'Come on, come on,' he murmured to himself.

Finally Webster appeared through the side entrance of the church, its door now reduced to ash. He walked back along the line of footplates to where they waited. 'OK, the pathologist is next to the body. We can get to within twelve feet of him on these footplates. Hard hats on, please.'

Jon glanced down at his white oversuit and heavy-duty rubber boots. Buchanon gave him a pained look as he donned his helmet. Jon imagined the kinks in the man's hair fighting to resist being squashed down. Slipping his own on, he stepped back to trail Buchanon as he followed Webster through the graveyard, blackened roof slates and charred beams now neatly piled at its edge.

As they got nearer the church the familiar sharp smell got stronger. Jon examined the walls. Big chunks of stone. No way they were about to fall down. Footplates formed stepping stones through a puddle in the porch. They moved into the ruined interior and surveyed the scene. A roof timber had crashed down on to the pulpit, breaking off the lectern. The left-hand side of the church still waist-deep in debris. The remains of the roof – a sodden layer of tiles, slats and sooty plaster – lay over the few pews that had survived the blaze.

The FIO led them along the uneven walkway stretching down the aisle. Ahead was a crouching figure, his white oversuit and hood contrasting with the grim landscape. Poking out of the mound of ash before him was a pair of blackened legs, little more than bone.

'I'd say the point of origin is right where the pathologist is,'

Webster stated. 'See the burn pattern on the wall?'

Jon looked for the V-shaped smear of soot the dumpy woman had described back at the station.

Webster pointed. 'Just above the layer of debris can you see a clean patch of stonework?'

Jon nodded. Curiously, there was a spot at the base of the V that appeared to be free of any smoke damage.

'That's what we call a clean burn. It's where the fire was at its fiercest, the high temperatures burning away all the soot laid down by the fire in its earlier stages. Chances are that's where it started.' He gestured across the aisle. 'The door to the vestry has been forced open judging by the damage to the lock. Usual routine – choir surplices, priest's robes, hymn books, all dragged out. They've smashed up several pews as well, then piled everything up against the side wall. There were wooden panels lining it, so they knew the flames would travel up to the timber roof relatively quickly.'

Buchanon's gaze was on the pathologist. 'So, effectively, it was a pyre – if that's where the body was.'

'I suppose so,' Webster replied.

Jon's boss gave a cough. 'DCI Buchanon, SIO.'

The forensic pathologist looked over his shoulder, face concealed by his mask. 'Doctor Richard Milton.'

'Can you see if it's a male or female?' Buchanon asked.

'Not at this stage, it's too badly charred, and the pelvis appears to have been crushed by falling debris. However, it's face down and lying directly on the floor, so the chest area may well be relatively unscathed. Once it's lifted I can look for evidence of breasts. There may be items of jewellery under there too. A necklace or pendant if we're lucky.'

'DNA?' Jon asked.

'Certainly. Complete destruction of a body requires temperatures in excess of a thousand degrees Celsius.' He paused. 'Portions of pelvic bone and dentition even survive the crematorium furnace.'

Jon wanted to roll his eyes. Typical pathologist. They loved giving out details like that.

The other man looked back down. 'Even in a body as badly burned as this, I imagine there'll be some liquid blood and relatively undamaged internal organs.'

Buchanon glanced around. 'So our arsonists entered in the usual way, only this time they leave their car jack and a body behind. Why?' He glanced at the altar with its gouges and chips. 'Sacrifice, or something that went wrong?'

Jon looked at the window frame and its bent grille. The sill was a good five feet high. 'If it was a sacrifice, how do you persuade your victim to quietly climb through a gap like that?'

'Maybe he was sedated,' Buchanon replied.

'Or maybe the person wasn't aware they were going to be the victim at all. Someone they'd picked out and set up. They could have been attacked once they were inside the building.'

Buchanon addressed the pathologist. 'Any sign of trauma to the head?'

The other man craned his neck forward. 'Oh yes.'

Jon was sure there was a trace of pleasure in his voice.

'However, not necessarily resulting from an external impact,' the pathologist continued, glancing at them with a glint in his eye. 'When a head burns, steam and gases build up inside the skull. Often it will burst, usually along the suture lines joining the skull's plates. The damage I can see could be as a result of that process, or debris falling or a blow from another person.'

'So you'll need to conduct a PM before you can say for certain?' Buchanon sounded disappointed.

'Yes. I can also check the lungs and airways. If there's any evidence of smoke inhalation, the person was alive after the fire was lit. If not, they could well have been bashed over the head, then placed on the pile of combustible materials post-mortem.'

'OK.' Buchanon turned round on his foot plate. 'Just need to work out who the poor bastard was.'

Jon surveyed the top end of the church. Just visible on the blackened walls behind the altar was a series of symbols, including a couple of inverted crosses. His mind went to the tattoo on Serberos's forehead. What if Mr Robson was on to something with his theory about his son being murdered? He looked at the corpse's claw-like feet and sighed. It would be worth calling the man and asking him for a DNA sample.

Back in the church car park Buchanon's phone began to ring. Jon watched his senior officer disappear into the mobile home that was the fire service's incident command unit to take the call in private. Jon looked to the crime scene unit, a far smaller caravan with Greater Manchester Police badges stuck on the side. He could see Nikki Kingston through the back window.

'Knock, knock,' Jon said quietly, poking his head through the open door.

She looked up. 'DI Spicer.'

God, thought Jon, she's still angry with me. 'Can I come in?'

She shrugged, continuing to sort out evidence forms.

Jon stepped inside. 'How are you doing?'

'Fine, thank you.'

'It's good to see you back at work.'

She didn't answer.

'What did you get up to on your time off? I tried ringing you a few times.'

Now she looked up, fixing him with a hostile stare. 'Attended quite a lot of counselling sessions actually. Didn't really feel like chatting with you after them.'

Jon felt himself flinch. 'Because of that night ...'

'Yes, Jon, because of the absolute sheer terror you put me through.'

He took a step closer. 'Nikki, I'm sorry. If I could have known what was going to happen—'

She waved a hand. 'Forget it. I'm trying to.' Raising her chin, she ran both hands roughly through her straggly hair, as if trying to yank the remnants of that terrible night from her brain. Jon looked at the smoothness of her throat, the faint blue lines just visible beneath the white skin. But then an image of Derek Peterson appeared, his windpipe slashed to ribbons by those claws.

She sighed. 'The bloody memory still haunts me, though. Doesn't it you?'

He looked down, unable to answer.

'What?' he heard Nikki say. 'Are you having nightmares too?'

He looked out of the window, watching the firefighters as they sipped their tea. He thought of the night sweats that regularly soaked him, of waking up with both hands clamped over his face, trying to cover his eyes from the sights he'd seen. 'Kind of.'

He felt Nikki's hand on his arm. 'Jon, have you seen a counsellor, talked about it with anyone? Alice?'

His wife's name twisted in Nikki's throat. He turned to her, a dry laugh catching in his own. 'How can I tell her, Nikki? Even if I could, I wouldn't want to. I don't want it mentioned. Just to speak about it would ... pollute my home. I don't want that.'

Her eyes had softened and he turned away, not wanting her sympathy. Not wanting to be a victim.

'Jon, you mustn't keep this inside. Not something so traumatic. What about my counsellor? She's very good.'

Jon placed a hand over hers, then gently removed it from his arm. 'I'm OK. My career prospects are hardly brilliant without it getting round that I need therapy. I'll deal with it.'

She flipped her hand over, keeping hold of his fingers. Squeezing them. 'So you'll just force it all down. It doesn't work, Jon. It creeps back. At night, in your dreams. It does, doesn't it?'

Her voice had a whining note. Or was it the hopeful tone of a fellow sufferer seeking solace? 'I'm all right.' He pulled his hand free and retreated to the door, knowing she'd seen through his lies.

'Then talk to me. Let's meet for a drink. How about that? Jon?'

He paused in the doorway to look back at her. God, the prospect was tempting. Just to open up and share it all with someone. He stepped from the caravan without a word.

# Chapter 7

Jon scrubbed at his nails once again. The damned smell from that fire. Would nothing shift it? He washed his fingers under the tap and held them to his nose. Finally the acrid aroma had been obliterated.

He looked down at Holly who was sitting on the kitchen floor. The way she stared silently up at him caused a wave of affection to flood his chest and the grime of the day was forgotten.

'What are you doing down there?' he asked in a singsong voice.

She flapped her arms in response, the action causing her to slide forwards fraction by fraction across the smooth lino floor.

'Come here.' He crouched down and lifted her up so she dangled in front of his face. 'Give me a kiss.'

He brought her closer and pressed his lips against her cheek. So smooth. So perfect. He plonked her back on the floor and looked at his wife. 'When's Ellie due?'

'I said to come round at eight. The food will be ready for about half past.'

Jon glanced at the clock. Quarter to. 'I'll look over some bits and pieces before she gets here.' He took Robson's dossier from the kitchen table and went through to the sitting room. Punch was lying in the corner, and as Jon slumped into his armchair, the dog raised its head. 'You OK, stupid?'

Punch's brown eyes swivelled upwards and the stump of his tail wagged briefly. Jon looked at the upper page of the dossier, a print-out of the band's homepage from a website called MySpace, whatever the hell that was. Skeletons with red eyes sat amid flames springing up from the large Gothic letters spelling out 'Satan's Inferno'. Bunch of freaks, Jon thought, putting the sheet of paper aside.

Next was a close-up of the lead singer. An address had been added in biro, the letters precise and uniform. Below that was a heading that read, 'Exits', followed by a list of dates and times. Jesus, Robson was really stalking him. No wonder the guy was taking out a restraining order against him.

Next sheet was a photo of another band member. Ed Padmore, drummer. He was obviously in his early twenties, wearing the obligatory black clothes, eyes hidden by a thick mop of unruly hair.

Jon flicked to the next sheet. A photo of the third band member, Alec Turnbull. Support guitarist, joined fifteenth May. Again, he was wearing black, hair down to his shoulders. Jon studied his face. Twenty years old, if that. Jon guessed the slightly pained expression was meant to be that of an artist in torment, but the guy was too young to pull it off. He looked more like an anguished teenager.

He went to the next sheet. A building by a car park. Their recording studio, according to Robson's notes. More dates and times. Occasions when they'd rehearsed, Jon guessed.

Below that was a gig schedule, mostly venues around Manchester. Night and Day Café. Jabez Clegg, Band on the Wall, Rockworld. Jon scanned for any dates in May. Diabolic on the twenty-seventh. That was tonight.

Punch's head went up and a second later Jon heard a key turning in the front door. The dog jumped to his feet and padded over to the doorway.

'It's me!' his younger sister called out. Punch's tail bobbed to and fro. 'Hello, Punch, how are you?' Ellie glanced into the room. 'Hi, Jon, heard you on the radio earlier. Did they really find a body in that church?'

'Yup.' He placed the file on the coffee table.

'So was it a sacrifice by devil worshippers?'

He crossed his arms and gave her a look.

She wrinkled her nose in disappointment. 'OK, I know the score. You can't say.'

'So how are you, anyway?'

'Not so bad,' she replied, already heading towards the kitchen. Next thing he heard was the sound of cooing. When he entered the kitchen a minute later Ellie was sitting down, Holly on her lap. He looked at his sister.

Brown hair was held back by a big purple band. Her pale green cardigan was open and Jon could see a fold of flesh poking out of the gap between her white T-shirt and jeans. She had always been prone to putting on weight. Though it bothered her, Jon thought her rounded features made her beautiful.

'Ah, she's gorgeous,' Ellie said, squeezing the baby close.

Alice was smiling. 'Well, you just made it. It's time for her bed. Come on, darling.'

Ellie lifted Holly to Alice's outstretched hands. Jon grabbed one more kiss as she was carried past him, then sauntered over to the table and looked in the Bargain Booze carrier bag his sister had brought with her. A bottle of white, a bottle of red and a DVD case. He lifted it out and read the words Ellie had scrawled on the side. 'Buffy the Vampire Slayer. Christ, Ellie, aren't you a bit old for ghost and ghoulie stuff?'

She cocked her head. 'Actually, Alice asked me to bring it. She missed last night's episode, too.'

Jon sighed with resignation as he examined the bottles. 'Shall I crack one open?'

'Go on then.'

As Jon uncorked the white he wondered how to bring up the subject of the family argument. 'Spoken to Mum recently?'

'No. I've been rushing round a bit,' Ellie replied warily.

Jon nodded, not believing her. 'She called last night. I think she's ready to make up.'

Ellie laughed bitterly. 'Make up? Yeah, right. You know she'll never be able to accept any of us following another religion.'

Us? Don't include me in this, Jon thought, I couldn't give a shit what anybody believes. It's all a load of bollocks. 'Maybe,' he replied, handing her a glass, 'but you could ring her back. She's upset. Worried too, I imagine.'

Ellie took a sip, her eyelids lowering slightly as she swallowed. 'I'll give her a buzz.'

Job done, thought Jon with relief. 'Ever heard of a local group called Satan's Inferno?'

'Yeah. Death Metal aren't they?'

'Have you ever listened to their music?'

Ellie's expression soured. 'Only on the radio. It's so violent, so negative. Couldn't stand it.'

'They're into magic and all that, aren't they?'

Ellie glanced at him. 'If you're implying their music is linked to my beliefs, you are very, very wrong.'

Jon held up a hand. 'Sorry. I just thought, you know, because they go on about hating Christians and the Church.'

'I don't hate the Church.'

'You weren't that in favour of it at Mum's the other day.'

Ellie winced. 'I only came out with that stuff to get back at her. She can be so bloody sanctimonious. I'm not anti-Church.' She paused. 'Well, I am a bit, but I don't want it destroyed like satanists do.'

'Destroyed?'

She placed a forefinger on the base of her glass and began to rotate it slowly. 'Satanism is simply an inversion of Christianity. They believe everything Christians do. They accept the duality of good and evil. In their minds Christ exists, but rather than revere him, they believe he must be fought. They worship Satan and so turn the cross upside down, substitute black for white, spell out the names of deities in reverse. Their whole belief system is locked into that of Christianity.'

Jon leaned back against the edge of the work surface. 'So this Wicca thing you follow ...'

'Is far, far older than Christianity. It's a pagan set of beliefs that sees no division between good and evil. Having said that, I think there's a lot to commend Christianity. Its problem is most of the people who promote it.'

Alice walked back into the room. 'People like your mum, you mean?'

'To an extent, yes. How can she be so intransigent? As I said,

Wicca is a far older religion than Christianity, but it doesn't try to dismiss every other belief.'

Alice removed a casserole dish from the oven and the smell of curry filled the room. 'Her hands are tied, aren't they? Isn't it in the Catholic catechism? Any other religion but theirs results in eternal damnation for its followers.'

'So all Muslims, Hindus, Buddhists, Animists, Taoists, Wiccans – we're all misguided, wrong, deluded. A few hundred years ago we were heretics, and we all know what the church did to them. It's such an unreasonable stance to take. No wonder it's been the cause of so much suffering.'

Jon was taken aback. His sister had so many new viewpoints, new words even. Sanctimonious. Intransigent. It didn't sound like her speaking. He thought about her new friend, the girl from the shop on Oldham Street. 'Why the decision to follow this Wicca religion?'

Ellie frowned in contemplation. 'It found me really. I've been feeling a kind of emptiness for a long time. Then I read an article about this college that's opened up in the Northern Quarter. The Psychic Academy.'

Jon lowered his glass. The place Henry Robson mentioned. Where his son fell in with the singer from Satan's Inferno.

'It offers courses in psychic development, that sort of stuff,' Ellie continued. 'I went along, read some of their literature, signed up for a course and that's where I met Skye.'

'The one who works in this New Age shop?' Alice asked.

'That's right. We got talking about pagan religions. So much of it connected with me.' She pressed a hand against her sternum. 'On a really deep level.'

Jon cringed inwardly. Why did she have to be so airy-fairy? His thought was broken as Ellie started speaking again.

'Society is so driven by greed. People are obsessed with material things – and they've lost their affinity with the natural world as a result. We're all judged on our ability to purchase, to consume. Look at the misery it's generating. People are in debt, trying to keep up, as if buying things can ever lead to long-term happiness. It's absurd.'

She took a sip of wine, then purposefully placed her glass on the table. Get ready, thought Jon. Here comes the profound bit.

'Well, I want to assign more value to myself than just a bloody credit rating. Wicca gives me that sense of worth, of fulfilment.'

'You're talking about spiritual needs,' Alice said, pouring herself a glass.

'I suppose I am.'

'Isn't your mum doing the same thing by going to church?'

'Yes, but churches don't have that meaning for me. The organisation is nothing more than a real estate conglomerate. Their buildings are closed in, stifling. Joyless hymns, droning sermons, cloying clouds of incense, the relentless organ music. It all separates you from what's important. I want to be outside, feeling the grass beneath my feet, breathing clean air, in touch with nature. That's what life's about. That's why I'm joining a coven.'

Jon coughed in mid-sip and felt wine trickling into his nasal passages as he swiftly put his glass down. Sniffing loudly, he wiped a tear from his eye. 'You what?'

'I'm joining a coven.'

'When?'

'In four nights' time. On May Eve, or Beltane as it's known to Wiccans.'

'And what happens on Beltane?' said Jon, sampling the word as if it was foreign.

'We celebrate the coming of spring and summer, the coming regeneration.'

Regeneration, thought Jon. I hope this isn't heading where I think it is. 'How do you celebrate it?'

'A bonfire will be lit. There's dancing and some singing.'

Jon could tell she was being deliberately vague. 'A bonfire?'

Ellie nodded. 'Fires are an essential element of pagan celebrations.' He caught an impish look in her eye. 'You need a bit of warmth if you're outside. Naked.'

'What?'

She grinned. 'Oh come on, Jon, you were asking for that. I can see it in your face. You think this is all about sex.'

'I don't know what it's about. All I know is that you're becoming a witch.'

'A Wiccan. The word witch carries too many negative connotations.'

'And this Skye person. She's a Wiccan too?'

'She is.'

'And she's a member of this coven?'

'Maybe.'

The word echoed in Jon's head. Maybe. 'And she's introducing you to all the magic stuff?'

Ellie frowned. 'All the magic stuff? I'll be learning how to connect with the life force of the planet. Mother Nature, if you will.'

Jon shook his head. Fuck, Mum is going to flip.

'What's the problem, Jon? You think I'm losing the plot?'

'No, I'm thinking Mum will lose the plot when she hears this. Tapping into the planet's life force. Sounds like a load of hocus-pocus to me.'

'As opposed to Mum, who goes to a large cold building and sends telepathic thoughts to a bearded old bloke who lives up in the sky?'

Jon held up his hands. 'Hang on. I didn't say I believed in Mum's stuff either.'

Ellie leaned forward. 'But you don't believe in the planet's life force.'

'Planet's life force. Come on, Ellie, what do you expect me to say?'

'Remember the ouija board we had as kids? That one made by Waddington's, I think.'

'Yeah,' Jon replied, seeing a brown board marked out with the letters of the alphabet in a shallow arc. One to ten across the base, yes and no in the middle.

'Who was pushing the glass round it?'

'You were.'

'Rubbish, Jon, my finger was barely touching that glass.'

'So Dave was.'

'Dave freaked out when he took his finger off the glass and it still carried on moving. And you insisted that you weren't pushing it.'

'OK, that was a bit weird.'

She sat back. 'So you admit there are forces in this world you can't explain. Why be so sceptical about worshipping such a force?'

Alice tapped her foot slowly in thought. 'You're saying this life force was responsible for pushing that glass?'

'No. I can't say what pushed that glass. According to the message that was spelled out, it was a person who'd died five centuries ago. Maybe it was. When someone dies you bury the body, but you don't bury the person. That person – the spark that gave their body movement, warmth, thought – doesn't die. It returns to wherever it came from.'

Jon rubbed at the back of his head. This was all too much on an empty stomach. 'Can we eat?'

Half an hour later and the food was finished. As Jon stacked their plates in the dishwasher his thoughts went back to why they'd invited Ellie round in the first place. 'So when will you ring Mum?'

'Tomorrow.'

'And this Wicca stuff.' He glanced over his shoulder. 'Maybe it's best you don't mention joining a coven.'

'I'm not hiding my beliefs from her, Jon.'

'Just for the moment, OK? Let her get used to the fact you're interested in something other than Catholicism first.'

She looked away. 'Why? She was only too happy to ram her beliefs down our throats when we were kids.'

A sudden rush of anger caused Jon's hand to clench. He slammed a plate into the rack, almost causing its neighbour to fall out. 'For fuck's sake, Ellie. This is what it's really about, isn't it? Getting back at Mum. Of all the beliefs out there, you pick the one that will aggravate her most.'

'Oh sod off, Jon. Now you're being pathetic.'

'Bollocks I am. Pilates, yoga, Buddhism – there are countless other things you could fixate on. But no, it has to be this Wicca shit. You're paying her back for all those Sunday school sessions when you were a kid. Admit it.'

Her bitter tone caught him by surprise. 'How would you know? You were never there.'

She bowed her head, but he'd seen the tears spilling down her cheeks. Registering Alice's look of shock, he turned to stare at the top of his sister's head. Something in her voice had set an alarm bell ringing. 'What did you mean by that?'

She sniffed loudly. Opened her mouth, then shut it.

'Come on, Ellie. What were you going to say? I got it easy? You and Dave had the rough ride? Bullshit. You didn't cop a fraction of the crap I had to deal with. Mum and Dad had forgotten the meaning of the word strict by the time you were a teenager. You can't—'

'You don't get it, do you!' Her face was bright red. 'The oh-so-clever cop. You do not fucking get it.'

He held his hands out. 'What don't I get?'

'That Sunday school.'

'Oh, you mean the hymns? Playing the tambourine. Tinging the triangle. Really tough on you, yeah.'

She looked directly at him, eyes burning with more emotion than he'd ever seen. 'The man who made me sit in the corner. The one who told me I was dirty, worthless, evil. The one who took Dave off into that side room for his special lessons.'

His vision blurred and Ellie's face was all that he could see. 'You what?'

'You heard me. I was a Jezebel. I remember that was the word he used. Years later I looked it up.'

A sense of dread rose up and Jon felt ill.

Ellie's eyes were now closed. 'I sometimes think the reason why I'm single and twenty-eight years old is because I deserve it. I know it's why Dave turned out so fucked up.'

He tried to swallow. 'He touched you?'

'No. Just said things.' She palmed away a tear about a drip from her chin.

Jon felt the muscles in his throat seizing up. 'And Dave?'

'I don't know. It was the look on his face when the man led him back out of that side room. I suppose I always knew, but I didn't understand what had really happened to him until I was much older.'

Jon wanted to shut it out, sit in front of the telly, have a normal end to the day. 'You think he was abusing Dave?'

She gave a single nod. 'He was always so quiet in the back of the car on the way home. We'd exchange looks, but neither of us dared say anything.'

Jon found himself turning away. He picked up a plate and started bending down to put it in the dishwasher. What the fuck am I doing? He put it back on the work surface, hand shaking. Behind him, he heard his sister sniff.

'Are you OK, Ellie?' his wife whispered.

Jon clamped his eyes shut. This is not happening. Please, this is not happening.

'Yeah, I'll be fine,' Ellie replied, but her words were ragged.

'Here, I'll get you a tissue.' Alice again.

'No, don't worry. There's one here.'

'Oh, Ellie.'

He heard the sound of a chair scraping and he knew his wife would be leaning across to hug her. His palms felt glued to the Formica surface. 'Hang on,' he said, head bowed to his chest. 'Where were the other staff and kids? When this man who put you in the corner, and took Dave off into … into that …'

'I often wondered that myself, but I figured it out. They'd gone home. It all happened after the class, when Mum was doing choir practice. This guy would look after us while she was in the main part of the church.'

His eyes stung as he opened them and slowly turned round. Alice was kneeling by Ellie's chair and they were holding hands. His sister's head was resting on his wife's shoulder. His vision began to swim. 'And you never tried to mention it to Mum?'

Ellie shook her head. 'How would I have dared? After all the lectures she'd given us on going to heaven and not sinning.'

Jon's mind reeled. He understood exactly what she meant and the fury moved slowly within him. His mother, so concerned with her pious contribution to her church, hadn't noticed the misery of her own children. He realised that if she was in the room now, he would find it hard not to pick her up and shake her like a rag doll.

'Don't say anything, Jon. Of all things, that would destroy her.'

The room felt stifling, like all the oxygen had been sucked away. 'What did it do to you and Dave? That bloody woman and her beliefs.'

'I'm OK, Jon. I can live with it.'

His mind went to their brother Dave. Living on the streets, begging, stealing, taking drugs. It explained so much. His moods, his love for getting wasted. He was trying to forget. Jon had to breathe in sharply. 'I need to get out.'

They both looked at him, eyes wide.

'Don't tell her, please, Jon,' Ellie whispered.

He waved a hand. 'I'm not going to Mum's.'

'Then what are you doing?' Alice asked. 'Jon, your sister ... what she's just said ...'

He could feel the blood pounding in his temples as he ground his knuckles against them. 'I just have to get out.' He looked at his sister. 'Ellie?'

Her head sank back on to Alice's shoulder. 'You go, Jon.'

He took a step towards her, hand half raised. 'It's just that ... all you've said.' The tears were nearly breaking from his eyes. 'I can't, I don't know. Right now, it's not something I'm able to—'

'I understand. Go, Jon. Get some air inside you.'

'Thank you.' With a last apologetic glance at Alice, he walked quickly from the room, grabbing his coat on the way out.

The streets were deserted as he drove along them, windows fully down. The rush of air buffeted his head and he welcomed the sensation. Ellie. Why did you never say ... the answer appeared before the thought was finished. His mum. The fear she'd sown in all of them. The fear of disgracing her God. He felt like he could rip the steering wheel clean off, fold it in two and hurl it through the windscreen. He breathed deeply, trying to force his thoughts away from what his sister had just said. But, like the point of a compass, his mind kept going back. 'Jesus!' he yelled, slamming a fist against his thigh. The car veered and he had to grab the steering wheel to avoid colliding with the kerb. Again, his sister's words played in his head and he reached for the radio, turning it up as far as it would go. Not loud enough. He wanted a barrage of noise. The song ended and the radio announcer started running through live music events in town that night. Satan's Inferno in Diabolic on Bloom Street, tickets on the door. That'll fucking do, Jon decided, turning left at the next junction.

The air in the tunnel began to tremble and he looked at the black candle's flame as it dipped and wavered in response. Finally the heavy rumble of the train passing overhead died away.

Silence returned.

He rearranged the flattened cardboard boxes, placing one against the brickwork to stop the damp creeping through his coat when he leaned back. The rest he spread out over the bare earth. Sliding the candle closer, he examined the blister on his finger. The skin was stretched taut by the fluid trapped beneath. It resembled, he thought, a full tick. From his army jacket, he produced a penknife and opened out a metal spike. He pressed its point against the surface of the blister, watching the skin bend inward as he gradually increased the pressure. Suddenly the metal pierced it and the sac deflated as a large droplet oozed out.

He raised the finger to his face, liking the way the candle made the fluid glisten as it ran downward. After wiping his hand on his sleeping bag, he picked up the candle and held his middle finger just above it, watching as the skin began to contract, then swell. The intensity of the pain grew rapidly and he gritted his teeth, trying to keep contact with the flame. But the hand holding the candle dropped it and the air hissed from his lips.

He placed the candle back on the cardboard surface and closed his eyes, shutting out the dullness of the ache that was now asserting itself, trying to keep the incredible sharpness of how it had just been alive. He wondered how it must feel to have your whole body wreathed in a sensation so intense. Was that how his mother would feel when Judgement Day came?

Eventually he opened his eyes and reached for the final edition of that day's *Manchester Evening Chronicle*. Starting at the back, he flicked past the sports reports and classified advertisements before reaching the entertainment section. There was the boxed announcement: Satan's Inferno, tonight at Diabolic. He stared down, focusing more on the gaps between the letters than the words themselves. Serberos and Ed. He had thought the three of them were brothers, in this together. But he was wrong. They believed their music was their aim, and with it sales, success and celebrity. He had thought so too. But slowly he'd realised the music was merely a step to something far more important. Better than that: when used properly, it was a conduit, a key, a mechanism to open the fissures of hell and flood the world with fire. To destroy the Church, his dad and the things his dad said.

Closing the paper, he looked at the front page. It was devoted to the discovery of the body in the burnt-out remains of the Sacred Heart church. His eyes paused at a subheading that read, 'A sacrifice to Satan?'

His free hand went to a strand of lank black hair hanging down over his face. Fingers began to roll it back and forth, back and forth.

Then he folded the paper over and flung it to the side. It skidded over the expanse of cardboard, coming to a stop by a ten-litre can of petrol.

# Chapter 8

Jon followed the A34 as it passed under the Mancunian Way, the concrete pillars of the flyover covered in skateboarder graffiti. Soon he was on Princess Street, heading for a small car park tucked behind the deserted office buildings lining the road.

As he parked, he glanced towards the fast food places dotted along the rear of Canal Street. Rick's flat was only two minutes away. That would be good, he thought. A bit of company, and someone who's oblivious to what I now know. He reached for his mobile and called his partner's number.

'Rick, it's Jon. I'm in town.'

'Jon, you all right?'

He took a breath, made an effort to sound relaxed. 'Yeah, 'course.'

'What are you up to now?'

Jon almost smiled at his partner's wary tone. 'Checking out the Death Metal band that Robson bloke was obsessing about. They're playing in a venue called Diabolic.'

'What, tonight?'

'Yeah, fancy coming along?'

'To Diabolic? That hell hole for goths on Bloom Street?'

'That's the one.'

'Erm, it's not convenient at the moment, mate.'

'What do you mean? I can practically see your apartment from where I'm parked.'

'I've got company.'

Company? Did that mean he was in the sack with another man right now? He pushed the thought from his head. 'No problem. I just thought ...'

'I know. Cheers for calling. You know, any other time I'd have been up for it.'

''Course. All right, I'll let you know how I got on tomorrow.' He pressed red, now relieved to get off the phone. Company. He could have just said he was busy or something.

He crossed the half-full car park and turned down the narrow side street leading to Diabolic. On one side was an old cotton merchant's building, on the other a hotel from the Victorian era – elaborate façade, arched windows, large plunging drainpipes. Water dripped from a broken gutter high above his head. Both buildings loomed tall, making Jon feel closed in.

Halfway down, two torches were mounted on the wall of the old cotton merchant's, gas flames flickering in the gloom. A heavy metal gate had been welded across the entrance, possibly the original, erected to protect the side entrance from nineteenth-century thieves. Above it a couple of gargoyles glared down. Those were definitely newer additions. A shaven-headed bouncer regarded him, hands crossed over his bulging stomach, legs planted wide apart.

Jon held up his warrant card. 'Mind if I nip inside?'

The bouncer stepped back. 'You're gonna stand out like a right knob wearing that gear.'

Jon glanced down at his old rugby shirt, jeans and battered trainers. 'Not a good choice for working undercover then?'

'You want to blend in here? Think zombies, mate, land of the living bloody dead.'

Jon clocked the Salford accent. How the guy must despise the types coming in here. 'I'll remember that next time.'

The bouncer extended a hand. 'Doors are straight ahead. Good luck.'

Jon stepped into the flagstoned entrance area. The walls had been stripped back to the bricks, many of which had been removed to create alcoves in which skulls sat. More torches were mounted well above head height, these with living flame effects. Jon looked at the triangles of red and orange silk as they bobbed and wavered. A girl with dark purple lipstick watched him from inside the ticket booth. Grabbing an ornate door handle, Jon stepped into the club itself.

Black. He stood still, waiting for his eyes to adjust to the near absence of light. A bar away to his left, softly lit by hidden bulbs. A stage directly in front, its edges a curved and writhing mass of . . . what? Tree roots? Snakes? The organic forms twisted upwards, creating an arch topped by a leering demonic head complete with shining red eyes.

Jon looked to the sides of the stage once again. Were those pigs' heads mounted on spikes actually real? Jesus, it wouldn't surprise him. A figure was on the stage, tapping drums, pressing foot pedals. In the DJ box someone else was bent forward, adjusting sound levels.

Jon stepped to the side and something moved from under his trainer. He squinted down. Someone's foot must have been poking out from an area of low seats. Faces and hands slowly materialised in the darkness. Pale, ghostlike. Eyes heavy with mascara stared up at him. 'Sorry about that,' he announced, not sure exactly who to address.

No reply.

And you lot are staring at me like I'm a freak, he thought, moving towards the bar. 'A pint of Stella, please.'

As his drink was poured Jon took another look around. Now he could make out the faint glow of green lights. Fire Exit. Toilets. Figures lurked in every recess, cigarette ends glowed briefly to reveal long black hair and darkly painted nails.

'Cheerful atmosphere in here,' Jon said, as his drink was placed on the counter.

The barman's eyes shifted to Jon's rugby shirt. What are you doing here, the look said. 'Three fifty.'

Jon held out the cash. 'When's Satan's Inferno on?'

'About half an hour.'

Jon dropped the coins into the barman's palm. 'Cheers.'

He took a stool to the corner of the bar, placed his back against the wall and examined the stage once again. It looked like something from the set of *Alien* and he guessed it was constructed from fibreglass or epoxy resin. Maybe even concrete.

Something strong enough to withstand bodies crashing against it anyway.

A couple sauntered up to the bar, both painfully thin. The girl's hair had been teased outwards, making her head seem too small. They ordered alcopop drinks, blue liquid that shimmered in the ultraviolet light. You two want a bloody good meal, Jon thought, as they melted back into the shadows.

Light spilled regularly into the club as more and more people came through the outer doors. The guy on stage approached the mike and put his lips against it. 'One two, one two, one two ...' The sound engineer made some adjustments and held up a thumb. The other man climbed off the stage and slipped through a concealed door to the side of the DJ box. From the speakers all around a drum beat started up, followed by a voice which snarled and groaned.

Sod this, Jon thought. He finished his drink and headed across the empty dance-floor. Aware that just about everyone in the club was watching him, he paused at the edge of the stage for a closer look at a pig's head. Plastic, but very realistic.

He reached the door and pushed it open. A narrow corridor led to another door. In front of it was the guy from up on stage. 'Out! This is private ...'

He found Jon's warrant card inches from his face. 'I need a word with the band members.'

'They're on stage in quarter of an hour. They're getting ready.'

Jon extended an arm and began opening the door. 'Best not keep them then.'

The small room was thick with marijuana smoke. A full-length mirror was on one wall, light bulbs mounted in its frame. In front of it Serberos Tavovitch was tying his hair back in a ponytail, a joint hanging from his mouth. Jon saw the inverted cross tattooed on his forehead. I can't believe he's done that.

Round a table were four other people. Jon recognised the drummer and the support guitarist. A bottle of Jack Daniel's stood in the table's centre. They all stared at him in silence. Screwed into the wall behind them a speaker relayed the noise coming from within the club. It sounded far busier than it actually was.

Jon heard the staff member begin to speak in the doorway behind him. 'Guys, I'm sorry. He wouldn't listen—'

'Who the fuck are you?' Serberos interrupted, still regarding his own reflection. His voice was surprisingly deep, but there was no trace of a foreign accent in it. Jon was almost surprised to hear him coming out with an actual sentence. He'd half expected him to start speaking in tongues.

'DI Spicer, Greater Manchester Police.'

No one spoke. Jon saw Serberos slowly raise his hand and move the joint out of sight.

'Just put it out while I'm in here,' Jon said, shifting a guitar case off a chair and sitting down. 'I appreciate you're about to perform, so I'll be quick. What can you tell me about Peter Robson?'

The other band members immediately turned to Serberos. The leader, Jon thought, watching as he carefully tamped down the end of the joint against the heel of a pointed leather boot.

'How do you mean?' asked Serberos, now adjusting the cuffs of his flowing black shirt.

Jon couldn't take his eyes off the inverted cross. As statements go, you didn't get more extreme than that. 'I gather he's been staying at your house. He still there?'

Serberos shook his head. 'He left a fortnight or so ago.'

'Where did he go?'

'We don't know.'

We, Jon thought. You speak for everyone in the band, do you? He looked at the table. The drummer, Padmore, was keeping his eyes down, the support guitarist, Turnbull, looked like a frightened school kid. Jon studied the other two men. 'Who are you?'

'We work here,' one replied, dragging himself upright, pupils heavily dilated. 'Front of stage security.'

What a joke, Jon thought, doubtful they'd be able to stop a determined five-year-old, the state they were in. His stare returned to the two band members. 'Either of you two seen him?'

The drummer shook his head.

'You?' Jon asked the guitarist.

'I've never met him,' he replied, speaking too fast. 'I joined the group after Pete left.'

Jon made a mental note. He was the weak link, no doubt of that.

'Alec joined us two weeks ago,' Serberos said, 'when it was obvious Pete was out of it.'

'Out of it?'

'This.' Serberos looked about. 'Gigging.'

'Why'd he give up?'

Serberos pushed his bottom lip up and held it there. Somehow the expression didn't seem British. Mediterranean, Transylvanian, something foreign. 'Trouble at home. Hassle from that crazy fucking dad he's got.'

'Henry Robson?'

'That's him,' Serberos answered. 'Head case.'

'A colleague informs me you're taking out a restraining order against him.'

'Too right. We've had to ban him from our gigs. He should be inside.'

'What was going on with him and Peter?'

'He didn't want Pete playing with us. He was doing Pete's head in, constantly going on at him with his God and damnation stuff. Pete couldn't handle it.'

'How did you meet Peter Robson?'

'We were both on this lame course. Started chatting about music and it went from there.'

'What was this course?'

'Some tarot-reading bullshit. At a shit heap called the Psychic Academy. I thought it would be a laugh.'

That place, Jon thought. I'll be paying it a visit. 'So he came to live with you.'

'For a bit. We had his old man camped outside my house and Pete was losing it big time. Couldn't rehearse. One day he just disappeared.'

Jon thought of the body in the church. Hopefully by tomorrow they'd have a DNA match off the national database. 'If he shows up can you get him to call me?'

He flicked a card on to the table, pretty certain it would end up as roach material in the next joint.

Back in the main part of the club he saw things were a lot busier. Several groups had emerged from the shadows to stand in front of the stage, and there was raucous laughter as a lad stumbled across the dance floor, thin legs struggling to hold him up. Jon reclaimed his corner and ordered another pint. Ten minutes, he thought. Just see if they've actually got any talent.

The music slowly died down and was replaced by a single funereal organ note as smoke began to swirl across the stage. A laser was switched on at the back of the club, its wafer-thin layer of luminous green bisecting the dance floor at shoulder height. People began to whistle and more bodies started to appear from the alcoves.

The side door opened and the three band members trotted up the stage steps. Padmore headed straight for the back and Turnbull kept to the edge, allowing Serberos centre spot. A beam of light bore down on him as he slid up to the microphone. 'Greetings.'

The crowd erupted in response and Serberos swelled at the applause. His right fingers ready on his guitar, he held a hand over the crowd and drew an upside-down cross in the air. 'Time to worship.'

The barrage of sound was immediate. The crowd began to leap up and down, tossing their long hair about as Serberos strutted around the stage, tensing his knees to bellow out lyrics distorted beyond comprehension by the amplifier's volume. Frequently his left hand went to his open shirt, his fingers caressing his nipples. The first song ended on a long scream and the drum immediately started again, this time even faster. Towards the end of it the drummer went into a frenzied solo and Serberos just stood there swaying, as if in a trance. Jon suddenly realised that his eyes had been fixed on him since the music began. Jesus, the guy certainly had stage presence.

The third song launched on the back of the second and Jon

continued to stare as Serberos tensed in a crouch, microphone held close to his lips. His body language was lascivious, heavy with suggestion.

'See how it tempts them?'

The comment had been yelled in his ear by a man wearing a black T-shirt and sunglasses. Jon turned back to the stage but the man tugged at his sleeve. He removed his mirror shades. Jon immediately recognised the manic stare. Jesus fucking Christ, it was Henry Robson in disguise.

He pushed back a long black fringe. 'I wear this because they don't want witnesses who are hostile to their cause. I'm surprised you've been permitted to stay.'

Jon was nonplussed. Serberos's words echoed in his head. The bloke should be inside. Jon could see his point. 'Aren't you banned from their gigs?'

Robson nodded.

'And isn't there a restraining order against you?'

Robson looked annoyed. 'That hasn't been formally served.'

'But Serberos has applied for one?'

'So I'm led to believe. Will you be arresting them soon?'

Jon shook his head. 'I'm still conducting my investigation. Mr Robson, you didn't tell me about the incidents with your son.'

The comment finally broke Robson's stare and his eyes dropped down. 'His soul was in mortal danger.'

The guy was standing too close. Jon leaned back on his barstool. 'Did an officer contact you for a DNA swab?'

'They did. It's my son's body in that church, DI Spicer, I know it. And the monster up there is responsible.'

Jon's eyes turned to Serberos, who was now kneeling at the front of the stage. He drank from what looked like a ram's horn, then let the dark liquid trickle from his mouth over the upturned face of a female fan. Jon could see Robson's frame was shaking as he opened his mouth. 'Such depravity.'

Jon finished his pint and got off his barstool. 'It's probably blackcurrant squash. The pig heads aren't real either.'

The muscles in Robson's jaw bulged out.

'Just don't do anything stupid, Mr Robson. I'll be in touch.'

As he left the maelstrom of sound behind him Jon decided on a new priority. Henry Robson was an individual who they should be watching very closely.

He slid over the low wall and dropped into the graveyard beyond. The grass was long and slightly damp. Crawling towards the nearest headstone, he felt the ground rise slightly beneath him. As he squatted on the grave he pictured the mouldering remains just six feet beneath. Would the person's clothes have rotted away by now? Had the skin shrunk on the head, leaving a mouth that gaped up at the eternal blackness above? What could those empty sockets actually see?

Peeping over the marble, he looked at the remains of the church, lit brightly by rows of arc lamps. Somewhere out of sight generator engines idled. Seeing it like that – gutted by fire, ravaged by heat – pleased him.

He wanted to look through the empty window frames, allow his eyes to linger on the ruined interior. The house of God, burnt to a crisp. Where was the Almighty's power now? He gazed up at the sky. You're impotent up there, aren't you? Unable to stop anything happening to you or your precious flock.

He ran a hand over the gravestone, felt the grooves on its surface. Letters, numbers, probably a prayer. Whatever it said, it meant nothing. An exercise in futility.

He moved round the outer edge of the graveyard, keeping a careful watch for any police. There was one, sitting in his caravan. The man was oblivious to what moved beyond his windows.

The presbytery lay in darkness. He cut between the graves and reached the wall that led into its garden. More confident now, he vaulted over, feet crushing a plant on the other side. The lawn was cut short and pleasant to jog across. At the living room window, he paused, trying to look in, but closed curtains blocked his view. Was he upstairs? He moved to the corner of the house, his footsteps crunching on the gravel path. The side door was locked. By shaking it, he could tell that it was only secured by a Yale halfway up. At the front of the house he tried the main door. Locked and, by the feel of it, bolted at the top and bottom.

That made the side door his best bet for getting in. He walked back round, crouched down and began to turn the handle again. Torchlight suddenly illuminated the panels before him.

'Stay right where you are!'

The voice was behind him, by the caravan. Not looking back, he sprinted across the garden and dived over the graveyard wall. Rolling on the other side, he jarred his back against an ungiving monument. His hand brushed something cold and metallic. Water sloshed over his fingers. He ripped the flowers from the vase and got ready to hurl it towards the shrubs at the bottom of the presbytery garden. But the torchlight was bouncing along in that direction. Bent double, he scurried to the outer wall of the graveyard, slid back over it and fled down a side street.

# Chapter 9

As Jon jogged round Heaton Moor golf course his stride seemed to be in perfect time with the drumbeat of a Satan's Inferno song. Alongside the monotonous pounding, three words repeated over and over. Dave and Ellie. Dave and Ellie. He searched his mind for something powerful enough to distract him and settled on his daughter's face.

She'd been sleeping through now for almost a month. When it had finally happened Jon realised that an uninterrupted night was among life's finest pleasures, ranking easily with winning at rugby, watching a good video with Alice or spending a night in the pub. Jesus, I'm getting old, he said to himself.

Punch bounded out from behind a patch of gorse bushes, his coat glistening with early morning dew. The animal's sudden reappearance snapped Jon's mind back to the Monster of the Moor case. The sound he and Nikki had heard that night up on Saddleworth. A shudder ran through him and the loop from the Satan's Inferno song finally dropped from his brain.

Jon glanced to the fir trees on his left, deliberately looking at the dawn sun as it glinted between the branches, trying to sear so much from his mind. Punch lolloped up to him, tongue hanging from his mouth. 'Come on, boy,' Jon said, cutting across the damp grass towards Peel Mount. 'I need to be at work.'

He dressed in silence, Alice watching him from the bed, their sleeping daughter in her arms.

His eyes kept going to the bedside clock. Seven thirty-six. That was good, he'd be in the office well before eight.

As he pulled a tie from the collection dangling from a coat

hanger in the wardrobe, his wife finally spoke. 'You haven't asked after Ellie.'

He focused on the thin length of silk. Cross it over, round the back, up, then down through the loop.

'Jon, are you listening?'

'She got home OK then?'

'Yes. She left about five minutes after you did. Said she wanted to be alone.'

He nodded, tightening the knot and then glancing in the mirror to check it was straight.

'How do you feel about what she said?'

He tried to swallow, but a lump had suddenly risen in his throat. Do something. You need to do something. Quickly, he skirted round the bed and retrieved his mobile from next to the alarm clock.

'Jon, talk to me, will you? How do you—'

He held a finger to his lips and then pointed at Holly. 'You'll wake her up at this rate. We can chat later.' He hurried from the room, anxious to be clear of her questions.

The incident room was busy, and after turning his computer on he headed for the kettle in the corner. He didn't know if the decision to get rid of the coffee machine in the corridor was a good one: all the clean cups on the brew table had already gone and he peered into the ones that were left, picking out the least dirty.

He spooned in granules from the large tin of Nescafé, filled his cup and walked over to his desk.

'OK everyone, gather round.'

Buchanon's voice. Time for the morning meeting. Without sitting down, Jon wheeled his chair over to the centre table, next to Rick who was already there. 'All right, mate?'

'Yeah, fine,' Rick replied, eyeing Jon's greasy-looking coffee with distaste.

Jon grinned, knowing how, if Rick had his way, a miniature Starbucks would be operating in the corner of the room.

'First things first,' Buchanon announced. 'There was an

attempted break-in at the presbytery of the Sacred Heart church. It happened at two forty last night.'

Jon lowered his cup. 'Was the priest there?'

Buchanon shook his head. 'The hospital had kept him in for observation. According to the uniform at the scene, it was a lone male trying to gain entry into the house. The officer came out from the crime scene unit, heard footsteps on the gravel by the house and spotted a figure lurking by the side door of the presbytery. His torch lit up the person, but he was dressed entirely in dark clothes, including a wool-type cap. Ignoring an instruction to remain where he was, the person sprinted into the back garden and escaped. The uniform put the person down as a young male, dark hair, about six foot tall. More than that, he can't say.'

'Nothing left at the scene?' someone asked.

'No,' Buchanon replied. 'Forensics will dust the side door for prints. This could be linked to the earlier attempt on the church which' – he glanced at Jon – 'was filed under attempted B and E. Or it could be some local lad trying his luck, knowing the presbytery is unoccupied.'

Jon sat back. Buchanon had a point. Someone had broken into the priest's car as well. Did it indicate a concerted campaign against the man?

'A person from the Bishop's Office for the Pastoral Support of Clergy was in contact yesterday. Full title, the Reverend Manager Canon Maurice Kelly. He was checking that it's OK if Father Waters is allowed to travel to a monastic retreat in Salamanca. A bit of rest and recuperation. The hospice have confirmed to DC Gardiner that Father Waters was there during the night of the arson attack, so I don't see a problem with him going. Does anyone else?'

Jon's finger tapped on his armrest. The priest deserved a holiday, no doubt about that, but if someone was specifically targeting him, they needed to know why. 'Will he be contactable at this retreat?'

'Yes,' Buchanon nodded. 'By phone.'

Jon shrugged. Maybe the man would be safer out of the country until they'd cleared this mess up.

'OK,' Buchanon announced. 'Next is the progress report from the crime scene itself. The corpse has gone to the MRI for an autopsy.' He glanced at his watch. 'I'm hoping to get that tomorrow morning. Meanwhile, the fire investigation officer has continued with the church excavation. All the tiles and roof timbers have now been removed and they're concentrating on clearing the right-hand side of the aisle around where the corpse was discovered. All debris is being sieved and magnets are being run over it. Webster hopes to have that side of the church completely cleared by tomorrow afternoon. That will enable forensics to focus on the point of origin.'

Buchanon stood up and turned to the board behind him. Photos of all four churches attacked so far covered it. 'As mentioned yesterday, each incident follows the same MO. Side window forced back by means of a car jack. The arsonist – or arsonists – then vandalise the church, including spray-painting the walls.' He tapped several photos of symbols and strange letters. Greek, Cyrillic or Arabic, Jon had no idea what. The five-pointed star, and simple diagrams – representations of the planets and their trajectories perhaps.

'The graffiti has been studied by an officer at the Met who worked on a similar case last year. He confirmed these are all things associated with satanic rituals, but used in a fairly random way. The work of amateurs or kids, in his opinion.'

'Amateurs hardly sacrifice people,' someone sitting to Buchanon's side murmured.

The SIO paused. 'True. But it's not yet been confirmed the victim was killed as part of some black-magic ceremony. The Met officer thought if that was the case, the victim would more likely have been left on the altar. He also says the victim would probably have been drugged, in order to be bled while still alive. The victim's blood, it seems, is often an essential part of a satanic sacrifice. The pathologist has been instructed to look for lacerations to the throat or wrists. A blood sample has already gone to toxicology.'

He glanced at the display once again. 'Now, going back to the incidents themselves. Samples from the first three scenes confirm petrol was used to soak the combustible material. Scorch marks on the floor then indicate a trail was laid back to the broken window. It was probably lit with a cigarette lighter, given the absence of any match remains recovered so far.'

'They can find a charred match in all that mess?' asked Rick.

Buchanon nodded. 'The lower levels of debris are swept away by officers using paint brushes. Not much escapes their attention. So, until we get an ID off the corpse, we'll continue with door-to-doors at each scene. Jon, you were looking at that band, what was it? Devil's something?'

'Satan's Inferno. Yes, I went over the dossier handed in to me by Henry Robson. I also went to a gig they were playing last night in a venue called Diabolic.'

'And how was it – diabolical?' Buchanon smiled at his own joke, earning a few obsequious laughs at the same time.

'Well, it was just a load of shouting to me,' Jon replied, 'but so were the Sex Pistols to my mum and dad. Didn't stop me thinking they were great, though. Maybe this style of music will get bigger, everyone there was loving it.'

'What sort of crowd is it?' Buchanon asked.

'A load of sullen spotty goths. The ones who'd managed to get a girlfriend all looked like they were planning suicide pacts together. What's his name, Marilyn Manson? You're about there with his look.'

'Jesus,' Buchanon muttered. 'I pray to God that stuff is long gone before my daughter hits her teens. And the lyrics – you'd describe them as inflammatory? Pardon the pun.'

Jon returned to his desk and opened Robson's dossier. 'I'll spare you the actual music,' he said, removing the CD. 'But this verse is worth hearing.' He read aloud the extract Robson had pointed out.

'That's a blatant instruction to burn down churches,' Buchanon said, outrage in his voice. 'They might not be attacking these churches in person, but they're encouraging others to do it.'

Let's see that stand up in court, Jon thought. 'I reckon it's just teenage angst, dressed up in black. Kids have always gone on about rebelling. They don't do much about it though, other than smashing up the odd phone box.'

'They did a bit more than that in Columbine,' Rick said.

Buchanon crossed his arms. 'And if the body found yesterday was that of Peter Robson?'

'We haul them in for some proper questioning,' Jon said. 'But they claim not to have seen him for a fortnight.'

'What else did they say about their missing band member?'

'He was scared of his dad. I have to admit, Henry Robson is a worrying man. He was at the gig last night, wearing a disguise.'

'Pardon?'

'Trafford Division mentioned that he's banned from seeing Satan's Inferno in person. He was in there though, wearing a black wig and sunglasses. Observing.'

'As long as that's all he does.'

'It's more his attitude that worries me. He has this assumption he's right, and takes it totally for granted we'll be on his side. The way he came up to me in the gig and revealed himself, it's like he thinks we're battling the forces of evil together. People like that believe they're justified in doing anything.'

Buchanon considered the comment for a moment. 'Any other satanic stuff from his dossier?'

'Some,' Jon replied, thinking of the Psychic Academy and the New Age shop on Oldham Street. 'I wouldn't mind looking into the whole occult thing a bit more. There are a couple of places where Rick and I could start.'

'Fine,' Buchanon replied. 'Let's meet again at four thirty.'


'Ticketless booking system nowadays.' Canon Maurice Kelly extended the print-out from bmibaby.

Father Waters took the sheet of paper, struggling to keep it steady in his hands. 'Thank you so much,' he replied. 'You don't know how much this means to me.'

'Nothing more than you deserve. Now, why not let me drive you to the airport? It will cost a fortune to park your car there for the next month.'

Waters looked at his Volvo, the back window of which had now been replaced. Standing on the tarmac next to it was a single brown leather suitcase. 'If you're sure.' He turned to the remains of his church. 'And Gerald at Our Lady is happy to welcome my congregation in? You'll get word to them that they're expected?'

'It's already happening. The lady who organises the coffee mornings was most helpful.'

'Agnes. Yes, she is.'

'And I'll place an announcement on the noticeboard at the front to explain exactly what's going on.'

Waters looked to the wooden structure standing to the side of the church gates. 'What if they don't look there? The police tape stops you from getting too close.'

'Then I'll put another one on the front door of the presbytery if you like.'

'Yes, that would be good.'

The bishop's assistant placed a hand on Waters' shoulder. 'Ben, we'll take care of everything. You can relax. Now we'd better get going, your flight leaves in less than two hours.'

Waters stooped to pick up his suitcase, then straightened up without it. 'And you're sure it's not too much trouble ringing round my hockey team?'

'Ben, I said it wasn't.'

'You've got all their phone numbers? I gave you the print-out and the keys to the clubhouse?'

'Safely in my briefcase. Really, Ben, stop fretting.'

Waters nodded. 'I can't believe I'll be there again. In just a few hours.'

'You've got your passport?'

He patted the breast of his jacket. 'Yes.'

Kelly unlocked his Saab, picked up the suitcase, and placed it on the back seat. 'Right. Away we go. Friar Ignacio is expecting you. He said that he's put aside the cell you stayed in last time.'

Waters sighed as he clicked his seatbelt in place. 'The one with the bougainvillea climbing the wall outside? That's so thoughtful of him.'

As Kelly drove down the close, Ben Waters watched the blackened ruins behind shrink ever smaller in the passenger wing mirror.

# Chapter 10

Jon and Rick headed up Oldham Street, passing an army surplus store with racks of walking boots outside. The buildings seemed to get older and the shops smaller as they walked further up the road. Soon, many were not much more than a doorway and a small window. A barber's. A tiny newsagent's. A vintage clothing store.

With green paint peeling from wooden window frames and a dimly lit interior, Magick looked more like an antiquarian book shop. Jon peered at the display behind the dusty window pane: a variety of books, crystals and tarot cards arranged on a purple velvet cloth. He could see numerous dead flies on the inner window sill and he realised the glass was probably dirtier that side, but that was what he liked about the Northern Quarter; it was still free from the presence of the sterile identi-kit chain stores that plagued every town and city centre across Britain.

He pushed the front door open and immediately the cloying scent of joss sticks hit him. Above the door frame a collection of wind chimes began to tinkle. Music drifted from ancient-looking speakers, whispering notes punctuated by the sound of waves crashing on a beach. It was the sort of stuff Alice used in the salon when she gave a reflexology treatment. Ethereal was how she described it. Insubstantial crap was more accurate, Jon thought.

'Welcome.'

The voice had come from behind a large desk to the left. A man wearing a paisley waistcoat over a white collarless shirt sat watching them. The trail from the joss stick beside him slowly righted itself, the line of rising smoke touching the leaves of the biggest cheese plant Jon had ever seen. It towered almost up to the ceiling, its larger branches supported by lengths of twine nailed to the walls. Leaves the size and shape of lions' heads hung down, some tilted to the side as if listening.

The man's sleeves were rolled up, exposing skinny forearms and a copper band around one wrist. What few strands of hair he had left were stretched back over his bald crown before bunching together in a sad and wispy ponytail. An image of a withered spring onion appeared in Jon's mind and he had to turn away to hide a smile.

'Hi,' Rick replied. 'Just browsing, thanks.'

'Be my guests.' The man turned back to his book.

Jon looked at a glass cabinet holding various sizes of crystal ball. Below them were packs of tarot cards. The next cabinet contained a variety of candles. Tall and thin, short and fat, white, swirly coloured and jet black.

The end of the shop was devoted entirely to books. Jon was just starting across the threadbare crimson carpet when Rick said, 'Interesting.'

Jon turned to his partner, who was nodding at the wall. A notice for the Psychic Academy dominated it. Jon looked at the pieces of paper pinned up around it. A handwritten note detailing the next meetings of the Glossop Pagan Society sat alongside a flyer for Satan's Inferno.

Jon turned to the desk and took out his warrant card. 'DI Spicer, Major Incident Team. Is Skye in by any chance?'

The man looked at it for a moment. 'Major Incident Team?'

'Just background enquiries. Is she around?'

'Not today,' the man replied. 'She's in all day tomorrow though. Can I help?'

'What do you think of this place?' Jon pointed to the Academy's poster.

'Well, some of the courses are outstanding. Especially the one I run.' He gave a crackly laugh as he took the top copy from a pile of prospectuses on the desk. 'Troy Wilkes,' he said, pointing to his name at the top of the page. 'I run the course on attaining a higher quality of spiritual health.'

'And how do we achieve that?' Jon said, keeping his face straight.

'I teach a lifestyle based on yoga, meditation and acupressure, combined with a strict organic vegetarian diet.'

Yeah, you look like a mung-bean muncher, Jon thought, taking in the lack of muscle in the man's shoulders. 'I thought the Academy was more concerned with magic. Casting spells, telling the future, making contact with the dead, that sort of stuff.'

'Yes, I suppose a lot of the courses give the impression you can learn about such things.'

'Give the impression? Something tells me you're not convinced.'

Wilkes sucked in his cheeks. 'My only quibble would be how some of the staff are happy to let students believe they can become a clairvoyant, psychic or medium by attending a few classes.'

Jon smiled inwardly. No organisation, it seemed, could escape a bit of antagonism among its staff. 'I don't follow.'

'You can learn about these things, but not how to do them. The Academy can be, how should I say, a little vague on that point.'

Jon lifted up a prospectus. 'How long have you taught there?'

'Since it opened last year. We've become the principal supplier of books for people taking its courses.'

'I'd never heard of the place until the other day. Popular, is it?'

'Incredibly. There are similar establishments popping up all over. The College of Psychic Studies in London is perhaps the most well known. Then there's the Academy of Psychic and Spiritual Studies in Swansea. There are others in Leeds and Glasgow. And of course the on-line ones.'

No wonder the church is dying on its arse, thought Jon. Everyone's going New Age.

'These are some of the main books we sell to students at the Academy.' He handed Jon a small paperback that looked like it had been printed in someone's garage. *Techniques for Out of Body Experiences*. Jon turned it over and saw the handwritten price sticker. Eleven bloody quid! A nasty bottle of vodka cost less and actually guaranteed a result. He put it back down. 'Well, thanks for your help. And you say Skye is in tomorrow?'

'She is.'

'Great, we'll pop back then.'

They emerged back on to Oldham Street, cut across the road and entered one of the narrow side alleys leading into the disorderly jumble of streets that made up the centre of the Northern Quarter.

White clouds of steam belched from an extractor fan mounted on the rear wall of a blackened building. The vapour was laced with the scent of washing powder.

'Makes a nice change from the sickly-smelling stuff in that shop,' Rick commented.

Jon raised his eyes in agreement. The angular struts of a fire escape's stairs cut into the narrow strip of blue sky above. A pigeon regarded him from the ledge of a window sill. 'What do you reckon to all this New Age stuff?'

'Probably grains of truth in it. The problem is sorting the genuine bits from the crap.'

'Which bits do you think may be genuine?'

'I don't know. You've got to admit some clairvoyants are capable of incredible things. Haven't we used them in investigations before?'

Jon shrugged. Rumours sometimes circulated, but no senior officer he knew had ever admitted to resorting to such measures.

'So what's the situation with this Academy place?' Rick asked.

'It's where Peter Robson, the missing band member, met Serberos Tavovitch, the lead singer of Satan's Inferno,' Jon replied, holding back on the fact that Ellie had enrolled there too.

'I thought they're not in the frame for these arson attacks?'

'They aren't. But I'd like to check it out, find out who else was on the course they attended. Get a feel for what the place is really about.'

As they navigated their way through the maze of narrow streets, Jon looked around with relish. He loved to imagine Manchester when it was establishing itself as the cotton-producing capital of the world. The city had undergone an astonishingly rapid and haphazard expansion of mills and warehouses – and the Northern Quarter was testimony to the chaotic growth.

Soon they were walking along the front of a grime-covered building, its heavy brick sides punctuated by a monotonous series of windows. Jon looked through those at street level. All had displays of thin garments hanging in them. Suspended by near-invisible nylon wires, the items' sleeves were held out to the sides in a beseeching manner, like trapped ghosts.

At the main door Jon examined the list of tenants. Where once the name of a single textile producer had stood, there now jostled a multitude of white plastic business signs. Stencilled black lettering revealed names such as 'Absolutia Collections', 'Paradise Couture (Retail only)', 'Plazio Fashion Import and Wholesale'.

Finally Jon saw the sign he was looking for. 'The Psychic Academy. First Floor.'

They climbed the steep stone steps and pushed through the heavy wooden doors into an enormous and deserted hallway, from which numerous doors led off into the ground floor shops. The first of these was locked and Jon glanced over the notice pinned on the other side of the glass:

Parkside Bailiff Services Ltd. Ref: P11757 Re: Sanjay Patel. Address: Unit 1, Knott House, Back Dale Street. Take notice: Under the terms and conditions of your lease, we as authorised agents acting on behalf of the landlord, have this day, the 22nd of March, re-entered these premises and the lease is hereby determined. Any attempt to re-enter will result in legal proceedings being taken against you.

'Classy premises,' Jon observed as they headed up the stone stairs, reaching a double set of doors on the first floor.

Rick pushed one open.

On the other side was a neatly decorated reception area. The green carpet led across to a simple wooden counter. Behind it, an elderly lady was chatting to a younger woman. Seeing the two visitors waiting, the younger woman said, 'Right, Valerie, I'll get you the information later.'

Jon gave the elder woman a quick smile as she hurried past, then he turned to the receptionist. The wall behind her was decorated with a row of circular wooden tablets. Chiselled into their surfaces were various symbols and letters. Jon immediately spotted a pentagram.

'Are you here to enrol?' The receptionist was looking up at him expectantly.

Rick stepped forward with a smile on his face and produced his warrant card. 'Actually, we're here to enquire about a couple of your students.'

'Oh,' she said. 'I'm not allowed to give out those details.'

'Then who is?' Rick asked.

A reverential note crept into her voice. 'Mr Arkell. He's our Academy Head.'

'Can we see him?'

She glanced at a timetable. 'He's working on the new time-table at the moment. The meeting is due to end in ten minutes. I can ask him when he comes out.'

'Thank you.' Rick turned to the seating area in the corner.

'May I?' Jon asked, taking a copy of the existing timetable from the stack on the counter.

'Of course.' The lady nodded.

Jon took the folded piece of paper, sat down next to Rick and turned his eyes to Monday's classes.

**In the Company of Angels**, Marianne Ash: How to use divine angelic guidance to empower yourself in everyday dealings.

**Advanced Healing Studies**, Rob Brown: Building on what

89

you've learned in earlier courses, Rob will use resonance healing powers to show how our presence as microcosms in the universe can nourish fellow human beings. This session counts towards the credits needed to attain healership status.

For fuck's sake, what a pile of rubbish, thought Jon as his eyes roved to that day's offering.

**Transfiguration for All**, Helena Hunt: Experience our medium as an ectoplasm mask forms over her face prior to her spirit guide making contact.
**The Real Deal**, Valerie Evans: Building on your understanding of Major and Minor Arcana, this class gives a deeper understanding of tarot.

Jon thought of the white-haired woman who had just walked away from reception. She had been called Valerie. He wanted to hang his head in his hands. Why does my little sister always seem to get mixed up in such loads of shit? Looking again at the sheet, he saw the prices being charged.

'All right, Jon? You're looking a little queasy.'

He handed the timetable over to Rick. 'Check what these people are paying for their enlightenment.'

At just after three o'clock voices were heard from beyond the set of double doors on the other side of reception. The doors opened and a group of people began spilling out. Jon was shocked at their appearance. A handful looked like veggies, complete with shaved heads or dreadlocks, and there were a few goths dressed entirely in black. But, outnumbering them all were elderly women in sensible M&S clothes, suited men in their thirties and, at the front of the group, housewife types probably rushing off to collect their kids from school.

'Jesus, I didn't expect a crowd like that,' Jon whispered.

'Me neither,' Rick replied, scanning the stream of pupils as they moved towards the exit.

The receptionist was replacing her phone. 'Tristan is on his way.'

Rick waited for her to look away. 'Tristan?' he said from the corner of his mouth.

Jon suppressed a smile. Tristan Arkell. With a name like that, this should be interesting.

A few moments later the doors to the inner corridor opened and a large man stepped out. He was well over six feet tall, with greying curly hair that receded right back to expose a high, bulbous forehead. His face was fat and there was a piercing quality to his piggy eyes as they swept the room.

The white woollen turtleneck he wore failed to hide the feminine swells of flab on his chest and, as he stepped forward, Jon could see the chunkiness of his thighs, despite the baggy brown cords he was wearing.

'Gentlemen, it's always a pleasure to assist the police. How can I help?'

The man kept his hands crossed over his paunch. Too bad, Jon thought as he stood up. You're shaking my hand whether you want to or not. As he held his right hand out there was a flicker of irritation in the other man's eyes. His fingers unlaced and he gripped Jon's hand. Soft, cool skin, the pressure kept light. A woman's handshake.

'DI Spicer, DS Saville. We were hoping you could answer a few questions about a couple of your students.'

Arkell inclined his head for a moment. 'Of course. Please, come this way.'

They followed him through the double doors and down the corridor. A wooden plaque had been mounted on the door at the end: Tristan Arkell, Academy Head.

His office was spacious with a large rug covering the floor. Jon looked at the interlocking patterns, guessing it originated from Tibet or somewhere similar. Its pattern was replicated by the silk banners that adorned the walls in the few spaces not occupied by shelves of books. In the corner was an enormous leather chaise longue.

'Tea? I have camomile, green or mint.'

Jon glanced at the corner table. No coffee in sight. 'I'm fine, thanks.'

Rick requested a green tea. After pouring out two cups, Arkell indicated they should sit in the chairs in front of his desk. 'Pass on my regards to DCI Summerby when you see him.'

The comment, with its suggestion of cosy familiarity, caught Jon by surprise. He looked up, notebook half out of his jacket pocket. 'You know DCI Summerby?'

Arkell smiled ambiguously. 'We had an involvement on a case several years ago. The little girl who went missing as she walked home from Bury train station.'

Jon's mind went back. The case was years old. What was her name? Anna? Amy?

'Hannah Sherry,' Arkell prompted. 'She disappeared in 'Ninety-seven.'

That's it, Hannah Sherry. Her body was never found. 'You were involved in that case?'

'Merely in an advisory capacity,' Arkell said with a modest lowering of his eyes.

Jon caught Rick's glance. 'In what way?'

Arkell adjusted his weight, as if broaching the subject caused him some discomfort. 'I have visions sometimes,' he sighed. 'And when Hannah vanished I received some very strong images of a red coat.' He leaned forward. 'She was wearing such a coat on the morning she disappeared.'

As the newspaper reports no doubt stated, Jon thought. He said nothing, knowing Arkell wouldn't be able to resist spilling the story.

The man's eyes were now shut. 'I saw the coat in a landscape that was bumpy, the soil sandy. Little pathways. I could see little pathways criss-crossing it. And the smell of the ocean. Sitting on her coat was a toad. Small, but with very distinctive markings. I looked it up in a book. It was a natterjack toad.' His eyes opened. 'DCI Summerby was leading the case, so I contacted him with this information.'

Jon crossed his legs. This should be good. 'And was it of any use to DCI Summerby?'

A pained expression came over Arkell's face. 'He was very sceptical at first. To the degree of even treating me as a suspect.

But, slowly, I like to think he came round to what I was saying. The natterjack toad is very rare you see. There are just a few colonies in the north-west of England. One is the sand dunes at Formby. I was sure the girl was buried there.'

'I believe no body was ever recovered,' Jon said.

'You're right,' Arkell sighed. 'Other avenues of the investigation got priority. The dunes were never searched, at least not by the police. I myself have wandered them many times over the years, but without success.'

'DCI Summerby retired at the end of last year,' Jon said.

'Oh? Well, if you ever speak to him, pass on my regards.'

I'll be speaking to him all right, Jon thought, but purely about you. He looked around the room. 'I hope you don't mind me asking, but how do you become head of a Psychic Academy?'

Arkell's lips twitched with the trace of a smile. 'I've had a fascination with such matters for many years. Inevitable, really, for those with second sight. I started learning more and more, even travelling abroad to further my knowledge of the mind's astonishing potential.'

'Where did you go?'

'I've spent time in the Himalayas of Nepal and the jungles of Brazil. I've been to many other places too. Transcendentally.'

Oh please, Jon thought. 'You must have had an understanding employer.'

'I'd given up work by then.'

'What did you do?'

Arkell shifted his weight on to his other buttock. 'Property dealings.'

'A surveyor?'

'Not exactly.'

'You bought and sold property though?'

He flicked a hand. 'Assisted in.'

'Residential properties?'

'Mostly, yes.'

Estate agent. He was a bloody estate agent. 'So, business doing well?' His eyes strayed to the paper-thin monitor on the corner of the desk.

Arkell paused before answering. 'Our courses are very popular, yes.'

Too right, Jon thought. Forty quid a pop, and none seem to last longer than a fortnight. Then all the pupils have to sign up again for the next stage. 'I didn't spot your name on the prospectus in reception.'

'I tend to find my time absorbed by administrative duties, I'm sad to say. I do make time for some mentoring, but increasingly on a one-to-one basis.'

'And how much do you charge for that?'

He waved a hand. 'What I ask varies according to how much help the individual needs.'

'But the Academy is a profit-making organisation, am I correct?'

'We have an active donation programme. The primary aim of the Academy is to further spiritual development.'

Well, that told me fuck all, Jon thought. 'We're making inquiries into a person who appears to have gone missing. I gather he was a student here recently.'

'His name?' Arkell reached for his keyboard.

'Peter Robson.'

The other man's hand stopped. 'Is this a trick question?'

'Not at all,' Jon replied.

Arkell's eyes swivelled round. 'Peter Robson's father had to be escorted from these premises not one month ago. He and a small group of Christian fundamentalists have waged a campaign of hate on this establishment from the moment our doors opened.'

'I'm sorry,' Jon replied. 'I wasn't aware of that. What has he been up to?'

Arkell opened a drawer and dropped a bundle of letters on to the desk. Jon immediately recognised the spidery handwriting. 'Hate mail promising our eternal damnation. They've picketed the front entrance, harassed staff and pupils as they come and go. I've had to take out a restraining order against him.'

You're not the only one, Jon thought. 'It seems odd his son would enrol here.'

'I had no idea they were related until the father stormed in here accusing one of my tutors of corrupting Peter. That's when we rang yourselves to have him removed.'

'That would have been officers from Booth Street. We tend to work out of Longsight,' Rick explained.

Arkell's eyes narrowed and he turned to Jon. 'DI Spicer. Was it you I heard on the radio yesterday morning? The church in Fairfield?'

Jon gave a nod.

'Is Peter Robson involved in the incident then?'

He might be more than that, thought Jon, an image of the charred corpse in his head. 'We're merely making inquiries at the moment. Had Peter Robson completed his course when his father called in?'

Arkell typed in a password, then began clicking away with the mouse. 'Let me see. Robson, Peter.' He entered the name. 'He first attended a tarot course, by Valerie Evans. Then he signed up for another of hers, the Way of Wicca, before going along to several one-off mediumship sessions.'

'What do those involve?' Jon asked.

'They're sessions hosted by our resident medium, Helena Hunt. She brings communications from the spirit world to members of the audience.'

Jon remembered the timetable entry about an ectoplasm mask.

'What? People wanting to speak with dead relatives?' Rick asked.

'Often,' Arkell replied. 'Though we discourage anyone from attending if their loved one has died within the last twelve months.'

The printer behind him began to whirr and Arkell rotated in his seat. 'Yes, the tarot and Wicca courses both lasted for two weeks,' he said, examining a sheet of paper before placing it on the desk. 'They had concluded well before the time his father turned up.'

Jon leaned forward to see where Arkell was tapping on the sheet. Robson's name was halfway down the list, followed by an entry that read 'Paid'. No grade or anything to indicate how he actually did on the course. Three names below Robson, Jon spotted Tavovitch's name. 'Serberos Tavovitch. How many courses has he attended?'

Arkell hesitated. 'How will this information be used? There are data protection issues I have to consider ...'

Jon looked him in the eye. 'You're all right. It's a murder investigation.'

Arkell blinked at the word, then tapped on the keyboard again. As he turned to collect more print-outs, Rick slid the attendance list for the Way of Wicca course towards Jon. With a meaningful look, he pointed to a name near the bottom. Ellie Spicer.

Jon gave a quick shake of his head as Arkell swivelled back round. 'Three other courses.'

Not interested in what the courses actually were, Jon scanned the names of the other students who'd shared a classroom with the singer. To his relief Ellie's name didn't feature on any. Examining the Way of Wicca print-out once more, another Christian name jumped out at him. Skye. Jon looked to the surname. Booth. Ellie's friend who worked in Magick.

'Tavovitch is an enigmatic character,' Arkell stated.

Jon sat back. 'Do you have many of his type turning up here?'

'His type?'

'Satanists.'

'Is Tavovitch a Satanist?'

'There's an inverted cross tattooed on his forehead. A pretty good indication, wouldn't you say?'

Arkell gave an odd movement of his head. Neither a nod nor a shake. Somewhere in between. 'There is a percentage of people who come here with negative intentions. We try to discourage people from pursuing that path. The Academy is all about positive development.'

'White, not black magic?' Rick interjected.

'Positive, not negative energy.' Arkell smiled back.

Yeah, yeah, Jon thought. Positive bank balance more like. 'Would it be possible to speak with this Helena Hunt? I notice from your timetable she's conducting a session today.'

Arkell glanced at a very expensive-looking wristwatch. 'Yes, she's normally in by now to prepare the room. Let me see if I can find her.'

As soon as the office door shut, Rick turned to Jon. 'Bloody hell,' he whispered. 'The guy's assisted in a murder investigation.'

Jon shook his head. 'There's a difference between someone wandering into a station claiming he's got information from the spiritual world and that information actually being used by us.'

'You're saying Arkell's was a crank tip-off?'

'I'll check with Summerby, but my experience of people like Arkell is they're desperate for any sort of official acknowledgement of their power. So he tries to help out with a case. Then he can claim that, because what he had to say was noted by an officer, he assisted us in our inquiries. Great publicity for him. Only problem is, it's bollocks. Summerby probably just had his claims taken down so Arkell would bugger off.'

Rick glanced at the closed door. 'Sneaky shit.'

As if on cue, Arkell opened the door and stepped back into the room. He was followed by a petite woman somewhere in her forties. Jon was taken aback by how ordinary she looked. Her hair was tied back and thick-rimmed glasses lent her a bookish air. Glancing down, he noted a white shirt collar poking over the neck of her mauve jumper. She could have worked in a library, or maybe a doctor's reception.

'Helena,' Arkell announced. 'These are the police officers.'

'DI Spicer and my colleague, DS Saville,' Jon said, getting to his feet. He realised that he towered over her. 'Thank you for sparing us a few minutes.'

She gave a tight nod, hands clasped nervously before her. You certainly don't look like a con artist, Jon thought. But then again, the best ones never do. Arkell slid over a chair from the other side of the room and they all sat down.

Picking up the print-outs, Jon said, 'Ms Hunt, you conducted a couple of one-on-one mediumship sessions with a Peter Robson.'

Her voice was squeaky and small. 'Yes.'

'How did Peter seem to you?'

Her eyes slid downwards before suddenly lifting and meeting Jon's. He didn't like their beadiness. 'He was in pain. Deep pain.'

'Physically?'

'No, his spirit. It was wounded. I sensed great upheaval in his life.'

'What did he want to find out from his time with you?'

She glanced to Arkell for a split second.

Don't look at that fat turd, Jon thought. 'Ms Hunt? Was he trying to make contact with his dead mother?'

'Yes.'

He carried on looking at her.

'We didn't achieve much in the first session. But my spirit guide discovered a very strong channel during the second.'

Naturally, thought Jon. Bad for business if you provide all the answers straight away. 'What sort of information did you give to Peter?'

'I cannot say.'

'Ms Hunt.' Jon leaned forward. 'There's a possibility Peter is linked to a murder. Any help you can give us would be greatly appreciated.'

'I cannot say,' she repeated, 'because when my spirit guide speaks, I am in a state of trance. Unless the conversation is recorded, I have no knowledge of what's been said through me.'

Oh fuck off, Jon nearly said. 'Did Peter make a recording?'

'No.'

'When you came back round, how did he seem?'

'Er ...'

Jon followed her glance to Arkell, who gave an almost imperceptible nod of his head.

'I suppose he was distressed.'

'Why did you think that?'

'He had been crying. But not through ... not in a happy way.'

You heartless bitch, Jon thought. What sort of shit did you feed to the poor bloke?

'I got the impression his mother is not in a nice place. He didn't stay in the room for much longer and, as he left, he was muttering about pain. Pain caused by fire.'

Jon studied her. 'Did you know his mother committed suicide?'

She looked horrified. 'She set herself alight?'

'No. Maybe Peter was talking about the fires of damnation?'

A hand went to her mouth. 'Oh no, he shouldn't believe that. There is no fire in the afterlife. We are simply reborn ...'

'Well,' Jon cut in. 'Maybe you could leave a note out for your spirit guide? Ask it not to mention fire and pain to a disturbed young man who probably believes his mother is languishing in hell.'

Her gaze was on the carpet as Jon gathered the print-outs. 'Could I borrow these?'

Arkell squirmed. 'The information is confidential—'

'And it will remain so, you have my word.'

The man's hands fluttered above the desk, then dropped to his lap. 'It seems I must trust you.'

'Thanks.' Jon stood up.


Serberos Tavovitch turned on his heel. 'There's no point ringing him. We have nothing to say.'

Alec Turnbull held up Jon Spicer's business card once again. 'I ... I'm not sure about all this—'

There was a crack and the card flew from his fingers, spinning to the floor. Ed Padmore sat back in his seat, now twirling the drumstick round in his hand.

Turnbull looked from one person to the other. 'When I joined this band, I didn't know it would involve all this. If we know where Pete is, we should tell the police.'

'You don't know where he is,' Serberos replied.

'But you do.'

'Who says?'

'When I first came round to rehearse, you said you were nipping over to see Pete afterwards. I remember you saying it.'

'Listen. You want to succeed, yeah? Because this band is going to make it. Have you ever played to the size of audience we get?'

Turnbull shook his head.

'Have you ever felt adoration like that? Don't tell me it doesn't give you a buzz.'

Turnbull began to smile.

'And the women,' Serberos added. 'Ever had so many staring at you? Wanting you?'

They all grinned.

'Right!' Serberos punched the air. 'This is just the start. We'll get signed, trust me. Forget fucking plod. Forget fucking Robson. He's lost it. We haven't got time to be looking back.'

'What if he's setting fire to these churches?' Turnbull demanded.

Serberos and Padmore exchanged a glance.

'What if he's the body in the Fairfield one?'

'What if he is?' Serberos shrugged, reaching for an engraved silver box and taking out a packet of King Size Rizlas. 'It's all publicity for us.'

Padmore crashed out a drum roll on the table top. 'Let's get fucking wasted!'

# Chapter 11

Jon placed the cup of coffee on his desk, checking the rim to make sure it had been properly washed up. 'What did you make of Arkell and that Hunt woman, then? Charlatans or what?'

Rick turned from his computer. 'More entrepreneurs.'

'Is there a difference?'

'A lot of the time, probably not.' Rick smiled. 'Looks like Arkell's hit on a lucrative gap in the market though.'

'You mean the market in spiritual need.'

Rick nodded. 'People have lost faith in the Church. Too much prejudice and prevarication over ordaining women and gay men. Can't seem to make its mind up about abortion or contraception either.'

'You're talking about the Catholic Church, surely?'

'Both. To the man in the street it's all part of the same thing. Society has moved on from those issues, but people still want guidance when it comes to bigger things. Who am I? Where am I going? Obviously spiritualism and the like promise a few answers.'

A fair description of my younger sister, Jon thought as he reached for his phone. 'Have a quick check on Arkell on the PNC. I'll give Summerby a call.' After consulting his address book, he dialled a number. The line double-buzzed, then went silent. Jon pictured the phone ringing in Summerby's cottage in Wales. His old boss picked up on the third ring. 'Edward Summerby here.'

'Boss, it's DI Spicer.'

'Jon, hello there.'

'How's things in Pembrokeshire?'

'Fine, thanks.' Summerby drew out his words at a leisurely

pace. 'I'm sitting here with the paper, watching seagulls wheeling over the bay. There's a few boats out in the breeze.'

Bored then, Jon thought. Sure enough, Summerby asked the question.

'How's the job then?'

'All right, thanks. There's been a few arson attacks on churches—'

'The Sacred Heart in Fairfield? It's linked then?'

Jon could hear the interest bubbling. 'We think so. One line of enquiry has led to a Tristan Arkell.'

'Arkell? The name rings a bell. Is he a man of the cloth?'

'No, he's head of a place in Manchester called the Psychic Academy. He claims to have visions ...'

'I remember the bloke. A salad dodger?'

Jon smiled. 'He does appear to favour a substantial diet.'

'What did the great oaf have to say?'

'He was keen to point out his role in the Hannah Sherry disappearance.'

Summerby's voice hardened. 'The man was clawing for an involvement; that he claims he had one makes me sick. He was a part-time healer in those days, but aiming for bigger things. You say he heads up some kind of spiritual college?'

'Coining it in. Loads of people signing up for classes on clairvoyancy and fortune-telling.'

Summerby snorted. 'A fool and his money are soon parted.'

'True. So his tip-off about the sand dunes at Formby was never followed up?'

Silence. Jon knew he was straying on to a sensitive subject. Unsolved murder cases always were, particularly those of children.

'Not officially, no. I had the dunes searched by four sniffer dogs at first light one Monday morning. Nothing.'

Jon could hear the bitterness in his ex-boss's voice. No doubt desperate for a result, he'd been taken in by Arkell too. Just like those grieving relatives who handed over cash to people claiming to be mediums. 'Thanks, boss, I thought as much.'

'How's he involved in this case?'

'A possible suspect attended a few courses at his Academy, that's all.'

'So how are things under Buchanon?'

Jon kept his voice neutral. 'OK.'

'One other thing, Jon. Arkell's got a record. Sexual assault, back in the seventies if I remember rightly. I seriously considered him for the Sherry disappearance, but he was working in an office when she was taken.'

'An estate agent's, was it?'

'Yes, why do you ask?'

'Just a hunch. Well, I'd better be going.'

'Yes, of course. Anything else, give me a call.'

'Thanks, speak to you soon.'

He hung up and saw Rick holding out a piece of paper. 'He's got a record.'

'Yeah,' Jon answered, placing a forefinger against each temple. 'Let me use my mind powers. Sexual assault, in the seventies, I think.'

Rick glanced towards Jon's phone. 'Twat. Summerby just told you. Did he know about the more recent ones?'

Jon rubbed his hands together. 'Go on.'

'Similar accusations were made in 2002 and 2003. Charges were dropped though.'

'Let me use my powers again. Neither woman was prepared to take it to court?'

'Correct. Although it was a man who dropped the charge in 2002.'

'A man?'

'Yup. It would seem our exponent of positive energy is AC/DC.'

Jon rolled his eyes, an image of the man's fat fingers fumbling at the clothes of his targets. 'Who were they?'

'People who'd contacted him for healing sessions. Maybe they have to surrender physically as well as mentally to be truly cured.'

As Jon caught the sarcasm in his partner's voice, he thought of Ellie, innocently picking her next course at the place. 'What about the one from the seventies?'

'Seventy-nine. That did go to court. Not guilty though. Lack of evidence by the look of it.'

'These more recent ones. What was he actually accused of?'

'Sexual assault. Both had gone for a private consultation. The female claims the attack took place in the Academy.'

Jon pictured the enormous chaise longue in the man's private office. He could see how her claims could have been twisted in court. The victims were probably advised not to take things further to save them from further humiliation.

'Thing is,' Rick said. 'How is this relevant to the arson attacks?'

Jon picked up a pencil and rolled it in his palm. 'Not sure.' Again an image of Ellie hovered in his mind. 'Unless he's one of these control freaks.'

'How do you mean?'

'What if the Academy is his little empire and the students are just there to be manipulated?'

'Like a type of cult.'

'I suppose so.'

'Why persuade them to attack churches?'

'He could be a Devil worshipper too.'

Rick tapped his pen against the edge of the desk.

Jon watched him, knowing something was on his partner's mind. 'You're not convinced, are you?'

'You must admit, it's taking an assumptive leap or two.' His eyes slid off to the side, then slowly worked their way back to Jon. 'Ellie's name was on that list. You're bound to be feeling protective about her.'

'What's that supposed to mean?'

'This Arkell business. It looks like he could well be a sexual predator. He's also cashing in on people's needs for spiritual fulfilment. But I can't see how he has anything to do with the churches burning down.'

Jon sat back and crossed his arms. 'Come on then, spit the rest out.'

'OK. You're letting your concern for Ellie and the fact she's enrolled at Arkell's Academy influence you. She's your little sister, Jon. You're trying to protect her, but it's at the expense of our effectiveness in this investigation.'

'No it isn't.'

Rick lifted the biro and examined the level of ink inside. 'Did you know Ellie's been going along to the place?'

Jon nodded. 'Yeah, she mentioned it the other day.'

'The Way of Wicca. She's into that stuff, then?'

'Until something else catches her attention.'

'But while she's dabbling in it, you'll be keeping an eye out for her. Jon, that's not what we're on this investigation for.'

Something hard twisted inside, pushing up into his throat. He heard a snap. 'Don't tell me what to do. You fucking understand?'

Rick's eyes dropped to Jon's hand and he sat back in his seat. 'OK.'

'Good.' He looked down to see what Rick had been staring at. The pencil lay in two halves on the table. He turned his hand over and saw blood welling up from a small cut in the centre of his palm. He curled his fingers over, hoping Rick would pretend not to have seen. 'I say we look at Arkell more closely. He's a fucking slime-ball.'

'Maybe. But that's surely a long way off brainwashing people into starting fires.'

Jon swept the pencil up and dropped the pieces into his bin. 'Still worth pursuing though.'

Rick raised his hands in defeat. 'Put it to Buchanon then, let him decide.'

Jon looked away. I'm not opening up the fact my sister wants to be a witch to the whole bloody office.

'What about Henry Robson being escorted from the Academy?' Rick asked. 'I bet the bloke omitted to mention that to you when he was handing over his dossier.'

'Funnily enough, you're right. There's quite a lot this dossier didn't include about himself.'

The door to Buchanon's office opened up. 'Right, ladies and gents, let's get started.'

Jon looked behind him. The table in the centre of the room was surrounded by people. He glanced at his watch. Shit, the four thirty progress meeting. He stood up to wheel his chair over. 'Coming?'

Rick nodded.

They positioned their chairs at a desk close to the main table as Buchanon began to speak. 'OK, we've got the pathologist's preliminary report back on the body in the church. He thinks that, at this stage, the most probable cause of death was a massive trauma to the head, though he still can't say if it was a blow delivered by someone else or the result of falling debris. Absence of soot in his airways points to the fact he was dead before – I repeat, before – the fire was started. He's also searched for signs of lacerations to the throat and wrists, but hasn't found any. So it seems he wasn't bled for any sacrifice.'

'Unless blood was collected as it dripped from his head wound,' an officer suggested.

'True, but that would be unusual in cases of satanic rituals,' Buchanon replied.

Someone else piped up. 'You're referring to the victim as a he.'

'Yes, what we can say is the victim is male. DNA tests aren't back yet, but the pathologist believes he was Caucasian, in his late teens or early twenties. The patch of skin on his chest was relatively intact, from where it was pressed against the church floor. Trapped in between was a necklace, hanging from which was an upside-down cross.'

Checking his hand to see if his bleeding had stopped, Jon wondered if they were talking about Peter Robson.

'The pathologist conjectures that, if a weapon was used to kill him, it had a curved edge. Maybe a candlestick, or a portion from the pews ripped up to make the pyre.'

'In which case it's now probably been reduced to ash,' DC Gardiner pointed out.

Buchanon nodded. 'Or a weapon the arsonist or arsonists

brought with them. In which case it could still be around somewhere. Now, regarding the remains of the church, forensics have concentrated on clearing the area to the right of the central aisle in order to get closer to the point of origin itself. On the floor not far from the point was a puddle of melted plastic. This, they believe, was a container that held the petrol used to start the fire. Tests are currently being carried out to determine if that's the case. Miss Kingston, anything further from the crime scene itself?'

Jon glanced at Nikki, who sat at the top of the table.

'Yes.' She raised a document, failing to make eye contact with the listening officers. 'The side window of the church was definitely smashed with the car jack. Fragments were found in its mechanism. We're now trying to determine if any fragments from the other churches are also caught in it. Also, the pathologist supplied us with a sample of cloth from the victim's underside. This, too, had fragments of the church's smashed window embedded in it. So he either broke it himself, climbed in over the debris or was dragged through while unconscious.'

Buchanon's eyes swept the room. 'Anyone with anything to add?'

The members of the Outside Enquiry team conducting door-to-doors all shook their heads.

'DI Spicer. You were delving into the city's occult scene?'

Jon looked at his SIO. 'Yes, DS Saville and I visited a New Age shop on Oldham Street which is the recommended supplier of books for an organisation called the Psychic Academy. This academy is located in a converted factory warehouse in the Northern Quarter. Head of the place is a man called Tristan Arkell.'

He caught a few smirks at his mention of the man's name.

'Student numbers are high at his college – Peter Robson and the singer from Satan's Inferno, Serberos Tavovitch, were two of them. It is, in fact, the place where they apparently met. Now, Arkell has three priors for sexual assault, though nothing has ever stuck in court. However, I think he merits some closer investigation.'

Our of the corner of his eye, he could see Rick give a shake of his head. Cheeky bastard.

'What sort of investigation?' Buchanon asked.

'I think it would be interesting to speak with the three people who accused him of assault – one of whom was male. I wonder how strong an influence this man may have over younger, more vulnerable people. He could be coercing them into all sorts of acts.'

Buchanon tapped his chin. 'Like burning churches?'

'It's a possibility. Arkell is a large man with quite a presence. He's also very good at spouting crap about having magical powers.'

'Sounds a bit shaky to me, Jon.'

'It's the fact Satan's Inferno met there too. There could well be undercurrents to the place that are relevant to the Sacred Heart being attacked.'

Buchanon mulled the information over. 'OK,' he said, not sounding totally convinced. 'Get the names of these three individuals and we'll get it actioned. I'll release a statement after this to let the press know the body of an as yet unidentified male has been discovered. I don't believe there's any point holding back on the satanic graffiti either, so prepare for media interest to move up a gear or two. Let's meet tomorrow at ten o'clock.'

# Chapter 12

Jon opened his front door then stepped back to allow Rick into the house first. 'Hi Alice, it's us,' he called out as they took their jackets off.

'I'll be down in a minute.'

Jon looked up the stairs. 'Changing nappies?' he asked.

'Correct.'

He led the way into the front room, took Robson's dossier from the shelf above the TV and placed it on the coffee table. Punch appeared in the doorway, his gaze snagging briefly on Rick before settling on Jon. The animal's brown eyes lit up and his stump of a tail began to wiggle.

'Hello, you stupid hound,' Jon smiled, dropping to one knee.

Punch reared up on his hind legs and placed a foreleg on each of Jon's shoulders.

'What you been doing today?' Jon asked, his eyes screwed shut as a wet tongue flicked over the end of his nose. He leaned back, unhooked the animal's paws from his shoulders and stood.

Rick was watching with a disgusted expression on his face. 'It's left saliva on your face.'

Jon wiped it off with the cuff of his shirt. 'Only a bit of dog drool, isn't it, boy?' He rubbed behind Punch's ears.

'Has he been letting that dog lick him again?' Alice stood in the doorway, a nappy sack dangling from her fingers. Her other hand was supporting Holly who was wearing a fluffy pink sleep suit. The baby's little legs were clamped round Alice's hip, her big blue eyes fixed on Rick. 'Want a cuddle?' Alice swivelled slightly to offer the baby to him.

Rick lifted Holly up in the air, a big grin on his face. 'You are looking good enough to eat, young lady, yes you are!' She began to giggle as he raised her towards the ceiling.

Jon stepped towards Alice, registering how her eyebrows were slightly raised in question. He knew what the look said. Does Rick know about Ellie? He gave a tiny shake of the head. 'Hi, babe. How's today been?'

'Fine. We did a bit of shopping, stopped in M&S for lunch.' She grinned impishly. 'Holly wanted a big slice of cherry cake, didn't you?'

Jon cocked his head to the side. 'Oh she did, did she? And was Holly able to eat her slice of cherry cake?'

Alice shook her head. 'Nope. She had to give it all to me.'

'Gosh,' Jon replied, feigning surprise. 'Well, at least it didn't go to waste.'

'That's right.' Alice smiled, patting her stomach. 'Fancy spaghetti bolognese, Rick? I've made a load.'

Rick took his eyes from Holly. 'Sure you've got enough?'

''Course.'

'OK, thanks.'

Jon reached out and plucked Holly from Rick's hands. 'Come here, gorgeous.' He placed a series of kisses on her cheek before pressing her against his chest. A layer of fine hair now covered her head and he breathed in the aroma of baby shampoo. God, she smelt so good. 'Has she had her bottle?'

Alice shook her head. 'I'll get it. After that she's ready for bed.'

Jon nodded at the dossier. 'Have a flick through. I'll be back in a minute.'

Alice reappeared in the doorway with a three-quarters full bottle. 'Cheers,' Jon said, taking it from her, and trudging up the stairs to the nursery with his daughter. Cuddly animals peeped down from the top of the wardrobe as he sat down in the armchair, positioned Holly across his lap and held the bottle to her lips. As she began to drink, he looked at the top of her head, studying her wispy strands of blonde hair. One day it would be long, probably tied back in pigtails. He imagined her five years from now, skipping through the local park. Would she prefer dresses or dungarees? A shy little girl or a confident tomboy? If she was anything like her mum, it would be the latter. An image of Holly as a miniature Alice, practising her kick-boxing moves on the boys in her toddler group, almost made him laugh out loud. Gazing down, he saw her lashes begin to droop lower as the milk made her drowsy.

Another day had passed for him, a lifetime for her. Every minute an adventure, every carpet a giant expanse to be explored, every object on it a thing of fascination. The world was awaiting her discovery. He looked at her tiny fingers curled round his thumb, saw the smoothness of her skin against his criss-crossed flesh. Suddenly he felt very old.

The teat slid from her lips and he placed the empty bottle on the floor. She was barely awake as he wound the key of the mobile attached to the head of the cot. 'Rock-a-bye-baby' began to tinkle out and the white fluffy sheep hanging over her mattress slowly started to revolve.

Jon stood up and laid Holly on the cotton sheet before tracing a finger down the side of her face. 'Night-night.'

As soon as he moved towards the door her eyes began to open. Quickly he stepped out on to the landing and, as he pulled the door shut, he could hear her struggling to turn over, an angry cry starting up. Wincing, Jon tiptoed down the stairs, but by the time he reached the bottom, she was in full throttle. He stood with his head bowed, analysing the noise. Though it was a frustrated cry, there was a shrill of tiredness in it too and he knew she wouldn't keep it up for long.

Hard as it was leaving her, he stepped back in the living room, glancing at the dossier as he closed the door behind him. 'Right,' he announced. 'Henry "the end of the world is nigh" Robson has been stalking the band his son used to play guitar for. This lot.' He sat down and slid the photo of the group to Rick. 'Satan's Inferno. You ever listened to Death Metal?'

'No,' Rick replied.

'Black Sabbath, Iron Maiden – that stuff is tame in comparison. This music has stripped out any actual tune. Sounds like something recorded in a torture chamber. Goes on about the

Devil taking over the world. Here.' He showed Rick the cover of the band's CD.

His partner examined the image of the demon towering over Manchester's skyline. 'I think I get the picture.'

Jon got up to listen at the door. Silence from upstairs. Relieved, he sat down again. 'So Peter Robson joins the band, leaves home and starts avoiding his dad.'

'Then he disappears.'

'According to the father.'

'And Peter Robson met the other band members on a course at this Psychic Academy?'

'Serberos Tavovitch at least.' Jon tapped the photo of the lead singer. 'This freak.'

Rick checked the door was shut, then quietly said, 'And Ellie's started attending courses at this place, too?'

Jon shook his head. 'Don't remind me. Thing is, what if the body in the church is Peter Robson's? What implications does that have for the investigation?'

'We'd need to get the rest of the band in.'

'Agreed. But what would their motive have been for killing him?'

Rick looked down at the photos. 'Which one is Peter?'

Jon flicked through to the press clipping Henry Robson had shown him. 'Here.'

They looked at the image of Peter, taking in the lank hair framing his mournful face.

'Reminds me of Neil from *The Young Ones*,' Jon stated.

'Who?' Rick asked.

'Neil. You know, the moping hippy one.'

'The hippy one. One what?'

'Jesus,' Jon murmured. 'I keep forgetting you're just a baby. Forget it. What I'm saying is, there's something sad about him. Like he's not totally happy about being on that stage. Maybe he started having doubts about continuing. I mean, he'd led a pretty strait-laced life up until that point. We know he's fucked up about his mum. Suddenly he's in a Death Metal band, playing gigs round the city and torching churches in the dead of night.'

'Wait up,' Rick interrupted. 'Torching churches? We've got no proof of that.'

Jon hunched forward. 'Just assume it, for the moment. They're torching churches, getting into all the messed-up satanist stuff.'

'So why kill him?'

'I don't know. He starts to waver, maybe wants out.'

Rick nodded. 'But they don't want him to leave.'

'Yeah,' Jon replied, feeling the familiar glimmer of excitement as a scenario started to take shape. 'Could even have been a kind of sacrifice, I don't know.'

Rick pinched a bottom lip between a forefinger and thumb. 'It's a theory. Not much more than that.'

Jon's shoulders dropped. 'Yeah, you're right. Until we get an identity on that body we could go on speculating for days.'

'What about Father Waters? Did you get hold of him when you called that retreat?'

Jon snorted. The instant the phone had started to ring, he knew it was going to be a nightmare. For a start the ring tone was a single beeping sound. He was just wondering if it was an engaged tone when his call was answered.

'Diga,' a croaky voice had said.

Jon was thrown into confusion. 'Hello. Do you speak English?'

'Un poco. A little.'

He realised his voice had slowed right down and increased in volume. 'I'm an English policeman, calling from England. DI Spicer.'

'Deeyie?'

'DI. Detective Inspector.' He paused. 'Spicer. My name is Jon Spicer. Is Father Ben Waters there?'

'Waters?'

'Yes. Is he there?'

'You have his message?'

'I have a message for him. Is he there?'

'Father Waters?'

'Yes. Can he call me?' Jon had read out his number, dreading what the person on the other end of the line was writing down.

Jon rubbed at his temples with both forefingers, then looked up at Rick. 'Put it this way, if Waters hasn't called back by lunchtime tomorrow, I'll try again. We need to know if he's met either of the Robsons, or Tristan Arkell for that matter.'

'Why not ring Henry Robson and ask him?'

Jon raised his eyebrows. 'And encourage a dialogue with that nutter? No chance.'

Alice's voice came from the kitchen. 'Food's ready!'

Jon and Punch stood simultaneously, the Pavlovian reaction equally strong in both of them. 'Let's eat.'

In the kitchen Alice was ladling bolognese sauce into three large white bowls. 'You can do the honours,' she said, nodding at the bottle of red on the side.

Jon gestured for Rick to sit, took out a corkscrew and began removing the foil from the bottle's neck.

'So who is currently on the receiving end of an Alice Spicer mauling?' Rick asked with a grin.

Alice brushed a strand of hair from her eyes, an innocent look on her face. 'What do you mean?'

'What do you mean?' Rick repeated incredulously.

Jon had to nod. Since the Monster of the Moor case the previous year, his wife had developed quite an activist streak. Local politicians, councillors, journalists, and figures from the business world all regularly received letters of complaint when Alice sensed duplicity, hypocrisy or dishonest statements. 'I might be sinking my teeth into the council at the moment.'

'What have those poor bastards done?' Rick asked breezily.

'They're withdrawing funding for a phone line that helps people suffering from mental illness. As if Manchester hasn't got a high enough suicide rate as it is. I tell you, it really pisses me off.'

Jon sneaked a look at Rick which said, you've gone and bloody started her now.

'They need to pinch a few pennies,' Alice continued, 'and the first thing they look at are those services which, by the nature of the people who use them, are less likely to draw criticism when cut. Someone in the depths of depression isn't exactly in a position to stand up for themselves. It's just plain cowardice on the council's part.' She paused. 'Anyway ... How's city-centre living treating you?'

Rick rearranged the salt and pepper pots in the middle of the table. 'Great, thanks.'

She picked up two bowls and placed them on the table. 'And how's the love life?'

Jon felt a sinking feeling. Why did she always have to ask? He glanced at Rick, who was smiling coyly.

Alice's eyes had widened. 'You've met someone. You have, haven't you?'

Rick hunched a shoulder.

Alice sat down and leaned forward over her bowl. 'Come on, tell me!'

He ground a little pepper over his food. 'He's an events organiser. Puts on private parties round town. For footballers, TV celebs, all sorts.'

'Never!' Alice's face was beaming. 'He organises parties for footballers? Like who?'

'Oh, I can't remember the names. Is it Fedrosa?'

'Sol Fedrosa?' Alice's eyes were almost popping out.

'That's it. He did his birthday bash. And that one they call Shrek.'

'He's done a party for him as well?'

'His girlfriend, I think. It was in Ebony. They hired the whole place.'

'I saw the photos in one of those magazines!' Alice exclaimed.

Jon reached for his bowl, knowing Alice had now totally forgotten about his food.

'Wait until I tell Melvyn. He'll be so jealous.'

Jon pictured the camp owner of the salon where Alice was due to go back to work. The news would cause him a chronic bout of hand-flapping.

'So what's he like?' Alice asked, now twirling spaghetti round the prongs of her fork.

'Late thirties. About six feet tall. Black hair, sort of brushed forward on top.'

'And his body?'

Jon glanced at his wife. For fuck's sake.

Rick grinned. 'Very nice, thank you. He works out most days.'

'Good firm arse, then?'

Before Rick could answer, Jon picked up the bottle. 'Rick. Red?'

'Thanks.' He slid his glass over.

'Ali?'

'Cheers.'

Jon filled hers up. As he poured his own he frantically tried to think of some way to change the conversation, but an image of Rick caressing another man's naked buttocks was now lodged firmly in his head.

Alice's eyes were still on Rick, an expectant expression on her face.

Rick drew in breath through his nose. 'Let's just say you could pop open a bottle of Stella with it.'

Jon slumped over his spaghetti. That, I didn't need to know.

A knock sounded at the door. Jon looked at Alice. 'Expecting anyone?'

'Nope.'

He walked down the passage, eyes on the pane of frosted glass. The top of a head was just visible and Jon recognised the silvery hair. Mum. Part of him wanted to retreat to the kitchen and pretend she wasn't there. He opened up.

'Oh Jon, sorry to come round like this, but we've really got to talk.'

She was standing on the step, clutching a small handbag against her coat with both hands, her face pinched with worry.

Bollocks, thought Jon, waving her in. 'What's up?'

'It's Ellie,' she said breathlessly, stepping into the hall. 'She simply refuses to see sense.'

'You've spoken to her?'

'Yes.'

'When?'

'Just now. Why?'

Jon met his mother's eyes, but it was obvious Ellie had said nothing about the Sunday school. 'So you've had another argument,' he said, walking back to the kitchen, his mother babbling away behind him.

'She doesn't understand what she's getting herself into. Really, she doesn't. I asked her what she believes joining a coven is all about.'

'She told you she's going to join a coven?'

'Yes, on the phone. Not a word about the dangers of worshipping false idols ... oh, hello Rick. I didn't realise you were here.'

'Hi, Mrs Spicer,' Rick replied.

'Have you eaten, Mary?' Alice asked.

'Yes, thanks. Don't mind me. You carry on.' She moved the local paper off the stool in the corner and sat down. Jon sank back on his chair and took a large sip of wine. 'So what did you say to provoke her?'

'I didn't provoke her. I went round with some information about the occult. Father O'Dowd kindly gave it to me.'

That old wino, Jon thought, picturing the red-nosed old priest who ran the Catholic church his mum attended. The guy knocked back so much Irish whiskey he wouldn't be able to look at a number six without seeing three of them. 'And what information was that?'

'He obtained some figures for me about exorcisms. Do you realise how many people come to believe they're possessed by the Devil after meddling with the occult? The Church performs dozens of exorcisms every year. In Italy it employs a couple of priests whose full-time job is to perform them. It's frightening, it really is.'

'But Mary,' Alice said. 'Practising a pagan religion isn't the same as worshipping the Devil. We went over this.'

Mary flicked a hand. 'It's the thin end of the wedge according to Father O'Dowd.'

Jon saw his wife's lips tighten and he knew she was having to bite her tongue.

Mary turned to Jon once again. 'I've done a bit of research

into this event when she wants to be initiated. May Eve is also known by paganists as Beltane. It's a festival of fire that celebrates the fertility of the coming year.'

Jon lowered his glass. 'Fertility?'

'Yes. Men and women go off into the woods in pairs to collect flowers for the festival. Then they light a bonfire and take it in turns to jump over it. It's meant to purify them and bring good fortune for the coming year. It's all about increasing fertility.'

Jon looked at Alice. 'They pair off and go into the woods?'

Alice sighed. 'These things are symbolic. It doesn't end up with everyone having sex. The maypole is a phallic symbol. Just because young girls will be dancing around it at village fairs up and down the country this May Day, doesn't mean they're warming up for an orgy.'

Jon turned back to his mum. 'What else did Ellie say about the festival?'

'She laughed at me. The girl in her house tried to claim the church is repressed, she came out with some nonsense about these stories being the product of sex-starved priests' imaginations.'

'Which girl?'

'I don't know who she was. She had beads in her hair and a tie-dyed top.'

Skye, Jon thought, liking the sound of his sister's new friend less and less.

'Jon tells me you used to go to the church at Gorton Monastery,' Rick said.

Mary's face softened. 'Yes, I did. Years ago now.'

'It looks like a magnificent building. Must have been a lovely place to worship in.'

She swivelled slightly to face Rick. 'Oh, it was. Did you know it's Manchester's highest single-storey building? They positioned it with the nave running north to south, rather than east to west as is traditionally the way.'

'Why did they do that?' Rick replied.

Mary's eyes drifted to a point on the wall above Rick's head. 'It was a declaration. Gorton, you see, is twenty feet higher than the city centre. In the 1870s – that's when it was built – there were many fields to the west of the city. The monastery rose up out of them.' She lifted her palms like a preacher addressing a crowd. 'The aim was to mimic Chartres cathedral, and it worked. The building towered above the skyline, dominating the view from Manchester. You know it was designed by Edward Pugin, son of Augustus, who was responsible for the Houses of Parliament?'

'No, I didn't.'

Jon glanced at Rick. Where's your interest in church architecture suddenly come from, he wondered. Then he realised the ulterior motive behind the questions. Rick was diverting the conversation from an argument about Ellie, and he was succeeding very well.

'You can see his father's influence in my opinion,' Mary continued, her fingers tracing shapes in the air. 'The intricacy of the stonework, the buttresses, and those gargoyles peering down.'

Now she was talking out of her arse, Jon thought. The Houses of Parliament didn't have gargoyles on its façade.

'How was it a declaration?' Rick asked.

'Well,' she replied, hands returning to her lap as she took on the tone of a schoolteacher. 'You must remember Catholicism in this country was banned by King Henry VIII. It took another three hundred years until the Catholic Emancipation Act was passed, allowing us to own property. We're back, the friars who built it were saying. Catholicism has returned to Britain.'

'You attended Mass there as a little girl, didn't you?' Rick asked.

'Yes,' Mary answered with a nostalgic smile. 'A lot of the congregation was Irish. The completion of the monastery coincided with the arrival of huge numbers from back home. They were the people who helped turn Manchester into a proper city. Jon's grandmother and all her sisters worked in the mills, and his grandfather and uncles helped dig the canals and build the aqueducts.'

Rick held up a forefinger and Jon could see he was now indulging Mary, encouraging her to reminisce. 'Wasn't Jon's grandfather – your father – the champion bare-knuckle fighter?'

Jon saw his mother redden slightly. She didn't like to admit the family's passage out of Manchester's slums was bought with the profits of smashing in men's faces.

'That was my great-granddad, Padraig,' Jon said. 'Huge bastard he was.'

'Jon,' his mum chided, 'no need for language like that. You know, at its peak the monastery had a congregation of thousands. The sunlight would flood through the stained-glass windows on the eastern side, lighting up the apostles on their pedestals lining the nave. The reredos – that's the carved screen behind the altar – would be shimmering with candles, and the air was fragrant with the incense that floated up into the vault above our heads.'

Fragrant, thought Jon. That's one way of describing the stink. And you're forgetting the line of miserable people waiting their turn in the confessionals. The clouds of guilt filling the place.

'How did it end up as a derelict wreck?' Rick asked.

Mary's face fell. 'It's a shameful story. The slum clearances of the seventies meant the congregation was moved away. New housing estates in Hyde and Hattersley and Wythenshawe. By the nineteen-eighties there were only a few dozen of us going back to attend mass. They decided to close it and move the remaining friars to a monastery in Somerset. The last Mass was celebrated, if that's the word for it, in nineteen-eighty-nine and the place was sold to property developers shortly after.'

Jon topped up their glasses. There was no stopping her now.

'The plan was to turn it into flats, but the company went bust and the monastery was left unguarded. It was a tragedy. Vandals and looters moved in and all the artefacts and anything else was stolen. The twelve statues of the apostles went, the reredos was smashed, the pews were ripped out. It was scandalous. That building is a world heritage site.'

Rick looked at her, clearly taken aback by the story. The silence was broken by Alice collecting the plates, the noise stirring Mary from her reverie. 'Anyway, Jon, what are we to do about Ellie?'

'Mum, she's an adult. There's no law stopping her from joining a coven. A couple of hundred years ago, maybe ...'

'Don't be flippant. This is serious, she's in danger.'

Jon sat back. What, like she was perfectly safe in that fucking Sunday school you dumped her and Dave in? He glanced at Alice and saw the look of warning on her face. I have to admit, he thought, I don't like the sound of this Beltane festival either, and I don't like the sound of this Skye Booth. 'I'll ask some questions tomorrow, all right?'

Troy Wilkes stepped from Magick out on to Oldham Street. Night had fallen and the road was almost deserted. A couple stood in the doorway of the *Big Issue* offices further down, bickering over how to divide up the day's takings.

Wilkes pulled the front door shut, deadening the pips of the alarm inside. He locked the door and waited for the last elongated beep. Satisfied the alarm was properly activated, he slotted the keys into his pocket and set off down the narrow alley that cut through towards the Manchester Arts and Crafts centre. Another jinking side road would take him to Shudehill tram stop and his journey back home to Altrincham.

As he started down the alley his mind was on the big policeman and his partner who'd dropped into the shop earlier that day. What could members of the Major Incident Team want with Skye? He knew they only handled the serious stuff like murders and rapes. Maybe he'd better call her, he thought, taking his mobile from his pocket. Then again, he was working with her in the shop tomorrow. He could tell her then and save himself the price of a phone call.

As he slipped the mobile back in his jacket he was unaware of the figure stepping out from the doorway behind him. Pain mixed with surprise as fingers were suddenly clamped round his neck, and he felt himself being yanked backwards into the shadows, unable to cry for help.

# Chapter 13

Holding his mobile to his ear, Jon sipped black coffee, eyes glued to the front door of Magick across the street. The café he was waiting in formed part of a delicatessen that appeared to specialise in ethical foods – organic this, Fairtrade that. Jon had scanned the shelves while ordering his drink, unsure of what many of the packets contained. Pulses, powders, more varieties of lentil than he ever knew existed. The only items that were familiar were jars of Tiptree jams – Blackberry Jelly. Now that brought back childhood memories of scouring the bushes by the side of the canal ...

'Nothing else then?' Carmel said again. 'Just what's in the press release.'

'That's right. A young male, probably died from a blow to the head. If you want some background stuff, it's worth looking into the Death Metal scene.'

'He was a follower of Death Metal?'

'I didn't say that. It all seems closely linked to Satanism, that's all.'

'OK. I'll see what we've got on the Psychic Academy and send any articles over.'

'Cheers, Carmel, speak to you soon.'

The two women behind him were discussing a Harry Potter book. The one who was reading it was describing a scene where the would-be witches and wizards were learning about potions and spells and roots of mandrake that shrieked when pulled from the ground.

A petite girl was walking up from the direction of Piccadilly Gardens. Though her thick locks of raven-black hair were adorned with beads, it was her choice of clothing that caught

Jon's attention. Her oat-coloured cardigan was of a thickly woven knit, flecked with brown dots and hanging down to her knees. It had the appearance of something fashioned in a crofter's hut on some distant Scottish isle. Her skirt was russet-coloured, long and flowing, almost obscuring a pair of brown suede boots. Hanging over her shoulder was a large canvas handbag, the strap plaited from thick braid.

As she stepped round a waste bin, he caught a glimpse of the wide belt at her slender waist, its buckle of an interlinking Celtic design.

What's the betting, Jon said to himself, that you stop at Magick?

She came to a halt at the front door and reached into her bag. Thought so. He finished his coffee and got to his feet. As he edged past the two female Harry Potter fans, he contemplated leaning over them and whispering, Professor Snape did it.

The door to Magick hadn't even fully closed behind her as he pushed it open again. She turned round and Jon was struck by her strange beauty. Heavy eyebrows curved over large brown eyes that seemed fractionally too far apart. A button for a nose and wide, sensual lips. One of those eyebrows arched slightly as she swept a beaded strand of hair away from her face. Though his sudden entry had obviously taken her by surprise, there was no alarm showing in those languid eyes, just curiosity as she calmly held his gaze. He had the sudden feeling she was assessing him far beyond his external appearance.

'Morning. Would you be Skye Booth?'

Her eyebrows buckled slightly and he wondered if she knew how attractive that made her. 'Yes. And you are?'

'Sorry. DI Spicer, Greater Manchester Police.' He fumbled for his warrant card. 'My ID is here somewhere.'

'Ellie's big brother.'

Jon looked at her, giving up his search. 'That's right.'

She stepped behind the counter, flicking on the shop's lights. Crystal balls began to glow in their cabinets. 'She has a beautiful soul, your sister. No artifice or acting; what you see is what you get.'

Right, thought Jon. Why couldn't you have just said you like her?

She turned the till on, then released the drawer. Jon heard the sound of coins shifting as the plastic tray jarred to a halt on its runners. He waited for her to say something else but she was now tidying the pamphlets on the counter.

'You two met at the Psychic Academy, Ellie tells me.'

She didn't look up. 'Yes, we got to chatting one break time.'

'What do you think of the courses there?'

'They're pretty good, certainly as a basic introduction to many subjects.' She reached under the counter and placed a small square of wood and a packet of joss sticks by the till. The leaves of the cheese plant hanging above her head seemed to be watching her as she slid a stick out, then flipped a cigarette lighter. Once a dull flame had taken hold at the tip she blew it out, snapped the lighter shut and placed it so deftly on the counter, no noise was made. She guided the end of the joss stick effortlessly into a tiny hole in the wooden block and regarded the thin wisp of smoke as it spiralled up towards her face.

Jon caught a whiff of the cloying aroma, which brought instant memories of Mass. 'Only an introduction? I thought you'd end up more than a novice, given the prices they charge.'

'Depends what you're studying.'

'What are your favourite areas?'

'I'm interested in alternative health, homeopathic medicines, reconnecting with the natural world. What about you?'

Somehow there was a suggestiveness to her question. He looked for confirmation in her face, but saw none. 'I'm interested in this whole New Age thing as part of an ongoing investigation.'

'Not just checking up on your little sister?'

The comment cut through the small talk. Jon paused, considering how to play it. He turned to the wall and spotted a new flyer up for Satan's Inferno. It announced a gig they were playing on May Eve. The venue was Diabolic once again. Takings must have been good for their last appearance.

'You a fan?'

She giggled. A genuine sound from deep down, not just the front of her mouth. 'No. Have you heard their stuff?'

Jon smiled back. 'It's, it's ... I can't think how to describe it.'

'Horrible?'

'Yeah, that'll do. For starters.' He relaxed, leaning on the counter, about to continue in a less formal way. Careful, a voice inside him said, she's drawing you in. He looked at her face, his eyes lingering on the remains of the smile still on her lips. In the dimness of the shop's interior her pupils appeared fully dilated. 'How about the singer? I understand he's attended a few courses at the Psychic Academy too.'

She shrugged. 'I rarely speak to him. He pops in here every now and again to pin up posters.'

'Peter Robson?'

She raised her eyebrows in question.

'He played guitar for the band until a few weeks ago.'

She shook her head. 'Sorry.'

Jon looked around. How do I steer this towards what she's planning with Ellie? Her earlier comment about checking up on his younger sister meant she'd already sussed him. To some extent at least. 'What is alternative health anyway?'

'Well, I'm training to be an acupuncturist.'

A voodoo image flashed into Jon's mind. 'Who do you use for a pin cushion?'

For the first time a negative look crossed her face. A spark of irritation. 'It's a four-year course.'

Jon straightened up. 'Seriously?'

'You need to learn the body's complete nervous system, its muscles and skeleton. There's more knowledge of anatomy involved than most GPs come close to possessing.'

'Sorry, I didn't mean to belittle it. I know it can have amazing results, cured a guy at my rugby club of his shoulder pain just like that.' He clicked his fingers. 'What about homeopathic medicines? Do you mean mandrake, stuff like that?'

She smiled. 'You've been reading Harry Potter.'

He spread his palms. 'Guilty.'

'Mandrake's well known for is medicinal properties. You'll never learn the power of every plant though, there's so much knowledge to absorb. That's not counting the huge amounts that have been lost over the last couple of centuries.'

'Since the days Merlin was around?'

Her eyebrows tilted again, but he'd made sure not to smile. 'Druids knew a lot, yes. Still do. But it was the wise women who were traditionally responsible for the health of their communities.'

'Wise woman being another way of saying witch?'

Her face darkened. 'They were classed as witches by the emerging, male-dominated, medical establishment. It was a concerted campaign to wrest power from them by discrediting and questioning their abilities. Tragically, it culminated in tens of thousands of women being burned at the stake across Europe.'

Ah, here's where Ellie's new-found views are coming from, thought Jon.

'You have a baby, don't you?' she asked.

The change in tack caught him by surprise. 'I do. Holly, almost ten months old.'

'Tell me, in the hospital, who gave the orders in the delivery room?'

'The doctor, of course.'

'Describe him.'

Jon frowned. 'I don't know, late twenties maybe. Kept checking the read-outs from the machine monitoring the baby's heart.'

'And who did most in the actual delivery of your baby? Before, during and after her birth?'

'The midwife.' Jon remembered her well – a middle-aged woman who exuded a reassuring warmth. She'd been brilliant, calming Alice and keeping him informed of exactly what was going on. Now he thought about it, there had been more than one occasion when the doctor had turned to the midwife for advice. 'I get it – before doctors muscled in, it was wise women who took care of everything, including childbirth.'

She nodded. 'Glad to enlighten you.'

He grinned. 'You'll be telling me you read fortunes next.'

'I do a passable attempt.'

'Really?' Jon glanced down at his hands.

'Though I warn you, I'm no expert.' Without waiting to be asked, she took his hand in hers. The touch of her fingers sent a warm sensation through his wrist. It carried in waves up his arm as she lifted the back of his hand and examined it. 'So much damage to your skin.' A fingertip traced the scar that ran over his thumb.

Jon wanted to sit, her caresses made him feel so weak. 'Rugby studs. Sometimes they had sharp burrs on – before they brought in the Kitemarks. A kind of safety ...' His words trailed off. She wasn't listening to his babble. Christ, the way she was probing at his palm felt good.

Slowly she flipped his hand over then beckoned for him to hold out his other. Just as he was about to extend it, his mobile rang. 'Sorry.' He stepped back, breaking contact to take out his phone. Rick's name was on the screen. 'What's up, mate?'

'Buchanon's just announced there's a DNA match on the body in the church. Where are you, by the way?'

He glanced at Skye whose chin was now propped on the heel of her hand. Her brown eyes didn't break from his. He swallowed. 'Just following up some inquiries on Oldham Street.'

'You're questioning the witch?'

Jon quickly turned away, afraid she'd have heard the comment in the silence of the shop. 'That's correct.'

'Don't tell me. She's next to you, isn't she?'

'Absolutely.'

'OK. Well, you'd better get back here. Ten o'clock meeting, remember?'

Jon glanced at his watch. It had just gone a quarter to. 'Will do,' he replied, cutting the call and looking back at Skye. 'I have to go.' He stepped towards the door, then paused. 'Listen, here's my number. I may need to speak to you again – about the Psychic Academy.'

She took the card by its corner. 'OK. We could finish your palm reading too.'

Jon nodded, and hurried outside. He crossed the road and cut down a side street to where his car was parked. As he approached the vehicle he flexed his fingers back and forth. Jesus, there was something electric in her touch, his skin was tingling even now. He shook his head. Think clearly, man. She's getting your little sister to join in some dodgy fertility rite just a few nights from now. Consider that, rather than what she'd be like in the sack.

He drove towards Piccadilly Station, aiming for the main road that would lead him back to Longsight. On his left were the mock castle battlements marking the exterior of the Piccadilly basin car park. As he passed the entrance, flashing blue lights caught his eye. A couple of police cars and an ambulance. They were all standing at the edge of the canal, looking down at something in the water. Another homeless person, Jon thought. Poor bastard probably rolled in there while off his head on meths.

# Chapter 14

He made it back to the incident room just as Buchanon was calling for silence. Once again, there were no seats at the central table, so he skirted round to his desk and perched on its edge.

Rick was watching him from his chair just down from Buchanon. Their eyes met and his colleague tapped a forefinger on his wristwatch. Jon acknowledged the gesture by wiping an imaginary bead of sweat from his brow.

'OK everyone,' Buchanon announced. 'A DNA sample from the body in the church was run earlier this morning, resulting in a match on the National Database.'

He held up a sheet of paper, swivelling it from left to right like a magician setting up a trick. 'Luke Stevens, aged nineteen. Date of birth, second of January, 1983.'

Well, thought Jon. Henry Robson's theory just went up in smoke. He stood up and stepped towards the table for a closer look at the victim's mug shot. Thin ratty face, eyes like piss holes in the snow, lanky strands of black hair hanging down to his shoulders. Another one of the undead.

'His record shows up several cautions for possession. Cannabis, acid and, on one occasion, magic mushrooms. From the sound of it, he was a bit of a loner. Unemployed and living at home at the time of his last arrest. I want to know who his friends and acquaintances were – if he had any – where he hung out, what interests he had. Let's get his last twenty-four hours mapped out. He wasn't in the church alone, so anyone he was with on that last day is top of our priorities. I'll take a team over to his house after this, inform the parents, and bag up the contents of his room.'

'Sir,' Jon said, sitting back on the edge of his desk. 'I'd better tell Henry Robson that the body isn't that of his son.'

Buchanon nodded. 'Make it quick. You, Rick and ...' His eyes settled on a couple of officers on the other side of the table. 'DC Gardiner and DC Adlon. You four can accompany me over to Luke Stevens' address. We'll need plenty of evidence bags too. Let's get going.'

Everyone rose to their feet, a sense of purpose in their movement. News of the victim's identity had infected the room with energy. It was, Jon thought, the best stage of any investigation. The promise of answers soon to be within reach.

Jon dug out Robson's number and punched it into his phone. 'Hello, Mr Robson?'

'Yes.' The man snapped the end of the word almost clean off.

'DI Spicer, from the Major Incident Team.' In the background, he could hear voices intoning a Gregorian chant. Cheerful, it wasn't. 'Sir, I have some positive news. The body in the Sacred Heart church was not – I repeat not – your son.'

Breath was let out. A release of tension. 'Are you sure?'

'There's been no formal identification made as yet, but DNA analysis has confirmed it wasn't Peter.'

'Who is it then?'

'I can't say at this stage.'

'They still have him though.'

'They still have who?'

'The Satanists. They still have my son, under their power.'

'Sir, I have to go. Of course I'll be in touch if your son crops up as part of this investigation.'

'Oh, he will, DI Spicer. He will.'

Jon hung up. 'Jesus, the bloke's possessed. I think he wants his son to be dead. It would confirm all his prejudices.'

Rick was standing on the other side of the desk, coat already on. 'Buchanon and the others are already in the car park. Let's go.'

As they crossed the room, Jon overheard two officers talking about an incident from earlier that morning. A body had been pulled out of a city-centre canal.

He turned his head. 'At Piccadilly Basin?'

'Yeah, the edge of the car park.'

'I passed it earlier on. Suspicious then?'

'Unsure at this stage. The guy was naked, though.'

Jon stopped, curious to know more.

'Come on, for Christ's sake!' called Rick, holding the incident room doors open.

They hurried down the stairs and jumped into Rick's black Golf. 'Where's this guy live?' Jon asked, clipping in his seat-belt.

'Ninety-two Fenney Street, Blackley,' Rick replied, following Buchanon's Peugeot out on to the A6.

'Nice,' Jon grimaced.

They arrived at the house less than thirty minutes later. As Rick parked up, Jon examined the street ahead. They were in a fairly typical run-down Manchester neighbourhood, two rows of Accrington brick houses staring at each other across a narrow road. Satellite dishes peppered the fronts of those on the left-hand side. No doubt the houses on the right had their receivers round the back.

They followed Buchanon to number ninety-two, but all hung back as he knocked on the front door itself. An overweight and balding man, probably in his early fifties, answered. As he looked from Buchanon towards the street, Jon dropped his eyes. Thank God telling him isn't my responsibility.

Buchanon spoke quietly for a few seconds and the man looked back into the house. 'Jean, it's the police. They've got some news.'

A dumpy woman with a puffy face and short blonde hair appeared. Jon could see the black of her roots showing through. As she waved Buchanon in, their SIO turned and gestured for DC Gardiner. She stepped towards the house.

'Unlucky, Susan,' Jon whispered from the side of his mouth.

A couple of minutes later Buchanon reappeared. 'Bring the evidence bags.'

DC Adlon retrieved a pile of polythene sacks from the back

seat of Buchanon's vehicle and they trooped inside. The house was heavy with cigarette smoke, and on the way up the stairs Jon could hear the woman half coughing, half crying.

Opening the door to Luke Stevens' room was like stepping into a grubby pub during a power cut. Pitch black and reeking of ashtrays and stale beer. Buchanon turned the main light on and a red bulb lit up. Keeping the door wide open, he picked his way through the gloom. Halfway to the drawn curtains, he stepped on a plate. Metal clattered on porcelain. 'Shit.' He made it to the other side and drew the dark purple curtains back. Daylight flooded in, illuminating a floor that was awash with objects. They surrounded the unmade bed in the corner as if laying siege to it. Dirty bowls, cups, music magazines, CDs, clothes, King Size Rizlas, a large ashtray, army boots, socks, food wrappers, empty cans of Red Bull and Tennent's Super.

As they all began pulling on latex gloves, Jon studied the walls. Posters for bands were pinned up edge to edge: 'Cradle of Filth', 'Dark Throne', 'Sodom', 'Morbid Angel', 'Cadaver Inc'. Directly above the bed was a huge enlargement of the Satan's Inferno album cover, *Raging Spires*. The headboard of the bed was plastered with ticket stubs. Jon leaned closer. They were all for the band's gigs.

'Look at this, Boss,' DC Adlon said, finger pointing to a desk in the corner. Newspaper cuttings covered it, spreading up the wall behind. Each report was concerned with the spate of arson attacks on churches.

Rick was flicking through a stack of CDs by the side of the music system next to the bed. He turned one over and began reading the track listing. '"Die like this", "In the Shadow of the Horns", "Black Goddess rises". Nice music for sending you off to sleep. Sweet dreams and all that.'

'Helped by this, no doubt.' Buchanon was crouched at the ashtray, the end of a large joint held between his finger and thumb.

'She couldn't stop him and he just ignored me.'

They all turned to the balding man in the doorway. Buchanon stood. 'Mr Stevens, we'll need—'

'Cooper. My surname's Cooper. I'm not his dad. He walked out years ago.'

'And you are?'

'Jean's partner.'

'Sorry, I had just assumed ...'

'Don't worry. Fair mistake to make.'

'How long have you known her?'

'We've been seeing each other around four, five years. I still have my own place, round the corner. Can't sleep here most nights, not with his bloody music.'

'Liked it loud, then?'

Cooper's nose wrinkled. 'When he did put on headphones, he'd still tap away. Biros as drum sticks. Almost applied for an ASBO to make him keep quiet.'

Buchanon held out his palm, the remains of the joint still in it. 'Were you aware he was smoking cannabis?'

'Oh aye, puffed away on it morning, noon and night, he did.' He held Buchanon's gaze for a second and then shrugged. 'As I said, he wouldn't listen to me or his mum.'

Buchanon's disapproval was plain to see. 'Well, sir, perhaps it would be better if you were there for Jean. Let us take care of things in here.'

Once Cooper had disappeared back downstairs, Buchanon turned round. 'Right, let's get the lot bagged up. I think we've got a few good avenues to explore here.'

They'd cleared the floor and desk when Jon's phone started to ring. He walked over to the brightness of the window. An unknown number was on the screen. 'DI Spicer here.'

'Hello. It's Skye Booth – from Magick on Oldham Street?'

'Yeah, I remember.' A young lad was making his way along the street below, posting brightly coloured oblongs of paper through letterboxes. Another crappy takeaway place for the neighbourhood, just to ensure everyone's diet was swimming in plenty of fat. 'How can I help?'

'There's been a report on the local radio. About a body being found in the Rochdale Canal just near here.'

'Go on.'

'My colleague hasn't shown up for work this morning.'

Bloody hell, that's a bit pessimistic. 'Have you tried calling him?'

'There's no reply.'

'And you think?'

'It's him. In the canal.'

Jon blinked. 'Why do you think that?'

'I can just ...' She paused. 'Will you check for me?'

'You can just what?'

'Nothing. Please, can you find out?'

'Skye, that's a worrying conclusion to make just because he's not answering his phone.'

'No, there's more. I can't explain it.'

'You can sense it's him. Is that what you're trying to say?'

'Yes,' she said, reluctance making the word stick in her throat. 'It's an image I had.'

Right. An image, Jon thought. A vision. A revelation from the cosmos. 'I'm really busy, Skye. Let me get back to you later, OK?'

'Please. Can you just make a call? Troy's got some scars on his left knee where he had an operation last year. Left and right sides of it. He wears a copper wristband too. It doesn't come off without being prised apart.'

Jon remembered. 'You're talking about the guy in your shop. Skinny bloke, hair in a ponytail?'

'Yes, that's him.'

'I talked to him yesterday. He worked at the Psychic Academy too. What's his full name again?'

'Troy Wilkes.'

I must be bloody mad, Jon thought. 'OK, I'll call you back in a bit.' He hung up and dialled the incident room. 'DI Spicer here. Who's this?'

'Sergeant Naylor, sir.'

'Sergeant, a body was found in the canal by Piccadilly Basin car park this morning. It's probably gone to the MRI now. Do me a favour and write this down. Lightly built Caucasian male, early thirties, thinning hair tied back in a ponytail, scars on each side of his left knee, copper band on one wrist. Got it?'

'Yes, sir.'

'Good. Now, can you find out for me where the body from the canal is and see if that description matches?'

'OK, give me a minute.'

Jon glanced behind him, feeling Buchanon's inquisitive stare. 'Sir, that call was from a female member of staff in the New Age shop on Oldham Street I mentioned. She has reason to believe a body found in the Rochdale Canal this morning was that of her colleague.'

'Reason to believe?'

He looked down at his feet. Bollocks, I'm going to sound a right idiot if I mention the visionary stuff. 'He hasn't turned up for work and his phone's not being answered. The canal is very close to the shop's location.'

'So that means he's drowned in it?'

Jon took a deep breath. 'She has a very strong feeling it's him.' Great, now he's looking at me like I've lost the plot. A voice on his phone broke the silence.

'DI Spicer?'

'Yes. Any luck?'

'It's a match. Description fits perfectly.'

Jon tried to hide his relief. 'Right. You need to let the investigating officer know it's a Troy Wilkes, works in Magick on Oldham Street. Can you find out who's handling things?'

'It's a murder investigation. I already know who's handling it.'

'Murder? Why?'

'His hands were tied behind his back, thumbs bound together by wire. Same for his ankles.'

Jon looked out of the window. That meant the case would have been referred to the Major Incident Team. 'So who's SIO?'

'DCI McCloughlin, sir.'

Jon's head went down. Shit, that's all I fucking need.

★

Skye Booth stood behind the counter. Her arms hung at her sides and her eyes were closed. But for a tiny pulsing movement at the side of her throat, she could have been a statue. Or dead.

Her focus was turned inwards, examining thoughts, emotions, impressions. She didn't like how things felt. Not in her head or in the world outside. Troy was dead. Of that, she was sure. After all, she had stared down at his pale torso, had seen his tightly folded limbs as their whiteness faded away below the brown surface.

A creeping sense of foreboding was gathering in the distance. She opened her eyes and glanced towards the window. Grey cloud filled what little of the sky she could see. A shiver gripped her shoulders and she looked at the phone again.

Come on, call me back. You said you would.

The phone remained silent. She considered ringing DI Spicer again, then contemplated getting out her rune stones and casting them on the counter. Maybe they would give a hint of what was about to pass.

# Chapter 15

Jon's hands had begun to sweat inside the latex gloves. He looked at his watch. Ten to five. He'd have to get something to eat soon. Spread out on the white Formica surface before him were the evidence bags collected from Luke Stevens' house.

He tried to clear his mind and concentrate on the process of sifting, but the photos of Troy Wilkes wouldn't go away. Seeing a body stretched out on the autopsy table had never seemed strange before. Pathetic, or stomach-turning, maybe. But never strange. It was Ellie's fault. Her comments about burying the body, not the person, when someone dies. What had she said? The spark, the thing that made the body alive, never dies.

Shaking the echo of her words from his head, he turned his thoughts to Troy Wilkes's corpse. Only yesterday, the man had been sitting behind the shop counter, chatting away. He'd picked up the prospectus for the Psychic Academy, laughed, blinked, shaken his head. Apart from the wire marks on the thumbs and ankles, the person lying on that mortuary slab was identical to the person in that shop. Even the water that had flooded his lungs had been removed. But Wilkes was cold and lifeless, the vital spark, the electrical pulse, lost for ever. Was that, Jon wondered, what a person's soul was? A minute charge of electricity?

'Anyone in?'

Jon felt himself flinch. 'You what?'

'Anyone in?' Rick repeated. 'I was saying, I'll start this end of the table.'

'OK.' He looked to his side. A bag containing a black, hooded top was sitting in a grey plastic tray, ready to go to forensics for analysis. Tiny fragments of glass were just visible embedded across the chest area. Glass, Jon guessed, from at least one of the other three churches to have recently burned down. He wondered if the arsonists realised that the act of breaking a window caused minute particles of the stuff to fly out in all directions. Plenty of burglars had discovered it to their cost, once forensics had a chance to go through their wardrobe with a fine-tooth comb.

Rick was carefully prising the lid off a cylindrical pot designed to hold camera film. He took a sniff of the contents. 'Christ. Smell this.'

Jon didn't need to step any closer. A pungent aroma was already filling the room.

Rick replaced the lid and sealed the container in an evidence bag. 'Skunk. Strong enough to really mess with your head, especially if you're not that stable in the first place.'

Jon considered the canister. 'You think the government should think again about reclassifying the stuff?'

Rick didn't bother replying; the answer was obvious to both of them. A bag containing signed photos of Satan's Inferno caught Jon's eye. He lifted it up and examined the sallow faces inside. What was it with this music? Death, cannibalism, necrophilia and torture. He thought back to his teenage years. King Kurt, Bad Manners and Madness. Music with a bit of fun to it. Stuff you could jump around to. OK, The Damned could be a bit darker, but even their songs weren't dragged down by this doom-laden morbidity.

He placed the bag next to the one containing the press cuttings and band reviews Stevens had carefully harvested. Was the bloke just a fan, or had he got closer to the band members than that? Did they invite him backstage, actually talk to him? If he was going to find out, the fastest way would be to pay Serberos another visit. 'Definitely no stuff from the Psychic Academy?'

Rick moved a bag containing all Stevens' CDs to one side. 'No, not a thing.'

Bollocks, thought Jon. It would have linked everything together a bit tighter. 'We should still go back there. Arkell will have records of him attending courses, if he ever did. I'd also like to know if Troy Wilkes taught him, or any member of Satan's Inferno.'

Rick replaced a torn pack of Rizlas on the table. 'If he did, then we definitely should be paying the Psychic Academy some serious attention. But just because Arkell's in charge of the place, doesn't mean he's behind all this.'

'Where there's smoke, there's fire.'

'Don't judge a book by its cover.'

They stared each other out in silence until a knock on the door caused Jon to look away. DC Gardiner's face was at the window. Obviously not wanting to go through putting on protective clothing all over again, she spoke through the glass. 'Just came off the phone to the female who dropped the assault charges against Arkell last year.'

'Yeah?' Jon said, also raising his voice. 'What did she say?'

'She still believes Arkell drugged her. She'd been having some private tuition classes with him, said he was guiding her towards some sort of transcendental experience.'

'And?'

'In the final session, she has no memory for the three hours she was in his office. Her head felt groggy as she walked home, which Arkell said would be quite normal. It was only when she got undressed to have a shower that she realised the fastening on her bra wasn't done up properly.'

'Did she have the shower anyway?'

'Afraid so. There's no evidence – she only mentioned it to an adviser in the Students' Union two days later. Even then, she could only say it was a feeling, an instinct that he'd abused her.'

'Why did she believe he'd drugged her?'

'At the start of the session, she'd applied some flying ointment to her forearms and throat area.' She caught his look. 'Er – it's to do with witchcraft. A concoction that contains hallucinogenic ingredients to facilitate the experience.'

'Those being?'

She examined a piece of paper. 'She says it contained henbane, belladonna and hemlock, mixed with safflower oil.'

'What are henbane and hemlock?'

'Native British plants. Belladonna, of course, is also known as Deadly Nightshade.'

'Hemlock's a poison,' Rick said. 'Didn't Socrates die from drinking it? Punishment for challenging the religious order of ancient Greece, wasn't it?'

'Fucked if I know.' Jon shrugged. 'Are these plants legal?'

'I'm checking with one of the drug squad's chemists. He's getting back to me,' DC Gardiner replied.

'No wonder it never went to court,' Jon stated. 'She'd have had more chance of proving fairies lived at the bottom of her garden. What about the bloke who made an allegation?'

'Can't trace him as yet.'

'OK. I've got details of some other people who've recently attended courses at the Psychic Academy. If I get you their names, can you start phoning around to see if any of them have had similar experiences with Arkell?'

'Is this on Buchanon's time or my own?'

'Your own, but just when you get any spare moments.'

She rolled her eyes. 'All right then.'

Jon held up a thumb while thinking of one list that he wouldn't be giving to Gardiner: the one with his sister's name on it. That was a piece of information he didn't need getting out.

Susan turned to go, then looked back. 'By the way. McCloughlin's brought in the girl you mentioned. The one who rang you about seeing the body.'

'Skye Booth?'

'That's her. She's in interview room two. He's giving her a right grilling.'

Jon's foot was already on the pedal for the bin. The lid sprang up and he dropped his gloves into it. Shit, he thought, I forgot to call her back. She'd probably still been waiting for me to phone when McCloughlin steamed through the door. You dickhead, Spicer.

He marched down the corridor and slipped into the observation room. On the other side of the one-way mirror Skye and McCloughlin were sitting at a table. In the corner a female officer stood silently watching.

McCloughlin's head was jutting forward, bristly hair sticking out of the ridges of skin at the back of his skull. His voice sounded tinny as it came through the speaker mounted on the wall above Jon. 'For the fifth time, Miss Booth, how did you know Troy Wilkes was in that canal?'

Skye looked remarkably unruffled as she tilted her head to the side. 'Officer—'

'Detective Chief Inspector.'

Skye's eyebrows rose slightly, revealing her exasperation just for a second. 'Whatever. Sometimes it happens to me. It runs down my mother's side of the family, skipping a generation each time. Grandma had it, so did her grandma, so did—'

'Spare me the second sight nonsense will you? This is a murder investigation. Take me through your whereabouts last night.'

'Again?'

'Again.'

As Skye crossed her arms and started speaking, Jon turned to the members of McCloughlin's syndicate who were watching. 'Is she under arrest?'

'No, just helping with inquiries. Though I don't think she realises that. McCloughlin played it heavy with her. Murder investigation and all that. She was happy to come along.'

'How long's she been in there?'

'About forty minutes.'

God! He should have guessed McCloughlin would have latched on to her like an attack dog.

'And she's sticking to her story?'

'Yeah. Not even the tiniest wobble. She had an image of her colleague's body just below the surface of some brown-coloured water.'

'But she'd heard the radio report. Every canal in Manchester is full of brown water. When you can actually see it through the layer of rubbish, that is.'

The officer smiled. 'Her problem is, she also knew the body was naked. That wasn't mentioned in any news bulletin.'

Jon turned back to the window. McCloughlin was hunched over his notes, head down, shoulders tight. Skye was sitting back, chin up, hands resting on her lap. Something approaching amusement was showing in her face as she looked at the top of her adversary's head.

McCloughlin stabbed his pencil at his pad. 'And this friend of yours, Valerie Evans. When I ring her, she'll vouch that you stayed at her house last night?'

Skye nodded. 'I said, call her. You've got her number. She'll be at home.'

Eyes still on his pad, McCloughlin crossed his arms, saying nothing.

'You've got a lot of negative energy, if you don't mind me saying.'

McCloughlin's head bobbed up like someone had pulled an invisible string. 'Spare me your spiritual analysis, missy.'

'Oh, I don't think your frustration comes from spiritual deficiencies. More a lack of sex, I suspect.'

Silence. Jon heard someone whisper to his side. 'Did she just say …'

All eyes were on McCloughlin as they waited for his reaction. It was common knowledge he'd been divorced over five years ago and no one knew of any girlfriends since. He blinked a couple of times, colour now flecking his cheeks.

'I notice you don't have a wedding ring either,' Skye blithely continued. 'Surely there's someone who could relieve some of that tension.'

Everyone in the observation room fought to control their laughter as McCloughlin patted a palm on the table. 'Please, Miss Booth. You're killing me with your wit.'

Skye shrugged as she looked away. 'According to what I've seen on TV, shouldn't you charge me with something or let me go? I have a shop to run.'

McCloughlin sat back. 'Why, Miss Booth, you're not under arrest. You've been free to go at any time.'

She looked confused. 'But when you came into the shop, you

said it was because you had reason to believe ...' Realisation dawned.

'At no point did I say you were under arrest. I am sorry if I somehow gave that impression.'

Skye's jaw was set tight. 'So I can go?'

'Allow me to find an officer to show you out.' McCloughlin stood, a gloating smile still on his face. 'I'm sure we'll be seeing each other again. Very soon.' He opened the door and waved the female officer out before him. A second later they heard his voice as he passed the observation room. 'Someone sling the smart-arsed bitch back out.'

A young-looking officer started for the door. Jon put a hand on his arm. 'I'll do it. She's spoken to me before.'

Once the other officers had gone up the stairs, Jon stepped into the interview room.

Skye's eyebrows lowered as her expression turned to one of tired hostility. 'Thanks for calling me back.'

He took the other chair, recoiling slightly at its warmth. Heat created by McCloughlin's backside. 'I'm really sorry. When you called I was in the middle of something. Then, when the identification was correct, things moved faster than I realised.' He wiped a hand across the table. 'Sorry you went through all that stuff. I had no way of knowing McCloughlin was getting the case.'

Skye gave a humourless smile and shifted her gaze to the mirrored wall. 'Of course! Good cop, bad cop. Didn't realise you actually used those tactics. Behind there is he, watching?'

'No. No one's there.'

'Yeah, right.'

Damn it, Jon thought, I've completely lost her trust. 'Actually, I've probably got two minutes before he hears I'm with you and bursts back in.'

'Why?'

Jon rubbed a hand at the back of his neck. 'Long story. We don't get on.'

'But he seemed so nice.' Sarcasm distorted her voice.

He grinned. 'You really rattled him with that sexual frustration comment.'

'What's the quote from that film? Never in the history of mankind has someone been in more need of a blow job.'

Jon glanced down. She had absolutely no embarrassment about referring to sex. Did her attitude, he wondered, extend to the act itself? Suddenly he could see her naked in a field, her body lit orange as she danced and whirled round a bonfire. 'You can understand why he was on your case though, can't you?'

'Because I knew it was Troy in that canal.'

'Not just that. You knew he'd been stripped. It's the sort of detail you wouldn't have known without having been there.'

She held his gaze for a long second, saying nothing.

Eventually Jon blinked. 'So you were there?'

'No. It was something I saw in my head. It happens some-times.'

He resisted the urge to groan. She was sticking to her story, for the time being at least. 'Fine. But you can't expect someone like McCloughlin to accept an explanation like that. He'll be on your case.'

'I'll have to live with it.'

'Listen,' Jon lowered his voice. 'Ellie mentioned she's joining a coven. You're introducing her to it tomorrow night, is that right?'

She looked at the mirror window. 'There really isn't anyone back there.'

'I said there wasn't.'

She nodded. 'Now I believe you. I'm sure you wouldn't want to be discussing this in earshot of your colleagues.'

'Skye, I don't know anything about your religion, apart from seeing films like *Rosemary's Baby* and *The Wicker Man*.'

'No wonder you're worried.'

'First she does that course, the Way of Wicca, now there's this ceremony to become a witch.' He paused, but she didn't object to his use of the word. 'What will she have to do?'

She was just about to answer, but then cocked her head to the side, eyes on the partially open door. It was pushed fully open. McCloughlin stood glowering in the doorway. 'DI Spicer, get out.'

Jon stood. 'Sir, this woman is known to me as part of the investigation—'

'Out. Now.'

Jon shot an apologetic glance at Skye, who was also getting to her feet.

McCloughlin didn't budge, making Jon step awkwardly around him. Squeezing past, he thought how easily he could lift the other man up and throw him against the wall.

As soon as he was out in the corridor, McCloughlin closed the door and half turned his head. 'Don't you ever try and interview one of my suspects like that again.'

'Sir.' Jon set off for the stairs.

'Oh, and DI Spicer.'

He caught the tone in McCloughlin's voice and, reluctantly, looked back.

The other officer nodded towards the interview room. 'What was all that talk about witchcraft just now?'

Fuck, Jon realised the door had been open for their entire conversation.

# Chapter 16

Peter Robson lifted the square of cardboard, pausing a second to study the worms half-buried in the compacted soil beneath. The creatures sensed they were now exposed and slowly began to probe at the earth, seeking safety below the ground.

Robson dug his fingers into the cold layer and hooked one out. Immediately it contracted to half its length and began writhing about in his hands. He could feel the ridges of its skin catching on his palm.

The magic mushrooms he'd eaten three hours before had now worked their way fully into his bloodstream and he stared at the creature, marvelling at its bizarre construction. A tube of goo; eyeless, limbless, hairless, yet a thinking creature all the same. After a few seconds its movements became calmer and it tried to extend its front tip between two of his fingers.

'Tickles,' Robson smiled, saliva glistening on his lower lip as he dropped the creature. He placed the flattened-out box against the bare brick wall then turned to retrieve that day's late edition of the *Chronicle*. It lay on the other side of the expanse of cardboard he'd spread out across the floor of the tunnel. He looked at the writing on the boxes.

Prince's tuna. Sharwood noodles. Kellogg's Frosties. The tiger's chest puffed out as he gave Robson an approving nod. The young man lowered himself on all fours for a closer look.

'They're grrreat,' he murmured, extracting a few more mushrooms from the tangled clump in his pocket. He popped them in his mouth, keeping it open and chewing quickly, trying to swallow them before the dusty flavour enveloped his tongue.

The layer of boxes undulated slightly as he picked up the paper then crawled back to his improvised seat. The headline on the front page was studied for a second, then the page was quickly turned, the rustle of paper deadened by the tunnel's confines. At page three he paused to bring the black candle closer.

As usual, the flame took his attention and minutes passed as he gazed at the source of light, watching tiny flecks as they were drawn across the pool of wax and into the wick. Eventually his eyes swivelled back and he had to think hard to remember what had originally caught his attention. The report on the church arson. The words kept trying to drift off the page and he had to anchor them down by running a finger below each sentence.

*Following the discovery of the body on Monday morning, police are now considering the possibility that the victim died as part of a satanic ritual.*

Robson violently shook his head. That was wrong! They were spouting a load of bullshit. They had fallen for the lies. He carried on through the report, banging a fist against the floor when he read about how the murder victim was believed to be a fan of the Death Metal scene. It was, the paper attested, an evil form of music inextricably linked to Devil worship.

You want evil? I'll show you the meaning of evil. He looked at the candle once again. When the flames are licking at your feet, you'll know what hell on earth feels like. And it won't be the pain that makes you scream, it will be the knowledge of what's waiting for you once you're dead. He looked to Tony and the tiger winked back. Vengeance is mine, sayeth the Lord. Oh no, you're wrong. You're very fucking wrong. Vengeance is anyone's. Vengeance belongs to those who are prepared to take it.

His German army coat felt good as he put it on. He folded the paper up and slipped it into an inner pocket. Then he crawled across to the plastic container. Petrol sloshed inside as he lifted it. Plenty for what he wanted to do. He stood up and, keeping his head bowed, walked unsteadily to the mouth of the tunnel. With his free arm, he lifted the curtain of tarpaulin masking his lair and stepped out into the night.

Movement in the air above him. A black form skittered across the dark orange sky. A helper, sent from below to look out for him. An empty train rumbled past along the embankment on the other side of the railway junction. Robson made his way through a thicket of bushes before emerging at the side of another track. The line was clear and he stepped carefully between the rails, his feet crunching on the thick gravel between the sleepers.

On the other side he followed the fence, knowing the tracks would lead him to within half a mile of the Sacred Heart. Ten minutes later, he squeezed through a gap in the wire, scrambled down a shallow slope, then crossed the Ashton Old Road. The streets were deserted as he strode quickly towards his target, cutting across the playing fields to approach the graveyard the same way as he had done before. Somewhere nearby an owl hooted, telling him it was safe.

Next to the police caravan and the blue Volvo parked next to it, arc lights shone towards the remains of the church. He cradled the container in the crook of an arm, not wanting it to swing against the perimeter wall as he followed it to the corner of the presbytery garden. He waited for any activity, either in the house or near it. Nothing. Carefully he climbed over the wall and ran across the lawn.

At the front door he began balling up pages of the newspaper, then sloshing petrol over them. Once they were soaked, he forced them through the letterbox, listening as they landed on the other side of the door.

Putting the last sheet of newspaper aside, he held the container up, pressed its neck against the letterbox and tipped more liquid through. Then he rolled the final page into a taper and inserted it below the metal flap. From his pocket he produced a bronze Zippo lighter. He flicked the wheel and a dirty yellow flame popped up. As he held it towards the twisted end of the paper, a notice pinned on the door frame caught his eye. He pulled it off and held the lighter close to the typed message.

While arrangements are made for the future of the Sacred Heart, Father Ben Waters would like his congregation to know that a very warm welcome awaits them at Our Lady in Abbey

Hey. Father Waters is currently taking a well-deserved rest for
a few weeks at a Catholic retreat near Salamanca in Spain.

The Reverend Canon Manager Maurice Kelly

So that's where he's hiding, thought Robson, stuffing the notice
in his pocket. He touched the flame against the end of the taper
and it instantly took hold, burning normally for a second before
making contact with the damper paper. Suddenly the flame
surged towards the door. Blue rivulets of fire began coursing
down the wood. By the time the taper fell through the letterbox, Robson was at the corner of the house. A soft whump was
audible as the mound of newspaper on the doormat ignited.
Yellow light flared up behind the glass panel in the door. He ran
for the garden wall, empty container flapping at his side.

# Chapter 17

More arc lights had been set up, illuminating the two firemen who were playing streams of water over the front of the presbytery. Jon looked at the blackened door frame and soot-covered bricks above it.

'It was lucky really,' Dean Webster said. 'The bobby on duty in the caravan spotted it early and called us straight away. A few more minutes and the flames would have been up the stairs. As it happens you've just got a ruined ground floor.'

'What caused it?'

'Someone shoved flammable material through the letterbox. Newspaper soaked in petrol, judging from the fragments of ash that carried up to the first floor. No sign of matches on the front steps, so most probably lit with a lighter.'

'Just like the fires in the churches.'

Webster tipped his head up at the night sky. 'Yup,' he sighed.

'What if anyone had been upstairs?' Rick asked.

Webster looked speculatively at the bedroom windows. 'They probably would have lost consciousness from the fumes. No smoke alarm, despite all our attempts to educate people.'

Jon glanced at the fire investigation officer. 'So it had the potential to be fatal?'

'Yes. The house is old. Those wooden stairs would have gone up in no time, and the smoke alone would have seen to anyone on the first floor.'

Jon turned to Rick. 'So first we've got someone trying to break in, now we've got someone trying to burn it down.'

'Attempted murder?'

Jon dipped his head to the side, weighing the comment up.

'Depends if the attacker knew Father Waters wasn't in. It would be hard to prove.'

'Not if he'd read the notice,' Webster said.

'What notice?' Jon asked.

'The one the other bloke from the church put up. Here, on the noticeboard by the front gates. Come to think of it, there was another at the side of the presbytery front door. Probably disappeared in the fire.'

At the front gates to the churchyard, Jon and Rick read the sheet of paper pinned to the middle of the board.

'This,' Jon said, pointing to it, 'gives anyone who's after Waters a very good idea of where to find him.'

'There can't be that many retreats near Salamanca,' Rick added.

'Bollocks,' Jon replied. 'And I forgot to ring him. Tomorrow, can you get on to this Canon Kelly? See if he speaks Spanish; he may have more luck than I did when I phoned.'

Webster looked at the pair of them. 'You reckon the priest could really be in danger?'

Jon glanced at the presbytery. 'It's looking more and more like it.'

'Any idea why?'

'Not a bloody clue,' Jon sighed. 'Apart from the fact he's a priest. Jesus, imagine if something happens over in Spain. What a nightmare of an investigation that would create.' His eyes moved towards the burned-out church, then returned to the crime scene caravan. 'Where's Waters's car gone?'

Webster looked confused. 'It was there earlier today.'

Jon called over the officer loitering by the caravan. 'The blue Volvo that was parked there. Do you know where it's gone?'

He shrugged. 'No. I remember seeing it this evening.'

'When exactly?'

'Ten o'clock, when I came on shift.'

'So it disappeared around the time the fire broke out?'

'When everyone's attention was on the presbytery,' said Rick.

'I don't like this. Someone's after the priest, and we need to know why,' Jon replied, turning towards the church. 'How's the excavation going?'

Webster extended a hand. 'I'll show you.'

They walked down the flagstone path leading to the side door. Webster crouched down and flicked a couple of switches on a junction box. Floodlights within the church came to life, bathing the interior walls with their glare. Webster led them through the porch and into the main part of the building.

Jon found himself staring at the altar, gouges in the stone-work now clear to see. On the walls behind, the graffiti had been circled in chalk and each arcane symbol neatly numbered off. His eyes caught on a small wooden square by the wrecked pulpit. Soot-covered cards were still in place, the numbers on them just visible. Forty-seven. Sixty-three. One hundred and twelve. The hymns sung in the last service before the attack took place.

The floor to the right of the aisle had now been completely cleared of debris, exposing rows of damaged pews, progressively more charred as they approached the seat of the fire itself. Those at the front were completely missing.

'You can see how they ripped up the first couple of rows for firewood,' Webster said, stopping halfway down the aisle and pointing over a ribbon of tape that barred their way.

'Anything more to indicate exactly what happened?' Jon asked.

'Some. See where the floor is burned most badly?'

Jon peered towards the jagged crater at the base of the wall scarred with the V-shaped burn mark. 'Yeah.'

'That's where the fire started. The floor has been burned most severely there and for the longest period of time. Now, what's odd is the lack of pool marks to the right of that, leading back to the window they got in through.'

'Sorry. Pool marks?'

'When you start a fire using a liquid accelerant such as petrol, you'll be carrying it in a container, usually with a neck or a spout.' He stepped away from them and mimicked sluicing out liquid from an imaginary container. 'You throw liquid forwards, over your target. But as you bring the vessel back towards your body, a trail of droplets will lead back to your feet. These trails can let us map out the actual movements of an arsonist within a room.'

'I like it,' Jon grinned. 'You're a crafty bunch of bastards, aren't you?'

Webster inclined his head. 'We do our best. Now, in the attacks so far, the arsonist has left a trail of droplets that lead back to the window. The trail has then ignited during the fire, after the arsonist has escaped back out through the window. OK?'

Jon and Rick nodded.

'Look to the right of the point of origin. You'd expect to see where splashes of petrol caused burn damage to the top layer of the wooden floor. Effectively scorching a puddle shape.'

The area was peppered with jagged black marks, including the area directly below the window.

'Burning debris has created a lot of the damage you can see. What's missing are the distinctive pool marks I'd been expecting.'

Jon nodded in agreement. 'So what do you conclude?'

Webster pointed at the left-hand side of the aisle. Though the roof tiles and timbers had been removed, a thick layer of ash still filled the gaps between the surviving pews. 'Until we examine what's under that lot, nothing at this stage. Could just have been a more careful person's turn to splash the petrol.'

'Surely it's a definite change in MO,' Rick said.

'Plus the car jack was left behind,' Jon added. 'Something must have happened to break their routine.'

'Possibly,' Webster replied. 'We'll work on clearing the rest of the floor, then I'll get a hydrocarbon dog to check it over.' He clocked their puzzled expressions. 'A sniffer dog, trained to identify the location of accelerants.'

'Great,' Jon replied as they retreated up the aisle. 'In the meantime, I'll get another couple of uniforms posted. Let me know if you discover anything more.'

Webster laid a hand on the stone arch of the inner porch.

'Oh, there'll be more to come all right. Every building has a tale to tell. It's just a question of teasing it out of her. Isn't that right, old girl?'

The sound of his palm slapping on the cold surface echoed within the silent walls.

Valerie Evans checked the table again. The tarot cards were on one side, a jug of water and two glasses on the other. Her Persian cat jumped up on to the guest's chair.

'Graymalkin, you naughty imp! That's for our visitor, not you.' As she lifted the animal up, the doorbell went and she glanced at the clock. Bang on time. That's a relief, she thought, not accustomed to giving readings at such a late hour. Keep it to thirty minutes, she told herself, and you can be tucked up asleep by eleven thirty.

The head of her visitor was visible through the glass of her front door window. She turned the Yale lock and opened up. 'Come in, come in. Everything's ready through here.'

She turned and began to walk back down the hallway but fingers closed on the back of her neck. Before she could react, she was thrown violently against the passage wall, her head slamming into an ornate mirror. The glass shattered and she felt shards of it pierce the side of her face. The grip on her neck didn't loosen as she was yanked backwards.

Her cat flew from her arms, twisting in the air and landing on all four feet. It looked up to see its owner being dragged screaming across the floor. It tried to dart one way, but a flailing leg obstructed its escape. Cutting across to the other side of the passage, it shot out the front door and into the night.

# Chapter 18

Leaves crackled slightly as the beast's paws connected with the forest floor. It was now so close he could hear the air blasting from its muzzle. Jon stumbled onwards through the dense tree trunks, another part of his brain fighting desperately to end the dream.

Come on, come on, wake up. Do not look back, just fucking wake up. The animal was now right behind. Stop this! Stop this! The sound of its footsteps abruptly ended as it sprang off the ground. He knew its jaws would be open wide, yellow eyes fixed on the vertebrae of his neck.

His strangled groan finally brought him out of it. The pillow. His bedside table, mobile phone next to the alarm clock. He waited for his breathing to slow, then turned over. Alice's hair brushed against his face. She was facing away from him and he hooked an arm over her waist. Beyond her, the faintest of glows showed at the edge of their curtains. Not time to get up quite yet. He let his hand rest there, drawing comfort from her warmth.

The top she wore in bed had ridden upwards in the night, exposing her midriff. He traced his fingers over it, feeling the small grooves in her skin as he reached the waistband of her knickers. Stretch marks. The consequence of carrying Holly around for nine months.

They were similar, in his mind, to the scars he carried from a lifetime of playing rugby. Marks to be proud of, signs of having put your body on the line to achieve something special. He smiled. Alice would have something to say if he compared injuries from a game she couldn't see the point of to the trauma of motherhood itself. You haven't a bloody clue, he could hear her say. He brushed his fingers back upwards, moving towards her breasts.

She stirred, turning her head to press a cheek against his nose.

'Morning.'

'Mmmm,' she murmured, pushing her buttocks back against him. 'Someone's feeling perky.'

He found her ear lobe with his lips. Knowing the effect it had on her, he began to run his lower teeth gently along its edge. As Alice's hand slid over his thigh a cough sounded from the nursery.

They froze, ears straining for any more sounds. Please let her be asleep, Jon thought.

The next cough was followed by a whimper.

No, no, no. He visualised the tickle in his daughter's throat. A spidery-shaped speck that he hated with all his might.

Another cough, this one turning into a cry. Bollocks, she's awake.

They heard the bars of her cot rattle as she struggled inside it, her cry getting ever louder. Alice sighed and the welcome pressure of her hand on his thigh disappeared as she got out of bed. 'Unlucky.'

Seconds later she reappeared with Holly in her arms. Jon flicked the duvet back for them, glancing at his daughter's little face. Dried snot was crusted above her lip. 'Thanks for that, Holly, you little monster.'

'Gah,' she replied and he couldn't help but grin.

Alice placed her between them and sat back against the head-board.

'So have you got your head round what Ellie said yet?'

He took a deep breath, held it, then spoke as he exhaled. 'Do we have to discuss this in front of Holly?'

'Why not? She can't understand anything.'

'It doesn't feel right, that's all. What are you up to today?'

His wife was silent for a second. Please, just drop it, Jon thought.

'Taking Holly over to the Sunshine Nursery. They're holding an open day.'

Jon stared at the ceiling. 'So you're signing her up.'

His daughter's face appeared inches from his and she tried to stick a finger in his eye.

'Yes. It's a lovely place. The kids from St Thomas's school have helped paint all these beautiful murals on the walls. It's so bright and cheerful.'

'What kind of murals?' Jon replied, eyelids tightly shut as a little finger tried to poke between them.

'You know, the usual stuff. Noah's ark and all the animals going in. Jonah and the whale. Baby Jesus in the manger.'

'Religious stuff then. To get started on them nice and early.'

'Jon, it's all very innocent. There's no harm in it.'

'Of course,' he replied lightly. 'I bet they haven't got pictures of the seven-headed beast, or the Devil trying to tempt Jesus out in the desert. What about firestorms engulfing Sodom and Gomorrah? They'll spring the nasty stuff on them later, will they?'

'Now you're just being ridiculous. It's a toddlers' play area, for God's sake.'

He pressed his jaws together. What could you do? If it was the best place, the religious stuff was the price you had to pay. 'I'd better grab a shower.'

He wandered through to the bathroom and turned the shower on. Waiting for the hot water to come through, he regarded his reflection in the full-length mirror. His penis hung limp – shrivelled and disappointed. Not my fault, mate, he thought. Blame it on the little baby girl in there.

When he got downstairs they were in the kitchen, Holly in her high chair watching Alice as she stacked up plates from the dishwasher. Punch sidled over and Jon cupped his dog's head in his hands, rubbing a forefinger behind each ear. 'Hello, boy.' He let the animal go, then grabbed a box of muesli and sat down.

'Just found a text from Ellie. She must have sent it late last night.'

He kept his eyes on the bowl before him. 'Oh yeah?'

'She was popping over later this morning, but now she's meeting up with Skye.'

Jon started tipping cereal into his bowl. The whole situation was becoming a serious worry. Something was obviously going on at the Psychic Academy and Magick – the tutor in the canal was proof of that. 'What are they up to?'

'She said they're going to scout for herbs and flowers for this Beltane ceremony. They don't actually pick them until nightfall, because that's when their potency is at its strongest.'

'Did she mention where?'

Alice gave a nod. 'Alderley Edge.'

'Should have guessed,' Jon replied. 'It's a favourite haunt for weirdos.'

'I thought it was a mega-bucks place to live?'

'Not the village, the Edge itself. It's a sandstone hill surrounded by woods. You've never been?'

'No. But now you mention it, I remember something in the paper about loads of people gathering there each Halloween.'

'There was a scandal back in the seventies, I think. The papers got hold of some photos of a witches' coven meeting at the top. It's meant to be a mythical area. There's a stone circle and a waterfall called the Wizard's Well. There's even a legend about King Arthur and his knights hiding in a cave beneath the hill, ready to ride out on to the plains of Cheshire to save England in its hour of need.'

'And witches use it on Halloween?'

'Not any more, they don't. More popular with pissed-up teenagers apparently, though it sounds like the witches still creep back there when it's less busy. Did Ellie say where this ceremony is happening?'

'No. But if they're looking for herbs up there, it would make sense that's where it'll be.'

Jon toyed with his spoon. 'I think this Skye is bad news.'

'Just because she's a bit different.' Alice tutted.

'Ali, I've met her.'

'When?'

'As part of this investigation. It's all a bit complicated. But

Skye, she's a child of the sixties, going on about Ellie's beautiful soul. I don't think she's malicious, but I don't think her head's screwed on straight either.' He thought about Arkell and the claims of sexual assault hanging over him. 'People like Skye and Ellie have trusting natures. They make easy pickings for the scrotes I have to deal with. We don't need her getting Ellie involved with all this stuff.'

'Don't be so tight on your sister. She, of all people, has every right to look for a bit of meaning in her life. God knows, enough people are left feeling empty by society today. Look at the increasing incidence of mental illness.'

Jon glanced at her bottle of pills on the window sill.

'Not post-natal depression,' she said. 'Depression full stop. People feel sad, they look for reassurance. Traditionally the Church provided that, but nowadays it seems to be falling apart.'

'Well, she could join a bloody hockey team. A swimming club. She'll get all the sense of purpose and belonging she wants from that. Might lose a bit of the weight that so bothers her too.'

Alice rolled her eyes. 'Sport. Jon Spicer's cure for all of life's ills.'

'It would sort out a lot of them. Boxing clubs – make attendance at them a condition for these ASBO kids. Reoffending rates would plummet, I bet you.'

'Maybe bring back National Service too?'

Jon shrugged. 'Maybe.'

Alice turned the kettle on. 'You sound like an old man.'

'You know, there's sense in it. What's the saying, the Devil makes work for idle hands? People need to get more going on in their lives.' He thought about Arkell again. There was a person playing on people's needs for his own gain. Whether financial profit or something more sordid. A thought occurred. 'The coven Ellie wants to join. Has she mentioned who else is in it apart from Skye? Is Skye like, well, the head witch, or is someone else in charge? Do covens have wizards or warlocks or whatever they call male witches?'

'I don't know, I haven't asked her.'

'Give her a buzz, will you? Casually, that's all.'

'She'll know I'm asking for you. Do your own dirty work.'

His mobile started to buzz. He disconnected it from the charger and looked at the screen. The station. Christ, it wasn't even eight o'clock. 'DI Spicer.'

'Morning Jon, it's Mark Buchanon here.'

'Sir, everything OK?'

'The radio room just contacted me with something. I'll need you to check it out, I'm just going into a status meeting with the Super.'

'No problem. What is it?'

'A body's been found. It could be linked to the one in the canal.'

'But that's McCloughlin's case, isn't it?'

'Yes, but there's a strong possibility it has a bearing on our case too. The victim has a tattoo of a five-pointed star.'

'Hang on.' He paced down the corridor and shut the door of the TV room behind him. 'Why do you think there's a link to Troy Wilkes?'

'Victim is naked.'

'Arms and legs bound?'

'No. She'd been forced into a barrel.' He paused. 'This is where it gets bizarre. Nails had then been hammered through the wood. It appears the barrel was rolled down a hill. Multiple puncture wounds. There's a massive amount of blood.'

'She'd been rolled down a hill? Where?'

'Alderley Edge.'

Jon felt his heart jump. 'Who is she?'

'No ID at the scene.'

'Any description?'

'Probably in her fifties. Big mane of white hair. That's it.'

His heartbeat slowed a fraction. 'Won't me turning up there tread on McCloughlin's toes?'

'It's not even been given an incident number yet, let alone had a syndicate assigned. I'd prefer a member of my team to be on the scene first, but just shout if you're not happy with that, I'll try and find someone else.'

'No, that's fine, sir. I'm on my way.' Once Buchanon had given him what other information he had, Jon hung up, reflecting on the piece of manoeuvring his SIO had just displayed. Maybe, he thought, that's why he's a DCI and I'm not. 'Alice!' he called towards the kitchen. 'I've got to go. Tell Ellie she has to stay away from Alderley Edge, OK?'

Jon saw Rick waiting for him on the pavement in front of Longsight station. He turned his hazards on and slowed to a halt in the middle of the road so his partner could jump straight in. Holding up a hand to the car beeping away behind, he quickly accelerated away.

'Where's Buchanon and McCloughlin?' Jon asked.

'Still in with the Super,' Rick replied, clipping in his seat-belt.

Jon flicked the siren on, and soon they were clear of the city, hurtling along a dual carriageway past fields that were dotted with sheep and their newly born lambs. Jon watched the young creatures as they chased each other about, their exuberance in total contrast to the grazing adults. A massive John Lewis and M&S loomed up on their right-hand side. 'For the landed gentry who live in these parts,' Jon commented.

The turn for Alderley Edge appeared a few minutes later and, as they took it, Jon spotted an expensive-looking hotel restaurant at the side of the road. The Merlin. Next came the high street itself, a strange mix of small boutiques and traditional charity shops.

'Best place in the country to pick up cheap designer gear,' Rick stated.

Jon peered at the shop they were passing. The items in the window looked anything but reasonably priced. 'What in there? Tangerine Dreams?'

'No. The Red Cross place next door. All the footballers and their wives who live around here need somewhere to dump last month's fashions.'

They got to a Threshers and Rick pointed across to it. 'According to the guy I'm seeing, that off-licence sells more bottles of champagne than any of their other branches in the country.'

Jon whistled. 'Marvellous, darling.'

The sign for the B5087 was on their left, and Jon swung the car into the far narrower road. The road began to rise and the houses grew further apart, high walls or hedges screening them from passing traffic.

'The rendezvous point is in the National Trust car park, somewhere along here.' Jon looked to his left. The field now bordering the road ended at a row of pine trees, the ground beyond dropping sharply away. They were on the Edge itself.

'There you go.' Rick pointed ahead.

Jon swung into a small car park – the oak leaf emblem of the National Trust on its gate posts – where three patrol cars and a pale blue Rover were already stationed. Jon could see an officer taking a statement from an elderly woman, whose spaniel stared eagerly out of the vehicle's back window.

They climbed out and Rick paused to look at an information board. 'Says here this place has copper mines that date back to almost two thousand years BC.'

Jon gave a nod. 'It's an interesting spot all right.'

Uniformed officers were gathered outside an old barn that had been converted into a café called the Wizard.

'What is it with this wizard business?' Rick frowned.

'It's a local tale. I learned about it on a school trip out here. A wizard waylaid a farmer hundreds of years ago, needing a horse for one of King Arthur's knights. They're all meant to be in hibernation somewhere beneath the hill.'

'Right,' said Rick. 'Along with a few dragons and ogres, no doubt.'

Jon headed for the nearest uniform, ID badge out. 'DI Spicer, DS Saville, Major Incident Team. What's the situation?'

Before he could answer, a middle-aged man with brown hair in a side parting turned round. 'Sergeant Dodd, sir.' They quickly shook hands. 'She was found at ten past seven by the lady in the Rover. Or the barrel was. It had rolled into one of the shallow open-cast pits further up. Lying on its side in a large pool of blood. She rang nine nine nine.'

'Who was first on the scene?'

'Constable Norris, sir. Kevin, run through what happened.'

The officer was in his early twenties, hair cut short and flattened down by gel. 'Well, I arrived at seven twenty-five. There was just the dog walker waiting for me here. After speaking with her, we headed up the path and I approached the barrel. As Sarge mentioned, blood was leaking out of it and running into a dip in the ground. The lid of the barrel was nailed shut, so I used a screwdriver from my pen knife to prise it off. I thought it would be a dog or something inside. As soon as I saw the body, I retreated from the scene and called for assistance.'

'I got here twenty minutes later,' the sergeant cut in. 'Had a look myself. Not a pretty sight. That's when I spotted the tattoo on her shoulder.'

'The five-pointed star?' Jon asked.

'Yes.'

'And she's naked?'

'I think so. There's a heck of a lot of blood.'

'How old does she appear to be?'

'Middle-aged, a bit older maybe. Long white hair, the bits not matted with blood anyway.'

'Who's up there now?'

'Three constables, sir. We've sealed the pit off,' the sergeant replied. 'About two hundred yards up that way.'

Jon looked at the wide sandy path rising up into the wooded slopes. 'OK, show us the way please.'

The sergeant led off and within seconds they were among beech trees, smooth trunks rearing up around them. Birdsong trickled down and the loamy smell of soil filled the air. Sunlight was breaking through the newly formed canopy above, freckling bluebells that seemed to float like mist just above the forest floor.

Glancing about, Jon was struck by the sheer force of life bursting out all around him. Things were, he thought, at a tipping

163

point. That brief period as spring segues into summer. Within days the new foliage would have lost its delicate shades of lime and the countryside would sink in on itself, darker, heavier, denser. Ready to soak up the days of sunshine ahead.

He looked at the beech trees again, suddenly realising where architects of religious buildings found inspiration. The trunks were as impressive as those of the columns in any cathedral he'd visited. Ellie's comments came back, how she wanted to worship outside in the open air. She had a point, this wood was far more pleasant than any fume-filled church.

They emerged in a large clearing, the area dotted with bowl-shaped depressions. Striped tape surrounded one, and two officers watched them in silence. At the edge of the shallow pit, Jon glanced down.

The barrel looked like it had come from a brewery. Curving lengths of dark brown wood were held in place by rusted metal bands at each end. He could just make out the shiny heads of nails peppering the woodwork.

'They're nine-inchers, big and sharp. Must be over fifty of them. She'd been thrown around inside like a rag doll. It's a right mess.' The sergeant crossed his arms and planted his feet apart.

Not on for a second look then, thought Jon, also glad to put it off until forensics gave the all clear. His eyes travelled to the other side of the flat clearing where the slope resumed. 'What makes you think the barrel was rolled down from higher up?'

'Marks in the soil. It's left a visible trail down the path.'

'Anyone been up to the top yet?'

'I've posted another officer up there,' the sergeant replied. 'But he's been instructed to keep well back from where the barrel began its journey.'

'Good work.' Jon took out his phone and called Longsight. 'DCI Buchanon, please.'

'He's en route to a crime scene. Shall I patch you through to his mobile?'

'No, don't worry. Is McCloughlin around?'

'En route to the same incident.'

'Thanks.' He pressed red and looked at Rick. 'This'll be interesting. Buchanon's on his way, McCloughlin too.'

'Dogs fighting over a bone.'

'Yeah, I just hope we don't get bitten in the process. Shall we take a little wander? See what's up there?'

Rick looked sceptical. 'I don't know ...'

'Come on. We'll keep off the path, there's not going to be much evidence we can contaminate in the undergrowth.'

'Go on then.'

They walked round the cordon and crossed the grassy clearing. Now the beech wood was interspersed with oaks and Scots pine. The path rose gently, gouges in the sand clearly marking the barrel's route down.

Stepping through the ankle-high layer of undergrowth at its side, they eventually reached a steep mound. Standing off to the side was another officer.

'Morning,' Jon announced. 'Major Incident Team.'

'Morning, sir.'

'Something at the top of this thing then?' Jon said, looking at the swathe of crushed bluebells leading down from the mound's summit.

'We reckoned so.'

Jon and Rick circled round and carefully climbed up the other side. At the top a pile of clothes lay next to a concrete plinth.

Rick peered at its inscription. 'The Armada Beacon. Highest point of the Edge and site for one of a chain of fires to signal the anticipated arrival of the Spanish fleet in 1588. Jesus, this place has a long history.'

Jon was looking at the pile of clothes. The cardigan and blouse were smeared with blood, the stains heaviest on the left collar. Droplets spattered the pair of shoes. 'She was injured prior to going in the barrel then.'

Rick took a breath. 'How do you force someone into a confined space like that? It must have taken some coercion.'

'Perhaps what the blood on the clothes is all about. The threat of a worse beating if she didn't obey. There's no way she could have guessed what was being planned.' He noticed several nails on the sandy earth and felt the skin across his back tighten. 'Imagine being trapped inside when they started hammering those things through.'

Rick turned away. 'Horrific. And what a bizarre way to kill someone. What the hell is it about?'

Shrugging, Jon pulled on a pair of latex gloves and lifted up the cardigan. A bracelet fell out of the folds. Attached to the links was a collection of silver charms. A moon and a sun. A small fish. A frog. A leaping figure. A little cat. In the middle of the tiny sculptures was a rectangular panel, words etched in the metal.

'Allergic to penicillin,' Jon murmured.

'Fat lot of good that'll do her now,' Rick replied, also crouching down.

Jon turned it over. 'Ah-ha, here we go. Valerie Evans, 33 Woodlake Avenue, Didsbury.' He looked at the shifting leaves above them. 'Where've I heard that name before?' He continued to stare at the canopy, but nothing came.

Rick looked at the path they'd followed up. It carried on past the mound and snaked off into the trees. 'Where does the trail lead? Another way up here?'

'Possibly.'

They picked their way back down and followed it along. A short distance on was a stone circle. Jon regarded the arrangement of moss-covered boulders, then examined the vegetation springing up around it with a sense of trepidation. Ellie was planning to be ferreting around here, searching for bloody herbs. Not any more she won't ...

A hundred or so metres further on, they stepped out of the trees on to a rocky ledge. Below, the Cheshire countryside stretched away, an occasional church spire rising from the rolling green fields. Far off to the left, the grey tower blocks of Manchester's outer estates glowed dully in the sun. He breathed in the clean air, imagining the existence people scratched out in the shadows of those ugly structures. A different bloody world. 'I doubt they came up this way,' he said, his glance shifting to the steep incline at their feet. The wail of sirens carried up on the breeze. 'That'll be the cavalry. We'd better get back.'

As they neared the clearing, they could see the number of people gathered in it had increased.

'There's Buchanon,' Rick said.

'And McCloughlin,' Jon added. 'He's going to be delighted at finding us here.'

They emerged from the trees. Buchanon was talking to Sergeant Dodd. McCloughlin had ducked under the tape and was stalking silently round the barrel.

'Sir, we've just been up to the top,' Jon called out.

McCloughlin's face soured. 'DI Spicer,' his former SIO spat. 'What are you doing here?'

Buchanon glanced over his shoulder. 'I sent Jon when I realised I couldn't make it here straight away.'

McCloughlin's scowl deepened. He turned back to the barrel and its puddle of blood.

'Anything up there?' Buchanon asked.

'A pile of blood-stained clothes.'

'Female?'

'Yes. Seems like she was made to strip and then climb into the barrel. I'd guess the lid was then sealed and the rest of the nails hammered in through the sides.'

Buchanon shook his head. 'It's a very particular way of killing someone.'

'Ritualistic, wouldn't you agree?' McCloughlin called over.

Jon picked up on the implications of the comment. Same as the body in the canal, therefore McCloughlin's case. He waited for his former SIO to look back at the barrel. 'There was an identification bracelet with her clothes,' he whispered to Buchanon. 'Name and address.'

'Really?' Buchanon mouthed.

'We could pay a little visit. While you're sorting things out here.'

Buchanon's eyes slid to the floor, creeping across towards McCloughlin. He was leaning to the side, trying to see into the barrel. 'OK, then. Ring me with what you find.'

'Sir.'

As they set off towards the car park, McCloughlin suddenly stood. Breathing deeply he took a few steps back, looking like he wanted to puke.

# Chapter 19

The drive to Didsbury took half an hour. Number thirty-three was set back off the road, window frames and porch painted in cheerful lime. As they walked up the drive Jon noticed a battered old orange Citröen 2CV parked by the garage. The choice of Green Party voters. Rick rang the front doorbell and they waited for a reply.

'Try the back?' Jon eventually said.

'Suppose so.'

They walked round to the rear of the building. A huge green-house filled most of the garden, rows of plants visible through the dirty panes. After knocking on the back door of the house, Jon tried the handle. It opened on to a kitchen done out in a rustic style. Pots and pans hung from a succession of black hooks above an open range stove.

'Hello! Police, is there anyone in?' The silence was unsettling. Cautiously they stepped inside. Racks of glass pots lined one wall, each one full of herbs. To the side of the door was what looked like a framed tea towel. Jon scrutinised the poem woven into the fabric:

*Poplar makes a bitter smoke, fills your eyes and makes you choke,*
*It is by the Irish said, Hawthorne bakes the sweetest bread,*
*But Ash green or Ash brown, is fit for a Queen with a golden crown.*

*Elmwood burns like churchyard mould, E'en the very flames are cold,*
*Apple logs will fill your room, with an incense-like perfume,*
*But Ash wet or Ash dry, for a Queen to warm her slippers by.*

Old Saying

A bell began tinking from further inside the house. It was getting closer. Jon and Rick stared at the door on the other side of the room as it began to inch open. A grey cat stepped through the gap. Rick let out his breath. 'A moggy.'

It made a beeline for Jon and began to rub itself against his shins, purring loudly. 'How do they do it?'

'What?' Rick asked.

'Work out who can't stand them, then bother that person most.' He pushed it away with his foot, but the animal didn't seem perturbed. It snaked between his legs, dipping its head to rub the side of its face on his shoe.

Rick was squatting by a tray on the floor in the corner. He snorted.

'Found something?' Jon said, high-stepping away from the creature.

Rick held a forefinger towards the name painted on the food bowl. 'Graymalkin. The name of the witches' cat in *Macbeth*.'

'You and your posh education,' Jon replied. 'Finally proving good for something. Do us a favour and give this thing something to eat.'

Rick held up a box of cat biscuits and shook them. The animal immediately ran across to him.

Jon eased the door fully open with an elbow and looked down the passage leading to the front door. Fragments of mirror littered the carpet and a table was overturned. 'Signs of a struggle here.'

Rick appeared at his side. 'Those look like droplets of blood on the carpet leading back to the front door. Blood on the door frame too.'

Jon tilted his head back, assessing the scene before him. 'Someone attacks her here, drags her out of the house and drives her to Alderley Edge. Someone she let in, or someone who forced his way in when she answered the door?'

Rick was peering into a side room. 'Someone she let in, I'd say.'

Jon glanced round his colleague. A small table covered with crimson velvet stood in the centre of the room. A deck of tarot cards were on one side, a jug of water and two glasses on the other. 'More bloody New Age stuff.'

Rick picked up a business card from a stack next to a crystal ball on the sideboard. 'Valerie Evans, Fortune-Teller.'

Jon pursed his lips. 'Not much good, I'd say.'

'How so?'

'She didn't see this coming.'

'Three words, Jon. Out. Of. Order.'

'Come on, you've got to keep a sense of humour, mate.' He tried to step into the room and almost tripped over the cat. It looked up at him with an adoring expression. 'That's why I can't stand the things,' he cursed. 'Its owner has been snatched a few hours ago and it doesn't care. All those sad people who reckon their cats love them are fooling themselves. Cats don't give a shit about anyone, they're only affectionate when they want something. Usually food. Isn't that right, you fickle little bastard? Want some more biscuits, don't you?'

Its purr sounded like a distant helicopter.

'Give me a dog any day.' He stepped over the animal and examined the spines of books lining a shelf on the wall. *Secrets of the Shaman. Celtic Myths. Witch Hunt: A History of Persecution. Tarot, the Oracle of Angels. The Magic of Wicca.*

His eyes lit on a collection of slim booklets. 'These are the ones for sale in Magick.' He pulled a couple of leaflets out from the shelf below. Details of courses at the Psychic Academy. There in the list of tutors was her name. 'Valerie Evans – the Real Deal. She taught at the Psychic Academy, just like Troy Wilkes.'

Rick looked directly at Jon. 'Yeah, I remember now. She also taught the Way of Wicca course, the one your sister and that Skye Booth were on.'

Jon shut his eyes. Christ, Rick was right. He glanced about. 'I've heard her name mentioned in connection with something else. What the hell was it?'

Rick was walking his fingers along her collection of CDs. 'Beethoven, Tchaikovsky, Verdi, Schubert. Satan's Inferno, Raging Spires.' He turned the case over. 'Signed.'

'What?'

'It's been signed. "To Valerie, thanks for everything. Serberos Tavovitch."'

Jon narrowed his eyes. 'So he knew her too. Time we hauled that freak and his band mates to the station. I'll call this in, we're going to need forensics.'

As he reached for his mobile, Rick stepped across to Valerie's phone on the table in the corner. A red light was urgently flashing. He pressed 'Play' and an electronic voice announced there were three new messages and one saved. First new message had been received yesterday at five fifteen p.m.

Jon and Rick's eyes locked as McCloughlin's voice came on the line. 'Miss Evans, this is DCI McCloughlin from the Greater Manchester Police. Could you call me at the earliest opportunity please.'

As McCloughlin read out his number, Rick whispered, 'What the hell does he want with her?'

Jon's sense of unease was rapidly growing. Pressure against his legs. That bloody cat again. The electronic voice continued. Second new message, received yesterday at six twenty-four p.m. McCloughlin again. 'Miss Evans, DCI McCloughlin, Greater Manchester Police. Sorry to bother you. Can you call me as a matter of urgency please.'

As he read out his number again, Jon racked his brain. How had McCloughlin linked her to his side of the investigation? A connection to the first victim, surely. They were colleagues at the Psychic Academy, after all.

The machine began to speak again. Third new message, received today at eight thirty six a.m. 'Miss Evans.' McCloughlin now sounded impatient. 'It's imperative that you call me as soon as possible. My number again.'

Jon resisted the urge to boot the cat across the room. 'Shit. This is going to McCloughlin's syndicate, he was on to her first.'

The electronic voice carried on relentlessly. 'First saved message, received on Wednesday, twenty-eighth of April at five eleven p.m. "Hi, Val, it's me, Skye."'

Jon's eyes latched on to the blinking red light.

'Give me a buzz about tonight. Blessed be.'

His mind clicked. Skye Booth. That's where he'd heard Valerie Evans' name mentioned. In the interview room at Longsight. His eyes swept the room, eventually finding a small photo on the window sill. Facing the camera was a middle-aged woman with a shock of white hair. It curled over her shoulders and hung down to her waist. It was the woman who they'd seen in the reception of the Psychic Academy. 'Fuck, I know why McCloughlin was calling. Skye Booth claimed she was staying here the night Troy Wilkes was murdered. McCloughlin is trying to check out her alibi.'

Rick's mouth was slightly open. He looked around his feet as if suddenly realising he'd wandered into the middle of a minefield. 'When he finds out we've been tramping around in here ...'

Jon's phone was already in his hand. As he scrolled through for Buchanon's number he thought about Skye Booth. A vision for one murder victim and an alibi that depended on the second. McCloughlin wouldn't go so easy on her this time.

# Chapter 20

Serberos leaned back in his chair, wrists draped over his thighs, hands almost cupping his crotch. He tilted his head at the tapes revolving round in the Neal twin-deck. Next to him a duty solicitor rotated a silver fountain pen between his finger and thumb, his eyes fixed on Jon.

'What's the speakers on that thing got?' Serberos asked. 'Can we put on some music after this and see?'

Jon was looking down at his notes. 'It can only record.' At the edge of his vision he saw Serberos's right hand slide out on the table top. He began tapping up and down with all four fingers. 'Could you stop that?'

Serberos's fingers paused in mid-air, then fell in sequence against the hard surface. A last little tattoo. If it was meant to wind Jon up, it worked. He kept his eyes on his notes, taking his time. Eventually he looked up. 'What is your connection to Valerie Evans?'

Serberos examined the nails on his thumb and forefinger. They were long, pointed and varnished black. 'She works at the Psychic Academy. I did her tarot course. Crap tutor she is. Waffles too much.'

'Do you know her in any sort of context outside the Academy?'

'How d'you mean?'

'Ever visit her house?'

He sniffed. 'No.'

'There's a signed copy of one of your CDs there.'

'Oh yeah, I gave her it at the end of the course. As I did everyone in the class. Spreading the word, you know?'

'So you've never met her outside the confines of the Academy?'

'No.'

The duty solicitor sat up straighter. 'When you arrested my client, it was on suspicion of arson. What's that got to do with Valerie Evans?'

Jon ignored his question. 'Who else was on Valerie's course? Was Luke Stevens?'

'I don't know. I've never seen the guy, as I've already stated.'

Yes, you have, thought Jon. And I don't believe you. 'Do you remember the names of anyone else on that course?'

He tipped his head back to stare up at the ceiling tiles. Jon knew them well. Brown water stains formed rings on the ones directly above the table. 'Let's think,' Serberos sighed. 'Older guy, Pierce something. Two middle-aged dears. One was called Margaret.'

As he spoke, Jon watched his Adam's apple bob up and down.

'Good-looking chick. Bit hippy-dippy. Saffron ... Celeste ... Skye? Something like that, I think.'

Skye Booth. Surprise, surprise, thought Jon. 'See any of them outside the classroom?'

'The hippy chick. She works in a New Age shop on Oldham Street. I've been in to put up posters for our gigs. Offered her a free ticket once or twice.' He gave Jon a look. 'Never snagged her though.'

'Thing is Serberos, Luke Stevens had a poster of your band above his bed and a collection of ticket stubs from dozens of your gigs. What I'm wondering is this: was he just a regular fan, or something more? Don't groupies get invited backstage occasionally? Cross the line from just a member of the audience to something a little more familiar?'

Serberos sneered. 'If they're girls, yeah. Not skinny little lads.'

Jon's pen paused. Serberos had just fucked up. 'I didn't say he was skinny.'

The singer raised his eyebrows. 'Every bloke at our concerts is skinny. The only fat goths you get are female.'

Jon reflected a moment. The bloke was bloody right. The ones he'd seen were emaciated to a man. 'So where's Peter Robson at the moment?'

'Yo no se, amigo.'

Jon stared at him.

Serberos kept the Spanish accent. 'I know notheeng.'

Jon kept on staring. Yeah, he'd make a good waiter on the Costa del Sol. Where the hell are you really from? 'Why aren't you telling me the truth?'

The other man's nonchalant expression was back. 'Isn't that your job to find out, officer?'

Jon's nails pressed hard against his pen. You cocky shit, I'm going to steamroller you. Not yet, but soon. 'Is Peter Robson burning down these churches?'

A pause that lasted a nanosecond too long. 'No idea.'

There was a knock on the door and Buchanon poked his head in. 'Jon.'

He caught the note in his SIO's voice. 'Rick, suspend the interview please.'

A group of officers were gathered in the corridor outside. As Jon closed the door behind him a couple parted and he saw McCloughlin's face. It was red with anger.

Buchanon turned to face him. 'Progress?'

'Some,' Jon replied. 'I'm about to spring the news that Valerie Evans has been murdered. His body language is giving away quite a bit so far. What about the other band members?'

'Padmore's just giving us the no comment treatment. However, Turnbull is another matter.'

Jon nodded. 'I thought he would be. The guy looked like he was shitting himself when I spoke to him backstage that time.'

'He wants to leave the band,' Buchanon continued. 'Says he didn't join it to get in all this. In his opinion Tavovitch, Padmore and Robson torched the first two churches.'

'How so?'

'Subsequent comments made by Tavovitch and Padmore. No outright admissions, just a hint that it's all good for publicity. Tavovitch and Padmore also seemed genuinely surprised on hearing about the third and fourth attacks. Padmore was worried, according to Turnbull. He says he overheard Padmore asking Tavovitch if it could have been Robson. Tavovitch just shrugged.'

Jon leaned against the wall, aware that McCloughlin's eyes were boring into him. He avoided the stare, just to aggravate him a bit more. 'Interesting. What about Luke Stevens? Does Turnbull recall ever seeing him backstage?'

'No. But there are a few more developments.' Buchanon held up a document. 'Analysis of the glass fragments found in the front of Luke Stevens' hooded top. The bit protected from the fire by the weight of his body.'

Jon leaned forward slightly in anticipation.

'They match the glass from the smashed windows of the Sacred Heart and the third church to be attacked, All Saints in Whalley Range. Nothing from the first two though.'

So was he a part of the first two attacks, or just copying them, Jon wondered. 'What about the glass fragments from the car jack found at the Sacred Heart?'

'Those results are in too,' Buchanon replied. 'A match for the Sacred Heart and also All Saints. Again, nothing on the first two.'

Jon turned the information over. 'So if Luke Stevens wasn't a part of the first two attacks, surely that means we've got more than one arsonist at work?'

Buchanon looked unsure. 'Well, he certainly wasn't working alone when he was killed.'

'And an association with the band members from Satan's Inferno is extremely likely,' Jon added.

'Extremely likely, but not by any means a certainty.' This from McCloughlin.

'He was a regular at all the gigs they played round town,' Jon answered. 'I know some of those venues. A crowd of more than a dozen and you're doing well. He must, at the very least, have been a familiar face.'

Buchanon turned to DC Adlon. 'Follow that up when we resume the interviews. Now, all the band members' clothes are at the lab. If any of them crawled through one of these church windows recently, we'll soon know. DC Gardiner, what have you got?'

She opened the topmost plastic sleeve in her hands. 'First is the nails in the barrel. I got on to our contact at the Met, the expert on the occult. It rang a bell with him and he tracked down a passage from a book called *The Philosophy of Witchcraft*. By the way,' she lowered her file, 'he's sending me his copy, along with various other titles from his collection which he thinks will be of help. He's also put together some fact sheets on the occult, witchcraft and satanism, they came through on the email just now.'

'The nails, detective,' McCloughlin said, as if cajoling a doddery aunt.

Jon saw Susan frown as she looked down. 'Sir. The passage describes how there's a stone in Perthshire called Witches' Crag. The name stems from an event where a suspected witch was forced inside a barrel. Sharp nails were then driven through its sides and the barrel was pushed down a hill.'

McCloughlin looked puzzled. 'It was a technique used for killing witches?'

'Yes. Quite common in Scotland during the sixteen-hundreds.'

He scratched the bristly hair on his head. 'But witches were executed by representatives of the Church, surely?'

Jon thought of Henry Robson and his manic stare.

'When I described how Troy Wilkes was killed,' Gardiner continued. 'With his thumbs and ankles bound by wire, he immediately said that was a recognised technique for swimming a witch.'

'Which means?' McCloughlin demanded.

'When they were thrown in ponds or rivers. You know, if they floated they were guilty. A sign of God's water rejecting them, like it was some sort of baptism. If they sank, they were innocent.'

'But probably drowned anyway,' Jon added.

'As did Troy Wilkes,' Gardiner replied.

Jon glanced at his SIO. 'They burned witches too. Was that what happened to Luke Stevens?'

Buchanon was now looking lost. 'Hang on. Luke Stevens was into satanism.' He turned to Gardiner. 'Have a look at those fact sheets or get on to the guy who wrote them. Have satanists ever killed each other? If they have, do they imitate the methods the Church used for killing witches.'

'OK,' Gardiner replied. 'Next?'

Everyone nodded.

She swapped sleeves and brought out some sheets of A4. 'One of the chemists at the drug squad got back to me on the legal status of henbane, hemlock and belladonna. You'll like this.'

Realising not everyone was aware of the allegations against Tristan Arkell, Jon cut in. 'It appears Tristan Arkell, head of the Psychic Academy, drugged a student who had signed up for a transcendental experience with him.'

'A what?' Buchanon asked.

'Out-of-body experience. She has no memory of over three hours and suspects Arkell assaulted her while she was out of it. The "flying ointment" recipe he gave her contained henbane, hemlock and belladonna.'

Gardiner flexed her sheets of paper. 'All three plants are native to Britain and all are renowned in folklore and witchcraft for their magical properties. Let's start with henbane.' She started reading from the notes. 'Grows up to three feet tall, bell-shaped flowers, stem and leaves sticky to the touch. All parts of the plant are highly toxic, its leaves being the most poisonous. Smelling them alone can cause disorientation and stupor. This is due to several tropane alkaloids, the main one being hyoscyamine.'

'What exactly does it do?' McCloughlin asked.

'Affects the nervous system, causing a dry mouth, dilation of the pupils, hallucinations and, if the dose is high enough, coma and death. Interestingly, it was a pharmaceutical preparation of henbane that Dr Crippen poisoned his wife with.'

Jon crossed his arms. Arkell was really in the shit, especially if the fat bastard had anything to do with this bloody coven Ellie wanted to join.

Gardiner flicked over another sheet. 'Belladonna, otherwise known as Deadly Nightshade. A bushy plant, growing to about four feet high, bearing purplish-black berries in the autumn. In folklore it's known as the Devil's own plant. Tradition has it, he's so keen on its cultivation, it's only on Beltane night that he can be diverted enough from its care to allow others to harvest it. Hence its older name, the Devil's Cherry.'

'What is Beltane?' Buchanon asked.

Jon stuck his hands in his pockets and stared at his shoes. 'May Eve.'

'Tonight,' added Gardiner.

'Also known as Walpurgis Night,' Jon continued. 'It's one of the main dates in the pagan calendar, signals the coming of summer.'

'How did you know that?' McCloughlin again, the faintest hint of a sneer in his voice.

Jon looked up and caught the glint in the other man's eye.

'I asked Jon to look into all this New Age stuff as part of the investigation,' Buchanon stated.

Jon clenched his teeth together. McCloughlin, Beltane, witchcraft, the Devil and his plants. He didn't know which he disliked most.

Gardiner pressed on. 'Belladonna contains a number of psychedelic ingredients. Along with hyoscyamine, there's scopolamine which causes profound confusion and disorientation, along with atropine which is a nerve poison. Anyone ingesting it will experience pleasantly hypnotic, visionary effects to begin with. However, it can quickly lead on to confusion, anxiety and panic. An overdose causes vomiting, convulsions, heart failure and death.'

'Nice,' Buchanon muttered. 'And these plants grow in Britain?'

'Yes,' she replied. 'Including hemlock, though the chemist wasn't quite sure why that plant featured in the ointment. It contains no psychedelic properties, it's just a straightforward nerve poison.'

'What' – Jon heard the aggression in his voice and proceeded more calmly – 'is the legal position in regard to possessing this stuff?'

'If in their natural forms, no problem,' Gardiner replied.

'You what?' Jon demanded.

She held a finger up. 'But if they've been treated in any way, dried or mashed up for instance, they count as a herbal remedy. And under the Retail Sale and Supply of Herbal Remedies Act, you need a licence from the Medicine and Care Agency for that.'

'Has Arkell got a licence?'

'I've made the enquiry. They're getting back to me.'

'Right,' Buchanon said. 'Let's carry on with Tavovitch and Padmore. Jon, a bit more pressure maybe?'

'With pleasure,' Jon replied, reaching for the interview room's door handle.

'By the way,' Buchanon added. 'Word's obviously got out that you lifted Tavovitch earlier.'

Jon remembered the sulky-looking couple with raven-black hair hanging around outside Tavovitch's house when they'd driven him away.

'In fact, there's a bit of a gathering forming at the front of the station,' Buchanon continued. 'Chants of "Free Serberos", among other things.'

'For fuck's sake,' Jon replied.

'And another thing, DI Spicer.' This time it was McCloughlin's voice. 'Given the fact that Valerie Evans was murdered, I'm having another go at Skye Booth. Warming up to find out exactly who else is involved in – what do you call a group of witches? Ah yes, her coven.'

Jon opened the door without bothering to reply.

# Chapter 21

Once Rick had formally resumed the interview, Jon stared at Serberos for a bit, relishing the prospect of nailing him. 'Your guitarist isn't so keen on staying in Satan's Inferno any more.'

The news brought an angry shine to the eyes of Serberos. 'Give a fuck. Couldn't play anyway.'

'Ah, but he can sing. In fact he's singing away for us right now. Beautiful voice, telling my colleagues all about how you and Padmore talked about the first two churches that went up in flames. Though, according to him, news of the third and fourth seemed to come as a bit of a surprise.'

Serberos acted out a yawn, saying nothing.

Jon was loving it. Time to sow a seed of doubt about his other band member too. 'Padmore seems to suspect Robson's got something to do with the most recent arson attacks.'

Serberos's eyes flashed.

Jon consulted his notebook. 'Now, forensics have been busy since someone started setting Manchester's churches on fire. They've been taking samples of glass from each side window that's been smashed in. What do you know about smashing windows, Serberos?'

He glared back in silence.

'Not a lot then, as I suspected. When you smash a window, the bits don't just fall inwards and downwards. The pane of glass actually flexes slightly before breaking. Not something you'd notice with the naked eye, but it happens all the same. This results in the outer edge of glass snapping back and sending microscopic particles towards the person who broke it. And when that person then crawls through the window frame, they get a really good coating of fragments down their front. Just bunging the item in a washing machine doesn't get rid of it.'

He paused to let the information sink in.

'Still got nothing to share wtih us? Come clean now and it'll look far better in court. No? OK, I'll continue. Analysis of the remains of Luke Stevens' top – the one he was wearing when he was burnt to a crisp – has shown fragments of glass from both the Sacred Heart and All Saints in Whalley Range. At the moment we're going over all your clothes with a fine-tooth comb as well. When forensics find fragments of glass from churches one and two, I'm charging you with arson. If they find fragments from churches three and four, I'm charging you with murder too.'

The duty solicitor waved a hand. 'I'd like to speak with my client in private. These revelations have nothing to do with the pre-interview briefing you gave me.'

Serberos's hands lifted and he started massaging his temples with the tips of his fingers. A low moan came from his slightly open mouth.

Time to finish him off, Jon thought. 'Also, I omitted to mention earlier that Valerie Evans was found dead this morning.'

Serberos froze and his eyes met Jon's.

'I don't advise you to say a word more,' the solicitor snapped.

'Stuffed into a barrel, then rolled down a hill,' Jon said. 'This barrel's sides had been driven through with fifty or so nine-inch nails. The mirror in the hallway of her house had been broken too. The effect I just mentioned? There'll be bits of that mirror in her attacker's hair and clothes.' He lifted his eyes to the top of Serberos's head and made a snipping motion in the air. 'Your turn with forensics is soon. They'll be taking samples.'

Serberos placed his hands on the table, then turned them up to reveal his palms. 'Listen, Pete Robson had a fixation with fire.'

The solicitor leaned towards Serberos. 'I really must—'

Serberos flicked his fingers at him. 'The more his dad bullied him, the worse he got. Then he started reading up on Satanism, really getting into it too.'

Jon sat back, keeping his silence. The little shit was only too happy to start spilling his guts now.

'He started talking about attacking the Church. He really wanted to do it damage.'

'It?' asked Rick. 'A particular one, or the Church as a whole?'

There was a click as the solicitor replaced the cap on his pen, then sat back with arms crossed.

'The Church in general. Christianity, God, everything. He'd got this book by a bloke called Aleister Crowley. He's a real figurehead for Devil worshippers. Pete wanted us to hold a ceremony to try and summon up a demon. Fuck, it was really disturbed stuff, you know what I mean? We said we weren't interested.'

Jon nodded at the tattoo on the younger man's forehead. 'And you expect us to believe you with that thing on your face?'

'This?' Serberos touched a finger against the inverted cross. 'It's a stunt. I'll get it lasered off when I'm rich.'

''Course you will, Serberos,' Jon smiled. 'After all, I can really see *Raging Spires* topping the album charts.'

The skin around Serberos's eyes tightened. 'We've got a record deal practically on the table.'

'So where will you go with your wads of cash to get it removed?'

'The clinic next to the tattoo parlour on Shudehill. The same guy owns both places.'

Jon had seen the building. One half for putting the things on, the other for taking them off. The owner was a bloody genius.

Rick spoke. 'Convenient. Suddenly the whole Devil-worshipping business is just a bit of a laugh. You're not serious about it at all.'

Serberos was nodding back. 'I'm not.'

'And your concerts, the words in your songs, they're all just a bit of fun too? A harmless charade?'

Serberos took a deep breath. 'It's an act, OK? A stage act. Like my name.'

'Your name checks out on our system,' Rick answered.

'I had it changed by deed poll, that's why.'

'From what?'

'Dan Humphries.'

Jon had to bow his head to hide his smile. 'Not very Death Metal.'

'Exactly.'

Jon looked up. 'So you're not descended from Romanian gypsies?'

'Am I fuck! Dad's from Rochdale, Mum's from Italy. He worked the cabins on cruise liners, she was the on-board cabaret singer.'

'Was?' Rick asked.

'They're retired. Live in Whitby now. Some hideous caravan park on the cliffs.'

Jon shook his head. It was so good, it had to be true. 'But I've seen you up on stage. Don't tell me you're not really enjoying yourself.'

'Yeah, I enjoy it. The girls screaming, who wouldn't get a buzz? But I don't believe it. The actual music is shit. To be honest, I prefer older-fashioned stuff.'

'Like what?' Jon asked.

'Dylan, Cohen, Cash. Even Sinatra. I'll take their stuff any day over what I do. Those guys really use their voices. Me? I growl and scream. It's shit.'

Despite wanting to laugh, Jon kept his voice cold. 'I'm not convinced.'

Serberos sighed. 'Look, I can keep a distance between the stuff we rant about in our music and what's actually real. Pete couldn't. He was getting really confused, frying his brains on 'shrooms and acid. Losing the plot big time.'

Jon leaned forward. 'Is it Serberos or Daniel then?'

'Dan's fine.'

'Who burned the churches down then, Dan?'

His eyes dropped to the table.

'Who killed Luke Stevens, or should I say sacrificed him? Was it Peter Robson?'

No reply.

'You know where Pete is, don't you?'

He didn't move.

Jon slammed a hand on the table. 'Murder, Daniel! We're talking murder here! Now, do yourself a favour and start co-operating. Where is Peter Robson?'

Dan screwed his eyes shut, then pressed his fingers into the sockets. A mumbled reply emerged from his lips.

'Look at me and speak clearly.'

Dan's hand dropped and he straightened out of his slouch. 'I said it's hard to describe. Easier if I just show you.'

'Show us what?'

'Where he's hiding.'

Jon turned to Rick. 'We'll need a car. In fact, three. One for us, one for Robson and one for evidence. Let's meet out the back in five.'

In the corridor, he collared the first officer he saw. 'Has McCloughlin got anyone in for interviewing?'

'Yeah, he's in room four.'

Jon ducked into the observation room attached to four. Skye was on the other side of the glass. Her head was tipped back slightly as a female officer took a swab from the inside of her mouth. The officer backed away and Jon could see a tear running down Skye's cheek.

He half turned to his fellow observers. 'No solicitor?'

'Didn't want one. Not yet, anyway.'

Jon felt a pang of worry. Be careful, he found himself thinking, McCloughlin is one canny bastard. 'What's he charging her with?'

'Obstructing a murder investigation.'

His old senior officer sat immobile. 'Valerie Evans was a member of the coven you belong to?'

Skye nodded.

'As was Troy Wilkes?'

'No. It's a female-only coven. He happened to work in the same shop as me, that's all.'

'Who else is in this coven, then?'

Alarm spiked in Jon's chest as Skye licked her lips before

replying. 'The rules are, apart from the person who introduces you to the coven, you don't learn anyone else's real name. It goes back to the days when witches were persecuted for their beliefs. It was safer if you didn't know the identities of those you worshipped with.'

McCloughlin's jaw muscles worked back and forth. 'Would you care to tell me how many people normally belong to a coven?'

She shrugged. 'Twelve.'

'And it was Valerie Evans who introduced you?'

'Yes.'

'And what about the person you introduced?'

Jon picked at his lower lip with a thumbnail. *Please don't feed my sister's name to that bastard.*

'I haven't introduced anyone, as yet.'

'And you're certain you don't know the identity of a single other member?' McCloughlin asked.

'I didn't say that.'

'So you do know who your fellow witches are?'

'Only one.'

Buchanon's pen was poised. 'Who?'

'She's someone I see around town, that's all.'

'What, you pass her in the street?'

'No. Through her work.'

'Her name, please.'

'I can't say. I can ask her to contact you, but I can't give you her name.'

'Skye,' McCloughlin's voice was surprisingly soft. 'Your fellow witches are being murdered, one by one. How will the next execution go? We've had a swimming and a barrel roll. Maybe a burning at the stake? The Inquisition had some great ways of killing people. Spiked braces, nasty ratcheted machines. Valerie looks like a pin cushion. Shall I get a photo? Oh, I forgot. You've probably seen her already. In one of your visions.'

Another tear set off down Skye's cheek.

'What's going on, Skye?' McCloughlin suddenly shouted.

'You claim you were at Valerie Evans' house the night Troy Wilkes died. What were you doing there again?'

She wiped her face with her fingers. 'Performing certain rites. By the time we'd finished it was very late, so I stayed over.'

'Which room?'

'The spare one.'

'Where exactly in the house is it?'

'Top of the stairs, second on the left.'

'Sheets or a duvet?'

'Duvet.'

'Colour?'

'Dark purple.'

'So when I direct forensics to that bed, they'll find hairs from your head on that pillow?'

'I doubt it. I stripped it the next morning. It all went into Valerie's washing machine.'

'You're not helping yourself much here, are you? Don't worry, if you slept in that room, you'll have shed DNA evidence somewhere. You'd just better pray we find a hair somewhere. In fact, there's quite a lot riding on that little head of yours, isn't there?'

Skye's eyes were now closed.

'Jon!' Rick's voice from the corridor.

He took one last glance at McCloughlin. God, you're a prick, he thought as he left the room.

# Chapter 22

The crowd of teenagers looked over at the convoy of three vehicles as they left the station's staff car park. Jon stared back, taking in the black beanie caps, Satan's Inferno T-shirts, absurd chains looping down from belts, studded leather wristbands and ridiculous platform boots that bristled with buckles.

Traffic on the main road forced them to a standstill and the group edged closer. Daniel Humphries began to wave, revealing the handcuffs. Their cries of delight turned to shouts of dismay.

A lanky young male in a full-length black coat ran forward, acne peppering his chin. 'Let him go!'

He was joined by a white-skinned girl, black eyeshadow adding to her angry look as she yelled, 'Fucking pigs!'

Others joined her and they pressed forward as one, many holding up hands with just a forefinger and little finger extended. They gestured at Jon, eyes wide and hostile. Some sort of Satan thing no doubt, he thought. A bang went off in the vehicle like a rifle shot. Someone had slammed a hand on the roof. Jon lowered his window. 'Touch this vehicle again and you're under arrest. Now fuck off.'

They hesitated, some stepping back on to the pavement. A gap opened in the traffic and they sped off round the corner. Looking at Daniel in the rear-view mirror, Jon spotted his smirk. 'You think it's funny? Messing with their heads, encouraging them to worship the Devil?'

Dan shrugged. 'If they weren't so estranged from the world, they wouldn't be so interested in me. You should see the stuff I get sent through MySpace.'

'What is this bloody MySpace?' Jon growled.

'A networking website, granddad. Kids message me all the time, asking about the meaning of life. Me?' He laughed.

'Great bloody example you are,' Jon murmured in reply, eyes on the road.

Dan slumped back. 'They're not my fucking responsibility, I'm in the entertainment business. Where the hell are their parents? It should be their mums and dads offering them guidance, not me. How fucked up is them asking me for advice? Serberos Tavovitch, lead singer of Satan's Inferno, the one who beckons to the Beast, trying to draw him up to the surface of the earth. Fucking joke.'

Jon glanced at him in the rear-view mirror. 'So that crowd of morbid-looking losers back there. You're totally free of blame?'

'If they weren't left in their rooms with only a computer for company, my fan base would plummet. Give them something to enjoy in their miserable lives. Mum, Dad, a meal round a table for a start.'

'And your mum and dad, what do they think of what you do for a living?'

'They're not arsed. Mum asks how things are going sometimes.' He met Jon's eyes. 'You've got a wedding ring. Any kids?'

'Yeah.'

'What sort of hours do you work? Ever home to read them bedtime stories? I suspect not. That's what I do. My website, my songs: bedtime stories for kids whose parents aren't around.'

Jon focused on the road in front, thinking about the hours he worked. Christ, as Holly got older would he find the time to be at home for her? Any murder case soaked the hours up like a sponge. He heard the older officers when they worked late, murmuring in babyish voices to their kids back home. Despite cupping the receivers close to their faces, their sing-song intonations stood out a mile against the brusque work conversations going on around them. And when they hung up, they always looked awkward, having to pause slightly before switching back into work mode.

His eyes flicked back to Dan once again. The singer was now staring out of the window as they headed towards the city centre. 'So where do we go once we reach Ardwick?'

He followed Dan's directions and soon they were parked up by the edge of the railway. It was at a point where various lines merged together to form the final run of track in to Piccadilly Station. A train waited at a set of lights as another started clanking slowly along the raised embankment, below which was a series of brick arches.

'He's in one of those. They're tunnels, maybe thirty metres long.'

'Exit at the other side?' Jon asked, scrutinising the dark entrances.

'Not the one he's in.'

'Which is it?'

'Can't see it from here. You cross over the tracks and it's down the slope on the other side.'

It took almost twenty minutes before a staff member from the station ambled up. He unlocked a gate in the fence and ushered them over a designated crossing point by the nearest signal box. The grassy slope on the other side was peppered with litter thrown from passing trains. Dan led them to the second entrance, the mouth of which was shrouded by an expanse of black tarpaulin. 'Pete? It's Serb, I'm really sorry, mate—'

Jon pulled him away from the entrance. 'Peter Robson? It's the police. Can we talk?'

Away to their left a Virgin train slowed to a halt, its windows full of watching faces. Jon swept the sheeting aside and shone a torch in. Bare earth ended at an expanse of flattened cardboard boxes. A broken base of a bottle held the stub of a large black candle. Chalk graffiti covered the walls. The same symbols he'd seen on the walls of the burnt churches. The circle of torchlight picked out a small camping stove and a couple of upturned plastic crates. Next to them a sleeping bag lay like a shrivelled slug. Jon played the beam across to the other side of the tunnel. A large petrol container and a car jack were revealed.

'Is he there?' Dan asked from behind.

Jon glanced over his shoulder. 'No. DC Murray, we're going to need those evidence bags from your car.' He stepped back from the arch and looked at Dan. 'Where might he go during the day?'

'Anywhere warm, where they won't kick him out.'

'Like the library?' Rick asked.

'He's never mentioned the library.'

'Where then?' Jon demanded.

'Manchester cathedral. I know he hung about in there a lot.'

'The cathedral?' Jon said, incredulous.

'When he wasn't in the place itself he'd be in a day centre thing to the side of it, where the drunks and homeless go for tea and free food. The Booth Centre I think it's called.' He paused to glance at the audience watching from the stationary train above them. Slowly he lifted his manacled hands, a middle finger raised. 'Fucking wage slaves.'

A light in the display above the track changed and the train began to advance towards the terminal. 'He was really fucked up about his mum. She committed suicide, you know?'

'We'd heard, yes.'

'Well, ever since, his old man has been spouting off about how suicides end up in limbo. Like abortions.'

Here we go, thought Jon. The bloody Church strikes again. 'Limbo meaning?'

'The halfway house between earth and Hell. When the world ends – which Henry Robson believes will be very soon – Christ will carry all the faithful off to Heaven before tribulation.'

Jon shook his head. This was sounding like the same crap his mum liked to come out with. 'I know this bit. The rest of us get thrown down into a pit of fire.'

'Right. Purgatory. An eternity of torment. Robson drummed it into Pete that because his mum took her own life that's where she was going to end up.'

Jon closed his eyes for a moment, wondering exactly what Helena Hunt, the resident medium at the Psychic Academy, had told the poor bloke. And the Church. Christ, if the only consolation it could offer someone who'd lost his mum was that she was headed for Hell, it was no wonder he hated it so much. 'So why go and sit in the cathedral?'

'He'd admit to praying sometimes. When he was really low. He didn't want his mum to end up in the flames, did he? He couldn't get his head round the fact how, if God is merciful, his mum would be made to suffer for ever in Hell.'

Fair point, thought Jon. 'Right, your help is appreciated on this. I'll make sure it's duly noted.' He turned to the other officers. 'Joe and Paul, can you escort Daniel back to the station. Hugh and Mark, bag everything up in the tunnel. Rick, let's head for the cathedral.'

He turned to go, but Dan stopped him. 'When do I get released? I've got a gig to play tomorrow night.'

'Daniel, you've got no band for a start.'

'I've got backing tracks. There's an A & R man from London turning up. It could be my break.'

Jon looked over his shoulder. 'Let's get Pete Robson in and see where we stand.'

They parked in a cab bay by the enormous Marks & Spencers, then set off along the pedestrianised area leading towards the cathedral. On the way, they passsed designer shops: Ted Baker, Rockport, Lacoste, Reiss. Harvey Nichols loomed up on their left and, rising up behind that, another monstrous development of trendy apartments. As usual, Jon found himself reflecting on the speed of change the city centre was experiencing. Where was the money coming from to fund it? Not for the first time, he hoped it wasn't too much too fast. There was something fragile about a transformation that took place with this sort of speed.

Down a set of shallow stone steps was an old timber-framed pub, Sinclair's Oyster Bar. One pound thirty a pint. Prices like that made Londoners weep into their beers. The whole thing had been dismantled, moved a hundred metres and rebuilt to clear the way for redevelopment after the IRA bomb of '96 had triggered the regeneration of the city in the first place. Just visible behind the old boozer was the dark tower of the cathedral itself.

The bustle of shoppers quickly died away as they walked the flagstone alleyway running along the side of the pub. Seconds later, they emerged into the open area surrounding the cathedral and the impression of entering another century was complete.

It was a squat, ugly building, Jon thought. No dramatic buttresses or soaring spires. The stone used to build it was of a dark brown, or maybe that was the effect of traffic fumes from the nearby road of Deansgate.

Bickering broke out on the grass to their left where a bunch of drunks milled around, most clutching soft-drink bottles filled with suspicious-looking brown liquid: a way to carry on drinking despite the recent council ruling that banned alcohol from Manchester's streets.

He watched the sad collection. They looked like walking scarecrows, or living skeletons, their eyeballs swivelling in hollow sockets, their emaciated frames moving jerkily beneath their baggy clothes.

A man in a baseball cap rasped at an unshaven older man, 'You've got eight quid, right?'

'Eight?' The older man thrashed his head. 'Listen, listen. She owes me, right? I haven't got it.'

'Who? Her?'

They turned to regard a fat woman who was lolling on the grass, her skirt ruffled up so high her crotch was almost in view. The way she stared back made Jon suspect she was either heavily drugged or mentally ill.

'Who is she?'

'What's your name, lassie?'

She didn't reply.

The man with the baseball cap grew impatient. He turned back to the bearded man. 'Get to fuck! You've had my CD player, you owe me.'

His demand was waved away.

'I'll fucking do you, you bastard!' He made a feeble lunge, but his way was blocked by a newcomer.

'Please, you lot! This is a public area. Keep the noise down would you?'

This man was neatly dressed, blue shirt and navy jacket. The man with the baseball cap slid round him and hurled a disposable lighter at the one with the stubble. 'Cunt!'

The word bounded off the cathedral walls.

The lighter landed on the grass and the older one bent stiffly to pick it up. 'Half full, cheers.'

'Bastard.'

As their mates stepped in to mediate, Jon followed the smartly dressed man down some steps. He approached a wooden door with a sign to the side that read, 'The Booth Centre'.

'Excuse me.'

The man looked round, a bunch of keys in his hand.

'DI Spicer and my colleague, DS Saville, Greater Manchester Police. I wonder if you could help us?'

He looked embarrassed. 'I'm sorry, officer, I've told them a thousand times. The Centre will be open in five minutes and they'll all come inside.'

Jon glanced at the group who were all now smoking cigarettes, their conversation back to more normal levels. 'It's not a problem with us. Though that's some job, controlling that lot.'

He nodded. 'They're worse now because they've been speedballing. Heroin and cocaine. The dealers have started selling it as a package. They can forget to eat for days.'

Jon understood why they were all so stick-thin. 'Are you familiar with most of the people who use the Centre?'

'Most, yes.'

'We're looking for a youngish guy. Early twenties, dresses in black. Black hair, probably tied back in a ponytail. Peter Robson, or Pete.'

'Pete, yes. He's been around quite a bit recently.'

'Today?'

'No. What's the problem, if I may ask?'

'Just a few questions. When does he normally show up?'

'We open for eleven a.m. and five p.m. sittings. He only ever comes along in the mornings. He's a very troubled young man. I've tried approaching him a few times, but he doesn't communicate.'

'Yes, we're concerned for him too. Why do you say he's troubled?'

'He seems so alone. He doesn't mix and when he does speak, it's very stilted.'

'Speedballing?' Rick asked.

'No. They're charged up on that stuff. Something else. You could have a scout in the cathedral itself. On the days he does turn up, he always has a sit in the Regimental Chapel first. Just slumps down in there and stares.'

'Thanks for your help, Mr ...'

'Green. Norman Green.'

'OK, Norman. If you could keep the fact we were asking after him to yourself.'

He nodded. 'Has he any family? Someone who can take him in?'

Jon tipped a hand. 'We're in contact with his father. Maybe something will work out.'

They went back up the steps and in the side entrance. The air, noticeably cooler, had a tinge of mustiness to it. Jon examined the walls. Chocolate-coloured stone that rose up to a ceiling of equally dark wood. The surfaces sucked in the daylight shining through the narrow windows. Mounted on the ceiling was a series of spotlights. They shone on to brightly coloured banners that hung down the squat pillars lining the main part of the church. The attempt at cheeriness couldn't dispel the gloomy nature of the building.

To their side a couple of tourists spoke in hushed tones. Jon watched as they stepped across the floor of black and white tiles, rucksacks on backs, cameras in hand. You'll need a bloody strong flash to make out anything in here, Jon thought.

Rick led the way, taking them past various deserted side chapels. From a room somewhere above came the faint sound of a choir. Jon couldn't tell if it was a recording or not.

At the top end was a larger chapel with flags hanging from the ceiling. 'That's it,' Rick whispered.

They scanned the rows of chairs. Empty.

Jon stepped inside. The highly polished wood floor had a

molten glow to it. Jon raised his eyes to the source of light. The end of the chapel was dominated by a stained-glass window that swirled with oranges, reds and yellows. The colours gave the impression that a fire was raging just behind the mass of panes.

'That's why he comes here then,' Rick whispered. 'Contemplating the fate of his mum.'

Jon sighed. It made sense. He looked at the mouldering flags dangling from the tops of pillars lining the chapel. Most were so old their lower edges had begun to fray and perish. One or two were little more than squares of fine gauze, only fragments of material in their top corners remaining. He read a small wooden notice below one. *King's Colour of the 96th Regiment of Foot. Now 2nd Battalion The Manchester Regiment. Raised in 1824, carried 1824–1861.*

The existence of the chapel was beginning to strike Jon as odd. 'Why does the Church glorify the military? What about Thou Shalt Not Kill?'

Rick shrugged. 'There's plenty about the Church that has nothing to do with principles of acceptance or forgiveness or tolerance. You're talking to a gay man, remember?'

Jon shot him a sideways glance. 'I thought the Church had got a lot more understanding about all that – and ordaining women too.'

'Yeah,' Rick said. 'Like political parties really take green issues or the rights of the disabled or a whole host of other minority issues seriously. They might react if they feel a surge of opinion against them, but it's all superficial at the end of the day.'

As they got nearer to the side doors the noise of arguing grew louder and louder.

'It's a death trap. A fucking death trap. Concentrate on that, man!' The bearded man's voice.

'He took my CD player!' That was Baseball Cap. 'He's full of shite. Listen, right—'

'I never touched your poxy CD player!' The Beard again.

'You're fuckin' asking for it!'

Jon stepped out into the sunlight. The group stood around a

mountain bike that had been dumped on its side in the middle of the small lawn.

'It's top quality man. Give me twenty-five for it,' Baseball Cap said to someone on the other side of the group.

'Twelve. You owe me eight from last time.'

Jon stopped. He recognised that voice.

Baseball Cap pushed his visor up. 'Twelve add eight is twenty, innit? I said twenty-five.'

'Twenty. I'm not paying more than that.'

'Tommo.' He turned to a young lad with a face like Gollum's. Haircut matched it, too. 'How much have you got?'

'Seven.'

Jon craned his neck, fearing the worst as the bearded man stepped back, laughter bubbling in his throat. His younger brother Dave was revealed. I should have guessed, Jon thought. Drug addicts and the homeless. Dave's preferred companions. He'd lost more weight and his head was now shaved. There was a cut or sore at the side of his mouth. Oh Jesus, thought Jon, what are you doing?

Baseball Cap was shaking his head. 'It's top, man. Look, rear suspension see? Pure quality.'

Dave shook his head. 'Twenty.'

The other man's shoulders drooped. 'When can you get it us?'

'No time. Faster on this.' Dave grabbed a handlebar and yanked the bike upright.

Jon stepped over. 'Dave.'

Their eyes met and Dave blinked with surprise. 'Yeah?'

The addicts were turning round, suspicion spiking their faces.

Jon walked past the group to a nearby bench. He could hear the tick of spokes as his brother followed. 'What are you doing?'

Dave appeared at the edge of his vision. 'Nothing. What are you doing?'

Rick was hovering just behind, an uncertain look on his face. 'I'll catch you up,' Jon snapped.

'You sure?' Rick's eyes were switching between him and Dave.

'Yeah. See you at the car.'

He waited until Rick had walked off round the corner. 'Why does that man owe you money?'

'This and that. I'm busy, you know?'

Jon looked at him. It was a sore at the corner of his mouth. Oh Christ, Dave, he thought, please don't tell me you're dealing to this lot.

'Look at me like that and expect me to stay for a chat?' Dave started to walk away.

'You're going down, Dave. Sooner or later.'

'I'm buying a bike. All right?'

Jon stared at his back. 'You never rang Mum.'

Dave stopped and his bony shoulders rose and fell. 'What can I say?'

Jon was about to reply, you promised. But what was the fucking point? 'She needs to know you're OK. Or alive at least.'

'Tell her then.' He started walking once again.

'I spoke to Ellie. She told me what happened to you two.'

Again Dave stopped, this time turning around. Something like fear was in his eyes. 'You what?'

'She told me about the Sunday school, about the man there.' He saw his brother's entire body flinch.

'What's she said?'

Jon stepped closer. 'Dave, there's no need to live like this. What you went through – there's help we can get for you.'

His brother spat on the flagstones. His phlegm was dark brown. 'Fuck are you on about?'

Jon grabbed his brother's arm, sensed his fingers almost connecting on the other side. 'Listen to me. We can get you sorted out.' His brother's eyes hardened and Jon realised his mistake. 'I mean we can get the problem sorted—'

'Fuck off. Get your fucking hand off me.'

'Dave, trouble?'

Jon turned to Baseball Cap. 'Piss off.'

'Piss off, yeah? You reckon?' He clenched his fists and flexed his emaciated arms. 'Make me.'

Jon wanted to laugh. One tap to the chest would send the bloke flying. But for the possibility of stabbing his fist on a hidden syringe, the temptation was overwhelming. Dave wriggled his arm free and, as he jumped on the bike, Jon's phone began to ring.

'Meet me at Stewie's. Half an hour!' Dave shouted as he rode away.

Jon watched him go, then turned to the other man. Incident over, he had stepped back, his eyebrows mockingly raised. I can't be arsed, Jon thought, retrieving his phone. 'Yes?'

'It's DC Gardiner, sir.'

He strode across the lawn, just registering the word 'shitter' being hissed at his back. 'Susan, what's up?'

'It's like the buses. Nothing, then three turn up at once.'

'Sorry?'

'Females from courses at the Psychic Academy. Three who've had private tuition with Arkell have returned my calls in the last hour. All think they may have been assaulted by him.'

Once again, the enormous chaise longue in the man's office flashed in Jon's mind. 'Three? How many did you ring?'

'Twenty-four.'

'Christ, that's some strike rate.'

'That's what I thought.'

'None thought to come forward before?'

'No. Their experiences are all so similar though. Vague suspicions, a sense of unease, but nothing they thought warranted an actual accusation.'

'Any willing to do so now?'

'If the list grows longer, yes. Safety in numbers. It'll just take one to jump and the rest will follow. Up until now each one thought they were the only one to experience something dodgy.'

'OK, carry on digging.'

'I've run out of names to call.'

'I'm not far from his Academy now. Let me pay him a visit. I'll get some more attendance lists. Good work, Susan.'

'Thanks.'

'By the way, where's McCloughlin?'

'In with Buchanon at the moment.'

'Is he still holding the girl from the New Age shop, Skye Booth?'

'No, he bailed her about half an hour ago, told her to go straight home. He's also organising a car to sit outside her house.'

'He's putting her under surveillance?'

'Apparently.'


Skye Booth walked quickly up the path leading to her front door. As she reached for her keys she couldn't stop her hands from trembling. That bastard. He represented all that she hated about the male psyche. Aggressive, patronising, fixated. The way he'd gone at her, using the details about Valerie to upset her. Valerie. Oh, you poor soul. How you must have suffered. She felt tears springing up once again and she sniffed them back.

The key wouldn't go in the lock. What was up with the bloody thing? She tried again, but something was blocking it. Shit.

She crouched down to examine the keyhole. Some idiot had jammed tissue paper into it. As she tried to dig it out a shadow fell across her. Skye's head had started to turn when a hand locked on to the back of her neck. As she opened her mouth to shout, a palm that reeked of petrol was clamped over it.

# Chapter 23

'Who was the bloke outside the cathedral?'

Jon glanced at Rick, then turned back to the pavement ahead. 'No one.'

'Oh.'

Jon could tell more was to come.

'Alice mentioned one time that you've got a younger brother. Left home—'

'It wasn't him. That's just some scrote I use for information.' Rick breathed in and Jon could tell he wasn't convinced. Before another question came, he spoke again. 'So if Susan's got three names already, Arkell could have assaulted dozens of girls.'

Rick nodded. 'Seems likely.'

They rounded the corner and were confronted by the dramatic sweep of Urbis. Jon regarded the translucent panels making up the sides of the museum and was reminded of an iceberg, or a ski jump. A couple of skateboarders glided past, backs of their jeans so low that the upper half of their boxer shorts were revealed.

Their walk took them up the side of the Printworks and into the narrow streets of the Northern Quarter. Five minutes later they were trotting up the steps leading into the building that housed the Psychic Academy. The downstairs foyer was quiet, just a couple of Indian women browsing in the textile shop to their left.

Jon took the stairs two at a time, his hand on the Academy's door handle before he saw the sign sellotaped to the wooden panel.

We are now closed until Monday the third of May. This is

to give me adequate preparation time for Beltane. Blessed be,
Tristan.

'What the hell is this blessed be business?' Jon murmured, shaking the locked door. 'Skye Booth signed off with it on Valerie
Evans' answerphone too.'

'Susan Gardiner asked the guy at the Met about it. It's a salu-
tation traditionally used by witches.'

Jon's hand dropped to his side. 'To address one another?'

'I think so.'

Fuck. Did that mean Arkell was involved in the coven Ellie
was joining? Skye had told McCloughlin it was a female-only
coven, but did that apply to the big ceremonies like Beltane? He
reached for his phone. 'Susan? It's Jon Spicer here. The Psychic
Academy is now shut for the weekend. Are you in front of a
box?'

'Yeah, logged on right now.'

'Run me an address search on Tristan Arkell, would you? I
need to know where he lives.'

'OK, hang on.'

Turning away from Rick's look of disapproval, he listened
to the clicking of the keyboard. A few moments later her voice
came back on the line. 'No Tristan Arkell is on the system.
You know, the Medicine and Health Care Agency called too.
They've no record of any Psychic Academy of Tristan Arkell
either.'

'Manchester Council?'

'Contacted them. He's failed to register the Academy with
them as well.'

'How long has this place been doing business? Jesus Christ,
you'd have thought they would have noticed.'

'What, in the Northern Quarter? Places are popping up and
disappearing there all the time.'

Jon thought about the warren of roads and old warehouses
they'd just passed through. She was probably right. 'Well, at
least when we do find him we can lift him for more than the
supply of prescribed drugs. Contact the Department of Work

and Pensions – they must have him or his business listed some-where.'

'OK, boss.'

'We're heading back in, see you in a bit.'


As Longsight police station came into view they couldn't miss the gathering of youths hanging round the front entrance. It had now expanded to well over forty, the lot dressed in black.

'The word to describe a load of crows. Murder I think,' Jon remarked. 'Fits that lot too. A murder of Death Metallers. Look at the sight of them.'

Some were sitting on the pavement, others stood huddled in small groups of three or four. Many seemed happy just to be on their own, flicking cigarette lighters, studying mobile phones or simply staring off into space. At the far edge of the group, blonde hair stood out. Carmel, interviewing a couple of them.

'I'll get a uniform to move them on,' Rick said as they turned down the side street. 'They're causing an obstruction.'

Jon waved a hand. 'Let them protest. At least they're engaging in something mildly productive.'

When they got to the incident room Rick made a beeline for his computer. Jon walked across to Buchanon's office. He was on the phone. Seeing Jon at the door he raised a hand and beckoned him in.

Jon took a seat, his attention caught by the screensaver on his senior officer's monitor. The oval form that dominated the screen was made up of an incredibly intricate blend of colours. Speckles of dark blue at the top and bottom of the shape spread inwards, merging into greens, then yellows and oranges. Towards its centre the shades altered again to reds and finally a few purples.

Buchanon hung up, then gazed at the image for a second. 'Beautiful, don't you think?'

'What is it?'

'The universe, thirteen billion years ago.'

'Sorry?'

Buchanon smiled. 'My wife works for the School of Physics

and Astronomy at the University of Manchester. She's involved in a project called the Very Small Array. Its purpose is to analyse the cosmic microwave background.'

Jon groaned inwardly. There's no way I'm holding on to the thread of this conversation for long, he thought. 'Cosmic microwave background?'

'Or CMB. As far as I can understand, every element in the universe has a specific frequency that you can analyse through the radiowaves it gives out. Jodrell Bank, where my wife works, is basically a big ear, able to listen to those radiowaves at frequencies of up to thirty gigahertz.'

'That's a lot, I take it.'

'A television receives at around eight hundred megahertz. A gigahertz is made up of one thousand megahertz, so yes.'

'And this image is meant to be the universe how many billion years ago?'

'Around thirteen. The Big Bang occurred about thirteen and a half billion years ago, but you can't study it from day one because no elements existed at that point. They took another few hundred thousand years to start taking shape. That's what this image is – streams of radiowaves from that point, visually represented by colour. The dark reds are the warmest parts, dark blues the coldest.'

Jon studied the image again. Stuff like this, he thought, actually makes my brain ache. It reminded him of looking up at the night sky as a child and wondering where space ended.

'Scientists,' Buchanon continued, 'can analyse this data and gain real insights into the origins of our universe.'

How can people still believe in Heaven, Jon thought, when images like this exist? God has nowhere left to hide. Except, of course, within the confines of unstable people's minds.

'That was Nikki Kingston, by the way. The Crime Scene Manager at the Sacred Heart.'

'I know who she is,' Jon muttered, peeling his eyes from the screen.

Buchanon glanced at him. 'That sounded a bit ominous.'

Jon shrugged. 'Sorry. It wasn't meant to.'

'She's got some interesting news. Traces of blood have shown up.'

'Where?'

'She's bringing in a diagram to show us. The pathologist's final report is due any minute too. Looks like we're about to get some answers. Now, what's been going on with you?'

Jon crossed his legs. 'Serberos Tavovitch – real name Daniel Humphries – took us to where Peter Robson has been hiding out. DC Murray and Ashford should have brought in the evidence bags from the scene.'

'The container of petrol and the car jack? I've already seen them. They've gone straight to the lab.'

'Good. It'll be interesting to see where any shards of glass on them are from.'

'And the petrol in the can,' Buchanon added. 'With luck we'll be able to establish a link to the presbytery too.'

Jon felt a slight jolt to the chest. The presbytery. Father Ben Waters. He'd forgotten about him. Wasn't Rick meant to have rung the church representative to make sure the old guy was safe? 'Is there any chance of putting an alert out to the airports? And ferries too? If Pete Robson is the person targeting the priest, and he's stolen the man's car, he could try to track him down out there.'

'You mean attack him in this retreat at Salamanca? How would Robson know he's there?'

'I'm sorry, sir, it completely slipped my mind. A notice on Waters' front door revealed the fact.'

'I don't understand.'

'It was for the parishoners. It mentioned that Waters is recuperating in a retreat near Salamanca in Spain.'

'Bloody great, Jon,' Buchanon cursed, picking up the phone.

As he made the call, Jon's eyes strayed back to the image on the monitor. There was a sense of infinity in the frozen kaleidoscope of colours. And here we are, Jon thought, frantically scrabbling around on this little bit of rock.

Buchanon hung up. 'Let's hope that slip doesn't cost us.'

Jon's mind snapped back. 'Sorry, sir.'

'Now.' Buchanon breathed in. 'We're going to have to release the band members downstairs on bail.'

Jon shot him a questioning glance.

'Forensics need more time to analyse their clothing and we've held them for almost eight hours as it is. I don't want to eat up any more of the twenty-four hours we've got before having to charge them.'

Jon looked at his watch. Almost four o'clock. Buchanon had a point, fuck it.

'Don't worry, Jon. We'll drag them back once the evidence is in.' He turned in his seat and looked out of the window on to the street. 'Plus it'll clear that rabble away. It's like a scene from a horror film down there.'

Jon remembered what the bouncer outside Diabolic had said, and smiled. '*Night of the Living Dead* you mean?'

'Precisely. Oh, I sent a couple of officers among them earlier on. They asked anyone if they recognised Luke Stevens or remembered him having much contact with the band. Taciturn lot, they are.'

'No one had anything to say, then?'

'Unfortunately not.'

'The crime reporter from the *Evening Chronicle* is down there asking questions too. I could try her. She may have more luck.'

'You've got her phone number?'

'Yup.'

'And you trust her?'

'She's a hack, of course not. I'll be careful.'

Buchanon nodded hesitantly. 'OK then.'

Jon took out his mobile and selected Carmel's entry from the phone book. She answered after a couple of rings. 'Don't look now, Carmel. We're watching you.'

She turned her back to the station. 'And who says the country isn't turning into a police state?'

'Every move you make.' Jon laughed.

'Thanks for the heads-up on Luke Stevens.' Sarcasm was thick in her voice. 'I had to get it from the voice bank.'

Jon thought of the telephone service on which Greater Manchester Police's press department left announcements concerning ongoing cases. 'Sorry, Carmel, I should have ...'

'Yeah, yeah. I'd half a mind not to send those articles about the Psychic Academy over.'

'You dug some out?'

'Arranged for a junior to deliver them a bit earlier.'

'Cheers. What are you up to down there?'

'Background on Satanism and Death Metal. We're doing a feature on links between the two, just like you suggested.'

'Fair play. Listen, we're trying to work out if Luke Stevens had any connection to Satan's Inferno. None of that lot down there will talk to us.'

He watched her head dip as she processed the comment. 'You're charging Satan's Inferno with arson?'

'I didn't say that.'

'But you've got them in custody. What are the charges then?'

'None as yet. Can you ask around in the crowd? Do any of them remember Luke from gigs, how friendly was he with the band, were there any times he was invited backstage? Try the girls, I know the lead singer would invite female fans to hang around after gigs had finished.'

'And you'll reciprocate how?'

Jon glanced at his SIO, uncomfortable about cutting deals in front of him. 'I'll give you the identity of the victim from Alderley Edge a few hours ahead of any official announcement.'

'Which will be?'

'Once we've traced a relative.'

'But you know who she is, right?'

'Don't remember saying the victim was female.'

'Damn!' She laughed. 'Nearly got you. Will you give me cause of death too?'

'Let's see what you get on Luke Stevens first.'

'Done.'

He cut the connection.

Buchanon was rolling his eyes. 'Anything more on Arkell? DC Gardiner informs me his list of accusers is growing all the time.'

'We're trying to determine his address. Problem is, we don't even know if Arkell is his real name.'

'This fake name business seems to be catching.'

'And he hasn't registered the Psychic Academy with the relevant authorities. There's not much to track him by at all in fact.'

'OK. Carry on with it, I'll call a meeting once Nikki Kingston shows up.'

A few minutes later the sound of cheering started up outside. Jon and Rick wandered over to the windows overlooking the street. The three band members were obviously at the front entrance, just out of sight. A second later Alec Turnbull hurried into view, the crowd hardly noticing him go. Padmore and Humphries then appeared, the lead singer holding his arms up and milking the applause. Jon watched Carmel as she directed the photographer to get it all on film.

A voice started up and the chorus soon caught on. 'Serberos! Serberos! Serberos!'

'God, I'd love to open the window and let them know he's actually called Dan, son of a cabin boy from Rochdale,' Jon said.

Rich laughed. 'They wouldn't believe you.'

'No, you're right,' Jon said, considering a quiet call to Carmel instead.

As the dark mass moved off down the street with the reporter following, Jon and Rick returned to their desks and began typing up reports for that day.

At five o'clock Buchanon's voice rang out. 'Listen up, everyone. I have the final report from the pathologist and fresh information from the Sacred Heart. Miss Kingston, go ahead.'

Jon turned round. Nikki was standing next to Buchanon. She

glanced up for a second, then turned back to the evidence bags on the table before her. 'Erm, we've been conducting LMP tests on the floor of the church—'

Buchanon raised a finger and Nikki's speech immediately dried up. 'LMP – a test for human blood.'

'Sorry, yes. We impregnate wipes with leucomalachite and hydrogen peroxide. If it comes into contact with blood, the wipe develops a green stain.' She held up a bag. Inside was a piece of wood. 'This is a section of floorboard from below the window that Luke Stevens used to enter the Sacred Heart. Though its upper side shows extensive fire damage, its underside is relatively unscathed. The green lines you can see are where blood has run down between the floorboards.'

She held up another two bags. 'The neighbouring boards, also stained. We've taken up the floor right back to the seat of the fire. The most blood was pooled beneath the floor at that spot, but traces show up all the way back to the window.'

'This fits with what the pathologist had to say in his preliminary report,' Buchanon announced. 'Lack of smoke damage to the lungs suggests he was dead before the fire was lit. Toxicology has found no carbon monoxide in his blood. High levels of cannabis and alcohol though, but not enough to render him completely helpless.'

'His crucial conclusion is this,' said Nikki, turning to her copy of the final report. 'He's determined cause of death to be massive trauma to the head, as we expected. What he's been doing is analysing the skull at the top and bottom edges of the wound. The way fragments have been compressed on its lower edge, and the angle of the wound itself, suggest the victim was standing up when struck from behind. He estimates the weapon was curved, about four inches long by about two across and swung downwards, on a slight angle from right to left.'

Buchanon stepped over to the plan of the church interior pinned to a nearby display board. 'So Luke was clubbed over the head at the window. He fell to the floor where he was left to bleed, probably for several minutes. Then he was dragged over to the pyre, which was then lit.'

'Perhaps he was on his way back out when he was struck,' Rick said.

Nikki turned her head. 'I have my doubts. The fire was not lit while Luke Stevens was alive. As DCI Buchanon mentioned, we know this from the absence of sooty deposits in his lungs. So why would he be attempting to leave the church before the fire was properly ignited?'

'Maybe he was just standing by the window because it was someone else's turn to light it. Webster has already said the MO is different for this one due to the fact there were no pool marks leading back to the window they smashed,' Rick countered.

'Which all points to a sacrifice,' Buchanon said. 'Luke Stevens simply wasn't aware he was it. The pyre was complete, everyone ready at the window, then Stevens is clubbed.'

'Has Webster brought that sniffer dog in yet?' Jon asked.

Nikki's eyes connected with his for a second before she directed her reply to the room. 'It's not available until tomorrow apparently.'

'Right,' Buchanon announced. 'We'll hope for more news then. In the meantime, our priority is to find Peter Robson. Once you're up to date with your reports, get some rest. We'll go at it again in the morning.'

As everyone resumed what they were doing Jon turned to Rick. 'Did you get hold of that bloke who was ringing Ben Waters?'

Rick sucked air through his teeth. 'He was meant to get back to me.' He checked his in tray for messages. 'Nope. I'll try him again first thing in the morning.'

Jon picked at a thumbnail, hoping the priest wasn't in imminent danger.

'Hello, Jon.'

He felt his back muscles stiffen. 'Nikki. Good work – going under the floorboards.'

She gave a modest smile. 'Tricks of the trade, that's all.' Her eyes went to the empty chair at the next desk.

'Sorry,' Jon gestured. 'Sit down. I'd offer you a drink but ...'

She glanced at the brew table. Empty milk cartons stood among towers of dirty mugs. 'I'm fine, thanks.'

Now her eyes went to Rick. The pause became slightly awkward and Rick stood up, saying, 'Oh, the *Chronicle* have sent over a load of old articles for you. I'll go and get them.'

No! Jon thought. Don't bloody leave me. He fired his partner a wide-eyed look, but he was already on his feet.

'So.' Jon turned to Nikki, trying to smile. 'You're looking well.'

Her lips tightened. I know I'm not, the expression said. She leaned forward, voice low. 'Have you thought about what I said?'

Jon contemplated feigning ignorance, but he wanted the conversation over before Rick returned. 'Counselling? No, I'm all right.'

'When was your last nightmare?'

He made a play of trying to think. Lowering his eyes from the ceiling, he said, 'Not sure. A few weeks ago, at least.'

'Really?'

'Yeah, I reckon so.'

'Jon, I can sense your pain. I've been there too, don't forget.'

He turned from her beseeching look. Will you just fuck off, he thought, you sound like a bloody God Botherer. Let's share our suffering, find comfort from the cruel world together. 'Honestly, I'm fine.'

As she got up, she laid a hand on his forearm. He wanted to shake it off. 'Just call me when you're ready to address this.'

She walked off before he could reply. Directing a mental V-sign at her back, he saw Rick on his way over with a load of print-outs. 'Any luck?'

'Not sure yet.' Rick replied. 'I need to go through them. Want a few?'

'Go on then.' As Rick divided the pile in two Jon's phone rang. His younger sister's name was on the screen. 'Ellie, where are you?'

'At home. I've been trying to contact Skye.'

'She's at her place.'

'Well, she's not answering her phone. She's meant to be picking me up. We were going out tonight.'

Bollocks, that's all I need, Jon thought. Two officers from McCloughlin's syndicate following Skye Booth to my sister's flat. 'Ellie, Alderley Edge is a crime scene. One of Skye's associates died up there last night. She was a member of this coven you're wanting to join. I want you to steer clear of that place. In fact, I want you to steer clear of Skye Booth too.'

'We weren't going up there. I was taking her for a meal in town. She's really low at the moment.'

'Can't you leave it for a day or two until we clear this mess up?'

'No, I'm her friend. She needs support right now, not isolation.'

'Ellie, in the opinion of a few people here, she's a murder suspect. I'm asking you to keep your distance, understand?'

'Stop bossing me around like I'm a child. I rang you to say that she's not answering her phone. It's not like her. Not when we'd made arrangements.'

'Listen, she just got out of a nasty grilling from a colleague here. She's probably chilling out – in the bath listening to whale songs or something.' He thought about the car that would now be stationed outside her house. 'Trust me, she's not in any danger.'

'Well, I'm going round to her place.'

He swivelled away from Rick, speaking down towards his chest. 'No. Don't. I'll make a call, OK? Give me a minute.' He snapped his phone shut and glanced over his shoulder. 'Younger sisters. Twenty-eight and she's still causing me grief.'

Rick gave a half-smile, his eyes on the old *Chronicle* article in his hands. 'Jon, take a look at this.'

'Two seconds, mate.' He jogged down to McCloughlin's room on the ground floor. An officer was just emerging, heading towards the doors to the car park. Jon searched his mind for the man's name. 'DS Mills, can you do me a quick favour?'

The man turned and Jon saw he had a cigarette in his mouth.

'Not a big one, I hope. I was just nipping out for a smoke.'

Jon's gaze lingered on the cigarette hanging from his lips. Right now, he thought, that sounds about the best thing in the world.

'Unless you want to join me?'

Jon saw the other officer was holding out a packet of Marlboro Lights, the lid open. A neat row of filters were lined up inside. Jon felt the fingers of his right hand twitch. 'No, you're all right, mate. You've got a car outside Skye Booth's address?'

'Yeah, they just reported in. Everything's quiet.'

'Can you give me their number? I need to check something.'

They headed back into McCloughlin's room where Jon jotted down the mobile. He raced back up the stairs and immediately called it.

'Dave here.'

'Hello, this is DI Spicer, back at Longsight.'

'Sir.'

'How long have you been outside Skye Booth's address, Dave?'

'About an hour.'

'What sort of place is it?'

'A big house. She has the ground floor flat.'

'Did you see Skye enter it?'

'No.'

'You said it all looks quiet. Any sign of anyone inside? Lights on, movement in the windows?'

'No, all the curtains are drawn.'

'I'm concerned she's not even there. What about the front door? Free paper sticking out the letterbox, anything like that?'

'Hang on. There is something on the front step. Looks like a handbag.'

Jon felt his stomach sink. 'Check please.'

He heard the car door open. A loud whoosh as a vehicle went past. 'Crossing the road now. Yeah, it's definitely a handbag. And there's a set of keys next to it.'

Fucking hell, thought Jon. 'Try her door.'

'No. It's locked. There's something blocking the keyhole. An obstruction of some sort.' The sound of knocking. 'Miss Booth? Hello, Miss Booth, it's the police. Hello? Sir, no one's answering.'

'Call for support. Now!'

He hung up and looked at Rick. 'Skye Booth has gone missing. Handbag and keys have been abandoned on the front step of her flat.'

Rick's eyes flicked towards Buchanon's office. 'We just cut all three members of Satan's Inferno loose.'

Jon was punching in his sister's number. 'And we've no idea where Peter Robson or Tristan Arkell are, either. I wouldn't mind knowing where Henry Robson is too.' His sister answered. 'Ellie, it's Jon. Skye's handbag and keys have been found outside her house. She's not there. Can you go over to ours? I don't want you in on your own.'

'She's disappeared?'

'Seems so. Something's going on and it's linked to this bloody coven she's part of. Please, Ellie, go over to ours. I'll be back soon.'

'OK.' Confusion and fear in her voice.

'Ring me when you get there, all right?'

'All right.'

He cut the call. Rick hadn't moved, the *Chronicle* article still in his hand.

'What have you got?' Jon demanded.

'This.' Rick rotated the photocopy so Jon could see the main shot. It was of a crowd protesting outside the Psychic Academy. Arkell could be seen arguing with the small group. Jon read the words on a couple of placards: *Pyschic Academy – Devil's Play,* declared one; *Spare Our Children*, demanded another.

Scanning the faces, it only took Jon seconds to spot Henry Robson at the front. 'Robson again. I said the guy's a loony.'

'Read the headline and opening paragraph,' Rick replied.

### Academy won't win this Heart.

Jon's eyes moved to the copy beneath.

Father Ben Waters, priest at the Sacred Heart Catholic Church in Fairfield, once again led protests against the recent opening of the Psychic Academy.

Jon looked again. At the back of the grainy image were a few people wearing white dog collars. Jon looked more closely. Holding a placard above his head that read *Lessons in Evil* was Father Ben Waters.

The cords dug into Skye's skin, cutting painfully across her exposed breasts. She tried to flex her fingers, but all sensation had been lost long ago.

A hand gripped her jaw and forced her head up. She knew the powerful torch beam would hurt her eyes, so she kept them closed. Behind its cruel glare he would be lurking, a blurry form whose long robes whispered as he paced the wooden floor.

'Their names. I will have their names.'

She kept the tears back, but couldn't contain the sob as she breathed in. 'I don't know.'

'You filthy daughter of Satan, do not lie to me!'

She heard him circling her chair once again. 'There will be eleven others in your coven. Do not deny it. When you meet to worship the Devil, to fornicate and scheme, a thirteenth joins you. The Grand Master.' His voice was now in her ear, his breath hot on her skin. 'Give me their names and you shall not suffer.'

'I don't know of any coven, and even if I did, I wouldn't know any names. It's the rules. If I know that, you must do too.'

'I know you belong to a coven.'

'I don't.'

'Oh, you do. I know because Valerie told me.'

His words caused her to retch, and at that moment, she realised he meant to kill her, whatever she said.

A hand grabbed the bare flesh of her thigh. 'You have the witch's mark. You have pledged yourself to Satan.'

'It's a mole,' she choked. 'Please, you must see that. It's only a mole.'

'It is the *sigillum diaboli*. You use it to suckle your familiar, the creature you employ to do the Devil's bidding. Call it and it shall come to you.' He grabbed a handful of her hair and yanked her head back. 'Admit it!'

Her cry of pain was immediately met by a shout of triumph. 'See! See! It has come!'

His footsteps moved away and she opened her eyes. Oh no. Oh no.

He was flailing wildly at the bat that had flown in through the arched window. She tried to see his face, but the cowl covering his head kept it hidden. The tiny creature flitted beyond his reach then darted back outside.

He placed his palms on the sill and she saw his shoulders rise as he sucked in air. 'Your familiar has deserted you. Satan has deserted you. Give me the names of your coven and I shall spare you the agony of the fire.'

# Chapter 24

'Jon, you're twitching more than Punch does when he's asleep.'

His eyes snapped open. The image of the forest faded and, with it, the sound of the creature pursuing him. He stared at the bedroom wall with relief.

'Jon?' He felt his wife's cool hand. 'Your back is soaking.'

'Just a dream.' He raised himself on to one elbow, blinking at his alarm clock's screen. Six fourteen in the morning. The dreams were definitely pushing out from their three o'clock slot, now tormenting him throughout the night. He sucked in air, waiting for his pulse to slow.

'Do you remember it?'

He shook his head. 'Nah. Some anxiety scenario. Probably walking into my inspector's exams with no clothes on.'

'Mmmm, that wouldn't be such a bad sight.'

He grinned over his shoulder. 'I'll get a shower.'

The kettle had only just clicked off when Ellie shuffled into the kitchen, a yellow dressing gown wrapped round her. The sight of her caused a sudden ache in his chest.

'Morning,' she announced.

Jon registered her toneless delivery. 'Morning. How was the sofa?'

'Fine,' she sighed. 'I didn't hear you get in. What time was it?'

'Just after one.'

She sat down and started fiddling with her hair. 'Anything?'

'No. We knocked on every door and visited every pub in the area asking if anyone had noticed a disturbance outside her place. Then we did the takeaway joints at kicking-out time, but no joy.' He thought of the cigarettes he'd tapped DC Murray for as they'd trawled the empty streets. None in over six months then, what – eight or nine? In a single night. He passed the fingers of his right hand across his top lip and caught the aroma of tobacco ingrained in his skin. The smell made him want to punch himself in the face.

'Have you called the office this morning?'

'Yeah. No news.'

She scrutinised her own phone. 'Where can she be?'

Jon dreaded to think. 'They'll find something soon, don't worry.'

'But if her mobile was in her handbag, she can't call for help.'

'Ellie.' He handed her a cup of tea. 'There'll be a team of officers working the surrounding streets, asking questions at bus stops, contacting the local minicab companies, gathering tapes from any CCTV cameras in the area. Something will show up.'

She cupped her drink with both hands, her shoulders hunched forward.

'This coven you were going to join. Did she ever mention who else was in it?'

She shook her head, eyes on the floor.

'Or how big it was?'

'Eleven. I was to be the twelfth.'

Jon thought about the information sheets the officer at the Met had emailed up. Details of how witches were meant to possess an extra nipple with which to suckle their familiar. Descriptions of a typical coven, twelve regular members and a thirteenth, the Grand Master who only turned up for the main sabbats, or meetings. 'What about the person in charge?'

'Who?'

'The Grand Master, isn't it?'

'She never mentioned any Grand Master.'

'He's the person who leads the ceremony.'

'He? No way, this is a female-only coven, Skye was adamant about that.'

'I was under the impression each coven has a Grand Master. A lead figure who shows up, probably with the drugs.'

She looked up. 'Drugs? What drugs?'

'Flying ointments. Herbal stuff to alter everyone's state of mind.'

'You've been watching too many films.'

Irritation caused his face to tingle. 'I think you're the one who's misinformed. It's not some harmless skip around a bonfire, Ellie. Three people are dead, your mate's been snatched—'

'Snatched?'

Shit, wrong word, Jon. 'Has gone missing.'

'You think she's been snatched?'

'Maybe. Look, churches are being burned, we've got women coming forward who think they've been assaulted ...'

'Who? Which women?'

'It's ongoing, but the Psychic Academy is not the harmless place you think it is.'

'You can't make me give up my beliefs.'

'I'm not trying to, but I want you to be safe.' He bowed his head and shut his eyes. 'I feel so fucking guilty, Ellie. I wasn't there for you and Dave. I wasn't there.'

Seconds dragged by in silence before he eventually heard her voice. 'It wasn't your fault, Jon. How could you have guessed? Me and Dave didn't even admit it to each other.'

'I used to laugh.' He shook his head from side to side. 'When you tried to make excuses for not going. God, I thought it was so funny watching the pair of you squirm when Mum called up the stairs, telling you to hurry up.'

'Jon, stop it.'

He pinched the bridge of his nose between a forefinger and thumb, sniffed loudly and let his hand fall away. 'Who was he?'

'I don't know. One of the teachers in that place. The memories are so unclear.'

Jon took a seat opposite her. 'Did you ... when did ...' He stopped. 'Oh shit, Ellie, you never said a word. Why did you never say a word?'

'I was what? Five, six, seven?' She looked at him, eyes cold and bright. 'It was our strict secret, of course. He said I had to keep it quiet, or we would never be allowed back to the church. Mum would be angry, God would punish us.'

I will find this fucker, Jon thought, and rip his bastard head off. 'You and Dave. It was the same man?'

'Maybe. I was so young. I remember stuff from that time and I still don't know if it's real or not. Huge birds of paradise in the trees of our local park. They didn't really live there, did they? By a little lake?'

Jon smiled, tears in his eyes as his fingers closed over hers. 'They were peacocks, Ellie. Yeah, there used to be an aviary there.'

She stared off to the side. 'Peacocks? So I didn't imagine it.'

'No, that was real.' He paused, giving her a second. 'Ellie, which Sunday school? Mum took you and Dave to a couple, didn't she?'

'The first one. The second one I remember far more clearly. It was much closer to our house, so we walked there. The first was a car drive away.'

Jon strained his mind. 'You're right. I can still see your two faces in the rear window as Mum drove you off. It was a Zodiac, the car. Massive thing.'

'I remember the church. It had a big tower. Emerald. Like a turret in the castle from *The Wizard of Oz*.'

'The monastery in Gorton? The copper on its spire is green. That's where the memories are from? The Sunday school there?'

She closed her eyes. 'I think so. I remember the layout. There was a main hall, then some smaller rooms off to the side. One connected through to the main church, where the old guys in their robes were.'

'The monks? They wore brown cloak things.'

'Yes.'

'Was it a monk who ...'

'No. He wore trousers, a jumper. Maybe more of a helper ...'

'Why do you think that?'

'I remember him clapping his hands a lot. Calling us to the central bit for stories. And he sometimes played a guitar I think.'

'How old was he?'

'He was a grown-up. Looked the same age as Mum and Dad. Not elderly.'

'Thirtyish then?'

'I suppose. I've tried to remember his face but nothing solid ever appears. I've realised over the years that it's easier just to forget. I should never have even mentioned it.'

'Forget it? Fuck that. You reckon you were between five and seven when this happened?'

A sudden sigh ended in a shiver. 'I think so. But, Jon, it's so long ago.'

His mind was racing. Ellie was born in 1976. So it was someone – an assistant by the sound of it – who helped out at Gorton Monastery's Sunday school in the early Eighties. He knew the school had been knocked down a few years before the entire place finally shut, in '89. But there would be records somewhere. There had to be. And whoever the bastard at that Sunday school was, he would find him.

His phone started to ring, but he kept his hand over Ellie's.

'Jon, answer it, I need to eat something.'

He met her eyes and could see she was glad of the interruption. Reluctantly, he picked it up. 'DI Spicer.'

Ellie stood and went over to the toaster.

'Sir, it's DC Gardiner. Sorry to call so early, but I had a brainwave.'

'Go on.'

'I just logged on to yell.com and put in the name Tristan Arkell.'

His eyes were fixed on his sister's back, her bowed head and plump waist. The monastery. Early Eighties. A male helper, in his fifties by now.

'Sir, are you there?'

'Sorry, Susan, yes. You put his name in where?'

'Yell.com. The online version of the Yellow Pages.'

'And?'

'His address and phone number are right there. He lives in Chorlton.'

'Susan, you'll go far in this game.'

'Thanks. Can I bring him in?'

'Clear it with Buchanon, then go get the fat turd.' As soon as he pressed red, his eyes were drawn back to his younger sister. 'Ellie?'

She kept her back to him. 'Let's talk about this later. If you want to make me feel better, find Skye.'

# Chapter 25

The reports were piling up on Buchanon's desk. With the allocator at his side, he picked up print-outs, scanned them, then moved them to another pile. Welcome to the role of SIO, Jon thought.

Irritation danced in his eyes when he saw Jon at his door. He beckoned with a finger as if summoning a waiter. Jon opened the door and stepped inside. 'Morning, sir.'

'DC Gardiner came rushing in here earlier, requesting permission to bring in Tristan Arkell.'

'Yes, I asked her to clear it with you.'

'Clear it with me?' Buchanon spat. 'What other developments are occurring on this investigation that haven't been sanctioned by me?'

'Sorry, sir. It was sort of a spontaneous development. Susan had been ringing Arkell's ex-pupils to see if any others thought they may have been assaulted.'

'Again, something I don't remember requesting her to do.'

No, Jon thought. But I mentioned it yesterday and you seemed fine with it then. 'I asked her to. As long as it didn't impinge on any actions given to her.'

'I was warned of this aspect to your character.' Buchanon's eyes moved momentarily to the side.

Jon turned, tracking his glance. McCloughlin was sitting on the other side of the incident room, head down as he conferred with a colleague. The fucker was slipping in the knife again. 'Sorry, sir. As I said, it was kind of unplanned.'

Buchanon gave a curt nod. 'Care to bring me up to speed on what else you know that may be relevant to this investigation?'

'I'm not sure what you mean.'

'I mean, DI Spicer, that your real motivation for bringing in Arkell is to ascertain what risk he might pose to your younger sister.'

McCloughlin again, Jon thought. The bastard has told Buchanon about Ellie. 'Sir, my younger sister has attended a course or two at the Psychic Academy with Skye Booth. Yes, I'm concerned by the fact someone like Arkell runs the place. We all should be.'

'Is that it – she's only attended a course or two with Skye Booth?'

Jon kept his anger down. 'Yes. I'd describe them as course mates. Casual friends, at the most.'

Buchanon said nothing for a second. 'It's highly likely we'll need to talk with her. Especially if she was with Skye at any point during the twenty-four hours before she disappeared.'

'I realise that, sir.'

'So what are your movements from now on?'

'Well, DS Saville and I are heading back to the cathedral in a bit. The person running the day centre there said Peter Robson sometimes shows for the morning session.'

'Is this assisting us in tracing the whereabouts of Skye Booth?'

Jon paused. 'Isn't finding her McCloughlin's shout?'

'Finding that girl alive is all of our shout now, DI Spicer. As decided in a meeting with the Assistant Chief Constable this morning, our syndicates are working together on this. The arson attacks, the murders of Luke Stevens, Troy Wilkes and Valerie Evans, and the disappearance of Skye Booth: same investigation.'

I get it, Jon thought. You're now feeling the pressure to get a result ahead of McCloughlin. No wonder you're so wound up. Future promotions are on the line. 'If Peter Robson has snatched Skye Booth, then yes. Finding him must be a priority.'

'Granted.'

'Talking of the Robsons, has anyone been to speak with the father again?'

'Henry Robson? On what grounds?'

'He's unhinged. Overly zealous with religion, all that end-of-the world stuff the officer with Trafford Division mentioned. He's clearly developed an obsession with the members of Satan's Inferno.'

'None of whom have been abducted or murdered.'

Yet, Jon thought. 'I just think it would be prudent if we knew where the man was yesterday at—'

'We've agreed to focus manpower on questioning all of Skye's friends. And acquaintances,' he pointedly added.

Ellie's face flashed up in Jon's mind. *I should have known McCloughlin would do it.*

'Hopefully,' Buchanon continued, 'we'll get a hit when we cross-match with an associate or two of Luke Stevens. Now, I'll give you until lunch to find Peter Robson. Then I want you and Saville back here to help find Skye Booth.'

Back in the main part of the incident room, Jon sat down so heavily his seat gasped in protest. 'Heard the news?'

Rick nodded. 'One big happy team now.'

'Did that frigging bishop's assistant call?'

'No. I've already tried ringing. A secretary said he's in a meeting until late morning. Surely you don't think Waters is still in danger? Not now Skye Booth has disappeared.'

'Yeah, you're probably right.' He looked at his watch. 'The guy at the cathedral said Robson normally turns up at eleven. Buchanon's given us until lunch to find him.'

The door to Buchanon's office opened and he marched across the room. Jon raised an eyebrow at the allocator, who emerged a few seconds later. 'Where's he rushed off to?'

'Arkell's here. Interview room three.'

Jon frowned. 'Buchanon's doing it?'

The allocator grinned. 'I think he needed a break from my reports.'

Jon nodded. 'You do like to create a blizzard.' He turned to Rick. 'You coming down to watch?'

His partner tapped the books on his desk. 'I'll carry on with these.'

Jon looked at the books the bloke from the Met had sent up. 'OK, you know where I'll be.'

The observation room was empty. As Jon went to close the door behind him a foot appeared in the gap. He swung it back and McCloughlin stepped inside. Jon moved as far back as possible. Of all the people to get stuck in a lift-sized room with.

'DI Spicer. Keeping your fingers in all the pies, aren't you?'

'Sir?'

'Anyone would think you're still hankering after becoming an SIO yourself.'

'You had to mention it, didn't you?'

'What's that, Detective Inspector?'

'About my sister.'

McCloughlin continued looking through the observation room's window. 'We're talking to anyone who's had dealings with Skye. I believe your sister's name cropped up purely on the basis of her attending the same course as Skye at the Psychic Academy.'

Jon regarded the other man's profile. No it didn't, you weasel. I didn't give Gardiner the list with my sister's name on it.

'Really?'

McCloughlin nodded. 'I think you're running out of time to come clean with Buchanon.'

Jon looked through the one-way glass without replying. DC Gardiner was handing over her notes to Buchanon. On the other side of the table the head of the Psychic Academy was keeping his bulky form totally immobile, though his piggy eyes were darting between the two officers. Next to him was a solicitor. A thin-faced man who must have been about half Arkell's weight. Studying the two men, Jon couldn't help thinking of a bear and its trainer.

The seconds ticked by as Buchanon continued poring over the file in front of him. 'So,' he eventually said. 'We seem to have a few problems with the legitimacy of your business.'

Arkell smiled. 'My application was submitted to the council earlier this year.'

'But you've been trading since late last year, as I understand.'

'Not as the Psychic Academy. My original application was for a commercial premises. It was only when interest reached a certain level that I realised the creation of an educational establishment would be possible.'

Buchanon looked back at the notes. Jon cursed silently: his superior obviously hadn't had time to read them properly.

'And as regards your tax payments?' Buchanon's voice lacked conviction.

'My accountant is filing returns. Again, the change in the nature of my business necessitated an alteration of my tax status. I've been on an emergency code for a while now. It's been proving quite prohibitive in fact, but the Revenue seem to take their own time with these things.'

Buchanon breathed in. 'I'll need you to provide details of your accountant before you go.'

Jon gritted his teeth. Before you go? Lay into him, man!

'So what's your interest in Arkell?' McCloughlin whispered.

Jon kept looking ahead. 'He's up to his eyes in this. Somehow.'

Beyond the glass, Buchanon turned a page. 'You have how many students at this academy?'

'Numbers continually fluctuate, but on average about one hundred and fifty.'

'Has a Luke Stevens ever been part of that number?'

'He has not,' the solicitor answered. 'My client can provide a list of every student who has signed up for a course. Luke Stevens' name does not feature on it.'

'He's come prepared for this,' Jon said.

'Seems so,' McCloughlin replied. 'Unlike your boss.'

'And how many of those are female?' Gardiner cut in.

Buchanon gave her a withering glance and she sank back in her seat. Jon could see Arkell had clocked the exchange. A glint of pleasure in his eye, he directed his answer at Buchanon. 'There's a slight female bias.'

'We've received a number of allegations from female

ex-students. Many claim you've used certain ointments to in-capacitate them. Why would you do that?'

'I'm not sure I understand you. Ointments?'

'Salves, balms, creams. Substances rubbed into the skin that contain psychoactive ingredients, as I understand.'

'Many native British plants contain such properties. It's not illegal to pick them.'

Buchanon turned back to his notes. You've rushed into this, Jon thought. Idiot.

'This guy's running rings round him,' McCloughlin mur-mured.

Jon kept his mouth shut.

Buchanon raised a finger. 'But is it not illegal to administer those plants without an appropriate licence?'

Gardiner shifted uncomfortably in her seat, obviously sup-pressing questions of her own.

Arkell's solicitor cocked his head to the side. 'My client simply supplied students with the recipe for a flying ointment. A recipe, I might add, freely available in numerous books on herbalism. Ingredients were neither supplied nor administered by my client. The students used their own ointments, entirely of their own volition.'

Shit, Jon thought, seeing the prospects of nailing Arkell there and then rapidly vanishing. He wanted to burst in and ques-tion him about whether he belonged to any coven, grill him on his role within it. Buchanon's approach was as effective as bombarding the bloke with balls of cotton wool.

The door half opened, bright light from the corridor reducing Rick to little more than a silhouette. 'Jon? It's twenty past ten. We should get going.'

He turned back to the one-way glass. The solicitor made a show of looking at his watch. 'Do you have any further ques-tions for my client?'

Buchanon studied the file for a few more moments, face red-dening. 'Until I've clarified a few points, no. However, we'll need to speak to Mr Arkell again.'

'My client is being released with no further action?'

'At this time, yes.'

Jon shook his head. NFA. This was pathetic.

The solicitor produced a sheet of paper from his attaché case. 'All necessary contact details are on this sheet. Now, if you could allow us to be on our way.'

Bollocks, thought Jon, as he stepped out into the corridor, slamming the door behind him.


Daniel Humphries stared at the lifesize poster of himself. Serberos Tavovitch, lead singer of Satan's Inferno. Writer and composer of all their songs. Frontman for the band. Fame and the resulting financial rewards were so close. So fucking close.

Where was Padmore with the backing tapes? They could do without Turnbull on support guitar so long as they had those tapes. He couldn't believe the recording studio was charging to retrieve them from their system. The studio had just blown any further business from Satan's Inferno, once the band made it big.

He thought about the call from his agent. A talent scout was definitely coming up from London. OK, a two-man band was going to look shit, but he'd explain that hassle from the police was the cause. Shit, the pigs had only finished giving him the full treatment a few hours before. The crowd would love it and the A&R man would see the potential for reams of publicity.

Besides, two-man band or not, let's be fucking honest, Satan's Inferno is Serberos Tavovitch. One less person on stage will just make my presence that bit bigger. Bring it on!

He tapped ash from his cigarette, his knees jiggling nervously up and down. It was a shame about Pete. If only the guy could have kept a grip, this situation would never have happened. He dragged sharply on the Marlboro. What if the police finally did find him? Just not before tonight. We get this gig done, a deal signed, then Pete could paint a confession across the front of the town hall for all he cared.

They couldn't charge him and Ed for talking with Pete about torching a church or two. The three of them might have tried getting into that one in Fairfield, started smashing its window even, but the vicar had come out and stopped them. It was that headcase Pete, and maybe that little idiot Luke Stevens, who had actually gone ahead and done it for real. Shit, what a pair of losers.

He dragged deeply on his cigarette again, regret bringing his spirits down. If only Pete had held it together the band would be ready to go. Up, up and away. Straight to the stars. Instead, here he was, scrabbling around, lining up a pre-recorded play list he and Padmore couldn't deviate from once up on stage. Maybe a break halfway through, he thought. Give his voice a bit of a rest, have some banter with the crowd, spit some fake blood over a few of them. What a bunch of twats he had to perform to.

The knocking brought him instantly to his feet. Ed. At fucking last. He ground the cigarette out, hurried to the front door and pulled it open. 'Did you get—'

Henry Robson was standing on his front step.

'You are so fucking busted,' Daniel said. 'Wait 'til I contact the police with this.' He reached into his pocket and brought out his camera phone.

'Where is my son?'

'Haven't a clue. Now say cheese, you mad bastard.'

As he started to raise his arm Robson smashed a fist directly into his face.

# Chapter 26

There were birds singing outside the window. It must be day. She opened her eyes and saw a patch of bright sky through the window. Not singing, chirruping. She recognised their comical noises. Those little fat ones. Not much more than a ball of brown feathers and two stick legs. Finches? No, not finches. What were their names? The word came to her and Skye smiled. Sparrows.

She remembered them in the hedgerows when she was a little girl, their animated discussions breaking into angry squabbles. They seemed to tumble down through the branches, half flying, half falling, but all the while keeping up their high-pitched chorus.

Footsteps echoed in the corridor outside and her smile disappeared. He was coming back. Her head lolled forward and she looked down at her naked body. The punctures had stopped bleeding. When he'd pricked her with the needle-like implement, he seemed deaf to her words. How she'd begged him to stop. With the book held before him, he'd studied the text then, muttering to himself, examined her body as a vet might study an animal. He no longer thought of her as a person and she knew that made her death all the more certain.

The door scraped open and she licked her cracked lips. 'My name is Skye Booth. I'm twenty-seven years old. My mum is called Stella, my dad is called Clive. They live in the Cotswolds, on a farm. An organic farm. They make cheese and yoghurt.'

He walked past her and put his book on the table. Next to it he placed a large pair of pliers. The sight of them caused her to retch again, but her stomach was now completely empty.

Carry on. You must carry on. She dragged in breath. 'Can

you hear those birds? They're sparrows. When I was a little girl we had them on our farm. They'd bath in the dusty bits in the courtyard, where the cows' hooves had made a dip in the dry mud. When it was summer—'

'Silence.' He turned round, hood covering his bowed head.

She tried to swallow. 'We used to get house martins too, building their nests of mud under the eaves of our roof. Or were they swallows? Do you know the difference?'

His silence was terrifying.

'They fly from Africa, my mum said. Morocco, all the way across Spain. Have you been to Spain? Not the Costa del Sol, the proper Spain.'

His shoulders moved, dropping slightly. A softening of his posture.

'Seville, Granada, Salamanca, Barcelona? Have you seen the Sagrada familia? A beautiful—'

He whipped an open hand across her face. She felt her neck crack and the taste of blood flooded her mouth.

'Temptress! Your attempts at seduction fill me with disgust. You are no better than the succubi, sent to torment me in the night.' He turned on his heel and lifted the pliers from the table. 'Now I will have the name of that coven member.' The curved points of metal made a snicking sound as he approached. 'Or shall I begin tearing the flesh from your corrupt bones?'

Skye tried to shy backwards, but the chair she was tied to wouldn't budge. 'Please. For God's sake, please.'

'God? You appeal to my God for help? Let him help you then. Admit your sins. Tell me the name.'

She felt the metal beginning to pinch the skin of her breast. 'Stop. I'll tell you. Just stop!'

He leaned down and tilted his head. 'Her name?'

Peter Robson turned from the Psychic Academy's locked doors and sat down on the top step. Closed? Until Monday? He took the bag of mushrooms Arkell had given him out of his pocket. There weren't many left. Reaching a thumb and forefinger inside, he extracted a tangled pinch and popped it in his mouth.

The dusty taste conjured images of the grave. The lining of his mother's coffin.

He leaned to the side and banged his head against the wall, slowly but firmly. The pain made the memories of her go away. Pain was good. Sliding the bag of mushrooms back in his coat, he took out his Zippo. The flint sparked and a flame appeared from nowhere, like a genie out of a bottle.

He lifted a hand and passed his palm over the wavering sliver of yellow, just a tingling caress to start off with.

'What are you doing?'

Two men, on the landing behind him. He hadn't heard them coming down the stairs. Peter jammed the lighter in his pocket and hurried down to the ground floor. Outside the sun glared down. The hugeness of it was overwhelming, a bright, cruel ball that sent waves of heat crashing over his head. He cut across the road, heading for the shadows on the other side.

The shade led him towards the city centre and he emerged on to Market Street, just by Debenhams. A tram rocked past on its rails, the shriek of its wheels giving off streams of black needles. They filled the air about his head and he waved them away with both hands.

Next came music from the open entrance of HMV. People are strange, a man sang, notes undulating wildly up and down. In front of him was a cart. The man beside it had a small plastic gun with a hoop at its end. The thing whirred and a glistening sausage welled up out of it. He flicked his wrist and the balloon detached itself, quivering for a moment in mid-air. Abruptly it vanished.

Peter stood transfixed as the man made another appear. This one hummed slightly as it led him across the cobbles, its sides bowing slightly as the air shifted. He tried to touch it, but it had drifted too high.

Shoppers moved out of his way, forming a tunnel that made it easier to follow the balloon. He wondered where it might be taking him but it disappeared outside Music Zone. The song playing inside had hurt it. A woman, wailing. No words, just sharp sounds. He knew the track. Padmore liked to play it. Pink

Floyd. The pain in her voice was mounting. Oh God, be quiet. He put his hands over his ears and hurried towards a side road. Her scream felt like an octopus about his head. Everyone still stepped aside, even though the balloon was no longer there.

He turned a corner and a metal monster blocked the road in front of him. It was squatting on a mound of rubble, caterpillar tracks rocking as its massive jaws bit at the side of the building. Whole sections of brick were falling away, exposing twisted lengths of metal. The creature's head rotated to the side so it could clamp on the struts and tear them off too.

Only a thin fence was caging the thing in, not enough to contain it. Peter looked around, but everyone was just walking by, talking on mobile phones, chewing on sandwiches. The man selling the *Evening Chronicle* shouted out a headline, oblivious to the fact a monster was ripping central Manchester apart.

There was a person standing next to the beast, easily within range of its terrible jaws. Maybe the owner. He was wearing an orange bib and yellow helmet. Perhaps the creature was scared of such colours, like giant squid are attracted to them. That's why so many survivors of torpedoed ships were never found during the war. The man held a hose at waist level, playing a jet of water over the building's open wounds, drenching the crumbling brick and mortar. He moved the arc of liquid across the monster's head, then switched it back to the building.

Peter stared at the drips cascading from its iron teeth and he wondered if this was the beginning of the end. Judgement Day. Had those who were to be chosen by God already gone? These crowds of shoppers, were they like him: damned? He looked around. Surely there should be other creatures? Colossal ones, spewing fire, ripping whole tower blocks from their foundations, tracks wider than a motorway.

He backed round the corner, into the sunlight that filled the street. It's not real, he said to himself. No one is running, everyone is calm. The monster's not really there. But he could hear girders groaning and the taste of destruction was on his tongue. He needed darkness and quiet. Pulling the hood of his coat over his head, he set off for the cathedral.

# Chapter 27

The living scarecrows were by the cathedral again, sitting on the top steps, showing the backs of their hands as they sucked on cigarettes clutched in their fingertips. Why do they always smoke like that, Jon wondered. The door to the Booth Centre was shut.

'One second,' Jon said to Rick, walking past the cathedral's side entrance to where they were gathered. 'Dave about?'

A few glanced over their shoulders, took in his suit and turned away.

'Is Dave about?' Jon said again.

Baseball Cap flicked his cigarette down the steps. 'Away to fuck, policeman.'

Jon looked at the bloke's scrawny neck, saw the grime caught in the creases of his skin.

Rick appeared at his side. 'Boss?'

'Come on.' Jon turned round and headed back to the cathedral's side entrance. His phone rang. Carmel's name was on the screen. 'Morning.'

'Morning, Jon. How's things?'

How's things? My lungs ache from bloody cigarettes, I've got a sister who wants to become a witch, I've got a brother ... He closed the train of thought down. 'Mustn't grumble. How did it go with the fan club for Satan's Inferno?'

'Not a lot, I'm afraid. A few remembered him from the gigs, but I don't think they were being honest. Now it's common knowledge it was his body in the church at Fairfield, he was suddenly everyone's best mate. However, none of them could even agree what he looked like.'

'Nobody said they'd seen him going backstage?'

'One or two of the girls reckoned they had. Again, they were more interested in getting their names mentioned in the feature.'

'You took their details though?'

'Yeah.'

'Can you email them to me?'

'Okay.' She dragged out the word. 'What about the victim from Alderley Edge?'

Alderley Edge? Jon almost laughed, Carmel, you're so far off the pace. 'Still trying to contact a family member.'

'So we can't do a swap quite yet then; the fans' names I've got for the victim's ID.'

You merciless bitch, Jon thought, deciding the Luke Stevens line of inquiry could wait. 'You're all heart, Carmel. I'll call you.' He snapped the phone shut.

Inside the cathedral, a middle-aged man sat on his own, staring mournfully towards the altar, fingers linked across his lap. Jon's eyes lingered on his bald head and wondered what had drawn him to that red chair. A dead wife? A child claimed by drugs? A loss of direction in life? It certainly didn't look like he was there giving thanks for anything good.

Rick led the way across the top of the nave. Following behind, Jon looked at the stone walls on their left. The ancient surfaces were pockmarked and scarred, like cliffs pounded by a relentless sea. His partner paused to direct a nod towards the Regimental Chapel at the altar end of the aisle. Behind the wood balustrades separating it from the main part of the cathedral a lone figure sat, strands of black hair hanging over his shoulders.

'Bingo,' Jon whispered.

Rick pointed to the opposite side of the building. 'I'll go round the choir stalls and approach the chapel from the far end.'

'I'll wait at the corner until you appear.' Jon moved silently across the black and white tiles, keeping several stacks of shoulder-high chairs between him and the person they were closing in on. He reached the last pillar before the chapel itself and stood behind it, eyes on the far end of the cathedral. A few seconds later Rick appeared and raised a thumb.

Jon stepped into the chapel, his attention drawn again to the angry glow of the stained-glass window at its end. The person was sitting in the front row of chairs, head bobbing up and down. The movement had the repetitive insistence of the tormented. Jon walked halfway up the aisle and gave a gentle cough. 'Peter Robson?'

The person looked sharply to his left, but not far enough round to actually see Jon. He then tilted his head to the vault above, as if the voice could have come from up there.

Keeping his voice low, Jon spoke again. 'Peter? My name's Jon.'

Peter scrabbled to his feet and whirled round, arms out at his sides in readiness to run. Jon raised his hands in a placatory gesture. Shit, look at the bloke's eyes. Bloodshot, with big black pupils. Windows on a tortured soul. He opened his mouth, then paused. How best to speak to the guy? 'Be cool, Peter. There's no need to be frightened.'

Peter started edging towards the balustrades and suddenly Jon realised he might be able to squeeze between the gaps. Rick appeared on the other side. 'Calm down, Peter, we want to help.'

He jumped at Rick's voice, then raked a strand of greasy hair from his face. Jon started forward again and he bolted down the side of the chapel, just making it past Jon's grasping fingers.

Shit! He batted a chair out of the way and gave chase.

Peter raced to the last row of seats and hurdled a couple of ropes, army coat flapping like the wings of a bat. Rick was parallel to him, sprinting down the central aisle of the nave. Jon cleared the ropes, realising Rick was blocking the way out of the side entrance. Peter realised it too and cut away to his right. Bollocks, there were doors on that side too.

Jon reached them just behind Peter, shouldering them apart, then crashing through the next set beyond. Peter was in a stone porch that was fenced off by ornate iron gates. He made it up them, but the spikes at the top prevented him from climbing over. Jon grabbed a muddy army boot and pulled the man back down. 'Peter, give up, mate, you're not going anywhere.'

Robson tried to crawl for the doors leading back into the cathedral, one hand batting at the air as if warding off a phantom.

'For fuck's sake,' Jon muttered. 'What are you doing?'

He reached Rick's legs and tried to burrow between them, all the while babbling in some strange language.

'Cuffs?' Rick asked.

'Peter?' Jon leaned down. 'Peter, we're taking you somewhere safe. Do you understand?'

He shrank back against the wall, drawing his knees to his chest.

'Nah,' Jon said. 'We don't need cuffs.' He hauled the lad to his feet, recoiling at the stench of body odour. Then, keeping a firm grip on his arms, guided him back through the doors.

The man in the main part of the cathedral watched aghast as they walked Robson over to the side exit. Halfway across Peter started to moan, a desolate sound that echoed round the cathedral walls. They left the building and started across the grass, his cries of distress growing steadily louder.

The scarecrows were soon on their feet, sunken eyes gleaming. Baseball Cap started up the chorus. 'Leave him alone, you fucking pigs.'

'Yeah, you fuckers. He's done nothing.'

'Police state! Police state!'

'Filth.'

Jon directed Peter on to the flagstone path, but the addicts cut across the grass to get in the way. Robson stumbled on an uneven edge and Jon had to wrestle to keep him upright.

'See that?' Baseball Cap said, blocking their way. 'Couldn't even wait till they got him in a cell.'

Jon curled his forefinger in, making a sharp point of the knuckle. He shot his hand outward, catching the man in the solar plexus. Baseball Cap's mouth and eyes were wide open as he fell on to his back. Jon knew the pain would be excruciating. He surveyed the rest of them. 'There's room in our car for one more, if any of you fancy a visit to the station.'

They all kept an arm's length away.

Robson was in an interview room less than an hour later. The body search at the custody desk had shown up a handful of change, a brass lighter, a packet of Mayfair cigarettes and the remains of a bag of dried mushrooms.

'These why you're in this state?' the custody sergeant had asked, dangling them before Robson's unfocused eyes. Eventually he'd given a lopsided grin and the sergeant had glanced uneasily at Jon. 'Not sure he's up to being interviewed. I'd be surprised if he knows what his name is, let alone be able to sign over these possessions to us.'

But Robson managed an illegible scrawl and was whisked away for fingerprinting. While he was being processed, the office manager had phoned down from the incident room – forensics had been over the car jack recovered from Robson's tunnel beneath the railway tracks. Glass fragments from the first two churches had been lifted from it, but that was all. Immediately Jon had bagged up the German army coat Robson had been wearing in the cathedral and marked it as highest priority. They needed to know if Peter had been with Luke at the third and fourth churches to burn down.

Now Peter was in front of Jon, the interview table between them. Wondering how to get started, Jon said, 'Peter, for the tape, would you confirm that you have forgone the option of having a solicitor present?'

Robson kept his arms curled round his ribs, his hands lost in the folds of the white custody suit, head hanging limply forward.

'The suspect just nodded his head,' Jon announced, ignoring Rick's shocked glance.

'Now, Peter,' Jon continued. 'Did you ever spend time with Skye Booth at the Psychic Academy?'

Robson didn't move.

'Peter, we've searched the tunnel you were hiding in. We've found the car jack' – no response – 'the petrol container.' Jon saw a drool of saliva begin to stretch down. It broke off and made a bead on the Formica surface.

'Peter, we know you were at the Swinton Methodist Church on the sixth of this month and St Thomas's in Pendlebury on the eleventh. The forensic evidence proves it.'

Robson placed a tip of a finger on the blob of spit and dragged it through. Slowly he began to draw a five-pointed star. Jon looked at Rick, who gave him a pained expression back.

'Peter, we also found the notice from Ben Waters's front door. Why were you trying to attack him? You stole his car, didn't you? Were you planning on driving out to Spain?'

Robson didn't react.

'I don't know if he can even hear us,' Jon muttered. He leaned across the table, then brought his palm hard down on it. 'Peter! Was Luke Stevens with you when you set fire to those churches? Were you with Luke at the Sacred Heart in Fairfield?'

Peter's finger stopped. 'Sacred Heart.'

Jon glanced at Rick. At bloody last. 'Yes, Peter. The Sacred Heart. Someone was with Luke Stevens. Was it you? Was it Serberos Tavovitch?'

'He'll burn for it.'

'Who, Peter, who was there?'

'Day.'

Jon frowned. 'Day? Is that a name?'

'Our day.'

'Sorry, Peter, I didn't catch that.'

'Our day this.'

'Whose day is it? Your band's? Serberos Tavovitch's? Tristan Arkell's?'

'Us give Heaven.'

'Give what? Who gave what?'

'In art.'

'In what?'

'Who.'

'Who. Who are you talking about, Peter? Someone who was there when Luke was killed?'

'Father.' Finally he looked up. Their eyes met and Jon felt himself flinch. They were so blank, so empty. 'Father.'

'Your father was at the church, Peter? He was there?'

Robson started rocking back and forth. 'Oh yes, oh yes.'

The door opened and Buchanon stepped inside. He leaned towards the tape recorder. 'DCI Buchanon has entered the room and is suspending this interview at twelve seventeen p.m.' He hit the stop button and turned to Jon. 'This is going nowhere. The custody sergeant should never have agreed to book him in. We need a psychiatric assessment before continuing – nothing he's said will be admissible until then.'

Admissible, Jon thought. Who gives a toss about admissible? We're trying to find Skye. 'I was getting somewhere, sir.'

Buchanon waved a hand. 'The guy's a bloody teapot.'

Jon was on his feet. 'He just said his dad was there. Didn't you hear that?'

Buchanon sighed. 'He was reciting the Lord's Prayer, Jon. Backwards. Our day this, us give Heaven in, art who Father.'

Jon turned slowly to Robson. Bollocks, his SIO was right.

'Why would Henry Robson be burning churches and killing people?' Buchanon added. 'He's a Christian fundamentalist, for Christ's sa ... he's a fundamentalist.'

Jon searched for a reason. 'What if he'd followed the members of Satan's Inferno to the Sacred Heart? He was stalking them, that much we know.' He glimpsed a theory and lunged at it. 'What if he saw their ceremony? Maybe he tried to stop them and Luke Stevens got killed in the following struggle.'

'Then, after the rest escape, he decides to torch the church?'

'To cover his tracks. Destroy the evidence that proved he killed Stevens.' He glanced at Rick, but his partner's eyes were averted.

Buchanon shook his head. 'Doesn't add up, Jon. I'm sorry. Let's resume this when the lad knows what bloody planet he's on.'

'Sir, we don't have the time. Skye Booth has been missing for almost twenty-four hours. If she is still alive, how much longer have we got to find her?'

'Jon, this interview isn't happening. It's a waste of all our time.'

Jon turned to Robson once again. He had now craned his

head back, eyes cutting from one corner of the ceiling to the other. 'Peter, did your dad know Skye Booth?'

Buchanon stepped forward, hands raised. 'Jon, that's enough.'

Jon stepped round the table and shook Robson's shoulders. 'Peter, who killed Luke Stevens that night? Was it your dad?'

Robson's head rocked back and forth. 'Burn him. Burn him. Evil from us deliver. Burn him!'

Jon released him and turned to Buchanon. 'Sir, please let me bring Henry Robson in.'

Buchanon's eyes were still on Peter as his hands dropped. 'OK, do it then.'

# Chapter 28

The secretary at the printer's where Henry Robson worked looked embarrassed. 'I'm sorry, officer,' she said, replacing the phone. 'No one's able to locate him. His phone clicks straight through to voicemail, as does his mobile.'

'But he turned up for work this morning?' Jon's elbows were on the counter and he realised it was making her more flustered. 'I really need to know.'

She turned to the visitor's book as if a clue might be contained there. 'No one's signed in to see him. His diary is empty. Perhaps he's chosen to work from home.'

Jon led his officers away from the desk, out of the receptionist's earshot. 'I've got his address here,' he whispered, reaching for his notebook as he turned to DC Murray. 'Hugh, if you and Susan can stay here. I need to know Robson's whereabouts on the dates when incidents have occurred. If he's at home Rick and I will take him to the station. Let's all meet up there and we can go over exactly what he's been up to these last few days.'

As Jon pulled out of the car park and accelerated away from Robson's workplace, Rick's phone beeped. He pulled it out and checked the message. 'It's from the incident room manager. That bishop's assistant has finally returned my call. He's left a number.'

'Fuck him,' Jon replied. 'Peter Robson's in custody. There's a shit-load I'd like to speak to that priest about, but nothing that can't wait.'

Ten minutes later they pulled up outside Henry Robson's house, an immaculate-looking semi on a sterile seventies development. An Audi estate was parked in the driveway. Rick pointed to the metal symbol stuck below the rear window. 'A fisher of men.'

Jon raised his eyebrows. 'Is that what those things are? I thought it was something to do with the car owner's star sign. Pisces.'

'No, it's a Christian thing.'

'Should have guessed.'

They walked round the vehicle and up to Robson's front door. The faint sound of monks' chanting could just be heard from inside the house. 'He's got that bloody tape on again,' Jon whispered, pressing the button. A two-tone bell chimed, tinny and artificial. They waited a few seconds and Rick tried again. Jon then started banging on the frosted glass with his knuckles. Slow and steady.

A door opened somewhere inside and a hazy figure approached. 'Yes?' There was a trace of fury in the voice.

'Mr Robson, it's DI Spicer. I have some very good news for you.'

'I'm ...' His voice suddenly lost its harshness. 'I'm feeling a little under the weather right now. May I call you later?'

'It's about your son, sir.'

'Peter? What is it?'

'If you wouldn't mind opening the door.'

A hand moved up and the door swung inwards a few inches. Through the narrow gap, Jon saw that Henry Robson's hair was dishevelled. A sheen of sweat made his forehead shine. Glancing down, Jon noticed the man's shirt was flecked with bright red dots. 'Is that blood, sir?'

Robson tried brushing at a larger spot. His knuckles were an angry red. 'Er, I'm fixing something in the garage. I caught my hand.'

Jon tried to see the man's fingers again, but he'd moved them from sight. 'We've found your son, sir. He's at the station right now. In need of a good rest, but otherwise he should be fine.'

Robson looked nonplussed. 'Peter?'

'That's right.'

'He should be fine?'

'More or less.' Jon stepped back and gestured towards the road. 'We can drive you there right now.'

'That's a little, a little awkward.' He glanced over his shoulder. 'You're sure it's him?'

Jon studied Robson's face. The colour had gone out of it. 'Certain.'

'I can drive myself. Just give me a few minutes.' As he reached up to reclose the door, Jon saw his fingers. No skin was broken. He moved back on to the front step. 'Sir, in cases like these, we prefer to drive the relative. You're obviously emotional, it's safer that way.'

They stared at each other for a few seconds before Robson nodded. 'Very well. I'll just change this shirt.'

As soon as the door closed, Jon looked at Rick. 'His hand's not bleeding.'

'What do you reckon then?'

'I don't know.' He stepped to the side and, as Rick moved back down the drive towards Robson's vehicle, he examined the garage door. It was a pale blue expanse of metal with a handle at the bottom to pull it up and over. 'The music's coming from in there,' Jon murmured, leaning his head towards it as the chants rose and fell.

Rick spoke from behind him. 'Jon, there's blood on the back seat of the car.'

He was about to turn around when the choir's voices died away. Something metallic clinked. He pressed his ear against the cold surface and could just make out the ragged sound of a person fighting for breath before the next song began. 'He's got someone in there.'

Jon grabbed the handle and yanked. The door began to tilt and he pulled it up, extending his arms so it slid back onto its ceiling runners.

Daniel Humphries was hanging by his wrists from a roof girder. The length of chain binding his hands together clinked again as he revolved slowly round. Blood was streaming down his face and over the insulation tape sealing his mouth. Some was falling from his chin into a large puddle on the floor, some was snaking down his throat and across his naked torso before disappearing into the top of his leather trousers.

'Christ,' Rick whispered, stepping forward as Humphries dragged in more air.

They heard the sound of Henry Robson racing down the stairs. Jon moved quickly to the side door that led in from the house and stepped behind it. Moments later Robson burst in. Jon grabbed his wrist and twisted it round in one swift movement. His fingers then sought out the other man's thumb and bent it across towards the little finger. With the lock successfully applied, he attempted to move Robson away from the wall of shelves and anything he might try to grab.

The other man braced his legs and turned his head. 'Let go of me!' he demanded.

Jon rammed the heel of his other hand between Robson's shoulder blades, forcing him to his knees.

'Plea ...' The word ended in a shriek of pain as Jon increased the pressure a fraction more.

'Like giving it out, but you can't fucking take it, can you? Now, where is Skye Booth?' Jon snarled.

Robson's chin was pressed against his chest, eyes screwed tightly shut as the breath hissed from his lips. Jon pressed on his thumb a touch more and felt the joint beginning to give. 'Where is she?'

Rick was over by Daniel, arms wrapped round his thighs, trying to take some pressure off his purple, swollen wrists. 'Help me, Jon, for fuck's sake.'

Jon turned back to Robson's grimacing face, forced him on to his stomach, and jammed his face into the concrete of the garage floor. Glancing back at the shelves, he saw a packet of plastic sack ties. Like the ones used to restrain the prisoners in Guantanamo Bay. He grabbed one, looped it round Robson's wrists and yanked. The plastic teeth clicked as Jon bent forward. 'I see you even twitch and you'll wish this day had never begun.'

Robson remained motionless.

Jon jumped to his feet and followed the length of chain to

where it was attached to a strut in the side wall. The bloody monks were starting up again and he pulled the plug from the CD player, then looked over his shoulder. 'Got his weight?'

Rick nodded and Jon tugged the crow bar from the links. The chain unravelled with a sound like thunder. As Rick sank to his knees, the weight of Humphries safe in his arms, Jon took out his phone and called for help.

A few minutes later an ambulance appeared at the mouth of the cul-de-sac and Jon waved it over to Robson's drive. Once the paramedics had assessed Dan and lifted him in to the rear of the ambulance, Jon directed them back out. The lad, according to the driver, was lucky to be alive. The vehicle swung round then set off towards the main road, its siren sounding a few moments later. As the sound rapidly receded, Jon heard the shrill ring of his mobile coming from his jacket.

'Hello, sir,' he said, marching over to his car where Robson was sitting stiffly in the back while Rick kept careful watch by the side of the vehicle.

'Is this report from the radio room correct?' Buchanon's voice buzzed.

'It is,' Jon replied.

'Henry Robson kidnapped and assaulted Daniel Humphries?'

'Beat the shit out of him. Literally.'

'Jesus Christ. He had Humphries hanging by a chain?'

'That's correct.'

'No sign of Skye Booth, though?'

'No. But he could have a lock-up near here, or access to an empty property. Anything.'

'Bring him in then. Let's give him a grilling and see.'

A grilling? Right, Jon thought. You'll ask him politely and he'll tell you absolutely nothing. 'We'll be there soon.' He flipped the phone shut, desperately trying to think. 'Buchanon says we're to bring him straight in.'

'Let's go, then.' Rick stepped towards the passenger seat, then looked across the top of the car when he realised his partner hadn't moved. 'Jon?'

'He'll blow it, Rick. Robson won't say a thing and Skye will be found in a cellar days from now, starved to death.'

Rick closed his eyes. 'What are you saying?'

Jon glanced into the car. He'd removed the wrist restraint and Robson was protectively cupping his injured thumb like it was a prize budgie. It would be so easy to get what they needed to know out of him.

'Jon, you are not thinking that we ...'

He looked into Rick's eyes and knew his partner would never allow him to do it. He's right, Jon thought. Cool down, use your head. 'Let's just take our time driving back. See what we can get him to say before Buchanon takes over.'

Rich looked faintly sick as Jon opened the driver's door. He pulled out of Robson's close, but rather than turn towards the M60 and the fast route back to Longsight, he turned right. The A666 soon merged with the A6 and Jon followed it in silence, aimlessly heading towards the city centre while he racked his brains for something that would provoke Robson into talking.

Rick reached for the radio, found Classic FM and turned it up loud. As Mars from Holst's *The Planets* made the inside of the vehicle vibrate, he leaned across to Jon. 'Where the fuck are we going?'

'I don't know.'

'This is crazy. Utterly crazy.'

'We've got to try something.'

'None of this will be admissible in court. You're breaking every ... we're breaking every rule. Our careers, everything, will be fucked.'

'Ten minutes, Rick. Fifteen. That's all this is costing us. Come on, let's give it a crack.'

Rick crossed his arms. 'Go on then. I want no part of it.'

Jon kept going, mind blank as to what approach to take. Robson was trying to say something. He killed the music.

'I need a doctor,' Robson bleated.

'Yeah?' Jon replied. 'Serberos Tavovitch? He's really called Daniel Humphries and he's on the way to see a doctor right now. The paramedics reckon he has concussion, a broken jaw and several smashed ribs. Probable kidney damage too, judging by the blood, shit and piss in his trousers. You want to see a doctor? Tell us where to find Skye Booth.'

'I haven't touched her.' He raised his injured hand. 'Why are you doing this? I'm on your side.'

Slowly, Jon shook his head.

Robson sank back against the seats. 'But Tavovitch confessed. He burned those churches down.'

'You were torturing him. He'd have admitted to shagging the Virgin Mary if you'd told him to.'

Robson's eyes flashed. Unbelievable, Jon thought. A touch of blasphemy and the bloke instantly reacts. He focused on the road ahead. They were now approaching the Mancunian Way. Wasn't there a big church near here? St George's, that was it. Empty for years, it had recently been deconsecrated and turned into a development of luxury flats. As they approached the roundabout, the building came into view. Scrubbed clean by the property developer, the pale stone seemed to glow in the sunlight, turrets and spires looking as though they could have been carved from marble. He pointed towards it. 'Does it bother you? Things like that?'

Robson's eyes slid to the side.

'Your religion is dying,' Jon stated, pulling sharply across, cutting up the car behind. Their vehicle bumped violently as he mounted the kerb and skidded to a halt on the grass in front of the building. Rick stared at him in disbelief.

'Executive apartments,' Jon announced. 'The people living in there don't give a toss about the fact it was once a church. Except, of course, when viewed in the context of their investment. Those stained-glass windows are now a novelty feature for impressing their dinner guests. The Church is abandoning its properties left, right and centre. The organisation you so love is becoming a giant provider of housing for pigeons.'

As cars passed by in a steady stream, Robson shrugged. 'The Church is weak. Its leaders are pathetic. While they pander to the masses, people are bound to turn away. Only once the true word of God is heard will people realise the error of their ways.

God isn't your mate, someone you might just turn to when feeling low. God is to be feared. His wrath is terrible. It will be too late for most when the truth of this becomes apparent.' He turned his gaze on Jon. 'I pity you. I've pitied you ever since you wouldn't pray with me when I first came to see you.'

Jon unclipped his seatbelt so he could look Robson in the face. 'So come on, you pious prick. Enlighten me as to why Troy Wilkes, Valerie Evans and Skye Booth deserve to die. God doesn't speak to me, maybe you'll pass his message on.'

'Serberos Tavovitch is the person you should be interviewing,' Robson replied. 'Not me.'

Jon rubbed a hand over the back of his neck. They didn't have time for this shit. He couldn't help glancing again at Robson's thumb. He thought about the boot of their car, and the taser locked inside it. Hook the fucker up to it, and start pressing the trigger. Christ, it was tempting.

'Henry,' Rick said. 'You're a Christian?'

'Of course.'

Jon sat back. Go on mate, he thought, you're welcome to have a go.

'Circumstances have led you to make a terrible mistake. What you did to that young man in your garage cannot be excused. Not from any moral or religious standpoint. Do you agree?'

Robson glared defiantly back. 'I thought he had murdered my son.'

'So, an eye for an eye then?' Rick replied.

'No. I would never have killed him. I just wanted him to admit what he'd done. To admit the truth.'

Rick twisted round. 'But you did kill Troy Wilkes and Valerie Evans.'

Robson's eyes were shining. 'They were serving the Devil. I didn't kill them, but their fate does not sadden me. At least they are now feeling the true error of their ways.'

'They're in hell, you mean?' Rick asked.

Robson gave a satisfied nod.

'Like your wife?'

His eyes dropped momentarily. 'What she suffers now, she brought upon herself.'

'I thought there was a recent edict from the Pope clarifying that limbo doesn't apply to suicides or aborted babies?'

'The Pope,' Robson sneered. 'You cannot twist the words of the Lord to suit the sensibilities of a corrupt society. "And the sea gave up the dead that were in it: and death and Hell gave up their dead that were in them. And they were judged, every one according to their works. And Hell and death were cast into a pool of fire. This is the second death. And whosoever was not found written in the book of life was cast into the pool of fire." That is what the Bible says.'

'What sort of an effect did you think saying something like that would have on your son?'

'He needed to know the truth. It's all anyone needs.'

'The truth. So you tortured Tavovitch for it. Surely you realise that was wrong?'

'It was a necessary measure. I was dealing with someone who is evil.' He looked directly at Rick. 'And you, officer. There is a whiff of the homosexual about you.'

'What did you say?'

'Are you a homosexual?'

Rick glanced at Jon before his eyes fell. 'I do not believe this man.'

'"As Sodom and Gomorrah and the neighbouring cities, in like manner, having given themselves to fornication and going after other flesh, were made an example, suffering the punishment of eternal fire." Start praying, officer. End times are upon us, tribulation is coming.'

'Shut up,' Rick replied, turning round.

Robson pointed a finger at his back. '"Little children, it is the last time: and as ye have heard that Antichrist shall come, even now are there many Antichrists; whereby we know that it is the last time."'

'Henry, you're going to prison for this,' Rick said, staring at the windscreen. 'You understand what will happen to you there? You'll be anally raped. You will be sodomised.'

Jon spotted the tears glistening in Robson's eyes as he jutted his chin forward. 'Many good Christians have suffered far more than that.'

Oh for fuck's sake, thought Jon, he'll be saying God told him to do everything next. The last refuge of those who realise no one on earth is prepared to agree with their actions. 'Let's just drive him somewhere quiet and kick the living fuck out of him.'

'No,' Rick said quietly. 'Henry, if you hold your Christian beliefs so dear, tell us where Skye Booth is. Start putting right your mistakes.'

Jon could see Robson's jaw muscles working, but his mouth remained shut.

Rick sighed. 'Why, in your opinion, were Troy Wilkes and Valerie Evans serving the Devil?'

'They lectured at the Psychic Academy. They were luring people into diabolical beliefs. Encouraging people to try and see the future by conjuring Satan, letting loose evil that spreads further every day.'

'So, in other words, they deserved to die because no one is permitted to hold any religious beliefs other than your own?'

Robson sat up. 'There is more at stake here than what happens in this life. There is the welfare of our souls to consider. When Judgement Day comes, and it will be soon, mark my words, the Lord will decide which of us goes to be with him in heaven and which of us goes to hell. That decision is for all eternity. Ignore it at your peril.'

Jon wanted to hang his head in his hands. How do you reason with a person like this? He didn't know. The ring of his mobile shattered the silence in the car. DC Murray's name was on the screen. He climbed out and took the call. 'Hugh, what have you got?'

'It's not looking good, sir.'

'How so?'

'Henry Robson was down in Birmingham the night Valerie Evans died. His work confirmed he'd been sent down there to fix a printing press. Some new model made in Germany. The part he needed had to be flown over from the manufacturer outside Hamburg. It was easier for Robson to stay there overnight and do the job when it arrived the next morning.'

'So he was in a hotel on his own?'

'No. The production line manager put him up for the night.'

'You spoke to this person yourself?'

'Sorry, boss. It all checks out. The job took him most of the next day. He couldn't have been in Manchester when Skye disappeared.'

Jon looked down at the grass, soft and long. He wanted to lie back in it and shut his eyes. 'That fucks the chances of it being him then.'

Murray kept quiet for a moment. 'Oh, the office manager is asking where you are. The Bishop of Manchester is waiting for you upstairs.'

'Who?'

'The Bishop of Manchester, believe it or not.'

'He's waiting for me at the station?'

'He turned up about ten minutes ago. You've been phoning a colleague of his, Canon Maurice Kelly?'

'What does he want?'

'I don't know. He said he has information to share with you.'

Jon looked across at the converted church. 'The bishop? Well, he can wait. His colleague was in no hurry to return our calls.'

'Where shall I say you are?'

'Is Buchanon wanting to know?'

'No. He's in with the ACC at the moment.'

'We're ten minutes away. Anyone wants to know, we've been caught in traffic.' He climbed back into the car.

'I'd like to see my son now.'

'Would you?' Jon sought out Robson's eyes in the rear-view mirror. 'Believe me, the last person on earth he wants to see is you.' He pulled back on to the roundabout shaking his head. Henry Robson was deluded, his son was tripping. Humphries was sedated. Arkell was somewhere at large. And they were no nearer to finding Skye Booth.

# Chapter 29

As they marched Henry Robson up to the custody sergeant's desk, a uniformed officer called down the corridor. 'DI Spicer? A kitbag's been handed in. Found by a dog walker on waste ground behind the Sacred Heart.'

Jon paused, one hand clamped round Robson's upper arm. 'And?'

'It had a membership card for a hockey club in it belonging to Father Ben Waters.'

'That's great. You may have spotted I'm quite busy right now.'

The young officer blushed. 'It's just that the receiver said I should let you know.'

'Cheers. You've let me know.' He turned to Rick. 'Book him in, will you? I'd better go upstairs and see what his Holiness wants.'

He was halfway up when his mobile rang again. Pausing on the landing, he glanced at the screen. No number he recognised. 'DI Spicer here.'

'Detective, it's Dean Webster, the fire investigation officer over at the Sacred Heart.'

'Dean, can I call you back?'

'I've found something you should know about.'

Jon started on the next flight. 'I'm listening.'

'The hydrocarbon dog arrived a bit earlier. We took her into the church and let her have a good sniff around.'

Jon was now at the doors to the incident room. Buchanon was in his inner office, glaring at him through the glass. A fat bloke in a black robe with red buttons was in there too. 'What did it find?'

'Nothing of real note around the point of origin or the window that had been smashed. But when we took her to the other side of the aisle, we got a result.'

Jon saw Buchanon's impatient wave and turned away. 'Go on.'

'She identified a trail of droplets and splashes leading back to the vestry door. The one that had been forced open from the inside so they could drag out the books and surplices to help start the fire. It's where the trail was lit from, the door to the vestry.'

Jon was trying to think, but the noise in the incident room was too loud. 'What's the significance?'

'The dog also identified traces of accelerant on the handle and keyhole area of the vestry's outer door.'

'So the arsonist probably left the building that way?'

'But, detective, that door wasn't broken open. Whoever left the accelerant on it probably did so as they were locking up behind them.'

Buchanon appeared at his side. 'DI Spicer, my office. Now.'

'I'll call you back, Dean, sorry.'

As his SIO led the way across the incident room, Jon called over to DC Murray. 'Hugh, see if Henry Robson had any connection with the Sacred Heart that might involve him possessing a key to the building.'

Buchanon ushered him into his office and shut the door. 'Bishop, I'm so sorry you've been kept waiting. Jon, this is the Right Reverend Terence Doyle.'

The man stood, brushing his robe as he did so. 'Sorry for all the garb. I've come direct from an official function.' He proffered his hand.

Jon hesitated, thinking of all the Catholic churches, children's homes, schools and other organisations this man presided over. He wondered how much abuse had been carried out in them all over the years. He took the bishop's hand, feeling the soft, fat fingers against his. He overdid the squeeze before breaking contact. 'There was no need to come in person.'

'Ah, that may not be the case,' the bishop replied, flexing his fingers.

Buchanon gestured to the seats. 'Gentlemen, please.'

As they all sat down Jon took in the flesh bulging over the man's dog collar. It appeared to restrict his circulation, making his eyes bulge.

'Reverend Canon Kelly finally got through to the refuge in Spain, where Father Waters had been booked in.' He glanced awkwardly at Jon. 'There appears to have been a slight break-down in communication.'

'What's that code for?' Jon asked.

'It appears Father Waters isn't at the retreat.'

Jon sat up. 'When did he leave?'

The bishop raised a hand and coughed lightly. Jon noticed the gold ring on his right hand. Worth enough to feed a few African AIDS orphans for quite some time, he thought. 'He never actually arrived.'

'Never actually arrived?'

'No. Reverend Kelly gave him his plane tickets and drove him to the airport. He should have got to the retreat a few hours later. But the room put aside for him hasn't been occupied.'

'So where is he?' Jon demanded.

'I would like to know myself.'

Jon rubbed a forefinger across his top lip. Ben Waters was organising the group opposing the opening of the Psychic Academy. Everyone killed so far, with the possible exception of Luke Stevens, was somehow involved with the place. Luke Stevens was killed in Waters's church, possible by someone with a key to the building. 'How long have you known this?'

The bishop's eyelids fluttered. 'Well, my assistant made an initial call to the retreat possibly yesterday.'

'I said, how long have you known this?'

Buchanon directed a finger at Jon. 'Detective, show some respect with your questions.'

Jon kept his eyes on the bishop. 'How long?'

'The retreat didn't return our call immediately.'

Jon leaned forward. 'That is not an answer.'

'DI Spicer, this is not an interview,' Buchanon said. 'Bishop, I must apologise for my colleague's tone.'

'I found out yesterday afternoon.'

'Yesterday afternoon?' Jon whispered. 'You've sat on this for twenty-four hours? Skye Booth was snatched around this time yesterday afternoon.'

Buchanan cut in. 'Jon, I hope you are not implying that Father Waters is somehow involved in all this!'

'I am, sir.' He turned back to the bishop. 'I also intend to see your phone records. If you're lying about when that call was—'

'Enough, DI Spicer! Enough. Now before you get out, I want you to apologise for that comment.'

Jon stood. 'I've no respect for your kind, bishop. No respect at all.'

He stormed out of the office to see Nikki Kingston sitting by his desk. Jesus Christ, this is all I need, he thought.

'Jon, everything all right?' she asked, turning a small black book over in her hands.

'No.' He fell into his seat, then dug his fingers deep into the armrests. 'We've been pissing in the wind all along.'

'What do you mean?'

He shook his head. 'I'll tell you some other time.' The gold cross on the cover of her book caught his eye. 'What's that?'

'It was dropped off for Father Ben Waters. With the church and presbytery ruined, I didn't know what to do with it. I was hoping you could forward it on.'

Jon held out his hand and she passed it to him. 'Who dropped it off?'

'The relatives of one of his parishioners, a Mr Bouras. He passed away the other night. They've been sorting out his personal effects at St Mary's Hospice and wanted to give it back.'

Jon opened it up. A prayer book, with a label for the Sacred Heart on its inner cover. 'St Mary's Hospice.'

'Yes. Father Waters fetched it for him on Monday night. The relatives were keen to return it before they fly back to Poland.'

Jon rotated it in his hands, thinking back to what Ben Waters had said the night his church had burned down. He'd claimed to have been at St Mary's Hospice all night, at the bedside of a dying parishioner. The parishioner, evidently, was this Bouras person. But, if that was the case, how could the relatives be claiming Waters had nipped away to fetch a prayer book? 'You're sure the relatives said it was Monday night that Waters went to get this?'

She frowned. 'Yes. They said it was the last thing their dad was able to ask for, but by the time Father Waters returned with it he was unconscious. He died early on Tuesday morning.'

'Exactly what time did Waters leave to fetch this book?'

'I don't know. Christ, Jon, I only said I'd pass it on to you.'

Jon lifted his fingers to his nose. Petrol. His fingers smelled of petrol. He lifted the book and sniffed it. The same cloying aroma.

Murray was walking across the room. 'Robson insists he's never set foot in the Sacred Heart.'

'Forget him,' Jon replied. 'We need to find Ben Waters.'

'The priest? Isn't he in Spain?'

'He never went. And I've got a horrible feeling he's been here the whole time. DC Gardiner! You checked out Waters's statement with the staff at Saint Mary's Hospice. Who verified that he'd been there all night?'

Gardiner's face had gone white and Jon knew exactly what she was thinking. Please don't let this fuck-up be down to me. She scrabbled about then stood up, notebook in her hands. 'The nurse on duty that night. Here, Sister Caroline Morris.'

'She definitely said he hadn't left the building at any point?'

'Yes. It's here.'

'I think she was mistaken. Nikki, these relatives. They were flying back to Poland?'

'This afternoon.'

'From Manchester airport?'

'I assume so. There was a taxi waiting for them.'

'Were they a couple?'

'Yes, in their fifties. The man's son and his wife.'

'Hugh, Susan, get over to the airport. Flights to Warsaw, Kraków or wherever. Can't be many flights to Poland every day. A Mr and Mrs Bouras. We need to know exactly when

259

Father Waters left the hospice and returned to the Sacred Heart to get this prayer book.'

Rick was approaching their desk, looking puzzled. 'I don't understand. Waters is here, in England?'

'He's certainly not out near Salamanca.' Jon jabbed a thumb over his shoulder. 'The fat fuck in Buchanon's office just confirmed that.'

'So you reckon he could have ...' Rick let the question hang.

'With this case, who knows. But we have to find him.'

'DI Spicer, what's going on?'

McCloughlin. Jon made himself take a breath before answering. 'I'm not sure, sir.'

'Why all this activity?' The older officer was coming out from behind the desk he'd been sitting at. Sensing something afoot, wanting to be involved.

Fucking hyena, Jon thought. 'Just let me think.' He looked across the room, searching for the receiver. 'You mentioned Father Waters' kitbag was recovered earlier on. Where is it?'

'Here.' The man hurried over to a cupboard, opened the doors and took out a large polythene sack. Inside was a long blue Puma holdall.

'Put it on the table, can you?' Jon asked, snapping on a pair of latex gloves. He broke the seal on the sack and dragged the bag out. 'We need something to tell us where Waters may be.' He undid the zip and removed a hockey stick that had been jutting out. Next he started rummaging in the side pockets. A bottle of water, a referee's whistle, a muesli bar, a plastic A4-size file. He opened it up and saw a list of boys' names, phone numbers to the side. The next sheet was a fixtures list. Nothing else apart from a few photocopied pages on fitness exercises. Turning back to the main compartment, he yanked out a tracksuit, a pair of trainers, a hockey shirt and matching pair of socks. The smell of stale sweat rose into his nostrils. 'Shit, nothing here.'

Next to him he saw Nikki lift up the hockey stick. She turned it round in her hands and examined the end. 'Jon, this could be it.'

He turned properly to her and saw that look in her eye. The one that said, we're on to something. It had been too long since he'd seen it and a small smile broke on his lips. 'Could be what?'

She blinked. 'The murder weapon we've been looking for. A curved, blunt edge, approximately four inches by two.'

McCloughlin bent forwards. 'Jesus, she's right.'

Jon met her eyes again and saw they were alive with excitement. I know, he wanted to say. Isn't this the best feeling in the world?

'What is happening here?'

Jon looked over his shoulder. The door to Buchanon's office was open and their SIO was staring at him.

'Sir, we need to find Father Ben Waters. He wasn't present at the hospice for the whole of Monday night as he claimed. It appears he left at some point to fetch a prayer book from his church. I think when he got there, he saw movement inside, armed himself with this hockey stick, then let himself in through the vestry door.'

Buchanon half-looked back into his office, then shut the door. 'Spicer,' he hissed. 'You had better be very, very sure of this.'

A reckless sense of excitement had engulfed Jon and he wanted to laugh. It fitted! The pieces fitted! 'Inside the church, he surprised Luke Stevens as he was preparing to torch it. Seeing his church wrecked, Waters loses control, chases Stevens to the window and brings the hockey stick down on the back of the boy's head as he tries to climb back out. Nikki, this making sense?'

She nodded.

Jon turned back to his SIO. 'When he realises what he's done, he drags the body back to the pyre. Next, he picks up Stevens' container of petrol and lays a trail back to the vestry, lights it with the matches he probably uses for candles, grabs the prayer book, locks up and returns to the hospice.'

Buchanon stepped forwards, arms crossed. 'How the hell did you work all that out?'

'The fire investigation officer reckons that was the sequence of events inside the church. Waters didn't go to Spain. He's been here all along. Sir, it works out. I thought the guy was close to cracking that night, but the next morning in the hospital, he was totally calm. I remember, he even said something about it being God's will that his church went up. A way to free him so he could serve in some other manner. That's what his new mission has been, hunting down witches.'

Buchanon's eyes went to the hockey stick in Nikki's hands. He took another step forward. 'I think more haste, less speed. How are you so sure Waters wasn't at the hospice as he claimed?'

Jon sucked in air, picturing what might be happening to Skye Booth at that very moment. 'Sir, we have to to find Waters. Can we not go over the fine details—'

'I can help you.'

They all looked round. The bishop was standing in the door-way of Buchanon's office, a leather attaché case in his hand.

# Chapter 30

Father Ben Waters looked up at the clock tower on Manchester Town Hall. Almost four. He still had a good five hours of daylight. That was good: he wanted to have dealt with her before nightfall, otherwise the flames that would purge her soul might attract unwanted attention.

But first he had to check that she'd been telling the truth. He set off down Brazennose Street, looking with distaste at a poster giving details of the Trafford Centre's newly extended opening hours. One of his congregation had informed him that its car parks were pretty much full by ten o'clock on a Sunday morning.

The country had lost its way, spurning the teachings of God for the sin of greed. That was the nation's new religion and places like the Trafford Centre were where people went to worship.

He passed a florist's, the front of the shop bright with exotic blooms. That reminded him. He needed more bougainvillea for the vase on his window sill. Their purple petals took him back to the time he'd spent at the retreat in Salamanca. It was such a happy time of his life, everything had seemed to be progressing towards his dream of becoming a Franciscan. Until the order had rejected him. He'd return there soon for a vist, but not before he'd earned it.

He paused to peer in a shop window. Small bottles with cork stoppers were arranged on racks. He examined the contents and saw some were filled with powders, others with what appeared to be dried flowers, fragments of plant or broken pieces of bark. Gnarled lengths of root lay in an open tray.

He glanced up at the shop's name. Hubbard's Herbal

Remedies. His lips were taut against his teeth as he began reading the calligraphy-style lettering on each label:

*Aconite, to counter acute infections*
*Belladonna, to combat earache or sore throats*
*Dandelion root, assists with kidney and liver functions*
*Lycopodium, a remedy for digestive problems*
*St John's Wort, combats feelings of depression*
*Thuja, heals weak nails*

He looked beyond the window display to the shop's interior. A couple of middle-aged women were behind the counter. They wore green dresses and beige pinafores, and were chatting away without a care in the world. He stepped into the shop and began to browse a display of pills near the door.

The two women were discussing last night's telly and the episode of *Most Haunted* they'd both seen. A spirit had definitely been trying to make contact, according to the show's psychic. It had been a wet-nurse from the eighteenth century, falsely accused of smothering the infant who'd been placed in her care.

Waters stared at the bottles before him, oblivious of their contents. The influence of Satan was everywhere, permeating the high street, infecting the TV schedules. The country was in mortal danger.

'Can I help you?'

He turned to the assistant who had approached, taking in her welcoming smile. Jezebel. The badge said her name was Sally. 'It's more a case of how I could help you.'

The corners of her mouth contracted slightly and she took a small step back. 'I'm sorry?'

He raised a forefinger to her face. 'I know what you represent and there will be retribution.'

The remains of her smile had withered and she looked to her colleague for support. Waters held his finger towards her too, then walked out of the shop. He strode towards Deansgate, glaring at the people he passed. A godless society was a vulnerable society. He saw where the dangers of self-indulgence led, saw it in the afflicted and the addicted who banged on his presbytery doors; saw it in the lost who turned to places like the Psychic Academy to find direction in their lives. All the while the agents of Satan circled, waiting to lure them from the path. Astrologists, palm readers, fortune-tellers, clairvoyants, herbalists. Witches. That's what they really were, witches. And they had to be destroyed.

He raised his eyes heavenward, sensing approval radiating down from the blue above. 'Thank you, Lord, you give me strength.' He turned on to Deansgate itself. A bus passed him. On its side a picture of an old woman on a broomstick was silhouetted against a giant moon. The lettering said, *The Witch Way. Nelson − Burnley − Rawtenstall − Manchester.*

Waters looked up the street. There was the pub she'd described straight ahead. He stopped at the chalk board propped on the pavement.

*Psychic Night with Helena Hunt, 8 p.m., 2nd of May. Tickets £15 including dinner. Have you lost a loved one? Are you curious to know what the future may have in store? Join renowned psychic Helena as she answers questions by making contact with the other side this Sunday night.*

Waters bridled at the chosen day of her performance. How dare she use the Sabbath to spread the influence of evil? Sellotaped to the top of the board was a photocopied piece of paper. He squinted at its poor quality. A newspaper story, reproduced countless times no doubt, that recounted Helena's uncanny abilities. At the end was a web address and phone number to contact her for personal consultations.

Waters tore it free and stuffed it in his pocket. There would be no event this Sunday. She would be receiving a visit tonight and, once he had obtained the name of another coven member from her, she would feel how the power of God dwarfed that of the Master she served.

He nodded to himself. The Booth girl hadn't been lying. Helena Hunt really did exist. It was good she'd been honest though, of course, that wouldn't save her. Nothing could. The shop at the corner of the next side street caught his eye. Hike and Bike. The window display was full of camping equipment. Tents, sleeping bags, foldaway chairs, gas stoves. He walked towards the doors, confident he'd find firelighters for sale inside.

# Chapter 31

The incident room was silent as everyone stared at the bishop.

'I can help you,' he repeated, raising the attaché case up a fraction. 'I've got all the information I could gather on Father Waters here.'

Buchanon gestured towards the centre table. 'Thank you, bishop. If, perhaps we could go through what you have here ...?'

'We need to know where he's holding Skye Booth,' Jon cut in. 'Has he access to any sort of property in this area?'

'Jon,' Buchanon said, a hand raised to ward him off. 'Ease up. The bishop is doing all he can.'

'No, he's right,' Bishop Doyle interjected. 'There are a couple of places that spring to mind.' He sat down and took a file from his case. 'Father Waters has spent his entire career at the Sacred Heart, living in the presbytery, but he also owns a place in Buxton. The cottage his mother used to live in. He once told me he makes it available for holiday bookings but, maybe, there is no one in it at the moment.'

'Have you got the address?' Buchanon asked.

'Yes. It's here.' He held up a piece of paper.

'Good,' replied Buchanon. 'That's extremely helpful. You said a couple of places?'

'Yes. There's the Sunday school he runs. I know he has the keys to it – we were discussing how it was going a short while ago.'

'What sort of place is it?' McCloughlin asked. 'Do other people ever use it?'

'It's a hall, located behind Our Lady, the church to which Waters' congregation was transferred. I can't see it offering any sort of privacy. Father O'Farrell uses it all the time.'

'It'll need to be checked out anyway,' Buchanon said. 'Right, DCI McCloughlin, I suggest you take a team over to St Mary's. I'll take one across to Buxton.'

McCloughlin looked like he had just bitten on a lemon. 'The disappearance of Skye Booth is directly linked to the murder of Valerie Evans. It's my case – I should check out the cottage.'

Buchanon cleared his throat. 'We don't know if the attacks on the churches aren't connected to her going missing. And as the syndicate assigned to that case—'

'What about his role as a hockey coach?' Jon asked. 'He's in charge of a colts team, isn't he?'

Realisation hit the bishop's face. 'Yes! He gave a set of keys to Reverend Kelly for handing on to another of the coaches there.'

'Keys for the clubhouse you mean?' Jon asked.

'Yes. Now, what was it called? I think the coach's telephone number is here somewhere.' He began to leaf through the file.

Jon had to thrust his hands into his pockets, the urge to snatch the attaché case and empty its contents out on to the table was so strong. Nikki Kingston held up the folder from Waters's kitbag. 'It's here, at the top of this print-out. Failsworth Hockey Club.'

She held it towards Jon, but Buchanon plucked it from her fingers. His eyes scanned down. 'It says training is on Tuesday and Thursday evenings. Skye disappeared late afternoon yesterday.'

'A Thursday,' McCloughlin nodded. 'So he can't be holding her there, the club would have been in use yesterday.'

'Hockey seasons end about the same time as rugby seasons,' Jon said. 'The last match at my club was the other week and the place will have been empty since then. Same may be true for Failsworth Hockey Club.'

Buchanon clicked his fingers. 'Right, we need to get over there. Gardiner, Murray, Rhea, Ashford, Saville and Spicer, with me. Now.'

McCloughlin turned to the bishop. 'The address for this cottage in Buxton?'

He handed across the sheet of paper and McCloughlin turned to his team. 'Let's go.'

McCloughlin's syndicate surged across the room, the DCI's head reappearing for an instant before the doors swung shut. 'You'll need someone to visit that Sunday school.' He disappeared before Buchanon could reply.

Jon watched his senior officer as he surveyed the team. No, he thought. Do not pick me. Buchanon's eyes moved across the waiting group, settling on Jon. Fuck!

'DI Spicer, you hold the most senior rank below me. Take DS Saville with you.'

'You're giving us the Sunday school?'

'I am. Keep me informed. The rest of you, let's be on our way.' He turned to the bishop. 'Would you excuse me? I'll get someone to—'

'Please, don't concern yourself. You go.'

As the group marched from the room, Jon turned to Rick. 'Bollocks.'

Rick bounced a plam off the top of the chair in front of him.

Nikki placed a hand on Jon's arm. 'The hockey club was your shout. That's so unfair.'

Taking a deep breath, Jon flexed his toes inside his shoes, waiting for the adrenalin to drain away. 'Yup, isn't life shit?' he smiled, before glancing at Rick. 'Let's get it done. We might be able to catch them up at the hockey club if we hurry.'

Rick walked over to their desk and grabbed both jackets. 'What a bitch. We should be with them.'

'I know,' said Jon as they set off towards the doors. 'Where is this place anyway?'

'I can show you.'

Jon stopped. The bishop. Shit, he'd forgotten all about him. The other man was slotting the last sheets of paper back in his attaché case. 'It's not far.'

Jon weighed up the offer. The last person he wanted in his car was that fat bastard, but if it got them to this Sunday school quicker, he'd cope. 'OK, you're on.'

Father Ben Waters took the wilted bougainvillea blooms from the small vase and tossed them from the window. After putting fresh ones in their place he peered down into the overgrown courtyard. The setting sun lit the lopsided dovecote with a beautiful glow. Two pigeons were perched on its roof, contentedly cooing at one another. As he scanned the pile of pallets and packing crates he'd gathered up earlier, he remembered the days when the courtyard was properly tended. The neat rows of vegetables in the kitchen garden, the cluster of fruit trees in the tiny orchard. But everything had been abandoned as the power of Satan grew.

The monk's cowl was ready on his bed and he lifted the lower hem to slip it over his head. After adjusting the hood so it hung down his back, he stooped to lift the large book that was placed on his pillow. He knew the page that was required. It set out all the necessary steps for burning a witch. He read the text one last time, picked up a simple cotton nightie and walked from the tiny room.

As they drove towards Failsworth, Jon looked at the burning orange ball hanging just above the rooftops. Above it wisps of pinkish cloud hung motionless in the fading sky.

'So Waters runs this Sunday school?' Rick asked with a backward glance over his shoulder.

'Yes. He's done it since first becoming a priest.'

Jon's eyes flicked to the rear-view mirror. 'What did he do before that?'

'He was in the process of becoming a Franciscan.'

'A monk?'

'That's right. He got to the stage of novice, but he didn't progress to being initiated as a brother.'

'A novice is a trainee monk then?' Rick asked.

'Yes. He'd embarked on the first stages of the process, moving from an enquirant where you approach the order, wishing to explore your calling. If the order agrees, you become a postulant for a period of learning. Next you become a novice, at which point a spiritual director is appointed to work with you. Together, you draw up a rule of life prior to taking your vows of chastity, poverty and obedience.'

Rick had now almost turned in his seat. 'So why didn't he become a proper monk?'

The bishop brushed a knuckle over the tip of his nose. Jon caught the gesture in his mirror. He knew it from countless interviews when a suspect was hiding something.

'There were certain issues. It was agreed Ben should look at other ways of serving God.'

'What sort of issues?' Jon asked, his foot easing off the accelerator.

'Spiritual ones,' the bishop mumbled. 'Ones relating to his faith. I don't think it's appropriate for me to go into details.'

Jon pulled up at the side of the road and stared at the bishop's reflection. The man looked like he was sitting on a nest of ants. 'I'll be the judge of that. What issues?'

'Jon,' Rick whispered. 'Give him a chance. He's only trying ...'

Jon shook his head, then turned to the rear-view mirror again. 'What issues?'

The bishop squirmed in his seat yet again as he slid some notes from his file. 'The order declined him. It's not unheard of.'

'For what reason?'

'The notes are a little vague.' His head was bowed, eyes on the piece of paper.

'Bishop, stop pissing me around and answer the question. Please.'

His eyes connected briefly with Jon's before dropping again. 'It seems his spiritual director was concerned with the forceful-ness of some of his views.'

'The forcefulness? In relation to what exactly?'

'Franciscans are bound by their vows to help the marginalised, whatever their beliefs. What it says here is that Father Waters tended to be quite unsympathetic if those people belonged to other religions.'

Jon thought of Waters leading the protests outside the Psychic Academy.

'And,' the bishop continued, 'his thoughts in regard to women were, according to this, quite negative too. They became concerned about his attitude.'

'What? Women's role in the church?' Jon demanded.

'Both. He was reluctant to have contact with any female.'

A memory popped into Jon's head. Waters lying in the road the night his church burned down. How he grabbed the female paramedic's hand when she tried to help him. His strangled cry of anguish at her touch. Jesus, he'd thought it was the chest pains that had caused the sound. It had been a glimpse behind the man's mask instead. 'So Waters had a problem with non-Christians and women. And these views were so extreme the Franciscan order wanted nothing to do with him.'

'I think your wording is a little strong.'

'Tell me Bishop Doyle, when did the order send you their notes on Ben Waters?'

'Wednes ...' His words dried up.

Got you, you oily shit, Jon thought. 'You had suspicions about Waters as far back as Wednesday. You claim the retreat in Spain returned your call yesterday afternoon, but you failed to tell me when you first rang them. You've been sitting on your suspicions for days, haven't you?'

'I was merely concerned for someone, the welfare of whom is my responsibility.'

Trying to cover your arse and the whole rotten organisation you represent more like, Jon thought.

'Where does someone train to become a Franciscan?' Rick asked. 'Do they have schools or something?'

The bishop looked relieved to break from Jon's furious stare. 'Waters did his training at Gorton Monastery. There was an entire wing of cells at the side of the church for monks on retreat and for those looking into joining the order.'

Jon felt his fingers beginning to clench on the steering wheel.

'So what would he do?' Rick asked. 'Sit in a cell all day studying religious texts?'

'For many hours, yes. But the monastery was a community too. Everyone helped according to their skills. He would have played a part in church services, assisted in the kitchen garden, helped the poor and needy in the surrounding area. Of course, there was the Sunday school too – I know he played an active part helping out there. With his musical talent it was inevitable that he got involved.'

Jon's voice was leaden. 'Musical talent?'

'The guitar. His Sunday school classes always revolve around singing songs. It's what makes them so popular, I suspect.'

'He taught the guitar at Gorton Monastery's Sunday school?'

The bishop consulted his notes. 'During the early eighties. Really they were the years the monastery started going into decline.'

It's him. He's the fucker who abused our kid, Dave. Jon had never felt so certain of anything in his life. 'Get out of the car.'

Rick's head whipped round.

'I beg your pardon?' the bishop spluttered.

'I need you to get out of my car.'

'Here? You're asking me to get out on this road?' He looked at the dilapidated houses lining the street. A bunch of lads were sitting on a nearby garden wall, cans of drink in their hands, rat-like eyes watching.

Jon's voice was barely above a whisper. 'I'm not asking. Get out.'

'Jon, what are you doing?' Rick whispered. 'We can't just—'

'We're going directly from here to apprehend a violent suspect. Now, bishop, are you getting out or am I dragging you out?'

'Jon,' Rick said. 'Buchanon's ordered us to check the Sunday school at St Mary's. What the hell has got into you?'

Jon's eyes were fixed on his hands as they gripped the steering wheel. The knuckles were white, tendons like wire straining beneath the skin. 'You can get out of the fucking car with him, or you can come with me.'

In the periphery of his vision, he could just make out Rick staring at him in astonishment. His partner sank back in his seat. 'Bishop, you'd better get out.'

The car door clicked open and Jon's eyes cut to the side. The bishop climbed uncertainly on to the pavement. He closed the door, then stepped towards Rick's window, fingers curled, ready to knock. Jon lifted his foot off the clutch and floored the accelerator.

Skye Booth was slumped in the chair. Small folds of flesh were pushed out by the loops of rope round her midriff. He looked at her for a while, his eyes lingering on her breasts. Her nakedness disgusted him. Placing the nightie on the table, he crouched before her. The smell of urine was strong. Her eyes were shut and her breathing came in short gasps. He slapped her cheek, a brisk blow that sent her head lolling towards her other shoulder. She didn't open her eyes, though her cracked lips began to move. Even if the words had been coherent, he didn't care what she was murmuring.

Reaching down, he untied her feet, then loosened the cords binding her to the chair. She would have fallen to the floor if he didn't catch her. Propping her up with one hand, he reached for the nightie and pulled it over her head. It was loose enough to go over her arms which were tied behind her back. He stood and hauled her up, but her knees immediately began to buckle.

Grunting, he hefted her on to his shoulder, then stepped out of the room into the long corridor. Stairs at each end led down to the ground floor. He turned right, stepping over broken tiles from the collapsing roof above. More debris littered the stairs and he had to edge down sideways, careful to avoid several gaps where the wood had begun to rot away.

On the ground floor he moved along several cloisters until he reached a corner entrance to the courtyard. The grass hadn't quite obliterated the path that led to the wooden stake at its centre.

★

Jon raced round the M60, an image of Waters floating before him. He tried to press his foot down even further, but the accelerator was already on the floor.

'Jon.' Rick coughed uneasily. 'You OK, mate?'

'Fine.'

'You know what you've just done? Buchanon's orders, the bishop ...'

'I know what I've just done. I take full responsibility. I gave you no choice.'

'I'm not saying that. I'm with you. But I just need to know that you're in control of what you're doing.'

Jon breathed deeply a few times and dropped his speed a fraction. Rick was right. He had to keep a clear head. 'Don't worry, I'm in control.'

'Where are we going?'

'Gorton Monastery.'

He came off at junction 24, then sped along Hyde Road. With every passing second the monastery spire became an ever more dominant part of the view ahead of them. When it started drifting to their side Jon veered off the main road on to a secondary route. The road curved to the left and finally the entire building was revealed. Waste ground surrounded it and, in the gathering dusk, it appeared for a moment like an immense ship, trapped in a blood-red sea.

'It's huge,' Rick stated.

Jon nodded. 'She's somewhere inside, I'm certain.'

Standing before the monastery was an abandoned petrol station, holes in the forecourt's tarmac where the pumps used to be. Jon spotted a blue Volvo parked to the side of the single-storey building. 'Waters' car. He's here.'

He skirted round the edge of the forecourt and came to a halt by the vehicle. They jumped out and peered through its windows. Nothing inside. Jon turned to the derelict monastery itself. The spire was at the front end of the building. Stretching out a good hundred metres behind it was a grey roof. The upper section of the side wall consisted of a series of arched windows. Buttresses tapered between them, topped by gargoyles that stared down at a secondary, lower roof. It connected to another side wall of arched windows, this one dropping to ground level itself.

Most of the glass was missing, in many places leaving a criss-cross of struts. To the rear of the building was another structure, this one with little more than exposed beams for a roof. Chimney stacks rose up like sentinels at regular intervals.

'The wing of cells the bishop mentioned,' Rick commented. 'Where the monks were housed.'

Jon set off across the bumpy terrain, stepping over clumps of weeds until they reached a chain-link fence topped with coils of barbed wire. *Danger. Unsafe structure.* The signs had been attached to the barrier at ten-metre intervals.

'How the hell do we get in?' Rick asked.

'There.' Jon pointed. 'He's cut a hole through.'

They ran to the opening, ducked through, and jogged between stacks of timber and piles of bricks until they reached the wall of what appeared to be a courtyard. The branch of an apple tree hung over it.

'We need a side door,' Jon whispered, leading the way towards the front of the monastery. Most of the ground floor doors and windows were boarded over, but the last one before the main entrance had been removed.

They stepped through and found themselves in the main part of the church. Amber light was flooding in through the stained-glass upper windows, dappling the opposite wall with patches of red, orange, yellow and blue. Jon remembered his mum mentioning how the Franciscans had built the monastery on a north-to-south alignment so it would dominate the skyline from the centre of Manchester. Now the west-facing wall was being drenched by the sun's dying rays.

Before them a series of six massive arches on either side of the nave led back to the intricate reredos, many parts of which had been smashed or broken off. All the pews were gone and the floor itself was strewn with chunks of rubble, masonry, broken bricks and pieces of wood. Stalagmites of pigeon shit dotted the way ahead and Jon was aware of movement among the rafters of the wooden canopy high above their heads.

'I can't believe they just abandoned this place,' Rick whispered.

'Left it to the looters,' Jon replied, making his way forward and glancing up at the empty plinths where the twelve apostles used to stand.

Rick followed his gaze. 'They were all stolen?'

'Lying around in back gardens, reclaimers' yards, God knows where.'

Rick's eyes dropped back down to the mosaic of tiles at their feet. Two arms, one in a flowing brown sleeve, were crossed before a red crucifix. The letters below the image spelled *Deus Meus Et Omnia.*

'My God and my all,' Rick said.

Jon scanned the confessionals on his left before turning to the doorway leading off to the right. Footprints were visible in the dust. 'This way.'

They crept through into the gloomy corridor beyond. A flight of steps immediately on their left, a row of doors stretching away in front, and another flight of steps at the other end. Seeing scuff marks on the stairs by their side, Jon jabbed a finger and they silently began to climb.

Except for light shining in through the many gaps in the roof, the first floor was identical to the one below – just a narrow corridor of doorways. They advanced slowly forward, listening for movement before glancing into the first cell.

Inside the tiny room was a partially dismantled, rusty bed frame and smashed bookcase. The second cell was empty, as were the third and fourth. At the doorway to the fifth, Jon froze. 'Someone's been using this.'

A patch of intact roof tiles ensured the room was protected from the elements. Inside, the bed frame had been reassembled and a mattress placed on top of it. Blankets had been folded neatly back and resting on the pillow was a large book.

Rick crossed the room and picked it up. 'Shit.'

'What is it?' Jon hissed, noticing the copy of *Pilgrim's Progress* on the tiny shelf unit in the corner.

'*Malleus Maleficarum.* It's the same book the guy in the Met sent up. *The Witch's Hammer*. The textbook witch hunters used in the seventeenth century. It tells you all about how to identify witches, try them, record their confessions, then execute them.'

Jon stepped over. 'Fresh flowers in that vase.' He leaned forward for a better look at the large pink blossoms and there, in the courtyard below, he saw a cowled figure tying Skye Booth to a stake.

Ben Waters secured the ropes with a couple of tugs sharp enough to rock Skye's head as it hung down. When he stepped away from her, she began sliding slowly into a sitting position, the downward movement halted by the wood piled up around her legs.

He added more pieces, propping them against her sides before ripping open a large pack of firelighters and crumbling the white cubes into her hair, tucking pieces into the neck of her nightie, then wedging whole cubes into the stack of wood.

Next he reached for the three-litre bottle of white spirit and, pressing with both hands, started squirting a stream of liquid over the pyre. Minuscule droplets rebounded off the dry surfaces, misting his robe and peppering the surrounding grass. His fingers began to ache and he tilted the bottle. It sucked in air like a person being drowned.

'Father Waters, stop! You must stop!'

He whirled round and spotted the younger of the two officers from the night he had to burn his own church. The man was standing about twenty feet away, both hands raised up. Waters searched the shadows behind him, but no one else was there.

'Please, Father, you cannot do this to her.'

He stepped back, the pyre now at his side. One hand began playing liquid directly on to Skye, the other reached deep into the monk's robe. 'She is a servant of Satan and you will not stop me in my duty to God.'

'She's just a young woman, Father. Confused maybe, searching for some meaning in her world. This is not the answer. Show her the error of her ways, but don't kill her.'

'She is already beyond redemption. Don't be fooled by the physical form you see. It's merely a vessel that must be destroyed.'

He gave a couple more squeezes to the bottle, but the thing was now empty. Dropping it on to the pile of wood, he lifted up a box of matches.

Having crept along the first floor corridor, Jon made his way carefully down the other flight of stairs. He found himself looking into the adjacent corner of the courtyard to Rick, a row of waist-high cloisters separating him from the overgrown garden beyond. Waters was still in the middle, and in the half-light he could just make out the man's back facing him. Waters dropped a plastic bottle on to the mound of wood Skye was slumped on.

Jon went towards the archway that gave access to his corner of the courtyard, but fallen roof beams created a barrier in front of him.

'Is she still alive?' Rick's voice had a note of desperation in it.

'Yes,' Waters replied, both hands now held before him.

'And she has confessed? To being a witch?'

'She has.'

'Then it is your duty to strangle her before the fire is lit. That's what *The Witch's Hammer* says, doesn't it?'

Good, thought Jon, as he climbed through the waist-high cloister into the courtyard itself. Keep that sick fucker talking. He weighed up the distance. Fifteen metres maximum. If I go in low and hit him slightly from the side, we'll both end up well clear of the pyre.

Waters was now fumbling with something. 'She didn't accept God as her true saviour! The fire must take her, not me.'

Jon was now fully through. The long grass in front was dark with shadow and he couldn't see what obstacles might be concealed beneath. Slowly, he took a step forward.

The sound of a match striking caused him to look up.

'Ask her now! Give her the chance!' Rick shouted as Waters

held his hand out, yellow flame flaring up just above his bunched fingertips.

Jon broke into a sprint, his eyes fixed on the tiny beacon in the priest's hand.

'It's too late for her,' Waters cried, flexing his elbow in readiness to toss the burning match.

Eight metres away, Jon clicked into rugby mode, dropping his upper body low enough to snatch a tuft of grass at his feet. The strands were still between his fingers as his body straightened and a shoulder smashed up into Waters' kidneys.

He felt the man's torso folding over his back as, for a second, they were both airborne. Then the ground connected and he heard a soft whump off to his side. A veil of yellow was suddenly all around him and he felt his eyebrows begin to crackle.

Immediately he rolled off Waters and into a kneeling position. The man was beating at his robe which was sheathed in a delicate yellow flame. Trails of it were spreading back towards the pyre and Rick was desperately kicking away pieces of wood. But doing so only removed what was holding Skye up and she sank into the fuel-soaked grass, arms tied around the base of the stake. Cursing, Rick started fumbling at the ropes. Flames were now surging across the outermost pieces of wood, yellow flickers growing a blue centre as the fire took grip.

Jon jumped to his feet, realised the ends of his sleeves were alight and clutched his hands under his armpits. 'Pull the stake over!'

Rick grabbed it in both hands and started yanking back and forth. It began to rock as a bright form rose at Jon's side. He turned. Waters was on his feet, shrieking as his hair disintegrated, burning strands floating up into the sky. Two claw-like hands were attempting to pluck the burning robe off his shoulders.

Jon looked at him and thought of his brother and sister. This thing, he thought, this piece of shit, destroyed my family. He stepped clear of the flailing arms, then drove a fist into the side of Waters' skull. The priest's head snapped to the side and he hit the grass once more. This time he didn't move.

Jon bounded over to Rick, wrapped his arms round the stake

and started pulling with all his might. Looking down, he could see the fire was now on the lower part of Skye's nightie, tongues licking the flimsy material. He slammed himself against the heavy wood once again and with a creaking sound the stake finally began to fall. A last shove toppled it completely and together they dragged her clear, fell across her legs and smothered the fire with their bodies.

After a couple of seconds Rick raised himself up. 'It's out.'

The scattered remains of the pyre were burning brightly in the grass, shadows dancing over the courtyard walls. Beyond them another fire burned more steadily.

'Waters!' Rick gasped, jumping to his feet.

Jon raised his blistered fingers and used his partner's sleeve to pull himself upright.

'Our jackets,' Rick said, trying to shrug his off. 'We'll use our jackets!'

Jon didn't loosen his grip. 'Don't bother.'

'You what?' Rick said, still trying to pull his arm free.

'Look at him,' Jon replied, turning to the priest. What remained of the thick brown robe now seemed to have melted into the bubbling flesh below. 'He's dead.'

Rick stopped struggling. 'What happened? He got to his feet, didn't he?'

Jon looked up at the spire that towered above them. Just visible at its very tip was a thin cross. 'Fuck knows,' he replied. 'I was more interested in trying to save her.'

He crouched down and started trying to scoop Skye up in his arms. 'Make the call, will you? She needs a hospital.'

# Epilogue

Jon's eyes followed the thin tube that hung down from the small sack of clear fluid. It curled across the bedcovers before disappearing under the large plaster on Skye Booth's forearm.

'Are you sure you're OK with this?' he asked, as he struggled to open his notebook.

'I think so,' she smiled, eyes dropping to Jon's hands. 'Are you sure you're up to it?'

He glanced at the gauze bandages covering them. 'I'll manage. My writing might be a little hard to read though. So Valerie Evans was a member of your coven?'

'Yes. He – that priest – was trying to destroy it. But each of us only knows the name of two other members, the person who introduced you and the person you introduced.'

'And, in your case, Valerie introduced you?'

Skye nodded.

'And so Troy Wilkes introduced her?'

'No. We don't have any male members. I can't understand why Troy gave Valerie's name.'

Rick stirred in the seat by the door. 'Did Troy have any idea that Valerie was a witch? Maybe from the fact they were colleagues at the Psychic Academy?'

Skye considered the comment. 'She would never have said anything.'

'Maybe she didn't need to. She taught the Way of Wicca course for a start. She also offered tarot readings. Call it an educated guess on his part.'

'I suppose so,' she sighed. 'But why then did the priest go for Troy in the first place?'

'Ben Waters had an intense hatred of non-Christians,' Rick

replied. 'It was something he hid very well, but we believe, when he actually found a Satanist trying to burn down his church, that control left him completely. We think that, after killing Luke Stevens, he thought he was on some sort of divine mission. Next he focused on the Psychic Academy, which he saw as a breeding ground for satanic beliefs. If Troy Wilkes wasn't a member of the coven, my guess is that he was just unlucky enough to be the first person Waters was able to snatch.'

Jon nodded. 'And not being a member of the coven, he could only give Valerie's name.'

Skye closed her eyes and leaned against the pillows piled up behind her. 'And then Valerie gave Waters my name.'

'That's it.' Rick clicked his fingers. 'Because Troy Wilkes drowned having only given Valerie's name, Waters could only follow the chain of coven members one way – and that was to you.'

Jon looked at her. 'In the cell Waters had occupied at the monastery, we found a piece of paper advertising a medium called Helena Hunt.'

Skye winced and tears were squeezed from her eyes.

Jon leaned forward and placed a hand over hers. 'You had no choice.'

'He was torturing me,' she whispered. 'Stabbing me with this spike. I tried so hard not to tell him anything.'

'Skye,' Rick said quietly. 'Are you sure you want to carry on?'

She wiped the tears off her cheeks. 'Yes.'

'Can you tell us when you introduced Helena Hunt to the coven?'

'I didn't. It was my turn, but I haven't introduced anyone, yet.'

Jon and Skye's glances met. Ellie. A few days later, Jon thought, and you would have been giving Waters my sister's name. He looked down at his notebook.

Rick was now frowning. 'So how did you know Helena was in your coven?'

'Luck. I knew her identity because of psychic evenings she does in pubs around town.'

'My God,' Rick whispered. 'So if Waters had got to her, he could have forced out more names—'

'Skye,' Jon blurted out, trying to stop Rick from completing the sentence. 'It was incredible you lasted as long as you did.'

She lowered her head. 'The room he kept me in. Where was it in the monastery?'

'In a side wing the monks used to live in. Near the end of the corridor.'

'Yes.' she murmured. 'I could always hear his footsteps approaching.' Her hand clasped the neck of her pyjama top. 'How long was I there for? My memory seems to cut out after a while.'

'Almost two days,' Rick said.

'In that room, tied to that chair?'

Rick nodded.

'That's where you found me?'

'That's right,' Jon cut in.

'So what happened to you?' Her eyes were on his bandages again.

'There was a fire, as we tried to arrest Waters.'

Silence for a few seconds. 'He was going to burn me, wasn't he?'

Jon couldn't look at her.

'Oh God. I'm right, aren't I? He was going to burn me. Tell me, I need to know.'

No you don't, thought Jon. Not unless you want the same kind of nightmares that haunt me. 'When we arrived he had some wood, yes. But as we approached him, he doused himself in petrol. We couldn't reason with him, he was determined to set himself alight. We tried to put him out and that's when I got burned. Skye, he wasn't interested in you by then.'

She turned to Rick. 'Is that what happened?'

Rick peeled his eyes from Jon. 'Yes. He committed suicide.'

'Skye?' Jon asked. 'You said there are no male members of your coven.'

'That's right.'

'So Tristan Arkell has no connection with it?'

'None.'

'I was convinced he had a role,' Jon muttered. 'Did you ever have any dealings with him at the Psychic Academy?'

'I kept well clear. There was something about the way he looked at me. Lecherous, calculating.'

You nailed him there, Jon thought.

'He's under arrest, isn't he?'

'Oh yes. We now have almost twenty pupils or ex-pupils accusing him of sexual assault.'

There was a knock at the door and Ellie peeped in, a bouquet of flowers in her hand. 'Hi there.'

'Ellie!' Skye smiled. 'I'm getting outnumbered by Spicers here.'

'Not yet,' Ellie replied. 'I need something to put these in first.'

She disappeared back out of the doorway and Jon held his hands up. 'That's plenty for now. We'll leave you to catch up with Ellie.'

As he stood, Skye pointed at his notebook. 'The stuff about what Waters was doing. Does Helena need to know? I mean, I feel so ...'

Jon shook his head. 'No one does.' He glanced meaningfully at the door. 'All of this conversation, it can remain between us.'

Ellie reappeared with the flowers in a plastic jug.

'Good,' Skye said quietly.

'What's good?' Ellie asked.

Jon stepped away from the bed. 'Skye's progress. She'll be out of here in no time. We've got to go. You coming round ours tonight?'

Ellie rolled her eyes. 'The big reconciliation with Mum.'

'Come on, Ellie, she's apologised.'

'She hasn't. She says she regrets her words. She hasn't said sorry.'

Jon widened his eyes at her.

'OK, OK. I'll come.'

'Nice one,' he said, stepping out into the corridor, then craning his head back round the door. 'And we're agreed? Religion is off the bloody menu?'

'Absolutely.'

Jon and Rick walked towards the lifts.

'I wonder where the Psychiatric Unit is in this place,' Rick said.

Jon knew. His wife had almost ended up in it the previous year. He thought of Peter Robson. The young man was pretty much catatonic when the doctor had sectioned him. 'The other side of the grounds. Tucked well away.'

There was a ping, the lift doors opened and they stepped in.

'Daniel Humphries is applying for jobs on cruise ships,' Rick said. 'I spoke to his mum earlier.'

'With that bloody thing on his forehead?' Jon said incredulously.

'No, his folks are paying for it to be removed,' Rick replied with a grin. 'Serberos Tavovitch is officially no more.'

'He's lucky to have been let off so lightly,' Jon replied. In their last interview with the singer, he'd told them all about Luke Stevens, how the lad had hung around at their concerts. Eventually Peter Robson had invited him backstage and the two had struck up a weird kind of friendship. With glass fragments from the third and fourth churches now having been found on Peter's clothing, it appeared the two had begun working together. It was everybody's guess that Robson had got out of the window that night at the Sacred Heart – carrying the knowledge of what Waters had done to Luke with him.

They reached the hospital's reception and walked out to the car park. 'So what's in store for Robson senior?' Rick asked.

Jon raised his chin and drank in the sight of the blue sky above. 'Kidnap, false imprisonment, three counts of GBH, several of ABH, possibly attempted murder. I'd say he's looking at ten to fifteen. A good few years of not picking up the soap in the showers anyway.'

Rick laughed. 'Can you imagine him inside? Surrounded by blasphemers, adulterers, sodomites and murderers.'

Jon grinned. 'His own pesonal purgatory. By the way, can you drop me off in town? There's something I need to sort out.'

The lawns to the side of the cathedral were empty, so Jon trotted down the steps to the entrance of the Booth Centre. The wooden door was slightly ajar and he could hear voices inside. Laughter. Coughing. The chink of spoons in cups.

He stepped inside. The living skeletons were sitting round two tables, mugs of tea and plates of biscuits before them. 'Anyone seen Dave?'

Dead eyes and gaunt faces looked at him for a moment before turning away in silence. Jon was about to step back outside when a gruff voice said, 'The car park. Back of the Great Northern.'

He looked to his side. The arsehole with the baseball cap. The one Dave refused to pay more than twelve quid to for the mountain bike.

'And when you see him,' he added. 'Give him a slap from me.'

A biscuit hit the side of the man's head.

'Fucking grass! Zip it.'

Jon turned to see where the missile had come from. Wet crumbs were caught in the old pisshead's overgrown stubble.

'Fuck yourself,' Baseball Cap snarled, scooping up a biscuit of his own and hurling it across the room.

'Ya cunt!' A custard cream was slung back.

'Please! Please! Gentlemen, please!' The man who ran the place positioned himself between the tables as platefuls began to fly about.

Jon closed the door behind him and cut down on to Deansgate, heading for the massive building that once served as a warehouse for the Great Northern Railway. Now it housed shops, glitzy bars and a multiplex cinema. Soon he was striding past a ticket booth, heading for the doors leading to the overhead walkway that connected to the rear car park. Halfway across, two private security guards emerged through the double doors on the other side. The older held a dustpan and brush.

Jon raised his warrant card. 'Have you seen a young male? Six feet tall, skinny, shaved head, probably up to no good.'

'We chased a group off five minutes ago. Hanging about in the toilets.'

'Where'd they go?'

The man shrugged. 'Back to the sewers.' He held up the dust-pan. 'After leaving us with a few syringes to clear up. Scum.'

Jon looked to the car park. It was no good. He'd be long gone by now. 'Cheers.'

He turned round and went back into the main building, walking slowly towards the escalators that led down to the main entrance. Halfway along the spotless corridor, his phone went. Alice's name was on the screen. 'Hi, babe. Everything OK?'

'Yeah.'

'How's that girl of ours?'

'She's fine. Playing with the saucepans out of the cupboards. Can't you hear her?'

Jon listened. The sounds of metal clashing against metal were punctuated by high-pitched shouts of delight. He grinned. 'The little monkey.'

'Where are you?'

'City centre.'

'Good. Can you pick up some wine on the way home? We're out of red and your dad won't touch white.'

'No problem. Anything else?'

'Depends. Is Ellie going to tell your mum about the Sunday school stuff? Because if she is, you can get a bottle of brandy for me.'

'No. We agreed to steer well clear.'

'For the moment or permanently?'

'It's Ellie's shout,' Jon replied, shortening his stride and putting a foot on the top step of the escalator. He began to move forward.

'But she'll say something sometime?'

He placed a hand on the rubber rail. 'I don't know. Mum's over sixty. Why destroy her affection for something she holds so dear?'

He heard his wife sigh. 'Because it's the truth.'

Jon looked at the other escalator alongside his. The steps were gliding upward, glass panels revealing the oil-stained cogs that revolved beneath. The truth. Would it help his mum to know it? Would it help Skye to know she'd been dragged from a burning stake? Would Alice like to hear that rather than try to save Waters, her husband had sent the man to his death? He looked down at his knuckles. The sensation of them slamming into Waters' temple came back and he wanted to collapse on the metal steps and curl up. 'I don't know, babe.'

'Mmmm. I'll see you in a couple of hours.'

'Yup. Love you.'

'Love you.'

He closed the phone, eyes on the blackened cogs as he continued his descent. No one was on the other escalator, but those wheels carried on turning just the same.

# Author's Note

The story of how Gorton Monastery fell into a sad state of disrepair is true. In fact, it was seeing the magnificent – but derelict – building as I passed it on the train to Manchester that gave me the original idea for this book.

Unlike my books, however, there is an entirely happy ending to the monastery's story. To read it and see photos of how this amazing building rose from the ashes, just visit www.gortonmonastery.co.uk.

# Acknowledgements

For their skills during the editing process, a massive thanks to Jane and Emma. Also to Jon for an inspired adjustment to the plot, Jade for her amazing efficiency and Robyn for her deft touch with the copy-edits.

The following, in no order of preference, were also essential in getting this book done:

Deon Webber, Fire Investigation Team Manager, Greater Manchester Fire and Rescue Service.

John Edgley, RF Group Supervisor, Jodrell Bank Observatory. (Any failings to describe the CMB properly are all my own!)

Tony Hurley, David Gray and everyone at The Angels, Manchester.

Juanita Bullough of The Eagle Eye Inc.

Nessy, for all your Morse-like knowledge.